D1603010

DEBUNKED

VOLUME 1 OF THE TERRAVENUM CHRONICLES

DITO ABBOTT

Debunked by Dito Abbott

Published by Maxing Out Media LLC

Copyright © 2022 by Dito Abbott

Visit the author's website at: http://www.ditoabbott.com

Cover by Kirk DouPonce at DogEared Design
Map Illustration by Dito Abbott

ISBN: 978-1-958072-04-2 (Paperback Print)
ISBN: 978-1-958072-02-8 (Hardback Print)
ISBN: 978-1-958072-03-5 (Large Print Edition)
ISBN: 978-1-958072-00-4 (Ebook)

TERRAVENUM CHRONICLES

DEBUNKED

VOLUME ONE

DITO ABBOTT

To S, Z, and J.

Without you, this book wouldn't exist.
Well, it might...but it would be a run-of-the-mill romance novel about a
mad scientist who accidentally turned himself into a pretzel, then fell in
love with a donut. And every sixth line would rhyme with "turnip".

Thanks for endless hours of plotting.
Thanks for keeping me laughing.
Thanks for joy.

You are my favorite adventures.

CONTENTS

SCAN QR CODE TO VIEW LARGE COLOR MAP

https://ditoabbott.com/terravenum

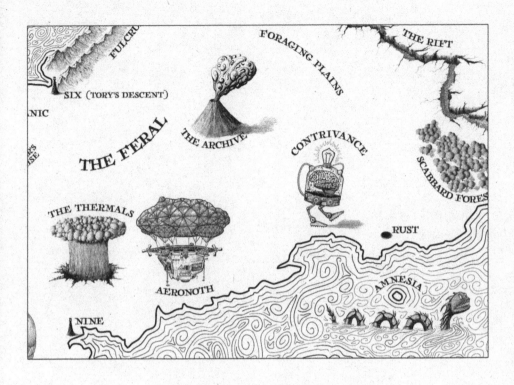

LOCATIONS IN *DEBUNKED*

CHAPTER 1
ANOTHER LETTER

Dearest Alexandria and Ozymandias,

If you are reading this, I have perished. My demise likely involved some manner of spiked pit or curiously fanged beast, so it's doubtful I suffered long. Do not try to find me—the path is too perilous, and I am lost to the mortal plane.

I bequeath to you my travel journal. Do NOT open it (but when you inevitably ignore my wishes and plumb its depths, remember: mystery and danger are jealous companions—you cannot flirt with one without courting the other).

You were my favorite adventures. I'm sorry I failed you.

With Love,

Your grandfather, Quidby Forsythe III

Ozzie sighed and folded the letter closed. Dying six times in two years had to be a record, even for an explorer as incompetent as Grandfather.

The journal's *FRAGILE* stamp had done little to protect it from a herd of stampeding buffalo somewhere between Peru and England, and a peppery aroma hinted at a layover in a Marrakesh spice market. Aged leather and the corner of an ornate metal frame peeked through tattered brown wrapping paper. Ozzie lifted the book with a grunt. Family secrets are always heavier than they look. He dropped the journal onto the lampstand by the door, triggering a shock wave that toppled chest-high document stacks cluttering the foyer.

Two months ago, Sir Quidby disappeared on an expedition to Siberia, then resurfaced in the Amazon rainforest. The time before that, an airport mix-up stranded the old explorer in the Moldovan Codru Forest instead of the grasslands of Outer Mongolia. How could one of the world's foremost map experts be so hopeless at using a compass?

Ozzie started up the main staircase, giving a wide berth to a tripwire that released a bone-bruising battering ram. Grandfather's dizzying collection of booby traps had turned St. Jude's, his lighthouse home, into a training ground for temple robbing. Mrs. Willowsby relocated the traps every few days, but Ozzie had cracked her rotation.*[1] He vaulted a bear trap at the top of the bannister without breaking stride.

Tattered red carpet lent an elegant backdrop to curiosities congesting the second floor. Ozzie straightened a rack of Masai spears, heard a telltale *swish*, then dodged a sandbag that dropped from a false ceiling panel. Careful footwork defeated a gauntlet of cunning snares as he advanced to the end of the hallway, where Grandfather's ramshackle residence connected to the lighthouse. Ozzie ducked under the archway and ignored the spiral staircase's complaints as he ascended the gently swaying tower. Groaning scaffolds, whistling drafts, and perpetual dampness are facts of life when you live in a one-hundred-fifty foot lighthouse perched atop a pinnacle in the North Sea.

He gave a cautious fist bump to a spiky suit of armor standing watch over the third floor landing. "What ho, Spikealot." The knight, focused on defending the stairs from pillaging hordes and ill-tempered wheels of cheese, didn't answer.

Ozzie paused at the threshold of his room. His desk was as he left it, groaning beneath a forest of research papers and textbooks. A shaft of light from the window speared his unmade bed, and a trail of dirty laundry stretched out of his closet like the tail of a slumbering dragon.

All clear.

Whistling under his breath, Ozzie strode across the room and swung an overloaded bookshelf away from the wall, revealing a hidden alcove. He slumped into a blue corduroy bean bag and pulled the shelf closed behind him. With the flick of a switch, Christmas lights painted his lair with unseasonably jolly shadows.

Ozzie opened a three-ring binder, flipped to the end, and slid the newest death letter into a clear protective sleeve. He scribbled *"Missing/Dead"* on the calendar, and after a moment's reflection, added a question mark. A year ago, Grandfather's disappearances rarely exceeded a week, but they had grown in frequency and duration over the last six months.

He chewed the marker cap and sank lower in his beanbag, scanning newspapers and articles that wallpapered his headquarters. Headlines touting "Eminent Explorer Missing, Presumed Dead" and "Forsythe Curse Claims Another Victim!" degenerated to photos of disgruntled search and rescue teams. From there, the Professor's misadventures migrated to gossip rags, bottoming out with "SCANDAL! Lonely Professor Weds Mail-Order Cartographer Bride." Ozzie smoothed the latest edition of *Treasure Hunter's Weekly* and trimmed a headline ("Fool Us Once, Sir Quidby") from yet another character assassination piece by Lord "Bully" Bulwerk, Head Stuffypants of the Guild of Borderless Explorers.

Sir Quidby was well-liked, but his unapologetic pursuit of debunking made him a pariah amongst his peers. The old explorer endured his exile with good grace and relished explaining the origins of his life's work to Ozzie. "In the Age of Discovery, every ship returning from the New World carried a wealth of knowledge that constantly forced cartographers to scrap their work. Many mapmakers succumbed to despair and exhaustion, refusing to get out of bed to receive daily dispatches—in the vernacular of their trade, they *bunked*. Only a tenacious few *de*-bunked, rising each day to greet a constantly changing world."

Ozzie smiled, remembering when Grandfather had cleared a

desk with a sweep of his arm, unrolled a dog-eared map, then pointed to labels on amorphous land masses. "*Terra Incognita.*" Whispered reverence breathed magic into Latin. "*Unknown land—* the white flag of an explorer who bunked."

Ozzie had struggled to decipher the scribbled name. "Ferdinand Magellan?"

"He went on to fame and fortune but lived a waking death, fenced by boundaries in his mind." Eager palms flattened another map. "*Terra Incognita.* Thirteenth century." A trembling finger traced ridges of mountains on the edge of the chart. "When Marco Polo reached the foothills of the Himalayas, he bunked."

"I've heard of him." At the swimming pool.

"My Guild colleagues lionize Marco Polo, but trust me, lad—he bunked."

"Mom says Lord Reginald wants to kick you out of the Guild."

Grandfather had snorted, then rolled the chart up. "Reggie Twixton regards any acknowledgment of his limitations as a personal insult. I was perfectly within my rights to name those mountains *Reggie's Blisters.*"

"Then why does he write you so many angry letters?"

The explorer's scowl was seared into Ozzie's memory. "Those are from his lawyers, who equally lack a sense of humor. You're missing the point, Ozymandias." He'd leaned closer, reflections from the fireplace dancing in his eyes. "Great men chase horizons. Exploring shows us who we are, but debunking whispers who we might *become.*"

Those golden conversations belonged to the old days—back when Grandfather's souvenirs were trinkets and trophies, not nightmares. Back before the "Accident" changed everything.

Ozzie's fists curled at the memory of the official police report.

Accidents didn't happen on purpose.

Someone…no, some*thing*…*took* his parents.

A creaky floorboard announced an intruder. Ozzie elbowed the bookshelf open and flopped on his side like a snail evacuating its shell. A sigh from the bed made him cringe.

Alex.

Ozzie propped himself up on one arm. "I didn't hear the door open."

His sister waved a calloused hand. "I free soloed a new route." The bedroom window swung open with an accusing moan as a breeze rocked the lighthouse.

People laughed when they learned the Forsythes were twins. Ozzie didn't blame them—aside from dark, wavy hair and piercing blue eyes, the siblings couldn't be more different. Alex limited her wardrobe to black leggings, black shirts, black beanies, and her ever-present Chuck Taylor sneakers—also black. Ozzie favored cargo pants and long-sleeve shirts that gave his arms sun protection on the rare occasions he went outside.

He was a constant source of disappointment to rugby and football coaches who hoped Alex's athleticism ran in her family. Once they saw Ozzie run—an act he approached with the grace of a newborn calf learning to walk—they left him alone.

As children, the Forsythe twins were inseparable. When you're undersized, book-loving, and named after an Egyptian pharaoh, it helps to have a sister whose punch rules the playground. But Alex lived for the moment, and a crowbar couldn't pry Ozzie's fingers from the past, so over time they drifted apart. Age fifteen found Ozzie spending his days scouring books for clues to their parents' kidnapping, while Alex notched first ascents on the sheer cliffs of Keeper's Rock.

He winced. "Don't let Mrs. Willowsby catch you climbing the lighthouse again." The housekeeper's disapproval had the half-life of plutonium.

Alex snorted. "I'm not the one making collages in a broom closet and hunting imaginary monsters."

Ozzie stiffened. "I'm just doing what's necessary."

"You're acting like a crazy person."

Arguing was safer than actual conversation, so he dove in. "I'm acting like the only person willing to admit something strange is going on!"

"The only thing strange in this house is your refusal to move on with your life!" she snapped.

That definitely wasn't true. The twins glared at each other across seven years of scorched earth. Silence was painful, but when your own sister doesn't believe you saw your parents kidnapped, what else is there to say?

Alex broke the stalemate. "This isn't healthy, Oz."

The truth hung over him like a storm cloud. She was probably right.

But she was *definitely* wrong.

Sir Spikealot rattled a warning from the landing. Ozzie lunged for the bookshelf, but Alex's cheetah-like reflexes beat him to the punch, slapping the secret door closed.

"Five minutes until dinner, children," snapped Mrs. Willowsby, in the tone of a SWAT team announcing a raid. She tapped a wooden spoon on the apron shielding her severe gray skirt and spotless white blouse. Her black hobnailed boot drummed the floor as she surveyed the room, cataloguing grievances. Ozzie kicked laundry into a basket, then straightened papers on his desk— anything to distract her from the red and green glow beneath his bookshelf. The housekeeper kept dim views on "poking into Sir Quidby's private affairs," and Ozzie was running out of secret hideouts.

"Thank you, Mrs. Willowsby," he said, trying for a winning smile and failing to place.

"Thank you, Mrs. Willowsby," Alex chimed in.

Ozzie concealed a gossip rag proclaiming "Crackpot Missing, World Shrugs" behind his back. "What's for dinner?" he asked.

The housekeeper squinted suspiciously over her spectacles. "Pea soup."

"Yum."

"Indeed." She lingered three excruciating seconds longer than necessary, then spun on her heel and marched down the stairs. Sir Spikealot rattled a metallic raspberry.

Ozzie plonked down on the mattress next to his sister.

"Ozzie—" Alex started.

"Just drop it. Thanks for closing the bookshelf." He offered an olive branch. "Another death letter from Grandfather came today."

6

"Exploding jellyfish or a hyper-territorial merman?"

"Spiked pit. Possibly a curiously fanged beast."

Mrs. Willowsby's voice cracked like a whip. *"Dinner!"*

The bed exhaled in relief as the siblings bounced to their feet.

Alex grinned. "When and where?"

Ozzie chewed his lip, running some quick math. "Seventeen days. Greenland."

"Four days. Tasmania," she countered.

"An optimist. I'll bet a week of dish duty we're talking Northern hemisphere."

"You already owe me ten days."

"For when Grandfather showed up in Indonesia? The equator doesn't count, it's hemisphere-neutral. Besides, he was wearing Arctic snow gear."

Dodging booby traps and needling each other, the siblings raced down the spiral staircase. Ozzie snickered when Alex jumped the handrail to take a shortcut through the study—she always forgot the quicksand pit. He slid down the bannister and pounded past the foyer without giving the book on the lampstand a second glance.

By Wednesday, the journal was buried and forgotten beneath a mountain of obscure manuscripts and crates of poison-arrow tree frog venom.

Twelve weeks later, the Forsythe children held a funeral and started a war.

---

1. The portable snake pit still vexed him on occasion, but he was fine as long as he didn't charge blindly into rooms.

CHAPTER 2

THE FUNERAL

The Professor's long history of dramatic reappearances kept an ember of hope burning in the weeks following his latest death. Friends and family waited patiently for another geographically absurd miracle, but after three months, hope dimmed and Arrangements were made.

Visitors from around the world descended on the sleepy seaside village of Lamswool to pay their respects to Sir Quidby. St. Jude's foyer overflowed with exotic flowers from a steady parade of gift-bearing tribal chiefs and despondent travel agents.*[1]

The Guild of Borderless Explorers typically honored former members with a funeral at their London headquarters, but in his pursuit of debunking, Sir Quidby accomplished the impossible: uniting his squabbling peers against a common enemy. The Professor's stubborn refusal to perish in a hail of poison-tipped arrows was widely regarded as selfish. As word of Sir Quidby's exploits spread, explorer clubs in every hemisphere disavowed and black-listed him.

And so it came to be that the funeral for Sir Quidby Forsythe III, world-famous debunker and disgraced archaeologist, was held at his favorite Lamswoolian pub: The Juniper Rhinoceros.

As usual, the coastal weather dressed for a funeral. Somber clouds cast a brisk chill in the air as Ozzie trudged up the hill, cursing the thin soles of his leather shoes. He ran a finger around his collar and lobbed dark thoughts at growth spurts, clammy sports coats, and undersized pants.

Alex and Mrs. Willowsby, irritatingly fresh after their climb, loitered in front of the Juniper Rhinoceros. Warm light spilled out of the pub's windows, painting cobblestones gold in the late afternoon haze.

"Let me look you over." The housekeeper straightened Ozzie's tie and brushed Alex's shoulders. Back at the lighthouse, the Battle of Formal Attire had been brief but fierce. When Alex finally slinked down the stairs in a black dress, Mrs. Willowsby wisely ignored his sister's sneakers and focused on subduing her unruly hair. A French braid kept the peace.

In what Alex described as "an outrageous and hypocritical abuse of authority," the housekeeper wore her standard ankle-length gray skirt and angular white blouse. As always, Mrs. Willowsby's silver hair was chiseled in a bulletproof bun. A red carnation pinned to her lapel was her only concession to the occasion.

Troop inspection complete, the old woman dabbed her eyes with a handkerchief. Ozzie squeezed Mrs. Willowsby's shoulder, then tensed when she clenched him in a tight hug. The awkwardness was beginning to fade when his sister's arms circled both their waists. Alex's rare display of emotion overwhelmed Ozzie. He hadn't cried since their parents' funeral seven years ago, but tonight, all bets were off. The three survivors huddled in the street, weeping unapologetic tears.

A loud crash inside the pub roused them from their grief. Guttural, foreign voices rose in a boisterous drinking song, and a wry grin turned the corner of Ozzie's mouth. His Mongolian was limited to swearing and street slang, but thumbing one's nose at the

Grim Reaper was a universal sentiment. The stout wooden door banged open and a raucous cheer chased a squawking ball of feathers into the night. The door clapped shut, muting the pandemonium.

"Was that a chicken?" Alex sniffled.

Mrs. Willowsby blew her nose. "I daresay it was." She cleared her throat and reforged her steely voice. "Let us enter the fray."

A blast of oriental spices and incense enveloped the trio as they crossed the pub's threshold. The Juniper Rhinoceros enjoyed a reputation for drawing an eclectic crowd, but Grandfather's funeral was more diverse than the buffet line at the United Nations.

A menagerie of mourners milled in the center of the room, trapped between the pub's weathered oak bar and rows of seated booths lining the walls. Ornate feathered headdresses, bright sarongs, and business suits dotted the crowd as dignitaries mingled with locals under the watchful glares of steely-eyed bodyguards. Warm chaos melted any reservations Ozzie had about the funeral. Grandfather would have loved this.

Leon, the barkeeper, slid an overflowing mug to a customer and waved a welcome with his washcloth. Ozzie nodded back. Mrs. Willowsby muttered something about ordering drinks and disappeared, leaving the twins alone by the shrine at the front of the room.

Candles, a hibiscus lei, and a mountain of sentimental baubles surrounded a framed photo of Sir Quidby—ground zero in a passive-aggressive culture war over the best way to celebrate the explorer's life. Ribbons and flowers battled an army of shrunken wicker soldiers for the honor of escorting the Professor's soul into the underworld.

Ozzie straightened the picture frame and smiled. His grandfather grinned back at him from the Serengeti plains, one foot planted on the chest of a big game hunter he'd knocked unconscious with a tree branch. "They used the poacher photo."

"I love that story," Alex said.

"Me too." He rubbed his nose with the cuff of his sleeve. "Grandfather against the world."

"It's how he rolled."

Alex inspected a jewel-encrusted octopus statue valuable enough to bankroll a dozen arctic expeditions. Even Russian oligarchs were paying their respects to Sir Quidby. She whispered their grandfather's motto, "The world is waiting—"

"—and it won't wait forever," Ozzie finished.

The twins claimed a corner table and indulged in the World Championship of people-watching. A troupe of Moko Jumbie stilt walkers milled through the crowd, crouching to avoid Leon's antique lighting fixtures. Two women at the bar casually twirled blowdart guns, staring openly at a trio of baskets guarded by a flute-wielding Indian man. In the center of the room, a sumo wrestler stood in a circle of empty chairs, waiting to strike a cartoonishly large drum.

Alex nudged Ozzie. "Did Grandfather know all these people?"

"Most of them rescued him."

"Excuse me!" Mrs. Willowsby weaved through the mob, burdened with sloshing mugs.

Sir Quidby's housekeeper was a subject of rampant speculation in Lamswoolian watering holes, and the rumor mill never stopped grinding. Edward Hunt recognized her from a live internet stream of an underground mixed martial arts tournament in Shanghai. The butcher's wife swore the housekeeper knocked out a charging bull in Flenderson's paddock with a single karate chop. Old Billy—well, you had to remember it was Billy, now— saw Mrs. Willowsby write cryptic messages in the sky with a flamethrower while wing-walking on a biplane. No one knew her full story, but local gossips practically dove out of the housekeeper's path when she walked to the farmer's market on Saturday mornings.

Mrs. Willowsby plunked three blackcurrant cordials on the table and clucked, "Bless her. Juney is going to make a mess of this." The children followed the housekeeper's gaze to the back of the room where Juniper, the pub's resident rhinoceros and namesake, nuzzled through the crowd like an asthmatic World War I tank. Ozzie grinned, pulled a sugar cube from his pocket, and whistled.

Snuffling, huffing noises quickened, accompanied by tinkles of broken glass and startled shouts from bulldozed victims.

"Juney!" he called.

The hip-tall beast brayed and loped to their table. Locals, used to the quirks of dining at the Juniper Rhinoceros, held their mugs aloft until tremors from the earthquake subsided. Juney swallowed Ozzie's hand in her eagerness for a treat.

"Hello, girl." He scratched the secret spot behind her ears, kindling a purr deep in her belly. How many tender moments like this had Grandfather shared with Juney after he discovered her wandering the East African plains, her mother slain by a poacher?

The baby rhinoceros made a keening sound and tilted her head to stare into Ozzie's eyes.

"He isn't here, Juney. Sorry." The wretched truth caught in his throat.

Mrs. Willowsby nudged Ozzie and scowled. "Steady on. Bully Bulwerk is making his entrance."

A pear-shaped man with a quivering handlebar mustache strutted to their table. Most people would balk at wearing a tuxedo and top hat to a funeral, but Lord Bulwerk rarely left his mansion unprepared to rub elbows with royalty. He belonged to an elite class of Gentleman Adventurers who conquered the Orient on the backs of cargo-toting natives while sipping brandy with wealthy benefactors.

Bulwerk's appointment as Chairman of the Guild of Borderless Explorers came courtesy of the Queen, and his lion-headed cane and the Rolls Royce idling outside the window were gifts from the Duke of Windsor. Explorers who challenged the silver-spooned chairman's lack of field experience soon found their expeditions defunded or bogged in a minefield of bureaucracy. If Grandfather hadn't defied the Guild and founded the St. Jude's Debunking Society, he wouldn't have been sanctioned to set foot beyond his own front door.

The fake explorer adjusted his monocle, cleared his throat, and grasped his lapels. "What a sad day for us all. The Guild of Borderless Explorers wishes to extend our deepest—" He caught sight of Mrs. Willowsby's stone face and faltered, "—er, sympathies…"

Alex slammed her mug down, flooding the table with a sticky tsunami of cordial.

Oh no.

"Are you *happy* my grandfather died?" she asked.

Bulwerk's eyes widened. "Not at all! Such a tragic loss for the explorer community."

"We are sitting in a pub because the *explorer community* and *your* Guild wanted nothing to do with him!"

The buzz of conversation faded, and heads swiveled. For possibly the first time in his life, Lord Bulwerk squirmed in the spotlight. "Certainly not! Quidby may have—"

"*Sir* Quidby!" Alex's shout turned more heads. The explorer recoiled, his face reddening. Ozzie raised his hands to defuse the situation, but his sister hadn't finished. "I wish you *had* offered Shambles House for Grandfather's funeral, so I could *laugh in your face.*"

Bulwerk puffed up to unleash a pedigree of tongue-lashing only centuries of meticulous breeding could muster. He got as far as "*How dare you?*" before self-preservation instincts tapped him on the shoulder and gestured to an attentive room. The pub was silent, except for munching sounds beneath the table where Juney had discovered a fallen bowl of pretzels. Bully Bulwerk seethed, "I see grief has overcome your reason. My condolences." He rapped his cane on the floor and stormed off to resuscitate his ego.

Mrs. Willowsby glowered at the chairman's receding back and called, "Good riddance, you pillock." Bulwerk stiffened, but he kept walking. "Well said, Alexandria. Those pompous blowhards at the Guild were unworthy of your grandfather."

The line of mourners at the shrine dwindled as people found seats for the memorial service. Ozzie drained his cup, then offered an arm to Alex. "I guess it's time. We're in the front row." A gentle touch on his shoulder stopped him in his tracks. A proud African warrior towered over the table, resplendent in an orange robe and crimson sash. Colorful beads stretched the man's earlobes to his shoulders. They jiggled as he bowed.

The warrior's voice rumbled like distant thunder. "I am very sorry for your loss."

"Thank you," Alex said. "You must be Noko."

The man smiled with a warmth that rivaled the sun. "Yes! Your grandfather and I grew up together."

Alex nodded. "He said you taught him bushcraft."

Noko's laugh shook the foundations of the building. "He was a wretched student! The man is a magnet for venomous snakes. It is a wonder he survived."

The group laughed, and Ozzie finally found his voice. "Grandfather would have been pleased you came."

"It is my honor and my duty. I am here to fulfill my friend's dying wish." Noko laid a silver metal box the size of a deck of cards in Ozzie's palm.

Mrs. Willowsby frowned and lowered her drink.

Alex tapped the box. "What's in it?"

"I do not know. Twenty years ago, your grandfather visited me and said he had made a very important and dangerous discovery— one that could cost his life. If he died, I was to deliver this box to your father for safekeeping." Noko paused and met Ozzie's eyes. "When your father passed, the burden fell to you."

"Burden?" Ozzie shook the box, but he couldn't hear any rattles over the noise in the pub.

"A dying man's last wish is rarely a blessing to the living." Noko pressed his fingertips together. "He claimed the fate of the world depends on what is in that box."

Ozzie grinned at his grandfather's flair for the dramatic. He tilted the box and the chrome surface flashed red. "Did he leave instructions on how to open it?"

Noko shook his head. "Quidby's secrets died with him."

"Then I guess we—"

Movement by the door caught Ozzie's eye. Someone screamed, then the pub exploded.*[2]

Mrs. Willowsby knocked the twins from their stools with a

diving tackle as a concussion wave swept through the room. Ozzie thrashed to free his arms, but the housekeeper disappeared before he could push her off his chest. He sat up, gasping for air. Lanterns flickered in the smoke.

"Alex! Are you okay?" High-pitched ringing drowned out his voice. Alex touched his shoulder and gave a thumbs-up. He shouted, "Are you hurt? We've got to—"

His sister reached down and picked up a cylinder that was spewing a column of white smoke. Ozzie frowned. A smoke grenade?

A bony apparition snatched the grenade from Alex's hand, flung it across the room, then pointed at the door. "Go!"

Ozzie said, "Mrs. Willowsby?"

A hulking shadow with glowing blue eyes wrapped the housekeeper in a bear hug. Mrs. Willowsby split her attacker's nose with a vicious head butt, then punched him in the groin.

"Mrs. Willowsby?"

Ozzie's first instinct was to check on the fallen man, but Alex had a death grip on his arm, her mouth agape at the deadly dance unfolding around them. Something fluid, predatory, and dangerous had replaced their housekeeper's Victorian reserve.

He yelled, "You're going to hurt yourself!"

Mrs. Willowsby gave Ozzie a look Lamswoolians reserved for Old Billy, then leveled a shadowy figure with a reverse spinning back-kick that folded the man in half. She flung a steak knife into the bicep of a would-be axe murderer and snapped, "If you're not going to leave, find a weapon and help!" She splintered a barstool, then chased two assailants into the smog.

"Let's go!" Ozzie tugged Alex toward the exit, but she wrenched him back, saving him from being stabbed by the stranger blocking their path. Their foe's luminescent blue eyes glimmered as he beckoned them closer with his knife.

"ROOOOOAAAAAAAAAAAAAAAAHHHHHHHHHH!"

Juney charged out of the smoke at a full gallop, demolishing floorboards with every stride.

SMACK

The baby rhinoceros plowed into the slack-jawed man. The killer's fractured body rolled across the floor and stopped, unmoving, at the twins' feet.

Ozzie slapped Juney's back. "Good girl." The rhino bellowed, then charged a shadow by the billiard tables.

Alex nudged their attacker with her foot. A silk hood concealed his face, but tattoos covered his jaw, neck, and collarbones. Interlocking geometric shapes gave the designs a tribal look, but they didn't belong to any culture Ozzie recognized. A dagger lay in the man's limp hand.

Find a weapon and help.

Ozzie reached for the knife, his pulse accelerating. The blade's three razor-sharp edges corkscrewed to a fiendish point, looking more like the horn of an evil unicorn than a functional weapon. The hilt was warm and slick with sweat. Adrenaline wrestled Ozzie's muscles for control of the trembling dagger.

Mrs. Willowsby's voice sliced through the chaos, "I was speaking to your sister!"

Alex snatched the knife from Ozzie's hand and shoved him behind her. He sagged against the wall, relieved and ashamed.

Five shadows sprang out of the smoke, forming a wall in front of the exit. Alex dropped into a defensive stance, twirling her knife with practiced ease. Unless they were close enough to see her ashen face, no one would know she'd only taken two months of Krav Maga before defecting to an ultimate frisbee league. Mrs. Willowsby limped to Alex's side. Judging from her confident grip on the broken stool leg, the blood on her blouse belonged to someone else.

The housekeeper taunted her opponents between labored breaths, "Come on, lads...who wants to dance...with an old biddy?"

Sapphire eyes smoldered like stars in the depths of the hoods. The shortest one hissed, *"Cuthorah!"* His comrades stretched out a golden, sparking net and advanced, using long spears to shepherd the children, while staying out of Mrs. Willowsby's reach. The Forsythes surrendered ground until their backs hit a stone wall.

To Ozzie's horror, Mrs. Willowsby doubled over in a coughing fit and dropped her weapon. Alex whispered, "I'll distract them. Go for the door." She braced her foot against the wall and coiled to lunge.

"Don't!" he said.

The men flung their net the moment she leapt. Alex never had a chance.

"*Yalyalay-tooooohhhh!*"

A stork-like figure leapt over the hooded assailants, shrieking a battle cry that petrified hairs on the nape of Ozzie's neck. Noko landed like a gazelle, sliced Alex free from the net with a stroke of his curved blade and spun to engage the spears.

Mrs. Willowsby waved Ozzie over. Sweat and blood ran down her face, but her voice was steady. "Get your sister. It's time to go."

He helped Alex to her feet. Aside from a bruised ego and superficial burns from the electrified netting, she appeared unharmed.

"Don't say *anything*," she hissed.

"Good work diving straight into their net. Solid plan."

"At least I did something."

"That's fair."

Mrs. Willowsby produced a machete from the folds of her skirt. She winked at Ozzie's shocked expression, then charged across the pub.*[3] Four adversaries blocked the door, but Juney flattened two of them before they could scream. Noko took advantage of the distraction to dispatch another foe, leaving only one—the leader—standing between the Forsythes and freedom.

The man hissed, his glittering eyes locked on the twins as the African forced him away from the door. Black robes stirred in the smoky background, picking up weapons. The odds were changing faster than Juney could charge.

Noko pointed to the exit. "Go! Remember your grandfather's wish."

Ozzie slid Mrs. Willowsby's right arm over his shoulder and grunted as she surrendered her weight. The housekeeper handed her machete to Alex, then succumbed to a coughing fit. Ozzie gritted his teeth—hadn't they *just* seen how knives encouraged his sister to do insane things? He made a half-hearted attempt to pry the blade from Alex's hand, but she pushed him away. The trio limped into the night.

---

1. Thanks to Sir Quidby's fondness for hazardous locales, nearly all the plants were carnivorous and had to be separated to prevent literal turf wars.
2. When police reconstructed events, the official incident report concluded: "The disturbance began when a loincloth-clad drummer grew impatient for the funeral to begin and took matters into his own hands. The concussion from his drum startled a baby rhinoceros into charging a woman who was breathing fire. She spewed a ball of flame directly at a snake charmer, who released three spitting cobras from baskets. Two blowdart hunters took advantage of a suddenly target-rich environment. Pub patrons responded accordingly, and panic ensued."

   The report circulated behind the scenes for years and became an urban legend at the Police Academy. Street-hardened cops used the phrase "pulling a baby rhino" to describe how the job plays tricks with your mind.

   Most Lamswoolians who attended the funeral refused to discuss that fateful night at the Juniper Rhinoceros. The few who loosened their lips became minor celebrities in local watering holes. After countless beer-soaked retellings, facts grew cloudy and exaggerated. Somehow—by unspoken agreement, greased palms, or drinking to forget—no one mentioned the assassins.
3. As charges go, it wasn't one for the record books. Mrs. Willowsby's injury limited their speed to a steady limp, but that's not the kind of thing you point out to a blood-spattered woman holding a machete.

CHAPTER 3
ON THE RUN

"All things considered, I've attended worse funerals," Mrs. Willowsby said, as they hobbled down the steep hill that led to the bay. A rhinoceros roar and the crack of splintering wood hastened their pace.

"Who were those people?" Ozzie said.

Mrs. Willowsby scowled. "Assassins, of course."

"What was up with their weird eyes?" Alex said.

"I've no idea. Would you like to go back and ask?"

Behind them, one of the pub's windows exploded.

Alex ducked under the housekeeper's left arm and doubled their speed. "Why did they attack us? Is the Guild involved?"

"Bulwerk lacks the nerve." Mrs. Willowsby coughed, spewing clouds of condensation like a locomotive venting steam. "Those lads knew how to handle themselves—two or three nearly cut me down."

The twins matched incredulous stares over the old woman's head. There wasn't a subtle way to broach the subject, so Ozzie leapt in with both feet. "Where did you learn to fight like that?"

"Just get to the boat," the housekeeper growled.

Rain, twilight, and adrenaline made the descent to Jackal's Cove even more treacherous than usual. Ozzie's shoes might as well have been ice skates, and he heaved a sigh of relief when slippery cobblestones gave way to crunchy gravel. St. Jude's lifeboat bobbed in ankle deep water, her fluorescent orange stripes gleaming in the dark bay. Ozzie glanced over his shoulder and his stomach fluttered. Hooded silhouettes were careening down the long ramp at breakneck speeds.

"They're coming!" he said.

"Keep moving," Mrs. Willowsby snapped.

Ozzie reached the rowboat first and pushed it until the North Sea swirled around his waist. He boosted his sister into the boat, and together they hoisted the cursing housekeeper on board. Alex fumbled oars into their locks as Ozzie stole a glance at the beach. A fleet-footed assassin reared back and hurled a knife, mid-stride.

Kling

The blade ricocheted off the hull, next to his shoulder.

Alex shouted, "Get in!"

An icy wave slapped the breath from Ozzie's lungs. Splashing sounds drew closer. He clung to the railing, kicking, while Alex and Mrs. Willowsby threw their weight against the oars. A hand seized Ozzie's ankle as the lifeboat nosed over a breaking wave. He screamed—or would have, if the ocean hadn't chosen that moment to drown him. Ozzie rolled onto his back, gasping and sputtering, but refused to surrender his grip on salvation.

The assassin's hood fell back, exposing a smooth-shaven, graffitied head. Pupilless eyes radiated blue light, like portals to another dimension—it was a face calculated to haunt dreams. The killer hauled himself up Ozzie's leg, gathered a fistful of jacket, and palmed the dagger clenched in his teeth. He screamed triumphantly and thrust the blade at Ozzie's belly.

THWACK

An oar clocked the assassin across his temple. He slumped into the rowboat's wake and was devoured by a wave. Ozzie looked up and saw Mrs. Willowsby, his avenging angel, silhouetted by lightning from a storm brewing offshore. She clicked the oar into its lock, then helped him scale the heaving gunwale.

"Row, children! We must see to our defenses."

Arctic wind sliced Ozzie to the bone as he struggled to match Alex's powerful strokes. "M-mrs. W-W-Willowsby," he stuttered, "*w-why* are people trying...to ki-kill us?" The twins stopped rowing, allowing the lifeboat to drift with the swells. Ozzie strained to hear over the howling wind and chattering of his teeth.

The old woman's face hardened. "Your grandfather traveled farther than anyone knows. I should have stopped him." Lightning flashed on the horizon.

Alex shrugged. "Is that all?"

Dramatic pronouncements about "exploring the ends of the earth" were a Forsythe family tradition, second only to dying under mysterious circumstances. Ozzie removed Noko's box from his jacket pocket. Its metal surface was inexplicably warm after his recent baptism. What did you drag us into, Grandfather?

"That is all you need to know," Mrs. Willowsby said.

Alex slapped her oar against the water. "People are trying to kill us!"

"And thus far, they have failed," the housekeeper snapped. "Now, row. Every second is precious." Her lips tightened as she glared at the box in Ozzie's hand, and he got the impression she was considering foisting Grandfather's gift onto Davy Jones. He slipped the silver box into his pocket and grabbed an oar.

The North Sea enjoys a well-deserved reputation as a watery graveyard, so no one complained when hundreds of years ago an anonymous private citizen built St. Jude's Lighthouse on a tiny island off the coast of England, where it served as a vital navigation aid until the Admiralty decommissioned it in the 1920s. Local opinion was divided about whether Keeper's Rock earned its name from the unbroken line of curmudgeonly lightkeepers who tended the property or the island's ever-growing hoard of shipwreck debris.

The central spire of Keeper's Rock rose from the ocean like a fist punching the sky. St. Jude's topped the island, suspended three hundred feet over raging water by a spiderweb of ropes, pulleys, and reclaimed yardarms. Sheer cliffs and a ravenous, ship-hungry reef offered only one sheltered approach to the narrow strip of beach on the southwestern shore. Alex and Ozzie timed the wave sets perfectly and surfed in on the back of a ten-foot roller.

At the first scrape of land, Mrs. Willowsby fell out of the boat, then limped up the footpath, clutching her side. "Quickly, children!"

Ankle-deep mud swallowed Ozzie's feet with a satisfied belch. He sighed, abandoning his shoes and socks to their fate. It was just as well—even numb, his bare feet gripped the ground with more conviction than those worthless loafers had. Bullets of rain pelted Ozzie's face as he stumbled up the path to find Alex waiting beneath Keeper's Forest, the island's long-suffering, solitary tree. Branches creaked and snapped overhead in a symphony of tortured fiber as violent gusts battered the exposed ridge.

His sister gaped at his feet. "Are you okay?"

He nodded, too cold to speak.

"See you at the top!" Alex said, bounding up the makeshift stairs with exasperating confidence. Why was Ozzie the only person with reservations about shoving planks of salvaged wood into a vertical rock face, then calling them "stairs"? He fumbled for the safety chain and followed his sister, stepping delicately to avoid collecting splinters as he circled the spire.

As much as he dreaded climbing them, the planks proved useful when Social Services visited St. Jude's for a welfare check after Grandfather took custody of the twins seven years ago. Exhausted from the strenuous row and perilous hike, the caseworker pronounced the island unfit for *any* inhabitants, including mountain goats. One look at the plank stairs sent her into hysterics, and she demanded the children return to the mainland at once.

Ozzie remembered the outrage dripping from Grandfather's indignant cries of, "Courting death? *Mountain goats?* Are you mad?" When the explorer stomped into the house and slammed the door, the twins barricaded themselves in the bathroom, ready for a siege.

"Children! Come here."

They found Sir Quidby in the kitchen, slicing vegetables with stiff-jawed intensity.

"We don't want to go!" Alex blurted.

Grandfather slashed crusts off a stack of white bread with four savage chops. "Don't fret, Alexandria. Cucumber sandwiches will disarm this young woman's nefarious ambitions, just as they did Queen Losweta of the Chompasca tribe."

Ozzie's curiosity momentarily outweighed his concern. "Who?"

"A rainforest tribe I discovered by accident whilst bathing in what turned out to be their sacred pool." Sir Quidby arranged the sandwiches on a tray and poured two cups of tea. "Their high priest challenged me to a belly flop duel for my life. The rest, as they say, is excruciating history." He nudged the front door open with his toe and floated down the plank stairs like a server in a posh restaurant. Ozzie held his breath while muttered pleasantries lofted to the lighthouse windows. Could cucumber diplomacy work a miracle?

"Am I *bribing* you?"

Uh-oh.

"By all means, inform the police—I myself wish to report an invasion by an obstructive, goat-hating bureaucrat!" Grandfather stormed up the staircase, red-faced and brandishing the silver tray like a shield. He stopped in the doorway and shouted down at his unseen nemesis, "Madam, if you cannot respect the sanctity of cucumber sandwiches, further conversation is pointless. My grand-children shall remain, now and always, *with me!*"

The Forsythes gathered around the observatory telescope to watch the caseworker row back to Jackal's Cove. The next morning, Sir Quidby called in a favor from a mysterious "friend in the government," and two days later, Mrs. Willowsby knocked on the front door.

Social Services dispatched a stream of caseworkers to Keeper's Rock, but only one—a retired alpine guide named Sigmund—conquered the planks. Fortunately, Mrs. Willowsby's cucumber sandwiches proved irresistible, and they forged a truce.

Ozzie scrambled up the last steps and lunged for the soggy patch of grass that moonlighted as the lighthouse's front yard. An ill-timed gust of wind knocked him off course, and only an eleventh-hour grab at the bronze bust embedded in the lawn saved him from getting blown off the cliff. Ozzie gave the statue a grateful peck on its wrinkled forehead. The sculpture was more than a handily placed tribute to a wizard-bearded, weather-worn lightkeeper—thanks to the Historic Preservation Act, it was the only thing standing between St. Jude's and condemnation by the Lamswool Housing Authority.[*1]

"Willowsby says to hurry!" Alex shouted, as she rappelled down the side of the main house to bolt a makeshift storm shutter over the dining room's thick-paned window. A hodgepodge of repurposed salvage gave the building a whimsical nautical vibe.

WHAP. WHAP. WHAP.

A ship's rudder broke loose and battered a fourth story light-house window, shattering glass and sending wood fragments tumbling into the dark ocean. Alex, oblivious to gale force winds and the consequences of gravity, scrambled up the side of the tower, then secured the thrashing board with a grin. How could she be so casual about dancing on the knife edge of calamity, yet freak out about wearing a dress?

Chock-Chock-Chock-Chock

Ozzie watched the lightkeeper pound a wooden stake into the edge of the northern bluff. It was a mystery why a decommissioned lighthouse needed tending, but Grandfather's purchase of St. Jude's had been contingent on retaining the caretaker who dwelled in the rickety shack on the south cliff. The cantankerous old salt had outlived local memory of his name, so everyone just called him Keeper.[*2] Tonight, Keeper had abandoned his yellow raincoat in favor of a red bandana, black sleeveless shirt, and a pair of bandoliers. Raindrops slalomed down the tinted lenses of his ever-present motorcycle goggles. Hammering stakes while dressed like a freedom fighter was a radical departure from Keeper's daily regimen of fishing, scouring the shoreline, and renovating his shack. There was no point asking what he was up to—on the loneliest crag in the North Sea, the man remained a hermit.

Come to think of it, Ozzie wasn't even certain Keeper spoke

English. On the rare occasions the old man engaged Grandfather in conversation, they used a baffling, long-vowelled language.

Keeper tested a spike with a satisfied grunt, then stood up. "They come tonight." An Eastern European accent colored his gravelly voice.

Ozzie released the door handle like it was dripping lava. A conversation with the lightkeeper was worth risking frostbite. *"They,* as in *the assassins*? Do you know who they are?"

Keeper shook rain from his bushy white beard, then battered another stake into submission. A tattoo of a Polynesian woman riding a dolphin danced on his bicep with each blow. The lightkeeper pulled a fresh stake from his pouch and glanced up. A flash of lightning reflected in his goggles, prompting a chill that had nothing to do with the frigid wind. He whispered, "Noctem."

Noctem.

Latin for "night."

Exhausted from six syllables of chatter, the lightkeeper resumed pounding stakes.

Ozzie conceded to his shivering extremities and entered the house.

He slid Noko's box into a pants pocket, then hung his sopping wet coat on a Burmese Weecho tree by the door. The plant's thorny, scarlet leaves were probably poisonous, but he was beyond caring. Carnivorous flowers snapped at Ozzie's legs as he blazed a trail through a jungle of gift baskets. He swept aside a curtain of vines and nearly impaled himself on the bolt of a steam-powered crossbow trained on the front door. Ozzie sucked his stomach in and tiptoed past the hissing medieval death engine, careful to avoid any contact with its scalding surface.

An arsenal of sharp-edged relics and outlandish projectile gimmickry lay in neat rows at the foot of the main staircase. Most, like the backpack-mounted catapult and two-handed throwing broadsword,[*3] were museum-quality examples of humanity's least successful attempts to diminish its ranks, but a few humdingers could wreak serious havoc when pointed in the proper direction.[*4]

Mrs. Willowsby limped from row to row, inspecting weapons like a warlord preparing for a barbarian invasion.

Ozzie stepped over a spiked mace and sidled up to Alex, who had returned from fortifying the house's exterior and was drying by the pot-bellied stove in the kitchen. She'd changed into black leggings, a black t-shirt, and fresh sneakers—a welcome glimpse of normality after the madness of the last two hours.

"Did Mrs. Willowsby say anything else?" he asked.

"She ranted about 'protecting our flank,' then rounded up enough cannonballs to sink the Spanish Armada." Alex pointed to the cargo bay, where they winched supplies up to the house. The barn door was open, allowing sheets of rain to drench a pyramid of cannonballs that was poised to repel attacks from the sea.

"This is crazy," Ozzie said. The twins pressed against the wall as Mrs. Willowsby stalked by, muttering about booby traps. When her footsteps faded, he asked, "Think the stories are true?"

Alex snorted. "After what she did in the pub? Definitely. I *told* you I saw her practicing nunchucks in the kitchen."

Ozzie lowered his voice, "Do you think she's killed people?"

"I think I want her to adopt me."

He rolled his eyes. "This isn't funny, Alex. Assassins—*assassins!* —broke up the funeral. One of them almost stabbed me! If it weren't for her and Noko, you would be—"

"I know." Alex wedged her hands into her armpits and rocked from foot to foot as she stared at the fire. "Whoever Willowsby is, I'm glad she's on our side."

"I didn't know we *had* a side until today," Ozzie muttered. Muffled hammering reminded him of his earthshaking news. "You're not going to believe this, but Keeper talked to me."

Alex's eyes goggled. "What did he say?"

"*They come tonight*—and he called the assassins *Noctem*."

"Noctem, as in *night*?"

"Yeah."

"Weird."

Mrs. Willowsby wiped her face with a blood-spattered handker-chief, then gestured for the twins to join her at the bottom of the staircase. "A battle is coming," she said, as if discussing the price of milk. She slalomed through her armory and disappeared into the foyer jungle. Bushes convulsed, leveling stacks of unopened mail. "Our adversaries are well-trained. They will neither surrender nor give quarter." Mrs. Willowsby grunted, moving something heavy. A crate fell open, spilling fragments of an Allosaurus femur—another random artifact in a museum curated by a hoarder. "Stay in Ozymandias' room until the fighting finishes."

Ozzie said, "Sounds good to me. Should we call the police?"

"In my experience, the authorities are useless in these situations."

Alex pounded the floor with her heel. "We can help you fight!"

A family of porcelain nesting dolls flew out of the bushes and shattered against the wall. "You would only get in my way."

"But, I can—"

"*No.*" Mrs. Willowsby emerged from the undergrowth, clutching a package. "Noko's box triggered the attack. We won't know the true depth of your grandfather's idiocy until we see what's inside it." Cities burned in her eyes as she thrust Grandfather's journal against Ozzie's chest. "Open the box."

---

1. According to Town Hall's spotty records, the lighthouse began life in the 1600s as a ninety-foot tapered pillar. In the 1700s, the light keeper built a shack next to the lighthouse. A rash of shipwrecks from an offshore naval engagement in the mid-1800s gave the lightkeeper raw material to expand his house. The 1900s brought style renovations and the addition of a second story, resulting in a glorified fisherman's farmhouse with Victorian-era appointments.

    The constantly-evolving structure delighted history buffs and crushed the soul of every Chairperson of the Lamswoolian Home Owners Association for the past four hundred years.
2. With the exception of Lamswoolian pub patrons, who preferred to use the slightly less formal "That Daft Bugger On The Rock".
3. Two-handed throwing broadswords died out when early adopters realized the inherent flaw in disarming themselves.
4. And considerably more damage if aimed poorly.

CHAPTER 4
THE ARROWHEAD

Alex paced in front of Ozzie's window. "Ridiculous!" she said.

"Agreed." He tossed Noko's box to his sister.

"I wouldn't have gotten in Willowsby's way."

"Oh, sorry—I thought we were discussing the idea that after eight self-defense classes, you were ready to fight assassins."

"I know enough to fight *you*," she growled.

Ozzie fled to his closet, where a dry pair of jeans, t-shirt, and a gray wool sweater transformed him from an ice sculpture into a human. Socks and sneakers summoned a barrage of pins and needles to his numb feet.

He re-emerged to find Alex investigating the box. "What do you think?" he asked.

"No hinges or lid." She ran a thumb over inscriptions on its surface. "This writing is weird—foreign, but familiar."

"I saw some like it in Dad's journal," he said.

Alex's pursed lips betrayed her skepticism.

Ozzie's shoulders tightened. Whether she believed him or not, he'd never forget the day he found his father's journal in the study. Dad had been amused by his curiosity, and Mom had been furious when she walked in and caught them flipping through the book.

Her shout—"Humboldt, you promised!"—still echoed in Ozzie's ears. It was the only time he'd ever seen his mother afraid.

After his parents died, he pored over every scrap of his father's research, but the pages with the cryptic writing were gone.

"I surrender." Alex tossed him the box, then tore a strip of packing paper off the Professor's journal.

"You give up too easily," he said.

"Deciphering ancient riddles is your thing. Call me when a temple needs robbing."

Ozzie examined the box's inscriptions under a magnifying glass, puzzling over the hybrid of Greek and Elvish runes. His quick glimpse at Dad's journal was so long ago…

Alex whistled. "Speaking of giving up…" She tilted the book, then flipped from cover to cover. Every page was blank…no sketches, maps, observations, or expedition notes—not even a doodled game of tic-tac-toe, which Grandfather swore was "a lost explorer's best friend."*1

Ozzie took the journal from her and chewed his lip. How many nights had he walked past the study and glimpsed the old explorer scribbling by the light of an oil lamp? He held a page up to the light. "Maybe he used invisible ink? It's not like Grandfather to go to so much trouble for an empty book."

The lighthouse swayed as the storm flexed its muscles. A blast of wind spit Ozzie's window open. Alex slammed it shut and flicked rain off her arms. "It's *exactly* like him," she said, "full of empty promises."

A cacophony of rattles and clangs suggested a train had derailed in the stairwell. Mrs. Willowsby tottered onto the landing and piled an eighteen-inch mound of chain at Sir Spikealot's feet. When the last loop *chinked* into place, she sagged against the doorframe, rubbing her ghost-white knuckles. The housekeeper straightened when she sensed the twins' stares.

"What progress have you made on the box?" she asked, in a tone that threatened to shank anyone who suggested she might need help.

Ozzie dropped the journal on the bed, as if he'd been caught pilfering state secrets. "Working on it." He picked up Noko's box.

A crack of thunder saved him from drowning in an awkward pool of silence. Seconds later, a projectile whistled overhead, sending Ozzie and Alex ducking for cover like frightened ostriches.

Mrs. Willowsby frowned. "Our guests have arrived. If they make it past me, push chains down the stairwell to clear a path, then lower the spare lifeboat and row for open water." She vanished, leaving the twins to play out the nightmare scenario in their heads.

Ozzie's hands grew clammy as he contemplated rowing on the open ocean in a storm at night. He was secretly relieved to see Alex's face blanch.

The housekeeper poked her head back in. "Just to be clear—when I said *guests*, you understand I meant *killers bent on our destruction*, correct?"

Ozzie nodded vigorously, as if giving himself a concussion might purge the memory of a dagger plunging at his stomach in the middle of the North Sea.

"Excellent. Open the box." Pep talk complete, she limped down the stairs.

Alex pressed her face to the window. "There are boats in the bay."

Ozzie squinted through the hazy glass. Between rain bursts, it was possible to make out dark shapes tossing and turning in white-capped surf, half a mile offshore. Dozens of spectral blue eyes returned his stare, like sinister stars. Orange light flared in a boat, and a trail of fire arced over the roof, accompanied by a buzzing rumble. An explosion made books riot on their shelves.

"That was a rocket launcher!" Alex said. "What did Grandfather *do* to these guys?"

Ozzie fought to quell the panic in his voice. "They won't be able to aim from a boat. That wasn't even close."

"We have to help Willowsby."

"You heard her—she needs us to open this."

"That was before we got attacked by a rocket!"

"Do you *want* to make her angrier?" he said.

Alex paced in a circle.

Ozzie steadied the box on his leg. Two smooth triangles flashed red in opposite corners of the lid.

Thumbs and corners.

Grandfather's habit of absentmindedly twiddling with corners of paper had cost his thumbs their fingerprints. When Ozzie asked why he kept doing it, the explorer claimed it was a custom he'd picked up in a town called Labyrinth, and he needed to practice in case he went back.

Ozzie pressed a thumb to each triangle and twisted, like he'd watched his grandfather do a thousand times. A soft *click* stole his breath.

"Alex, look! A keyhole."

A square, black hole waited patiently in the center of the lid, taunting him.

"How did you do it?" she asked.

"Thumbs and corners." Ozzie angled the box, keeping his fingers in position.

"Don't move!"

"I won't." The square keyhole jogged a memory. "I need you to get something from my, um, treasure bag." His cheeks blushed. Ozzie's persistence in calling their father's old messenger satchel his "treasure bag" was a perpetual target of Alex's scorn. Fortunately, a shock wave rattled the room before she could formulate a wisecrack.

"Where is it?" she said.

"My headquarters." He winced, but Alex was either too scared or too focused to mock him for having a "headquarters." "Check under the newspaper clippings about freak Aurora Borealis phenomena."

"You're such a geek." She heaved the bookshelf aside, then ducked into the nook. Alex emerged with their father's worn leather bag and shook it over the bed. Keepsakes and mementos from the Professor's expeditions rained onto the sheet. Where was it? Blowdart gun...clay balls...useless block of paper...yes!

31

"Grab the coin with the bronze cross and embedded emerald," he said. Grandfather gave him that artifact after a failed expedition to the Amazon basin. Ozzie had always thought it strange how the cube-shaped gemstone protruded far enough to spin the coin like a top. "Slide the emerald into the keyhole," he murmured, gritting his teeth as an explosion thumped Keeper's Rock.

The jewel slid into the lid and blinked bright green, like a lovesick firefly. A wave of energy rippled across the surface of the box, sending jolts from Ozzie's fingers to his elbows. He yelped, but held on as the emerald faded to its normal, dark luster.

Click

He tested the lid with a cautious finger tap, and the box creaked open, unveiling Grandfather's gift: a white arrowhead suspended in a bed of translucent red gel.

Alex wrinkled her nose. "Did something die in there?"

He plucked the arrowhead out of the box and wiped it clean of foul-smelling goo. "Noko said the fate of the world depends on this. Maybe it's a clue to a bigger puzzle."

"Or maybe it's just a fancy box holding a stinky arrowhead," Alex said.

Ozzie scraped the stone with his nail. He hadn't expected a map to El Dorado, but a garden variety arrowhead *was* a bit of a letdown.

Two thuds shook the lighthouse in quick succession—the rocketeers were finding their range.

"This is getting serious, Oz." Alex peeked out the window, then ducked. "Three boats landed on the beach."

Ozzie tried to ignore the ratcheting tightness in his chest. He slid to the floor and leaned against the bed frame. "Willowsby said we needed to figure this out."

"She told us to open the box. It's open! We need to get out of this tower!"

He poked the gel and watched it engulf his finger like cold molasses. "Give me a minute," he said. After so many years, he was finally on the verge of answers!

Crack

The lighthouse shivered. A support timber had snapped under the main house.

"Oz?" A note of disbelief in Alex's voice bent his ear. "I know why the arrowhead is special." She pointed at Grandfather's journal.

In all the times Ozzie handled the book, he'd never unwrapped the cover, out of respect for the old explorer's wishes. It was love at first sight. Ornate, embedded metalwork swooped in circular patterns that framed deep gashes in leather binding. The cover was a testament to a lifetime of adventure—and at its center was a shallow, *arrowhead-shaped* cavity.

Ozzie scrubbed the arrowhead on his pants. Was it his imagination or was the stone hotter? He reached for the cover, and when his hand was still an inch away, the arrowhead leapt through the air and snapped into the book with a *clunk*. A noise like tearing canvas pricked Ozzie's ears.

"Did you see it jump out of my hand?" He tried to pry the arrowhead out. "Must be magneti—"

FZZZZZT

Alex yanked the book away from Ozzie's face as a wave of blue energy rippled from the center of the cover. Electricity scorched his hands, and he dropped the journal to the floor. The book's glowing edges flared, then dimmed.

"Get back!" Alex scrabbled at the arrowhead, but her blunt fingernails couldn't dig the stone out.

Ozzie clenched his fist, wincing. "I'm okay...everything is okay."

"You don't know that! This stupid book could kill you." Alex numbered points on her fingers. "First, Grandfather died. Then, assassins crashed his funeral—but thankfully, Mrs. Willowsby is secretly a ninja. Now, creepy blue-eyed killers are invading St. Jude's, a magic arrowhead just electrocuted you, and our escape plan is to paddle into a hurricane." She poked the journal's cover, discharging a blue spark. "Everything is *not* okay."

Staccato rainfall splattered the window, applauding her

outburst. The overhead light flickered, and a faint scream trailed into the howling tempest outside.

Ozzie tested the book cover with his pinkie. All clear. The journal's spine snapped like cracking twigs as he pried it open.

Alex threw her hands up. "Are you even listening to me?"

He turned a page.

"I'm serious, Ozzie. We—" Indignation died on her lips.

The journal was alive with hand-drawn illustrations and notes in the Professor's unmistakable hand. A lump formed in Ozzie's throat as he scanned a random page.

Uncommon Badgadders target the hippocampus, feeding upon their prey's long-term memory.

NOTE: Wear a helmet and limit thinking to a minimum. I suspect they sense brain waves.

Ozzie frowned at the drawing below the text. Someone, presumably Grandfather, had sketched a corpulent, walking elephant trunk straight out of Salvador Dali's nightmares. He flipped through more outlandish drawings.

Fangorius Lumps
Petulant Drawlbeaks
Hatchclaws
Faulty Trills (WARNING: Do not gargle in their presence)

His initial thrill at Grandfather encountering such bizarre beasts was tempered by growing concern that these sketches were the ravings of a madman. For the first time, Ozzie considered the possibility his grandfather *had* gone crazy.

"Alex, what if—"

CRACK

A vertical blue fissure appeared in the space between the bed and the door, spawning a vortex that battered the twins with papers, books, and office supplies. Ozzie clutched the journal to his chest as the scent of burning ozone flooded his mouth with bile.

"Run!" Alex clawed Ozzie's forearm, but his limbs were carved from stone.

The rift sliced downward, as if a knife was cleaving the air. Flashes of light threw ghastly shadows on the walls. Within seconds, the fissure was tall enough for a massive leathery leg to step into the room. Two claws and a reptilian muzzle followed.

Every mental wall Ozzie had built over the last seven years crumbled.

Every therapist was proven a fraud.

Every emotional scar hemorrhaged.

It was happening again.

---

1. According to *An Incompetent Abroad*, Lord Ruffrib's unauthorized account of Sir Quidby's life, the explorer first discovered the saving grace of tic-tac-toe at the age of twenty-one on an expedition to Papua New Guinea:

   "Quidby and his colleague Reginald Katchoo ran afoul of cannibals and found themselves designated as ingredients for a stew. Whilst awaiting their fate in a large cauldron of water, the Professor doodled a tic-tac-toe game on the outer wall of their iron prison. Reginald Katchoo engaged Quidby in a spirited match of wits that drew the attention of their captors.

   The two explorers explained the rules, forming an impromptu tic-tac-toe league, which the cannibals embraced with their usual abundance of enthusiasm. As commissioners of the league and tic-tac-toe strategy experts, Quidby and Reginald Katchoo were deemed too valuable to snack upon, and thus, were released."

CHAPTER 5

MRS. WILLOWSBY'S FIGHT

Renata Willowsby sheltered behind the refrigerator as projectiles chunked into St. Jude's wood siding. Honestly, a Gatling gun? She checked her watch, then lurched into motion as the last round from the ammo belt slugged the wall. Mrs. Willowsby felled the gunner with a single shot from her repeating crossbow, then ducked behind the shredded window frame.

Of course, the assassins weren't using an actual Gatling gun, but aside from firing glowing bullets that sparked with blue electricity, the weapon's fundamental principles—spinning barrels and pointless machismo—were the same. A fresh onslaught of ordnance punched the walls with vigor and volume that overwhelmed the torrential rain, but the housekeeper had already ghosted to her next objective.

Mrs. Willowsby skulked to the far end of the house, weaving to avoid exposed sight lines. It was worrying how quickly the assassins had regrouped after the Juniper Rhinoceros debacle. Aside from their fondness for impractical weapons, these lads knew what they were doing. She risked a quick glance out of the cargo bay and permitted herself a satisfied nod—her cannonball blitz had dampened the attackers' enthusiasm for scaling support timbers beneath the main house.

Large-bore rounds—no doubt from an absurd siege weapon—pummeled St. Jude's. Renata grimaced and reloaded her crossbow with a backhanded slap. She'd plug holes as fast as she could, but there was only one way this fight was going to end.

For the tenth time that day, Mrs. Willowsby cursed the Professor for dragging the twins into his buffoonery. For the hundredth time, she cursed herself for not anticipating the attack at the funeral. She shouldn't have allowed herself to get emotionally attached to the Forsythes. Sentiment made her soft. The housekeeper worked her way back to the front door, sneaking shots through the skeletal remains of windows.

A discordant melody warbled on the wind. The lyrics were indecipherable, but Keeper's raspy baritone revved up and down the scale like a chainsaw. Her mouth twitched. Keeper was exactly the sort of wily codger she wanted in her corner when the chips were down.

Best get running, lads.

Two explosions rocked the island, knocking her to the floor. She scowled. Those were conventional detonations, not the space-age stuff the Gatling Boys were slinging.

Another blast swayed the house.

Wait—when she barged up the planks twenty minutes ago, Keeper had been pounding in ranging stakes and wearing his dynamite-fishing bandoliers. Renata thumped the floor with her fist and shouted, "Keeper!"

That bloody lightkeeper and his home-brew nitroglycerin were going to blast St. Jude's to pieces. What's the point in fighting assassins if you do their job *for* them?

BANG

The front door bounced on its iron hinges. Took them long enough—no home invasion was complete without a battering ram. She aimed a flare gun at three crates of antiquated Chinese fireworks stacked by the door. Another blow from the ram scattered splinters and bolts through the jungle like shrapnel.

Her finger whitened on the trigger, a hairsbreadth from giving her guests a welcome they would never forget.

Steady on, Renata. You've got one shot at this.

She didn't notice the static buildup in the air until her arm hair stood at attention. The temperature plummeted twenty degrees in the space of two horrified heartbeats.

A Breach.

A terrible rending sound, like a monstrous, slow-motion whip crack, echoed from the second floor. The sound jolted Mrs. Willowsby into action. She counted in her head, as Sir Quidby had instructed.

Two...Three...Four...

How many seconds did a Breach last again? Forty? Forty-five? She steadied her aim, hit the fireworks crates dead-on, then limped up the stairs.

Seven...Eight...

By the time the ancient bottle rockets ignited, the housekeeper was in the upstairs hallway. She tossed the flare pistol aside and wrested a broadsword from a suit of armor.

"Sixteen...Seven-*teen*, let *go!*" A rusty gauntlet surrendered the blade with a begrudging clatter. Renata stumbled backwards, catching her dress on a suit of sub-Saharan porcupine-quills. She yanked free and hobbled up the lighthouse's spiral staircase. "Twenty-one...Twenty-two..."

The broadsword trembled as fatigue sapped her wrist strength. Not the most practical weapon for indoor combat, but there wasn't time to be picky.

"Twenty-three...Twenty-four..."

The crackling, spitting hiss of the Breach grew louder. Beams of light streaked out the doorway like sunlight dancing on a lake. A blood-curdling roar from the room tightened Mrs. Willowsby's grip.

Her count reduced to a hoarse whisper, "*Twenty-six...Twenty-seven...*"

The housekeeper raised her blade and channeled the agony from her wounded leg into one of the Worst Battle Cries of All Time.

"*TWENTY-EIGHT!*"

Fortunately, broadswords have a way of making people take you seriously.

She charged, assessing and prioritizing threats as she crossed the threshold. The Breach hovered in the center of the room, threatening to scorch her retinas. Alex lay unmoving, sprawled next to the window. Ozzie was on the floor, pressed against the bed and clutching the Professor's journal to his chest, his face a rictus of terror. Papers, books, and furniture whipped around the room like debris in a tornado.

A sputtering cord of white energy led from the Breach to a seven-foot tall, long-tailed lizard encased in a grid-like suit of lightning. The beast reached for Ozzie.

"Hey!" Mrs. Willowsby planted her heel, translating momentum into a deadly pirouette. The brute sidestepped her blade, then raked her shoulder with an open-clawed slap. Pain tore the sword from the housekeeper's grip, so she threw a blind elbow strike to the creature's sternum. A *crack* confirmed contact, then fire seared through her forearm. Her newly fractured elbow had penetrated the exoskeleton, only to hit a concrete bunker masquerading as a breastbone.

The monster pinned the housekeeper's arms, lifted her off the ground, then ravaged her eardrums with a full-throated roar. Predatory, slitted pupils hunted for fear in Mrs. Willowsby's defiant glare, but found none. The beast snarled and squeezed like a garbage compactor, cracking Renata's rib cage. She swallowed a scream, knowing from experience that a deep breath would generate a fountain of pain. Her tormentor tossed her against the wall with a dismissive grunt.

Agony swept Renata to the brink of unconsciousness.

Shallow breaths.

She'd lost count, but it had to be at least thirty-five seconds now. If Quidby was right, the Breach wouldn't stay open much longer.

The monster crouched in front of Ozzie and traced a claw down the cover of the Professor's journal, purring with pleasure.

Mrs. Willowsby risked a gulp of air.

"Oy."

Her shout was a croak. She winced, then gutted out a deeper breath.

"*Oy!*"

Stabbing pain blurred her vision.

The window exploded in a hailstorm of glass. Another lightning-clad lizard beast splintered the window frame and fell into the room, trailing a fizzing rope of white energy. This creature was shorter, around six feet tall, and sported red-lensed welding goggles.

Mrs. Willowsby balled her fists and knuckled to her feet, scanning the room for weapons. She was calculating the destructive potential of a lamp when the goggled intruder bellowed and charged the first monster. The behemoths collided with a thunderclap, unleashing a furious clash of sparks that set fire to Ozzie's desk. They rolled across the room, biting and grappling like wild beasts.

The crackling energy cord leading from the Breach to the larger lizard's exoskeleton strobed red. The creature screeched and dove for Ozzie, but Goggles had a stranglehold on its tail. The trapped monster clawed at the floor, dragging both brutes toward the boy, one inch at a time. A warning buzzer blared and the blinking exoskeleton lit the room blood-red, like a murder scene in a Hitchcock film. The beast lunged for Ozzie's throat but fell short, writhing on the floor as its suit blazed brighter. A repulsive stench of burning flesh filled the room. The energy leash snapped taut, dragging the howling warrior feet-first into the blazing rift.

CRACK

The Breach sealed with a blinding flash, leaving a demolished room as the only evidence it ever existed. Mrs. Willowsby steadied herself on the doorframe and summoned what little authority her cracked ribs allowed to threaten Goggles with an unsteady finger. "Leave this house at once," she panted. "We are *not* your enemy."

The monstrous reptile snorted, gathered the trinkets on the bed in a sheet, and slung the makeshift bag over its shoulder. It reached for Ozzie, who screamed, battering the beast's head with the

40

Professor's journal. Renata felt a twinge of pride—at least the boy was fighting back. There was hope for him yet.

Goggles snatched the book from Ozzie's hand and dropped it in its bag. A screeching buzzer catapulted the creature into frenzied action. It whacked Ozzie senseless, gathered him under its arm, and stalked to the window. The beast's exoskeleton flashed red as it collected Alex's limp body, then climbed out the gaping hole in the wall.

"No!" Mrs. Willowsby cried. A blast rocked the lighthouse, but the assassins were of little concern now. Renata hobbled to the window in time to witness an immense rift of radiant light snap closed in the stormy sky.

The Forsythe Curse had devoured another generation.

Quidby, what have you done?

CHAPTER 6
THE HUNT

"A platoon of warriors guarded the book!" Lieutenant Vash whined.

Captain Skhaar's claws chewed divots in the stern rail as lightning raged around the airship *Revenge*. Flying so close to the Dome spurred his stomach to mutiny, but hearing such a pathetic excuse from an underling made him want to vomit. A downburst swatted the airship. Skhaar's death grip on the rail kept his feet on deck, but his scowl deepened with every pitch and yaw of the floundering vessel.

When Home Office assigned him to *Revenge* three months ago, the crew found it hilarious that one of the Fury King's Annihilators was uncomfortable with heights. After Skhaar unceremoniously executed their captain and rolled his carcass over the side, the laughter stopped.

Projecting an air of palpable menace came as naturally to Skhaar as skinning a murmoot. In the old days, sky jockeys cowered at the sight of the three red stripes disfiguring the left side of his face, branding him an Annihilator. But size and reputation didn't intimidate the new generation of Maelstrom clutchlings—they worshipped speed and vigor, the currencies of youth. The more foolish among them even mocked Skhaar's tail stump—an injury that would dishonor a lesser warrior.

That didn't last long.

The helmsman strained at the wheel and avoided eye contact with his captain. Around the ship, crew fought to stabilize *Revenge,* while subtly distancing themselves from Lieutenant Vash. All eyes and ears were locked on Skhaar.

Good.

Time for another lesson on the price of failure.

Annihilators are trained to unleash maximum destruction, but decades of warfare—and more importantly, survival—taught Skhaar to curate his rage. Instead of flaring out in a bonfire of glorious mayhem like so many of his brethren, he sculpted anger like an artist. When Skhaar focused his rage, the world bent to his will—and Lieutenant Vash had earned his undivided attention.

Skhaar scowled through a wave of nausea. "What of the book?" he snarled.

"I touched it, Captain."

"You touched it."

"My sivsuit timed out. I barely escaped!"

That much was true. Streams of blood oozed from a grid of ugly pink welts tattooing Lieutenant Vash's entire body. Skhaar's tail stump twitched, rattling a chain beneath his tattered red cloak. He unhooked a fist-sized metallic ball from his shoulder strap and dropped it to the deck with an ominous thud. Normally he wouldn't waste dynami on an object lesson, but this close to the Divide, there was plenty to spare. He activated a power stone on his belt, discharging a red stream of energy that burst from his tail stump and rippled down the chain to engulf the ball in crimson lightning.

A flick of his stump seared a curved line in the black hurtle-wood deck. The retrieval mission was a debacle, but at least it would breathe new life into the legend of Skhaar the Annihilator's Tail Mace.

The ball hissed and skittered in Skhaar's footsteps as he circled Vash like a shatterjoy taunting a gruffletrunt. The lieutenant's panicked expression gave the Annihilator a measure of workman-like satisfaction.

"You *touched* it?" Skhaar's whisper was barely audible over the groans of tortured rigging. "If you *touched* it, WHERE IS IT?"

Lieutenant Vash spat the answer. "The apprentice kept it."

Skhaar bellowed and twisted, whipping the mace in a blur that struck the Lieutenant's chest like a meteor, crushing his lungs. Vash dragged himself across the aft deck, gasping.

"Spare me your pitiful excuses," Skhaar growled. "Who defeated you?"

The lieutenant's eyes bulged as he sucked enough breath to wheeze, "The runt."

The Annihilator fixed the crew with a dead-eyed stare, then casually flicked his tail stump, ending Vash's agony with a crack of bone.

Once dynami burned the mace ball clean, Skhaar depowered and coiled the chain, humming his Deathsong.*[1] Vash's failure earned him a mention in verse eighty-one, between Olinth Dracoslain and Berlusk the Deceitful.

"Who is next?" Skhaar said.

"Next, Captain?" The watch commander hovered, a picture of military efficiency.

"Below the lieutenant—the next in line for promotion."

"Based on seniority: Master Gunner Trof, sir." The Commander beckoned a quivering, gray underling to approach. The gunner's missing claw didn't hinder him from turning his left palm skyward and clenching his fist in a passable *What-I-Take-Is-Mine* Maelstrom salute.

"Congratulations on your promotion, Lieutenant Trof," Skhaar said.

"T-thank you, Captain."

"Let your first act as lieutenant be to eliminate evidence of your predecessor's weakness."

Lieutenant Trof bowed his head and began disposing of Vash's remains.

Skhaar clipped the ball to his shoulder strap, dreading the

mountain of paperwork he had set into motion. To earn an officer's commission at such a young age, Vash was undoubtedly a blood relative of a senator, clan chief, or member of the royal court. The non-combatant know-it-alls at Home Office would be giddy with condemnation when they got wind of Skhaar's latest purge. *"We don't have an endless supply of warriors, Skhaar. Training costs time and money, Skhaar. That's the fourth lieutenant you disemboweled this week, Skhaar!"*

Maybe they were right. Maybe the old ways—*his* ways—were obsolete in the new, *improved* Maelstrom, but no one complained when he got results.

Revenge nosed out of the storm clouds and settled into the soothing rhythms of level flight.

"What heading, sir?" The helmsman's eagerness grated on Skhaar's nerves. The crew was always irritatingly relieved when they delivered their repticidal, airsick captain to smooth skies.

Still, it was a good question. If Lieutenant Vash was telling the truth about fighting the runt—and Skhaar, an expert at soliciting Famous Last Words, was certain of it—then Pascal had scrounged enough parts to build another sivsuit. The audacious act elevated the inventor a few notches in Skhaar's esteem—not all the way to Worthy Opponent, of course, but verging on A Minor Irritant.

If the inventor and the runt brought the book through the Divide, it might still be possible to redeem this mission. Skhaar put himself in the mind of his quarry—after spending months monitoring the Dome, Pascal would need supplies and information. This far south, that meant one place.

"Head northeast, for the last known position of Aeronoth."

There were too many greedy eyes and empty pockets between here and Aeronoth to approach the sky city undetected. Alone, a scout ship like *Revenge* was outmatched by a Smuggler's Alliance corvette or even a Merchant Guild trade galleon, but a small Maelstrom fleet would demand respect. Skhaar needed reinforcements.

He turned to the Avianmaster and barked, "Message *Dreck* and *Karkis* to join us. It's time the fleshlings felt the wrath of the Storm."

"Aye, Captain!" The bird handler scribbled two sets of orders, secured them in swallow pods, then fed each capsule to a vicious malark. The long-beaked raptors shrieked, reminding everyone that in addition to being efficient messengers, they were exceptional killing machines. The pair stretched their red-feathered wings with lazy menace, then launched like blood-soaked arrows. Skhaar smirked as his messengers disappeared into the haze. *Dreck* and *Karkis* were under orders to run silent, so ship-to-ship radio contact was forbidden.

It always came back to the old ways.

The helmsman spun the wheel with exasperating cheerfulness, and the horizon tilted. Skhaar's claws dimpled the railing. Just a little longer. The sooner he recovered the book, the sooner his stomach would stop trying to climb out of his throat. Until then, in typical Annihilator fashion, he'd make sure anyone who got in his way lived *just* long enough to regret it.

---

1. Sauracian warriors traditionally honor defeated foes by remembering them in Deathsong.

   Vanquished opponents are ranked in descending order according to their skill and courage in combat. Particularly brutal battles may earn an opponent an entire verse, while minor skirmishes merit only a name. A Deathsong is a warrior's penance for their destructive path.

   In the modern Maelstrom, Deathsongs are ridiculed as sentimentalism, since fallen opponents are unworthy of remembrance.

CHAPTER 7
THE DIVIDE

Ozzie's inner ear did backflips as his prison cell shuddered. He massaged life into his throbbing right shoulder and puzzled through the chaos of the past five minutes. The lizard beast had lugged him across a rickety gangplank suspended between his window and a crackling, shimmering...blimp? Dirigible? It was definitely an airship—the vessel hanging beneath the balloon was as long as two school buses and sported a dragon figurehead on its blunt bow.

Wooden deck planks complained as he fumbled blindly along the wall until he found Alex, unconscious but breathing. Ozzie clenched his fist and pounded the floor.

Thump

He was right.

Thump

All the slender threads he'd pulled, searching for answers...

THUMP

No one, not even his twin sister, believed an eight-year-old who swore a glowing dinosaur kidnapped his parents. Patronizing smiles and worried frowns led to psychologists and hand puppets. Eventually, it was easier to claim he'd made the whole thing up.

But he was right.

47

Vindication probably felt better outside a cell.

A bestial howl clamored above the wailing wind. The floor tilted abruptly, then dropped away. Ozzie braced in a corner as the room spun like a centrifuge. When gravity returned, he grabbed the door handle.

Click

The latch flipped up—the door was unlocked! He pushed it open as quietly as possible, gaping at the madness that greeted him.

Streams of emerald flames scorched an indigo sky. Grotesque, colossal shadows seethed and roiled outside a halo of light surrounding the airship. A flying whale with a dozen madly blinking eyes strayed into luminescence, bellowed an ear-bending roar, then peeled away. Lightning cascaded through rigging, outlining an enormous balloon overhead. Radiant white cargo netting blanketed the vessel, like a jumbo-sized, glowing exoskeleton.

Sparks skittered across the deck near the bow, where a bulky form crouched in a tangled mess of wires. The creature snarled, flung its welding torch aside, and punched a metal box. The netting flickered, then blazed twice as brightly, illuminating the airship like the Eiffel Tower on New Year's Eve.

"Whoa!" Ozzie shielded his eyes.

The beast spun. Red goggles glared accusingly. A spine-shivering growl promised pain.

"Sorry, I was just…" Ozzie stammered.

Crack

The vessel pitched sideways, sending him tumbling down the steep deck. A frantic grab at the railing offered a breath of hope, then his fingers slipped, and Ozzie plunged into an empty, infinite void.

He fell away from the ship in slow motion, flailing like an untethered astronaut on a spacewalk gone wrong. A stuttering purr drew his attention downward, where midnight-black monsters waited beyond the ship's halo. Their howls were eager, triumphant, and above all, *hungry*. Ozzie screamed and reached for the shrinking vessel, a million miles away.

A claw clamped his outstretched wrist, threatening to tear his arm off. He looked up and saw his reflection in a pair of opaque red lenses above a snout of bared teeth. His savior dangled from a long cable that spooled back to the airship. Ozzie shrieked as a tentacle slithered around his ankle, wrenching him down toward fangs and darkness. The lizard grunted and spun a dial on its belt, activating a winch that reeled them up into the globe of light, to the yowling dismay of the shadow beasts.

When they neared the ship, the lizard yanked Ozzie to eye-level and roared. Gut-wrenching halitosis vied with spleen-quivering volume for the honor of overwhelming his senses. The beast tossed him over the railing like a sack of potatoes. Before Ozzie could regain his feet, a calloused paw seized his neck and flung him into the open prison cell, where he collided with Alex and thumped his head on the wall. The last thing he heard as the door slammed was the snarled equivalent of *"And stay there!"*

Ozzie woke from a dream about a spaghetti monster, winced, and tried to massage his temples, but his hands were pinned to his sides. Brawny, leathery arms rasped his skin as they laid him on a cool, flat surface. Volatile chemicals and motor grease singed his nostrils. The faint chatter of flapping rigging and creaking wood jolted him fully awake.

A glowing orb swung on a wire, casting ominous shadows across test tubes and surgical instruments. Sweat trickled down Ozzie's forehead. He'd seen enough television to know nothing good happens to anyone who wakes up on a lab table. A deep-voiced creature snuffled and growled behind his head. Ozzie forced his eyes closed and inched his heel to the edge of the table. With a head start, he might outrun the heavy-booted lizard.

Come on, Ozzie. You can do this.

One.

Two.

Three.

He scissored upright, and a tail clotheslined his chest, mashing him against the table. Ozzie curled into a ball in a desperate bid for air. Between gasps, he got an unobstructed view of his captor.

The lizard was a cross between a professional wrestler and an overweight Komodo dragon. Red-lensed goggles perched above a pair of yellow, slit-pupiled eyes. A red stripe ran down the reptile's back, from its anvil-shaped forehead to the tip of the beefy, ridged tail crushing Ozzie's sternum. Stubby legs and a squat neck completed the look of a bombproof, walking tank.

Another creature leaned into the light, prompting Ozzie to do a double take. This one had knock-knees, a pronounced potbelly protruding from a single-sleeved trench coat, and a serpentine neck capped by an elongated head. There was something undeniably camel-ish about it—if camels walked on two legs, sported pros-thetic left arms, and wore World War I-era pilot helmets that offered a selection of flip-down magnifying lenses. A six-inch milli-pede slalomed between the camel's metal fingers, forming infinity symbols with the neon green stripe that accented its orange body.

Red Goggles snarled and jabbed a claw at Ozzie. The camel waved the millipede and belched. Ozzie eyed a collection of tools on a workbench—if he lunged, he might reach something he could use as a weapon. The camel huffed a command, and the lizard slapped its tail across Ozzie's lap like a roller coaster restraint. A paw forced his head sideways against the table.

Panic lubricated Ozzie's tongue. "What are you doing?"

Heat exploded behind his right ear. He screamed—first in horror, then pain. The lizard released Ozzie's neck, and he jammed his chin to his chest to stare at the millipede dangling over his abdomen. "Leave me alone!"

The camel's prosthetic hand opened, as if offering a gift, and the insect flowed onto Ozzie's stomach. It circled his belly button in a jumble of twitching limbs and snapping pincers.

"Let me go!"

The millipede turned toward Ozzie's voice, as if noticing him for the first time. It tested the air, then streamed up his shirt. Tiny feet tingled wherever they touched bare skin. Ozzie's frantic pleas jumped an octave as the insect rippled up his neck and behind his right ear. He heard, rather than felt, the grinding of bone. A thousand needle pricks radiated agony through his skull.

Ozzie clawed behind his ear and touched a lump that wriggled beneath his skin. Blood smeared his fingers—the millipede had burrowed into bone! He shrieked and thrashed, dislodging the lizard's tail from his lap. His torturers exchanged a surprised look. The camel touched a brass cylinder to Ozzie's temple.

Every nerve ending in his body screamed, and a flash of unbearable brightness forced his eyes shut. Ozzie clenched his jaw until the tide of pain receded.

"What was that?" The deep voice bordered the edge of gruff.

"A prototype surge quantizer." A second, higher-pitched voice fired words like a machine gun.

"What does it do?"

"It discharges enough dynami to jumpstart a frozen turbine. At least, it's supposed to—usually it overloads, then melts in my hand."

"That could kill him!"

Ozzie groaned. A bulging eye blinked at him through a magnifying lens. "Look how happy he is! He's fine. Let's do the other one."

The deep voice growled, "Hurry. I need to tend the ship."

Suffocating weight vanished from Ozzie's legs, but the shock from the quantizer had drained his energy. He resolved to meet his fate with a defiant shrug, or possibly a nap. His head rolled left, where his captors labored over an adjacent table.

"Incision complete," the lizard rumbled.

"Good. This little guy is frisky." The camel dropped a squirming millipede onto a black shirt. It circled, found its bearings, then rippled out of sight. The lizard clomped out of the room, revealing the person lying on the slab.

Alex!

Ozzie croaked, *Wake up.*

His sister didn't flinch when the millipede wriggled into the incision behind her ear. A bulge squirmed under her skin for three disgusting seconds, then lay flat. Alex's eyes shot open. She clutched her head and screamed. Experiencing a millipede burrowing into his skull was horrendous, but watching it happen to his sister was worse.

Ozzie grunted and jackknifed to a sitting position, steadying himself as the airship shuddered. He slid off the table and elbowed past the camel.

"Alex, it's me! You're okay!" Ozzie grabbed his sister's shoulder and lied to her face.

She blinked at blood on her hand, then stared glassily at her brother. "Ozzie? Where are we?"

There was no easy way to explain they'd been kidnapped by a lizard, were currently soaring through a monster-filled void on an airship, and a millipede had just tunneled into her skull. He settled for the truth. "I don't know."

Alex caught sight of the camel over Ozzie's shoulder and shouted, "*What is that?*"

The beast in question inspected a wiring harness under a magnifying lens and sniffed, "How quickly I become a *what*." He plonked the wires down on a workbench and raised an elastic eyebrow at Alex. "Not good at making friends, are we?"

Ozzie forced words through parched lips. "You speak English?"

"No," the camel nodded at a terrarium where an orange-shelled millipede snaked against the glass, "but translapedes do."

"Transla-what? Those things burrowed into our *skulls*!" Ozzie said.

Alex touched the incision behind her ear and her eyes widened.

The camel enunciated slowly, as if explaining to a toddler, "Trans-la-pede. Fascinating creatures. They instantaneously translate language and written words into your native tongue, all for the low price of feeding on your neocortex." He loped past the children and bolted the wiring harness to a wall.

"Feeding on my neocortex?" Ozzie said. "You put a *parasite* in my *head* that's *eating* my *brain*?"

"That's a negative way to spin things." The camel flicked an ear

52

forward and raised the side of his leather helmet, displaying a faded scar. "It's standard practice when you come of age, though there is usually more ceremony involved."

He flicked a switch with a triumphant flourish, and ceiling lights cast a clinical glow across the lab. Crowded workbenches lined the walls, overflowing with tools, gadgetry, and peculiar contraptions. A wall of terrariums housed a menagerie of bizarre and otherworldly creatures, most of them slimy. The camel beamed, then registered the twins' dismay for the first time.

"You'll be fine. Nearly everyone survives."

A gravelly voice from the stairwell scraped rust from the walls. "Given your fondness for courting untimely death, we did not think you would mind."

CHAPTER 8
ICARUS INITIATIVE

The lizard pushed its goggles onto its forehead and traversed the
room in four strides. Water streamed down ridges on the beast's
hide, forming puddles on the floor. The reptile focused a slit iris on
the Forsythes, then bared a mouthful of triangular teeth.

"Who are you and why are you so important to the Maelstrom?" it growled.

Ozzie cleared his throat, fighting the impulse to look smaller
and less appetizing. "I'm Ozzie Forsythe, and my sister is—"

Alex pushed past him, hands on her hips. "Who are *you* and
why did you kidnap us?"

"*Alex…*" Ozzie hissed, tugging her elbow.

The lizard's contemptuous snort ruffled his sister's shirt. "I am
the reason you are still breathing, child. Had I arrived seconds later
—" The reptile frowned, snatched Ozzie's hand, and inhaled with
vacuum cleaner suction. "*Forsythe*? You are progeny of Forsythe?"
It threw a perplexed scowl at its partner. "Impossible. They are little
more than hatchlings!"

The camel shrugged. "*You* brought them back."

"They had the Professor's journal and were under attack by a
Maelstrom warrior wearing *your* sivsuit."

The camel slammed its hoof on the counter, then jabbed at its companion with a dental mirror. "It's not like I intentionally *gave* them tech. I got hungry, didn't lock my lab, and my archnemesis stole my life's work—a tale as old as science. Can we please move on?"

Metal groaned overhead, and the airship rolled.

The reptile growled, "I hope it was a worthy sandwich. It hastened the end of the world," then stormed up the stairs.

"For your information, it was delicious!"

A door slammed.

The camel glared at the ceiling, then turned back to his workbench and spun valves on burnished copper pipes. Steam screeched, gears chattered, and gauges slammed red over a backdrop of bubbling liquid. A haunting, familiar aroma enraptured Ozzie's nostrils.

Coffee.

The camel teased hazel foam from a spigot into a steampunk metal thermos. As bizarre as the scene was, fresh-brewed coffee conjured a comforting illusion of normality.

Alex crossed her arms, unimpressed by the spectacle. "Who *are* you?"

"Depending on who you ask, I'm either a genius or the unwitting architect of an impending apocalypse. I prefer to think of myself as both." He took a generous swig and closed his eyes. "My name is Pascal, and I'm captain of the good ship *Angelus*." He gestured to a placard by the stairs that bore the vessel's name, which he pronounced as "Ann-jealous".

Ozzie blurted, "*What* are you?"

The question hung in the air like a foul odor.

Pascal sighed. "*That's* the sort of bold, forthright inquiry that provokes a tavern brawl or demands an honor duel. No, no, it's fine." He waved Ozzie's stammered apology away. "Best get the dangerously rude questions out. Purge, Ozzie Forsythe. Purge." He propped his elbows on the bench and slouched, potbelly bulging like a melancholy bean bag. "I'm Dromedarian. The closest comparable species on your world is a *camel*," Pascal's nose wrinkled with

55

distaste, "were it blessed with a quadrillion additional firing neurons and impeccable fashion sense."

A faint voice barked, "Brace yourselves!"

The room swiveled in a tight circle, twisting Ozzie's stomach into a Gordian Knot. When the merry-go-round slowed, he swallowed and asked, "Is this Earth?"

"Now *that's* the right sort of question. No, this isn't Earth—and yes it is, depending on—"

"You are in Terravenum, child, floundering high above the Barren and flirting with extinction!" The lizard charged down the stairs like an irate bull. "We have no time to waste on trite conversation. Maelstrom forces are undoubtedly searching for us, and *Angelus* is one envelope tear away from strewing the landscape with our corpses."

"Sorry, are we still trying to scare them?" Pascal locked his elbows and teetered like a zombie. In a robotic monotone, he said, "Children, divulge your secrets or I will harvest your internal organs with blunt utensils!"

Even Alex cracked a grin.

Pascal shrugged off the lizard's glare, opened the lid of a basketball-sized brass globe, and tinkered with wires. "Allow me to avert the inevitable crushing of your frail human anatomy by introducing my companion *before* you insult her." He nodded at the reptile. "This is Layla. She is Sauracian, and maintains the best traditions of her species by denying the existence of humor in the universe."

Sauracian.

The word was a good fit—aside from Layla's red-lensed goggles, utility belt, and thick-soled leather boots, she wouldn't look out of place destroying cardboard cities on a Japanese tv show.

"You saved me from the shadow monsters," Ozzie said.

"You were foolish to abandon *Angelus* while we were in the Divide," the lizard grunted. "Had the Belua captured you, they would have feasted on your flesh for millennia."

The somber proclamation prompted an exchange of silent stares.

"Thanks?" Ozzie said.

Alex raised her hand. "Out of curiosity, are we *currently* surrounded by flesh-feasting shadow monsters?"

"We successfully crossed the Divide," Layla said. "There are no Belua in Terravenum." She leaned over the children. "Now, what is your relationship to Professor Quidby Forsythe?"

The twins' jaws dropped in unison.

"How do you know my grandfather?" Ozzie said.

"We have known the Professor for years, ever since he discovered a path through the Divide."

"There must be a mistake," Alex said. "Our grandfather wasn't a *good* explorer—he mostly wandered around until someone rescued him."

A deep crease formed in Layla's forehead. "Are you not the progeny of Humboldt and Adeline Forsythe?"

Ozzie steadied himself on a workbench. "How do you know our parents? Did you kidnap them too?" His voice cracked, but he didn't care.

"There is no mistake. Your grandfather is well-known in Terravenum."

The Sauracian had dodged Ozzie's questions about his parents, and her gruff tone warned him not to push the subject. He grumbled, "If you say so."

"If you did not know of the Professor's adventures, why did you signal us by activating his journal?" Layla said.

"We weren't trying to activate anything." Ozzie's voice took on an exasperated edge, "Assassins attacked us, then a creature that looked *a lot like you* materialized in my room and tried to take Grandfather's journal. Or kill us. Or *something*." He threw his hands up.

"The Professor has many enemies who covet his research," Layla said. "Once activated, his journal became a beacon to anyone scanning for it. We monitored the Divide for months until we detected its signal—it was the Professor's plan, should he disappear."

"Grandfather is dead," Alex said, matter-of-factly.

Pascal raised his muzzle from the inner workings of the brass ball and cleared his throat. "That's not necessarily true."

A loudspeaker screeched in the stairwell.

"Proximity warning!" Layla stormed out of the lab. "The Maelstrom found us!"

The Dromedarian said, "The Professor isn't dead, he's missing. Welcome to the rescue party!" He vanished up the stairs, then craned his head back in. "Coming?"

Ozzie stumbled onto deck and steadied himself against the pilothouse. In the light of day, *Angelus* shared many of her ocean-going sisters' features. Between her plank deck, mid-ship steering station, and scads of high-tension rigging, she looked all the world like a snub-nosed schooner. A junkyard of gadgets littered her deck, and a propeller engine idled on each side of her stern, wheezing and belching smoke. Alex skipped to the railing and scanned the horizon with a smile, while a glimpse of the cloud bank below weakened Ozzie's knees.

Pascal tugged a line, flaring gas from the patchwork balloon. "Pitch for an emergency descent! Dive!"

"Our flank is vulnerable if they approach from altitude!" Layla snapped, spinning the helm. "We have to outrun them!"

"*Angie* isn't up to it. The powersieve over-torqued her ventral fins."

"I warned you not to pull heavy Gs in the Divide!" Layla tossed an electrical cable to Pascal. "Did you finish the stealth modifications, or were you too busy eating?"

"As if you haven't craved blobadillo tacos!" Pascal slapped three switches down. "And I built *this*!" He brandished the brass sphere proudly. Short tubes poked out of the ball in every direction, like an underwater mine.

"What does it do?" Layla flicked the wheel, and the deck tilted sharply.

"I'm not sure."

"You are an imbecile!"

"You have no soul."

58

Layla smashed a button, choking the alarm. Rushing wind filled the silence. "Activate it then," she said.

Pascal's brow furrowed. "I will."

"Do it."

Lightning flashed above *Angelus*. Three bird-like shapes torpedoed through the clouds, growing larger by the second. Airships.

"Um, guys?" Ozzie said, pointing at the incoming vessels. Bolts of red lightning arced from the middle airship, outlining the predatory, angular contours of its hull.

"Hey!" Alex tugged Pascal's arm, and the inventor bobbled his prototype.

"What?"

"Are those the ships you were worried about? Cause I'm pretty sure you should be."

Pascal tore a junction box open and spliced a river of wires faster than Ozzie could follow. Layla scurried up the starboard rigging with surprising dexterity and vanished behind the air bladder. She dropped to the deck a moment later, generating a mild earthquake.

"I recalibrated the ventral fins," she said. "Do not overstress them."

Pascal slapped the box closed. *Angelus'* twin engines stirred with resentful moans, their propellers chuffing the air. "Go!" he shouted.

Layla slammed the throttles to their stops, and the airship lunged like a thoroughbred charging out of a starting gate. Ozzie plunged his arm through a knotted tangle of rigging, determined to stay on board.

"Dive!" Pascal said.

"We are defenseless!"

"We have *this*!" The inventor flourished his brass globe. Tendrils of smoke wafted from tubes on its surface. "I have a really good feeling about it."

The Maelstrom airships were close enough to make out cutlass-shaking warriors at their railings. They widened into a three-pronged formation, fighting turbulence as their engines buzzed louder. Red lightning flashed.

Layla growled, "We are going to die," then wrenched a lever. *Angelus* lowered her nose.

Pascal whacked his prototype ball with a screwdriver until it kicked smoke production into overdrive. Within seconds, the airship was the head of an expanding triangle of fog. A smokescreen was a cool gimmick, but it didn't help them escape—if anything, they were easier to follow. The Dromedarian fastened a balloon to his invention, then released it into the sky. Ozzie didn't see the point—the cloud would mask *Angelus* from their attackers for one or two minutes, but then what?

The inventor kicked open a storage locker and bellowed, "Icarus Initiative!"

"Absolutely not!" Layla shouted.

"I'm open to better ideas!" he said.

The Sauracian smacked her tail against the deck. "Children, hold onto something and prepare for disaster."

Pascal loped past, dragging a clattering assortment of tubes.

Layla snarled, "If we survive this, I am going to make you suffer."

"That's reasonable," he said. "Commencing Icarus in 15 seconds!"

Angelus shivered and quaked under the strain of the dive, but there was no chance of reaching cover before the Maelstrom ships cleared the smokescreen. Ozzie searched the cluttered deck for something substantial to cling to as the rumble of six straining Sauracian engines pierced the veil of smoke.

"Over here!" Alex beckoned him to a rope ladder.

Pascal plugged a cable into the air bladder and counted down, "10...9...8..."

"Is this really happening?" Ozzie said.

Alex looped a line around his waist. "I've pinched myself twenty times and haven't woken up yet." She grinned and tested her knot with a hard tug. How could she smile at a time like this? Ozzie dusted off memories of fifth grade Greek mythology as his sister tethered herself to the rigging. Let's see…Icarus flew too close to the sun, accidentally melted his wings, then—

Oh no.

Layla cut power to the engines.

"2…1…"

Ozzie wedged into the ratlines and held his breath.

WHUMP

Angelus plummeted like a homesick boulder. Ozzie's feet raced his stomach to the sky as fabric flogged above him in a mess of limp rigging. Alarms shrieked, but the emergency was obvious— the air bladder had collapsed!

A blur of soupy clouds streaked past, and in a blink, *Angelus* was plunging through crisp, blue sky over desolate wasteland. Metal screeched, and a square panel tore out of Pascal's grip. He gawked at his empty hand, bellowed, "Moving to Plan B!", then stabbed an S-shaped handle into the deck and cranked it like he was starting a Model-T Ford.

Ozzie glanced over the side and yelped. Stubby, fan-shaped wings were extending from the hull! Layla punched the throttles, drawing indignant howls from the engines. Gravity returned as *Angelus* settled into a steep glide, her envelope flapping behind her like a flag. Ozzie scanned the sky for Maelstrom ships, but didn't see any telltale silhouettes.

"What is Plan B?" Layla said, straining at the helm.

"We're on Plan F now, keep up." Pascal wrestled a clunky contraption out of a locker. A pair of bellows at its base and a variety of hinges, holes, and handles suggested he'd weaponized an accordion. "I could use assistance, children!"

Alex hustled across the deck, her face flushed with excitement— as usual, she was never more alive than when she was nearly dying. Ozzie unknotted his restraint and grabbed one of the see-saw handles. A single glance at the godforsaken terrain below was motivation enough to pump for his life. The twins coordinated jumps like they were born for this singular task. They melded into a machine of concerted effort, a frictionless unit, a focused duo that—

"What are you doing?" Pascal said.

61

"Pumping," Ozzie panted.

"Why?" the inventor asked.

The twins stopped, and the bellows gave a half-hearted belch.

"Hold the pump down!" Pascal said. He jabbed a flexible tube into his prosthetic elbow, then clenched his fist. Incandescent blue fluid raced through the tube, into the machine. The handle screeched, see-sawing like it was manned by a pair of hyperactive sumo wrestlers. Ozzie and Alex threw their weight on the base to keep the bellows from bouncing across the deck.

For five long seconds, the air bladder sulked. Pascal twisted a dial on his arm and the pump shifted into higher gear. Metal wailed as the bellows wheezed like a short track sprinter in a marathon. The bladder stirred, inflating to resemble a limp cucumber.

With agonizing sluggishness, *Angelus* leveled off twenty feet above the ground, but glowing joints and plumes of smoke signaled impending catastrophe for the heroic pump. The twins scrambled away from the gyrating machine.

"No open flames!" Layla shouted.

Pascal increased the contraption's speed, provoking an outraged shriek of metal. "Fifteen more seconds!"

Three claws sliced through the blue tube, and the pump clattered to a grateful halt. Layla wrenched the cumbersome machine from the deck and hurled it over the side, where it exploded in a cartwheeling fireball that warmed Ozzie's cheek.

"We were nearly there," Pascal said, yanking the sliced tube from his arm.

"If you are referring to the afterlife, I agree." Layla expanded a spyglass and searched the clouds for signs of pursuit. "You risk too much, Pascal."

The Dromedarian tapped a red-lined gauge. "I built *Angelus*. I know what she can take."

Layla's scowl deepened. "*Angelus* is a stout vessel, but your genius ends where piloting begins."

Pascal folded his arms and surveyed the smoldering aftermath of the pump's last stand, as his airship scolded him with reproachful creaks. "I concede Icarus Initiative has a few kinks to work out."

Alex snorted. Layla's jaw worked, grinding her teeth like tectonic plates.

"Excuse me," Ozzie raised his hand, "did we escape? Are we safe?"

The Sauracian glared daggers at Pascal, then glanced skyward. "What the Maelstrom wants, they get—by the sword, if possible." A shadow darkened her face. "If the Fury King seeks the Professor's journal, no one is safe."

CHAPTER 9
FAMILY SECRETS

A cursory inspection of *Angelus* suggested she had weathered Icarus well, with the exception of a leak in the main air bladder valve. Pascal took one look, said, "Marvelous! I've got just the thing!", then bounced down to his lab.

That couldn't be good.

Ozzie sidled up to Layla, who was glaring at the hissing valve with animosity.

"Is that gas flammable?" he asked, remembering the alarm in her voice when the pump was overheating.

"Heliovapor is highly volatile, so most vessels carry as little as possible." She nudged a metal canister with her boot. "Thanks to Pascal's fondness for punching holes in her envelope, *Angelus* carries a surplus."

"Envelope?" Ozzie asked, newsreels of flaming zeppelins forming an orderly queue in his mind.

Layla gestured upward. "The balloon holding us aloft."

Pascal marched past, squeezing a corpulent, chihuahua-sized, purple slug with a pair of tongs. "Meet Wilhelm," he said. Slime from the creature's back dribbled a viscous pyramid of goo at the inventor's feet. "Droolug mucus is famous for sealing battlefield wounds, but through diet manipulation and motivational exercises,

I tripled the potency of his secretions. I've been looking for a chance to test it." He waved the slug, showering the deck in transparent goop. "Um, don't step in that."

"How do you motivate a slug?" Alex asked.

"Droolug," the inventor corrected her. "Positive affirmations, mostly—*You can glue it! Stick it to 'em! Great glob!*—that kind of thing."

"Just fix the leak," Layla growled.

Fifteen minutes of sloppy, disgusting work later, *Angelus* eased into a gentle climb. The crew tiptoed cautiously around the mountain of mucus beneath the valve. So far, so good—the repair was oozing, but holding. Immediate danger averted, the Forsythes retreated to the privacy of the bow as Layla chopped vegetables into a steaming cauldron at the helm.

"I didn't know slugs could scream," Alex said, "and so *loud*."

Ozzie nodded in wide-eyed agreement, ears still ringing from the droolug's howler monkey wails when Pascal squished it against the air bladder. He rested his elbows on the railing and watched the desert drift by.

"Screaming slugs, Dromedarians, Sauracians...I don't know what to think anymore," he said. "Yesterday, Grandfather was a laughingstock. Today, he might be the greatest explorer in history. Is it *possible* he's still alive?"

Alex snorted. "I don't know, but I'd give anything to shove this in Bulwerk's face."

"And what about Mom and Dad?" Ozzie said. "Did they know about Terravenum?" His sister flinched. In light of today's revelations, *I told you so* didn't seem sufficient, so he stared silently at the wasteland. Far below, a horse-sized spider spotted *Angelus* and burrowed into the sand. Ozzie shivered from a chill unrelated to the cool breeze and said, "At least we're safe for the moment."

Alex exhaled between her teeth like a leaking air bladder valve. "Yep, safe and sound on a slug-patched balloon piloted by a lizard with anger issues and a camel who surgically implanted insects in our brains. You really think we can trust them?"

"What choice do we have?"

"None. Just pointing out this is a weird version of *safe*."

"Dinner time!" Layla called.

Ozzie steeled himself as he meandered back to the helm, where Pascal had unfolded a table and set up chairs. As hungry as he was, in a world where droolugs exist, *anything* might be on the menu. To his stomach's shock and considerable relief, Layla handed him a bowl of steaming, mouthwatering stew.

"Delicious!" Alex said, between spoonfuls, "What's it called?"

A flash of white between Layla's lips hinted at a smile. "Scourge. It is the Professor's favorite."

Ozzie took a sip and grinned as foreign spices warred for his taste buds' allegiance. He chased a mystery vegetable with a spoon, mulling over Layla's triangular, carnivore teeth. "Is scourge a Sauracian dish?" he asked.

Pascal guzzled a pint of stew from his mammoth bowl. "Traditional Sauracian dishes include more protein," he said, smacking his lips.

"Protein, as in meat?"

"As in, whatever they kill."

Ozzie scrutinized chunks in his stew with suspicion and a dash of creeping horror.

"I am largely a vegetarian," Layla growled, her glare warning Pascal to play his mind games elsewhere. "Scourge is a staple of the Barren tribes."

"How did you meet Grandfather?" Alex asked.

Pascal reclined in his chair and cradled the back of his head. "On a supply run when a malfunction forced us to land in the Foraging Plains."

"Malfunction?" Layla snorted. "You tried to loop *Angelus*, and the rudder fell off."

"A malfunction that could happen to anyone sufficiently curious about aerodynamics," Pascal said. "*Anyway*, repairs were nearly complete when we heard a commotion in the distance. Fearing a raiding party, I threw my tools on board, and Layla began pre-flight. As we lifted off, a man scampered around a dune and sprinted for *Angelus* with Scatterling hoard wardens snapping at his heels." The inventor slapped the table and chortled, his potbelly bouncing. "I've never seen a human run so fast. Layla and I don't usually interfere in local disputes, but the man's desperation moved her to drop a ladder over the side."

The Sauracian grunted. "Scatterlings are not known for mercy. I could not stand by and watch them slaughter him."

"The Professor's leap for our rope ladder was short by at least ten feet," Pascal laughed, "so she swung down, grabbed him around the waist, and tossed him on board."

"A split-second decision that changed our lives forever," Layla said.

Pascal's grin faded and he nodded.

"Why were they chasing him?" Ozzie said.

Layla downed a gallon of scourge, then burped. "He stole an artifact from a Scatterling hoard."

"It must have been valuable."

"To Scatterlings, salvage is life. They have a saying: *Those who pilfer a hoard soon join it*, referring to their tradition of collecting thieves' heads."

Stealing from maniacal kleptomaniacs—now *that* had Sir Quidby's fingerprints all over it. "How did Grandfather discover Terravenum in the first place?" Ozzie asked.

Pascal flicked his blubbery lower lip with prominent buck teeth. "You'll have to ask him. Something about a secret gate."

"A *gate*?" Skepticism riddled Alex's tone.

"At least one path exists between our worlds," Layla rumbled, "but until the Professor's arrival, venturing into the Divide was certain death—if not from the monsters who dwell in it, then from the Noctem, who protect its secrets."

Ozzie bolted upright. "*Noctem?* Keeper said that name last night, before assassins attacked St. Jude's. Who are they?"

The Sauracian's bowl paused on the way to her mouth. "You were attacked by the Maelstrom *and* assassins last night?"

Alex said, "You didn't notice the army of tattooed, twirly daggered freaks with glowing eyes? There were explosions everywhere!"

"I assumed I was interrupting a local festival."

"Who is the Noctem?" Ozzie asked, desperate to veer the conversation back on track.

"A clandestine organization dedicated to preventing the recovery of the lost Borealis Stones," Layla said. "The Professor is their sworn enemy."

Ozzie's thumb traced his throbbing translapede incision. Two days ago he would have chuckled at the notion of Grandfather having sworn enemies outside of his life insurance provider or the Guild, but the idea wasn't so crazy now.

Pascal tilted his head. "Describe the assassins' weapons."

"I didn't see any up close, but their projectiles were neon blue and hummed like bees."

The inventor's hoof rapped a complex rhythm on the table. He said, "Dynami is difficult to collect in Terravenum, and nearly impossible to obtain in Urt. The Noctem wouldn't waste their supply."

"What did they want? The journal?"

"Possibly." Pascal rose from his chair and opened a locker.

"What is Urt?" Alex said.

"It's what we call your side of the Divide." The inventor dropped Grandfather's journal on the table with an impact that sloshed scourge from his bowl. He frowned at scorch marks on the book's binding, then sniffed its cover.

"Be careful," Ozzie said. "It almost fried my arm when it activated."

Pascal tapped the arrowhead with his hoof, discharging a blue spark. "I'm not surprised. The power stone is set for maximum discharge, to make the signal easier to detect through the Divide. Don't touch it until I can dial the setting down." He pushed the book aside and lifted a cloth sack onto the table. "Let's see what other bounty Layla collected on her accidental rescue mission."

All of Grandfather's trinkets were accounted for—as well as a shattered bedside lamp, a framed picture of the Forsythes, a stuffed monkey, an alarm clock, and Noko's box.

Pascal flipped a magnifying lens down and cracked the clock open. "Where is the detonator?" he whispered.

"That's a clock," Ozzie said. "It keeps time."

"Indeed it does," the inventor mused, examining a circuit board like it held arcane, dangerous secrets. "Can I keep this?"

"Sure."

The clock vanished into one of Pascal's jacket pockets.

Ozzie pretended not to notice when Alex quietly reclaimed Bobo McSmiles, her stuffed monkey.

Noko's box elicited a low whistle from the inventor. "Volantium —the Ancients used it to control and channel dynami. It's the only metal that can pass through the Divide without being inside a sivsuit or powersieve. Where did you get this?"

"From Grandfather, at his funeral," Ozzie said. "It held the arrowhead that activated his journal."

Pascal popped the lid with an expert twist of his mechanical thumb and hoof, then touched his tongue to the red gel inside. He grimaced. "Stale. That power stone was in there a long time."

Layla twirled the blowdart gun and laughed, a sound like roller skates on gravel. "Remember this Trovian slumberdart pipe? The Professor won it from a deputy apprehender in a game of tumble-monk, then used it to escape from jail."

Pascal was too enamored with a new discovery to answer. "It can't be..." He held a small ball of hard-packed yellow mud to his nose. Voluminous nostrils crinkled, then flared in shock. "Panacea clay! Where did he find it?"

"Why? What's it for?" Ozzie asked.

"Panacea clay is a universal antidote. It's exceedingly rare—I can't imagine where the Professor found *any*, let alone enough to ransom a kingdom."

Blood drained from Ozzie's face as he pictured the rash of yellow stains dotting the walls of his room from bored blowdart target practice. He cleared his throat. "So it's valuable and rare. Interesting." Ozzie craned his neck to peer inside the half-open velvet pouch. "Out of curiosity, how many are in the bag?"

69

"You have *more*?" Pascal checked the bag. "Blithering krump-nits, there are four!"

"Four. That sounds right. Yes. Four."

Layla scooped up a five-inch, square notepad. "And of course, Labyrinthian parchment."

"I spent half my life trying to open that," Ozzie said. The Saura-cian twisted opposite corners with her claws, and the square sprang into an accordion of flimsy paper tiers. "Whoa!"

Thumbs and corners, just like Noko's box.

Layla nodded. "Labyrinthian tools are favored by those who venture near the Divide. The Professor always carries some with him." Hundreds of cubes cascaded like a string of paper dolls from grade school art class.

"What does it do?" Ozzie crinkled a wafer between his fingers.

"This one is a glide chute. Careful!" A chain of cubes snagged a breeze and wrenched Ozzie forward. Layla's paw clamped his shoulder, anchoring him to the deck. She blocked the wind with her body and meticulously re-packed the wayward chute, one cube at a time. After corralling the final wafer, she performed the corner twist in reverse, rendering the square solid and seamless.

Pascal inspected an inch-wide silver bracelet. "Do you know what this is?"

"Grandfather gave that to me when I was ten," Alex said. "Let me guess...is it a secret decoder? A teleportation device?"

The bracelet flashed red in the lantern's pale glow. "Better. It's an armillam. The Ancients used them to channel dynami."

"You said that word before. What *is* dynami?"

"In a word that does it little justice: energy. Trace quantities of dynami power most Terravenum technology, but your armillam—what we call *Stone Tech*—can harness and control large amounts of it."

Alex frowned at the innocuous jewelry, no doubt remembering all the games of dress-up she and Ozzie had played. "How does it work?" she asked.

"No idea. This is the first unhacked armillam I've seen in

70

person, but the Ancients weren't in the habit of putting their symbol on trifles. Be careful with it." He offered her the bracelet.

Alex gasped. An engraved symbol on the band glowed turquoise. Four elongated arrowheads pointed at each other, like cardinal directions on a compass, overlaying a pair of concentric circles.

"Stella Signum," Layla rasped.

Ozzie's rusty Latin kicked in. *Star Sign.*

"It's on here, too." Pascal slid a chunk of metal across the table. A flash of scarlet hinted at its origins, and the Stella Signum radiating from its surface left no doubt it was Ancient technology. Ozzie frowned. He'd always considered the sword hilt quaint, but the glowing symbol gave the stubby handle a forbidding, businesslike vibe.

Layla lifted the artifact gingerly, mumbling to herself. She tapped the handle with the tip of a claw.

SSSSCCCCHHHHPPP

A tongue of metal flicked out of the hilt, extending to within an inch of Ozzie's forehead. There was no time to dodge, only a split-second to blink, before his sister tackled him. Alex scrambled to her feet and rounded on Layla, a mouse challenging an elephant.

"Are you crazy?" she shouted.

Layla dropped the hilt. The blade retracted instantly, and the handle bounced on the table. The Sauracian brushed Alex aside and kneeled before Ozzie. She rotated his head, searching for injuries. "My apologies. I have heard rumors of such a weapon, but never imagined—"

Ozzie pushed her paws away. "I used to chase Alex with that hilt, pretending I was a space pirate. It never did *that* before."

Pascal picked the handle up. "Volantium absorbs dynami—it started charging as soon as we entered the Divide."

SSSCCCCHHHHHP

He gave the fully extended sword an experimental swipe. The blade sang.

"Be careful!" Alex said.

The inventor adopted a fencing pose, with extra elbows thrown in. He dueled an invisible swordsman, stabbed a sandbag, then straightened with a grin.

Sssscchhkkkt

The blade retracted.

"Well-balanced," he said, "almost to a fault—I prefer my sword to fight me."

Layla slathered droolug mucus over a punctured bottle of heliovapor. "You are an infant," she grumbled.

"A sword is just a tool," Pascal said. "Jab the pointy end into the bad guy." He tossed the hilt onto the table. "It's dangerous, but we shouldn't *fear* it."

Alex white-knuckled the table. "*What is wrong with you?*"

Ozzie tuned out the drama and picked up the photo of his family. His father beamed through splintered glass, happy and proud of the eight-year-old son on his shoulders. Ozzie's mom was frozen mid-laugh, cradling a pouting Alex in her arms. Their last family vacation.

Pascal tapped the photo. "Humboldt was a good friend. Your mother too, although she hated when he loved my ideas."

Alex slammed her fist, bouncing artifacts across the bedsheet. "How many secrets does our family have?" She buried her face in her hands.

"More than you can imagine, and fewer than I wish," Layla answered. She threw a mournful look at Pascal, who dipped his chin. "As you have guessed, last night was not the first time the Maelstrom breached the Divide. Seven years ago, they used a sivsuit to kidnap a human." Her eyes flicked to the twins. "Your father."

Ozzie raked his treasures aside with a sweep of his arm, so nothing stood between him and the truth. He leaned forward.

"Start from the beginning."

CHAPTER 10
THE BOREALIS STONE

Layla settled onto her stool with a weary, rolling sigh. "To understand the sacrifices your family made, you must first understand what fueled their obsession. Legend has it that millennia ago, Terravenum and Urt were one world. Human kingdoms rose and fell, but none expanded beyond their natural borders, for fear of monsters who dwelled in the west. Then the Borealis Stone fell from the heavens, and scientists from one city-state discovered how to harness its radiation—a power source they called *dynami*—to gain a staggering technological advantage over their rivals."

Pascal broke in, "Dynami changed everything: agriculture, transportation, and weaponry. After asserting dominance over their neighbors, the Ancients set their sights on building an empire." He twisted a knob on his mechanical forearm until blue liquid flowed through tubes in his elbow. "Superior technology made them unstoppable." He clenched his fist, and metal and ceramic groaned under the pressure of his grip.

"The Ancients' thirst for domination turned west," Layla said. "But when their raiding parties ventured beyond the Fulcrum Mountains, they woke a sleeping giant: Sauracia. It was the first interspecies war in history. Individual Sauracian tribes fought ferociously but could not mount an effective defense. On the cusp of

73

defeat, a new leader emerged, replacing conventional Sauracian tactics with ambushes, scorched earth, and intricate gambits." Layla's expression hardened. "He formed the Maelstrom—a ruthless army willing to die for his banner. The tides of war turned and the commander's exploits earned him a name cheered in every Sauracian crag and dreaded across Terravenum: the *Fury King*." She spat the name like a curse.

Pascal paced in a tight circle. "The Ancients, accustomed to pressing their advantage in combat, now fought to survive. Their engineers became increasingly desperate in their efforts to develop new dynami-powered weaponry. Reckless science and radiation leaks rendered entire regions of Terravenum uninhabitable," he tapped his chest with a hoof, "planting seeds of mutation."

The Sauracian rumbled, "By the mid-point of the Cloud War, the Maelstrom ruled the sky, reducing the Ancients' empire to a single fortified city-state: Relik. Concerned the Borealis Stone would fall into the clutches of the Fury King, the Engineers projected an impenetrable dome of purified dynami around their capital. The humans prepared for a siege, but fate intervened. What happened next is a matter of speculation—"

"It was a traitor!" Pascal said.

"—some blame a traitor, but based on my experience, it was more likely a scientist run amok." Layla arched an eyebrow at the inventor. "Whatever the cause, the Borealis Stone cracked, generating an explosion that expanded the shield thousands of miles in every direction, bathing Terravenum in radiation, and decimating the Maelstrom forces. When the dust settled, a massive dome of pure dynami—the Divide—separated Terravenum and Urt."

"What happened to the Ancients?" Ozzie said.

"Nearly all perished when their city collapsed in the Abyss."

"What does this have to do with our family?" Alex said.

"Legend holds that Engineers who survived the Fracturing separated and hid the three fragments of the Borealis Stone. Whoever unites them will control the Dome and the Divide." She pointed at the sky with a claw. "The Fury King is hunting the

Stones. The Professor hopes to find them first—as did your parents."

"Wait," Ozzie said, "if the Cloud War was a thousand years ago, how is the Fury King still alive?"

"Sauracians live longer than humans," Layla said. "But the Fury King's dynami exposure in the Fracturing extended his life span even further. His most ardent followers believe he is immortal."

"Hang on," Alex said. "You're telling me a race of sentient lizards lived on Earth, and no one has found evidence of it?"

"The Professor theorizes that Urt-based Noctem operatives prevent such discoveries by sabotaging expeditions."

"Why would they do that?"

"They believe the Stones are too dangerous to be controlled."

"They're right," Ozzie said.

His sister scowled. "You're agreeing with assassins who launched a full-on invasion of St. Jude's."

"You didn't see the monsters that live in the Divide." He clenched his fists, remembering the slap of tentacles on his flesh. "If a dynami shield separates Terravenum and Urt, why isn't there a glowing dome in our world?"

Layla's shoulders jumped like hills in an earthquake. "Until the Professor's arrival, no one who ventured into the Divide returned. Our knowledge is limited to hearsay, speculation, and legend."

Ozzie picked up the family photo and searched for lies in his parents' faces. "So, reptiles had a war with humans, a magic rock exploded, and the world is at stake. Let's pretend that's not as insane as it sounds for a minute. What happened to Mom and Dad?"

Pascal deflated in his chair and began disassembling a brass pocket watch. Layla watched the inventor organize gears into neat rows, then said, "Your parents researched Stone Lore with the Professor until your mother became pregnant and was no longer willing to risk crossing the Divide. Adeline begged Humboldt to abandon his search for the Stones, but he ignored her wishes."

Ozzie remembered all too well the tension in the house when his father left on expeditions, and the barbed welcomes that greeted his returns. In her husband's absence, his mother expanded her expertise in swordsmanship to include forging her own weapons. Night after night, she pounded resentment into meticulously crafted blades, each hammer strike a lullaby to her dozing children. Sometimes Ozzie peeked out the window to watch his mother test new creations in the backyard, dancing through intricate footwork with an angelic smile and deadly ease.

Layla said, "When word of the Professor's Stone Lore expertise reached Sauracia, the Fury King dispatched his Maelstrom to kidnap your father, aiming to blackmail Sir Quidby into recovering the Stones for him." Her eyes flicked to Pascal, who was adjusting clockwork with tweezers. "Your parents never emerged from the Divide."

Clunk

The timepiece struck the table, and the inventor's head bowed low.

"What did Grandfather do?" Alex's voice was hoarse.

"The Professor searched for your parents for months, then threw himself into Stone Lore because the only way to protect you from his enemies is to find the Stones."

"What makes you think Grandfather is still alive?" Ozzie said.

Pascal flipped a magnifying lens up, but kept staring at the fragments of his watch. "Circumstances surrounding his disappearance are suspicious, and the alternative is unthinkable. Also—and this is just my opinion—the Professor's death will involve an explosion large enough to collapse the Dome."

Ozzie grinned. "If he's alive and has so many enemies, how do we find him?"

"It took us months to recover the journal, so his trail is now cold. We will visit Aeronoth—a city of vagrants, black marketers, and corrupt information merchants. If any clue to the Professor's location exists, we will find it there."

Pascal groaned. "Seriously? The Guild is dying to catch us harvesting dynami without a license and half the Mercenary League is gunning for me. Plus, I was counting on the healing power of time to mend my relationship with Bryce."

76

"Maybe next time you should not sell weapons to a mercenary who nicknamed himself *The Disruptor*." The Sauracian cocked her head sideways. "He wrote his own theme song, Pascal. Did he sing it for you?"

The inventor grunted noncommittally and tweaked gears in his timepiece.

Layla said, "Bryce could not rhyme with 'Disruptor,' so he shouted 'Aargh' at the end of each stanza. This is who you chose to arm with prototype weaponry."

"You clearly haven't spent much time with mercenaries, Layla. Compared to his colleagues, Bryce is an intellectual." Pascal stood up. "Let's get this over with. Punch the throttle—when rumor of the Fury King's search for the journal reaches Aeronoth, we'll have a bounty on our heads."

The Sauracian accelerated the engines. "It has been a long day. Pascal and I will alternate watch, but everyone will sleep on deck in case the Maelstrom finds us in the night."

With table folded and treasures stowed, *Angelus* skimmed moonlit clouds like a ghost ship. Ozzie huddled beneath a musty fur blanket and imagined his mother practicing swordplay on the deck until a headful of bad dreams came calling.

CHAPTER II
ANGELUS

Ethiopian coffee. Dad's blend.

Ozzie yawned and tried to rub yesterday's insanity from his temples. Alex stirred in her nest of blankets, stretching. Her grin said she recognized the smell, too.

"You're awake!" Pascal waved a mechanized mug. "Care for some life-giving elixir?"

Ozzie smiled. "Thanks. Is coffee popular in Terravenum?"

"Depends on the crowd. Scientists swim in it, but muscle-headed, stab-first/think-later types prefer drinks they can quaff." A twist of a knob propelled dark liquid through a maze of clear tubes and glassware. "Insomnians up north grow a tasty bean, but nothing close to your father's blend. The Professor brings me a bag whenever he visits." He tapped a beaker critically, then pumped an orange handle until a thermos overflowed. "Behold!"

The inventor pressed a cup into Ozzie's hand and filled it with blistering nectar. The coffee's floral aroma conjured memories of his father poring over books and charts in his study.

"Come with me." Pascal started down a hallway. "It's time I properly introduced you to *Angie*." The twins hurried to keep up. "She's built on the bones of a derelict dreadnought I found in the Crypt. Scavenge rights cost me four hundred klunklings." Pascal scowled at a structural rib in the ceiling. "Hang on, I need to adjust the torsion rectifier."

The inventor swiveled a wrench attachment from his prosthetic finger and crawled behind a rack of equipment. A mournful groan echoed through the ship's hold. "Got it. Next stop, the living quarters!" The narrow hallway scraped the inventor's belly, but was tall enough he could walk upright. "Last year a powersieve test generated a spatial rift that swallowed Layla's workshop—a completely understandable mistake to which she wildly over-reacted." He stomped on a dividing line between light and dark floor planks. "But I fixed it! See how the new hurtlewood blends in?" Pascal pushed open a narrow door in the opposite wall. "This is the Professor's cabin."

It was the smallest room Ozzie had seen on *Angelus*, aside from the broom closet on deck. A stained canvas hammock slung across the room at chest-level, just high enough to give its occupant a view out the cabin's single porthole. A desk ran the length of the wall next to the door. Ozzie scanned dusty volumes on the bookshelf.

Ghosts of the Divide
The Garrilus Codex
Combat Techniques for the Book-Laden Scholar
Tales of the Unread: Man, Myth, or Monster?
Debunking Field Manual (and Bathroom Companion), 6th Edition

Ozzie sat in the squeaky swivel chair and thumbed through *The Garrilus Codex*. Dog-eared pages were riddled with notes in his grandfather's distinctive hand. He skimmed a paragraph.

Garrilus' "Meditations Within A Puddle of Quicksand" is undoubtedly an allegory for the Lies of the Sixteen and the Fracturing. How deep does the conspiracy go? How long was the Fury King in league with the Sixteen?

Grandfather had circled the passage and scrawled: *Infantile spec-*

ulation. Ozzie flipped to the cover, curious what author had drawn the explorer's ire.

Knoxbleat Vouch

"Ready?" Alex leaned against the doorframe, hands in her pockets as Pascal's footsteps receded in the hallway. He returned the book to its shelf and jumped up. The corridor was too narrow to walk side-by-side, so he followed his sister in single file.

"Pascal said one of us could stay in Grandfather's cabin, and I told him you would want it," she said. "Did you notice the wall carvings?"

"No," Ozzie mumbled, half-listening, as he contemplated the bookshelf. Why was Grandfather reading about combat techniques?

"Make sure you check them out. I'll be next door," Alex paused, then added, "in Mom and Dad's cabin."

He snapped to attention. They had their own cabin? "What's in there?" he asked, feigning casualness.

"Two hammocks, some empty shelves, and a few sets of clothes."

"Oh." A handwritten apology note from his parents was too much to hope for, but it would have helped.

Pascal spun a corroded wheel lock on a grimy door. The metal slab swung inwards with a tortured wail as the scent of hot grease invaded the corridor. Layla's bulky form materialized in the smoke. The Sauracian slid a tool into her belt, then de-fogged her goggles with a scowl.

"What do you want?" she snapped.

"Just showing our guests around *Angie*," Pascal said. He tried to snake his head into the room, but Layla blocked him. A persistent clanging noise showered sparks across the Sauracian's back, but she didn't flinch. "Everything good down here?" the inventor asked.

"Yes." Layla snapped her goggles down and shut the door in his face. The lock *clanged.*

"The main engine room is unofficially Layla's domain," Pascal said. "Sauracians prefer warm environments, so she sleeps down here." He ducked a bulkhead and squeezed down the hallway. "Between you and me, she's a little overprotective."

The inventor tapped a code into a battered keypad. Hydraulics hissed as bolts *chunked* open. Pascal beckoned them to follow. "Dynami is expensive and difficult to store, so most vessels only transport a few gallons." He spread his arms. "I embrace an alternate philosophy." Racks of golden barrels lined the walls. Each container sported a red indicator light, except for a single green-lit barrel by the door. "These drums are usually full, but the power-sieve drained us dry."

"Why do you need so much?" Alex asked.

Blue light illuminated Pascal's face as he peered into the active barrel's inch-wide viewing port. "Experiments, prodding the unknown with a big stick, black market shenanigans...the usual."

Ozzie tugged a frayed nylon strap that secured a barrel. "Sounds dangerous."

"Only if you count sprouting an extra leg while slowly going insane as a liability." The inventor grinned. "But the bigger risk is getting caught harvesting and selling dynami without a license—the Merchant Guild discourages entrepreneurial spirit when it impedes their cash flow."

"So dynami is big business," Ozzie said.

"Dynami is *power*." Pascal pointed to a lipstick tube of glowing blue liquid in his prosthetic elbow. "Small amounts fuel engines, drive economies, and birth empires. Large amounts leave spontaneous, highly inconvenient craters." He slapped an empty storage barrel, which rang like a bell. "Dynami degrades most metals over time, but volantium is immune—making artifacts like your armillam and sword hilt extremely valuable. The Ancients manipulated dynami in ways we still can't fathom."

Alex twisted the armillam on her wrist. "Does anyone know how Stone Tech works?" she asked.

"If they do, they're sitting on a throne of klunk-tons in an underground lair, being fed grapes by bodyguards," Pascal said.

"Hackers modify Stone Tech to make it do a tenth of what it's capable of—weapons and industrial applications, mostly—but beyond that, it's a guessing game. Hack Tech is lucrative, but tends to malfunction in legendarily memorable ways."

Ozzie rubbed a metal drum, smudging the dull yellow finish. "This doesn't look like volantium."

"These barrels are made of noflexium, a durable alloy that can store dynami for six months without melting. Only the wealthiest power brokers—merchants, kings, and the occasional trust fund mime—can afford volantium. It's too precious to waste on barrels."

"What happens if dynami leaks out?" Ozzie said.

"With low-grade samples, nothing. But purified dynami is… much messier."

Ozzie frowned at a puddle of gently-glowing goo beneath a rack of blinking lights. "Should we be in here?"

"Just don't lick anything." The inventor keyed the door open and gestured to the hallway.

Despite Pascal redesigning and tweaking systems throughout the tour, a clear picture of the vessel emerged. *Angelus* was an eighty-foot-long, twenty-five-foot-wide lightning rod for scientific inspiration. A laboratory, packed with ongoing experiments and prototypes, occupied the largest cabin on the vessel. The only concessions to the necessity of income were an empty cargo bay, the dynami vault, and a half-filled smuggler's hold. Four crew cabins were an afterthought, squeezed into the stern, between machinery rooms and workshops.

Angelus was constructed primarily of hurtlewood, a dark brown timber that shared similar strength characteristics to steel, but at a fraction of the weight. The enormous envelope keeping the vessel aloft was sewn from a patchwork quilt of flame-retardant canvas.

Although Pascal built *Angelus* himself, the inventor begrudgingly acknowledged Layla's greater skill with engines and piloting. Their fluctuating power dynamic raised awkward questions about who officially captained the vessel. When Alex asked, Pascal declared himself in charge, prompting a fit of chuffing laughter from the Sauracian that echoed in Ozzie's ears for hours.

Layla throttled down at sunset, easing the engines into a low, steady thrum. "Without the proper bribes, a night-time arrival at Aeronoth will draw unwelcome attention. If we arrive at first light, we can blend into Guild traffic."

Alex said, "Is Aeronoth a Sauracian city?"

"No, but Aeronoth is managed by the Merchant Guild, so it is one of the few places in Terravenum Sauracians are welcome, provided they have klunk in their pockets."

"Pascal mentioned a bounty on our heads," Ozzie said.

"Many in Aeronoth would ransom their own hatchlings for a price. Word of our presence will no doubt reach the Maelstrom, but our primary concern is avoiding anyone who has a grievance with Pascal."

"Like Bryce the Disruptor?"

"Pascal claims his enemies spring up like weeds, but in truth, he cultivates them like flowers. Last time we berthed at Aeronoth, his garden of disgruntled customers included Bryce, half of the Mercenary League, the Alchemist Club, the Tumblemonk Federation, and the Society for Civil Discourse."

"He made weapons for all those groups?"

"Weapons, the occasional coffee machine, industrial prototypes...but mostly weapons." She checked the compass heading, then cracked her knuckles with the sound of snapping bones. "Pascal's pitiful business instincts are surpassed only by his abrasive customer service."

Ozzie settled into his grandfather's hammock with an appreciative groan and flipped through *The Garrilus Codex*. After a few chapters of mindless skimming, he snapped the book shut and stared at the ceiling. Even if the Borealis Stone legend was true—and given the fact he was currently flying on an airship piloted by a lizard and a camel, it was hard to dismiss it—every fresh revelation about his parents' secret life deepened his sense of betrayal.

"Did Grandfather write a memoir detailing his descent into madness?" Alex stepped into the room.

"Kind of," he said. "It's research about the Borealis Stones."

"Anything good?"

"Nothing worth destroying our family for."

Wood creaked as *Angelus* shuddered in a breeze.

"Did you look at the wall yet?" she asked.

Ozzie swiveled out of his hammock. A gimbaled lamp rocked overhead, illuminating carvings in the hurtlewood wall. He traced letters that spelled a name he knew by heart.

Humboldt

Dad.

His mother was next.

Adeline

Two more names lurked below.

Alexandria

Ozymandias

Groups of vertical slashes stippled the walls, as if marking days in captivity. Ozzie ran a finger across two weeks' worth of lines.

Alex strung a wrinkled hammock between two hooks. "Mind if I stay here tonight? Mom and Dad's cabin creeps me out."

"No problem." He slid into his hammock and cradled the back of his head. "I want to get another look at Grandfather's journal," he said. "Layla locked it in the smuggler's hold in case we get boarded, but I need to see it."

"This isn't our fight, Oz."

Ozzie ground his teeth. What happened to the hard-charging girl who earned the nickname 'Cannonball' in Lamswool's skate park? "I'm not suggesting we sharpen swords and rescue Grandfather from the clutches of lizard warriors. His journal will tell us what he discovered in Terravenum, and maybe we can retrace his steps."

Alex snorted. "Because his steps were so well-chosen the first time."

The names on the wall were shadowed, like tombstone epitaphs.

Humboldt

Adeline

Alexandria

Ozymandias

How many nights had Grandfather laid here, staring at what he'd lost, and was so desperate to keep?

Ozzie didn't remember falling asleep, but the cool light of dawn was meandering through the porthole when Pascal's shout catapulted him out of his hammock. "Get up! They found us!"

CHAPTER 12

AERONOTH

Alex pushed past Ozzie, took stairs two at a time, then slid to a stop on the main deck. Billowing mist shrouded *Angelus* in a thick fog. Pascal jogged out of the murk and thrust an electrical cable at her.

"To absolutely *no one's* surprise, the Maelstrom beat us here," he panted. "Plug this into that terminal when I tell you to."

Layla growled, "Is that for Mirror Mode? Pascal, we are in a *cloud*."

The inventor lurched to the stern and cranked a hand-powered generator. An ascending hum accompanied a dim orange glow. "*Now!*" he hissed.

Alex stabbed the cable into the terminal and yelped as a jolt of electricity stung her fingers. Strings of light outlined *Angelus'* envelope, turning the stained canvas smoky white.

"Idiot!" The helm squeaked as Layla's claws gouged its spokes.

Pascal winked at Alex. "I wove static-charged chromatic fibers into the envelope fabric," he whispered. "When current passes through the fibers, they mirror their surroundings. I got the idea from watching enneapuses*[1] camouflage themselves."

Alex reached over her head, marveling at her hand's blurry reflection on the envelope's surface. She waved at herself. "That's amazing. Why is Layla mad?"

"Mirror Mode has a few glitches."

"Let me guess: it catches fire when you turn it on."

Pascal looked hurt. "Why would you say that?"

"I'm starting to see a pattern."

He held up a scrap of canvas and spat on it. The fabric burst into flame. "It catches fire *only after direct exposure to water*—an important distinction."

"Aren't clouds made from water vapor?"

"In a sense."

She looked at the impenetrable mist surrounding them. "Then..."

"Pray this is a dry cloud."

Angelus bathed in sunlight, her envelope shifting dusk blue as she nosed into clear sky. When the spots in Alex's vision cleared, she gasped. Twenty airships were jockeying for position in three lines that led to a bucket-shaped flying city. Aeronoth was a hundred times larger than *Angelus* and suspended beneath an envelope the size of two soccer fields. Docks extended from the city's top level like spokes, home to a flock of cargo cranes that serviced a steady stream of freighters. Mammoth propellers groaned on each side of the vessel, cajoling the rusty behemoth forward at a leisurely pace.

Pascal said, "Aeronoth is the only sky city to survive the Cloud War—a deposed queen with a chip on her shoulder, bloody knuckles, and a fistful of klunk."

A Maelstrom vessel patrolled the head of each line, inspecting the parade of airships waiting to unload cargo. Pascal extended a comically long spyglass to scan the blockade.

"Uh-oh," he said.

Red lightning flared, and a dozen howling commandos boarded a vessel that aroused their suspicions. The inventor bared his lower teeth and whistled as the Sauracians herded the freighter's crew into a line. A warrior knocked someone to his knees.

"Why are they letting the Maelstrom do this?" Ozzie said.

Pascal slapped his telescope closed. "There are good reasons no one builds sky cities anymore—they're slow, difficult to defend, and easy pickings for predators. Unless the Smuggler's Alliance intervenes, Aeronoth is vulnerable."

Angelus drafted behind a dual-envelope, high-capacity ore hauler.

"Let's get out of here," Alex said.

"I would dearly love to, but Aeronoth is our best chance of finding a lead on the Professor."

"What is *that*?" Ozzie pointed at a brown mushroom cloud behind the city. Its base was miles wide, sucking sand into a sheer wall that erupted in the stratosphere.

"The Thermals—hurricane-force updrafts generated by atmospheric torsion from the Dome. Traders use them to reach altitudes with favorable winds for long hauls. See those eddies on top? She's snarling today."

Layla opened a panel on the helm, uncovering a speaker grille and microphone. Earth technology looked out of place in the Sauracian's paws.

"Pit Control, Pit Control, this is…" Layla hesitated, then continued, in a defeated tone, "Dragon Lady."

A jolly male voice leapt through the speaker, "Dragon lady! Welcome home, my love! To what do we owe the pleasure of your company?"

My love? Alex stifled a laugh as crimson colored Layla's cheeks.

"Good to hear your voice, Timble. Blankets and blindfolds in the hold today. Here to barter and hit the Thermals. Any chance of an escort?"

"For you, my dear, anything."

"We will wait at the western fuel hub."

"Aye. The Pit is jammed today, so I'll drop by around sundown."

"See you then."

The compass in the ship's binnacle swung east as Layla rolled *Angelus* toward a group of vessels docked in a satellite clump below the city. Chromatic fibers in the envelope blurred the line between clouds and canvas as they threaded the fleet. The Sauracian growled, "Mirror Mode *might* prove useful after all, provided no one sneezes and transforms us into a fiery comet."

Angelus dodged a small freighter that was drifting in a circle as its crew dumped cargo over the side. Pascal waved, and the man at the helm responded with a universally rude gesture.

"Why are they emptying their hold?" Ozzie said.

"Their captain does not know what the Maelstrom is searching for, but is certain he does not wish to get caught possessing it," Layla rumbled.

Alex tapped the compass. "Didn't you say *western* fuel hub?"

"Timble and I are old acquaintances," the Sauracian said. "When I mentioned 'blankets and blindfolds,' he knew to flip anything I said, in case anyone monitored our conversation. 'West' meant east. A simple deception to give us extra time."

"So when he said he was dropping by tonight—"

"He will join us shortly."

Ozzie touched the speaker grille. "You have radios in Terravenum."

"Random breaches occasionally drop Urt technology through the Divide," Pascal said. "Radio was one of fate's more generous gifts—unfortunately, Dome radiation limits broadcast range to line of sight."

"What other technology fell through the Divide?" Alex asked.

"Difficult to say—most breachfall lands in the Foraging Plains, where Scatterlings collect it for Market Days. They barter everything from vinyl music discs to super-heated corn seeds, but keep the best finds for their hoards."

Angelus slid alongside a floating platform. A coverall-clad Dromedarian threw a gruff nod at Pascal and secured the dock lines. His eyes widened when Layla stepped to the railing.

"We're out of order." A pipe danced in the dockworker's lips, claiming credit for his husky voice. "Routine maintenance."

"We require fuel and dockage for repairs," Layla said.

"No fuel. No space," he wheezed.

Three docked airships and a handful of empty berths called him a liar.

"Looks like there's room to me," Pascal said.

The dockworker nodded at the blockade above them. "Lizzies are searching for a light freighter with a mixed species crew. Don't need your kind of trouble."

Layla's voice hardened. "We will refuel, then be on our way."

"No fuel. No space."

Pascal smiled and reached into a pocket of his trench coat. "This seems like a simple misunderstanding between friends." He clinked a bag of coins. "We're happy to grease the wheels of commerce—just need a little dynami to top off our tanks."

"Leave." The dockworker reached for a microphone on his shoulder.

"Pascal!" Layla barked.

The inventor hurled his coin bag at the Dromedarian, catching him in the stomach before he could key the mic.

Kzzzrrrrrrk

A wave of blue energy laid the dockworker flat on his back, twitching.

Pascal shouldered a leather satchel and hopped onto the barge, beckoning Alex and Ozzie to follow. He checked the Dromedarian's pulse, then retrieved the bag of coins with his prosthetic hand. Sparks skittered across ceramic knuckles.

"Is that really money?" Alex asked.

"With slight modifications." Pascal tossed the pouch and caught it. Coins jingled and let off a faint burning aroma. "I call it a shock-bag. Grinding klunklings against each other generates an electrical charge, which stores in fibers of the bag until it hits a target." Pascal glanced at the bargeman. "It overloads the nervous system. He'll be fine, just paralyzed for fifteen minutes."

"What's a klunkling?" Ozzie said.

"A practical solution to a ridiculous problem. For reasons surpassing understanding, Terravenum's official currency, the klunk-ton, weighs 2,000 pounds." He loosened the mouth of the shockbag and displayed tarnished, misshapen coins. "Someone with a brain and a chisel invented klunklings." Pascal cinched the bag shut and turned to Layla, who was uncoiling a hose in the run-down fuel shack. "Top up the tanks and keep *Angie* running. We'll tickle Aeronoth's belly for word of the Professor and try to avoid a tearful reunion with the Guild."

"And the Mercenary League," Layla reminded him.

"Right."

"And the Slimebeast Coalition."

"Them too."

"And the—"

"*I get it.*"

A chubby yellow airship descended from the city, propeller chomping beneath a pancake-shaped hull. The no-frills sky tug wouldn't win any races, but its deep-throated engine huffed like a team of panting oxen. The pilot throttled down when his oily rub rail kissed the fuel barge.

"Pascal, you rogue!" Unfiltered by radio and speaker, the bald man's bombastic cry stopped just short of a scream. Alex ducked, but no one on nearby vessels glanced in their direction—life was hard enough without getting entangled in the Maelstrom's affairs.

Pascal gripped the pilot's forearm. "Jackby! Good to see you."

Jackby Timble would need a stepladder to see over Alex's shoulders, but he had the boisterous demeanor of a much larger man. With every seismic laugh, his belly threatened to split his grease-stained overalls. But the star of the show was unquestionably the magnificent, red handlebar mustache he twirled around his plump finger. "Where's Dragon Lady?"

"Patching holes on *Angelus*."

"Of course she is." Beady eyes probed the twins. "And who are these strapping children?"

"Tourists who want to see a sky city."

The pilot barked a laugh. "A tour guide? You've run into hard times, old friend." He thrust a pudgy hand at Ozzie. "Jackby Timble, at your service."

"I'm Ozzie."

Alex offered her hand. "Alex." Jackby's grip was firm—the handshake of a working man, but the way his eyes kept flicking to Pascal's satchel made her uneasy.

Angelus' crew squeezed around a smoking engine that occupied most of the sky tug's cockpit. With the tap of a throttle, the airship slid away from the fuel barge.

"Where can I drop you off?" Jackby asked.

"The Pit," Pascal said.

"Perfect, avoids attention from upstairs." He spun the helm and pulled a creaky lever, coaxing the airship to climb. "Lizzies won't storm the city so long as we don't give them a reason."

"When did they arrive?" the inventor said.

"Middle of last night, cannons blazing and horns blaring. A couple lads made a run for it, but that ended poorly." He nodded at the ground, where two columns of black smoke marked burning wrecks. "Word is they're searching for a mixed crew on a tramp freighter," Jackby's stare landed on Pascal's satchel, "and a book."

Hair on the back of Alex's neck stood up.

The inventor tightened his bag's strap. "I hope whoever they're looking for gets away."

Aeronoth's rust-stained hull loomed overhead, surrounded by dozens of blockaded ships.

"I didn't expect so much traffic," Alex said.

"The Thermals are good for business." Jackby pointed at the distant wall of sand. "As an official Trade City, Aeronoth caters to any creed or species, so long as your credit is good."

"What kind of trade?" Ozzie asked.

"Goods, services…most anything but slaving. The Merchant Guild monitors transactions and collects tariffs, but the city operates on the timeless economic principle that *if you don't get caught, it didn't happen.*"

Alex stared at the circus above them. "Why is everyone so afraid of three Maelstrom ships?"

Jackby's back stiffened. "Aeronoth's survival hinges on the begrudging suspicion that trade *might* be better than warfare." He massaged three brown scars that bisected the back of his neck. "Blink, and scout ships have a way of becoming an armada."

The pilot hovered the tug at the mouth of the city's lowest repair bay. He unearthed a stubby device from his pocket and turned to face his passengers. A flick of his thumb ignited the miniature cattle-prod. "What's in the bag, Pascal?" Jackby said.

Alex's heart sank.

The inventor rolled his eyes. "Put that away before someone gets hurt."

"Give me the book." Jackby's voice trembled, but his hand was steady.

"You don't want any part of this mess, Timble."

Alex stepped in front of Ozzie and braced to leap for the weapon.

"Don't make me do this," the pilot pleaded.

"No one is making you do anything." Pascal opened his palm. "Give me the scorch stick."

Now! She lunged as Jackby pressed the trigger. A burst of light and the stench of ozone swamped her senses. As she fell, two more *crrracks!* split the air. Bodies thumped as darkness rushed in.

----

1. Overachieving cousin of a standard octopus.

    Enneapuses (nine-armed cephalopods) are cocky, but humbler than deca-
    puses (ten-armed cephalopods) and *far* less pretentious than dodecapuses
    (insufferable twelve-armed show-offs, who invariably insist on juggling at
    public occasions).

CHAPTER 13
THE PIT

"What have you done, Jackby?"

"I had no choice. The Maelstrom will leave once they have the book."

A gruff voice said, "Did you see the heavyset lizzie without a tail? That's Skhaar the Annihilator. Annihilators don't just *leave*, they throw an aftermath."

Alex groaned. A pulsing ache in her jaw matched the throbbing in her temple. Someone heaved a shallow breath and pushed against her back.

Ozzie.

She tried to sit up, but her wrists were bound behind her. Alex closed her eyes and found her brother's fingers.

"Are you okay?"

A soft snore answered. She squeezed the fleshy base of his thumb.

"Ow!"

"*Wake up*," Alex hissed. Silent machinery towered overhead like statues, as industrial lubricants wrenched at her nose.

Pascal's voice drifted up. "This isn't necessary. We all want the same thing."

"Oh? What might that be?" the gruff voice said.

"Love?" the inventor guessed. "Daddy's approval?"

Leather creaked as weapons unholstered.

"Okay, fine. *Not* love."

Alex squinted through the floor grating, ignoring the non-skid biting her cheek. Pascal was bound to a chair and framed in a spotlight on the floor below. His leather satchel sat open on a table in front of him, displaying a strongbox covered with blinking red lights, a rainbow of wires, and a gramophone horn.

Jackby placed a machete on the table, locked his elbows, and leaned into the circle of light—a move designed to intimidate, but executed with the gravitas of an assistant middle school principal at detention. "Open the box," he growled.

Pascal whistled a quick two-tone melody. His bag made a *ftzzz* sound, then started ticking. A collective gasp from the edges of the room betrayed the presence of an audience. Jackby retreated into the shadows and said, "What did you do?"

"Activated fail-safe mode. Congratulations, you successfully kidnapped a weapon-designing genius. Release me and my passengers, or pick the fragments of your teeth out of the wall."

"He's bluffing," the gruff voice barked. A Dromedarian stepped into the light, arms crossed over a black tactical vest and scarred torso that hinted at military service. "Pascal will not detonate a bomb unless he's safely out of range. He would never sacrifice himself for something as fickle as principle."

Pascal feigned shock. "Is the Smuggler's Alliance so desperate to lick the Fury King's boots they sent the great Commander Rekpole on an apology tour? *Sorry about the skirmishes, everyone. Can we interest you in buying some illicit spices?*"

Rekpole grinned humorlessly and adjusted his red beret. "The Alliance prefers to choose our own battles. You brought yours to our doorstep."

"I only dropped by for information and fuel. Give me five minutes and I'll be out of your fur."

"Five minutes is a long time to share a sky with an Annihilator," Commander Rekpole said. "There is more at stake than your personal vendetta against the Maelstrom, Pascal. Diplomatic relations with Sauracia dangle by an ever-fraying thread."

"A thread the Alliance should have cut long ago, Rekpole."

Jackby cleared his throat. "Can we focus, please? We need to deliver the book before the Annihilator gets bored and torches the city. Open the box."

"You don't want me to do that," Pascal said. The satchel ticked louder.

A breathy voice undercut the tension, "You claim to seek information and fuel. What information?" A creature skittered out of the darkness like a germ-phobic wraith, each step calculated to keep the hem of its blue, shimmering robe free of grime. Black, unblinking eyes scrutinized Pascal while two antennae probed the air like divining rods. Alex grimaced. Insects didn't usually gross her out, but she'd never seen a four-foot tall cockroach before. Gold chains and a gleaming medallion clinked as the creature reared up to meet the inventor's eye line. "What information?" Its voice was scratchy and thick, as if two people with sore throats were speaking in unison.

Pascal sneered into the insect's shrunken face. "Baron Muk, deigning to descend into the Pit? I'm honored. I need contact information for your mother, so I can tell her what a disappointment you turned out to be," he said.

A red-robed cockroach scuttled around Baron Muk's elbows and pulled an abacus from its shoulder holster. It stood on two legs, spun, and walloped Pascal's chin hard enough to straighten the Dromedarian's neck. Wooden beads and splintered oak clinked across the floor, and the creature flung its shattered calculator into the corner.

Alex winced, straining against her bonds, but the cords only bit deeper. "Can you get your hands free?" she whispered.

"No," Ozzie said. "What *are* those things?"

"I have a bad feeling we're going to find out."

Baron Muk sighed. "That was Lojo's favorite battle abacus. I fear he might become irritable now. Tell me, Pascal—while you still have use of your tongue—what information is so valuable you would risk a Maelstrom blockade?"

The inventor worked his blubbery lips, then mumbled, "It's personal, not Guild business. I need to speak with Mercy Malicious."

"Everything in Aeronoth is Guild business," the insect said. He flicked his antennae at Commander Rekpole, who nodded and loped out of the room. "We shall summon Madam Malicious to the Pit. Now, disarm your device so we may examine this book that outvalues our lives."

"You don't want me to do that," Pascal said.

Lojo scampered to a wall and retrieved a pair of industrial tongs.

Jackby's mustache trembled as he cleared his throat. "Surely torture isn't warranted."

"It's only a splice joiner, Jackby," Pascal said. He bobbed his head at Lojo. "Keep it angled under sixty degrees or the flare will choke."

The tongs came together, igniting a white-hot, hissing flame.

Jackby took a half-hearted step to block the roach's path. "This is wrong."

"Morality can wait until the Council inquiry," Baron Muk said. "We need answers *now*."

Pascal leaned away from the hissing splice joiner. "You're asking the wrong questions, Muk. Ask yourself why the Maelstrom wants the book." His boots scrabbled on the slick grating, angling his chair back. "Then ask if helping the Maelstrom has ever accomplished anything other than raining destruction down on us."

"Last chance." Baron Muk raised his voice over the splice joiner's mad fizzing, "Open the box."

"Please, Pascal," Jackby said.

The inventor buried his chin and drew his neck back like a bashful snake. Lojo extended his hind legs to bring the tip of the joiner to Pascal's nose.

Sput

The white blaze extinguished like a birthday candle.

Pascal tossed his head and howled, "I *told* you to keep it below sixty degrees!" He waggled an eyebrow at Baron Muk. "You need to hire better help—"

Lojo swung the split joiner into the inventor's jaw, sending a tooth ricocheting off a wall.

Alex flinched, as Ozzie cried, "Oh!"

The Dromedarian licked his split lower lip, then spat a mouthful of blood on Lojo's robe. "Fine. It would be my *pleasure* to open the box." He pursed his lips, grimaced, and whistled a high-pitched three note melody. The lock snapped open, killing the ticking sound and leaving the room in uneasy, expectant silence.

The baron bowed politely. "Thank you." He reached for the satchel.

"What do you think you are doing?"

The ebony woman's ankle-length, fire engine-red dress and bohemian yellow blouse were more at home in a fortune teller's tent than an industrial dungeon, but she marched across the room like a conquering general. "Pascal! What have they done to you?" She shoved Lojo aside and seized the inventor's head in her hands. "You poor dear," she tutted.

"Hewo Mewcy," Pascal's clamped lips struggled to push words past her embrace, "good to see—"

Her finger shushed his swollen mouth. "One moment, love." Mercy rounded on her audience in the shadows, rekindling her fury with a single indrawn breath. *"How dare you?"*

Jackby lifted his hands. "Calm down, Mercy. This is not an affair for women."

Everyone, even the cockroaches, froze.

Mercy erupted, unleashing a verbal flaying of Jackby that rattled ductwork. Eventually, her anger subsided to a glowering, quickly obeyed demand that Pascal be freed from his bonds. Commander Rekpole jumped to attention, releasing the Forsythes.

Mercy fussed over Ozzie and Alex with grandmotherly concern. Thinning gray hair and canyon-deep wrinkles placed her in her early seventies, but a dizzying arsenal of muttered curses and a bejeweled eye patch warned not to underestimate her. "Are you injured, dears?" she asked.

Alex rubbed her wrists. "We're fine, thanks." Ozzie nodded, tenderly probing a purple bruise on his cheekbone.

"Touch that bag, Muk, and I'll decapitate your supply chains," Mercy snapped. "You won't traffic so much as a grape without my say-so."

The baron templed his segmented arms and drifted away from Pascal's satchel.

"I'm glad at least *one* member of the Council is present for this travesty," Mercy said, glaring at Commander Rekpole. "Although I don't know why you'd imprison a genius whose innovations improve Aeronothian lives every day."

Lojo sniggered.

She rallied in the face of skeptical stares. "True, Pascal's inventions have enabled a string of failed mutinies, but he would never intentionally bring the Maelstrom here."

"The lizzies asked for him by name," Jackby said.

Mercy scowled. "And since when do we do the Fury King's work *for* him?"

Rekpole crossed his arms. "Skhaar the Annihilator is here."

The woman's hand strayed to her eye patch before she caught herself. "That is...bad news," she said, "but it changes nothing. Aeronoth cannot align ourselves with the Maelstrom."

"What would you have us do?" the smuggler said.

"What we always do: survive. But with our honor intact."

"The Queen of the Black Market lectures *me* about honor?" Baron Muk hissed, antennae shaking.

Pascal poked his head between the three of them. "Sorry to interrupt this semantic debate about my kidnapping and torture, but I need a word with Mercy."

The old woman waved an admonishing finger at Muk, then spun on her heel and joined *Angelus'* crew in a huddle.

"*I cannot believe you brought the Maelstrom here, you gangrenous buffoon,*" Mercy whispered.

"Children, this is Mercy Malicious," Pascal said. "Mercy, meet the Professor's grandchildren: Ozzie and Alex."

The old woman steered Alex's chin from side to side, then grinned. "You're the spitting image of Adeline. I admired your mother, child."

"That's nice," Pascal said, throwing a furtive glance at Baron Muk, whose antennae were straying toward the satchel. "Any idea where the Professor is?"

"Quidby is missing?"

The inventor whispered, "For at least three months. He sent his journal and a power stone to the children in Urt. The Fury King made a play for them with a sivsuit, so Layla brought them across the Divide."

Understanding flared in Mercy's eyes. "So *this* is the book the market is buzzing about. Well, that's no surprise—the Fury King has been after the Stones for years." She drummed her fingers on her forearm, jingling bracelets, then stopped abruptly. "Vicarious has gone missing, Pascal."

"Again?"

"He launched an expedition to Amnesia."

"*Amnesia?*" Pascal hissed. "Perfect! Just what we need: Vicarious Quibble setting foot on an island *no one* returns from. You should keep better track of your husband, Mercy."

A storm darkened the old woman's face. "Mind your business, Pascal," she snapped. "It may be true Vicarious can't explore his way out of a canvas sack, but once he sets his mind to something, he won't be dissuaded." Her voice trembled, the first sign her steely exterior might be capable of cracking.

The inventor exhaled heavily, then bowed his head. "Sorry. I'm sure Vicarious will return soon. He's the luckiest man I know."

Mercy flicked an errant strand of hair from her face. "Unfortunately, the news does not get better. When Quidby visited Aeronoth four months ago, he agreed to join Vicarious' expedition."

Pascal's prosthetic hand made a hollow *thwap* as it slapped his forehead.

"You saw Grandfather? Was he well?" Alex asked.

"He was agitated—claimed to be on the verge of a break-through. Planned to stop at the Archive before joining Vicarious in Amnesia."

"The Archive," Pascal said, with a deadpan expression. "Wonderful."

Mercy lowered her voice. "Dark deeds are afoot, Pascal. The Fury King grows bolder every day and the Noctem are increasingly desperate to protect the Stones." Her bracelets jangled like warning bells. "Vicarious survived two attempts on his life last year. Trust no one."

"PAAASCAAAAL!"

A mournful howl echoed through the ventilation system. As one, the Aeronothians turned to the door. Mercy uncoiled a bull-whip from her belt.

"Oh no," the inventor breathed.

"PASCAL!"

The cry was closer now and dripping with menace. Heavy foot-steps sent mini-quakes through the metal grating. Alex scanned the room for a weapon and spotted a brown pouch next to Pascal's satchel. Yes! She palmed the shockbag and worked the coins with her fingers to build up a charge.

A battleship-chested, furry monster barreled through the doorway and skidded to a stop, claws screeching. Narrow, feline nostrils tested the air, then gave a contemptuous huff. The creature locked gazes with Pascal and stood on two legs.

"Pascaaaal." A predatory purr rendered the name sinister. The beast had the head of a mountain lion and a body of a steroid-laced action hero. Immense muscles jostled and twitched beneath beige fur as claws extended and retracted like knives. As if the mere pres-ence of a long-fanged, eight-foot tall apex predator wasn't intimi-dating enough, some fool had replaced its right arm with a soot-streaked cannon barrel.

"Bryce! Buddy!" Pascal chirped, "I was just coming to see you."

CHAPTER 14
HAVOC THE PLAGUE

Bryce? This was Bryce the Disruptor?

Bryce rumbled, "That is no longer my name. I am Havoc —*Havoc the Plague.*"

"You've got to stop changing your name, Bryce," Pascal said. "Mercenary work is all about branding."

The beast snarled and lurched forward, prompting everyone in the room to retreat two steps. Crossbows appeared in Rekpole's hoofs, and Lojo brandished what had to be the four sharpest pencils in history.

Pascal patted the air. "Easy, Bryce. We're all friends here."

Alex ground the shockbag klunklings harder. Static electricity levitated her hair—which was either a very good, or an extremely bad sign.

"*Friends?*" Bryce waved his weaponized forearm at Pascal. "Would a *friend* sell me a Triple-Action Bolt Cannon that overloads at high altitude?" He slapped a cluster of crimson burns that pockmarked his chest like moon landings. "I live in a flying city!"

"Did you try to save klunk by powering it with low grade dynami?" the inventor asked, in far too judgmental a tone, considering the circumstances.

"Your dynami is overpriced," the mercenary sulked.

"It's premium!" Pascal jabbed a hoof at his customer. "Did you read the manual? The power source has to be enriched. You voided the warranty, Bryce."

"It's a cannon! Point and shoot."

"So you *didn't* read it." Pascal turned to the twins and threw his arms up. "I don't know why I bother writing those things."

The mercenary threw his head back and roared.

Pascal rolled his eyes and reached for Bryce's arm. "Fine, I'll look at it—but don't tell anyone, or I'm going to get swamped by warranty-breaking dolts who can't be bothered to crack a book open."

When the inventor popped an access panel on the cannon barrel, Baron Muk snatched the satchel from the table. The gramophone horn blasted a shrill note, then spewed a stream of silver tinsel into the air. Muk slapped his neck and crumpled to the floor.

Alex's arm tingled from electrical buildup in the shockbag. She reared back to hurl it at Bryce with the form that earned her three consecutive Little League Pitcher of the Year honors.

Pascal shouted, "Don't!", but it was too late. The shockbag hit Bryce square in the chest and the mercenary folded like a house of cards, smashing the table.

Streams of tinsel drifted down like spider silk, coating the room. Pascal, Alex, and Mercy were the only people still standing as bodies spasmed and convulsed around them.

"Don't touch anything!" Pascal said.

"Ozzie!" Alex snatched two eighteen-inch silver strands from her brother's body. Her fingers went numb on contact with the tinsel. She brushed Ozzie's hair out of his face, and he stared back with dazed, uncomprehending eyes.

"Why can't I move?" he said. Groans around the room expressed similar sentiments.

"I don't know." She turned to the inventor, who was tiptoeing to Bryce. "What was in the bag?"

"A contingency plan," Pascal said. "I *told* them not to open it." He slid the mercenary's eyelids open, then grimaced. "Ozzie will recover. Those metal strands are coated in shempum*[1] saliva, which contains a potent nerve incapacitator. Don't touch them with bare skin."

Numbness crept up Alex's forearms like an advancing zombie horde. She asked, "Out of curiosity, is there an antidote?"

Pascal glared at her. "You touched one, didn't you?" The inventor cracked a compartment in the base of his prosthetic arm. "How have you and your brother survived fifteen years?" He tossed her a vial of red fluid. "Drink it."

"Ozzie needs it more than I do."

"The saliva will paralyze you when it reaches your heart," Pascal snapped. "I can't carry both of you." He gestured to the fallen mercenary. "And thanks to your brilliant shockbag gambit, Bryce the Unhinged here is going to wake up any second, twice as mad and three times stronger. Why would you throw a power supply at a bionically enhanced mutant?"

Bryce moaned at the mention of his name. He raised himself to his elbows and flexed his claws. Alex chugged the antidote. Pungent liquid scalded her throat and spread tingling warmth to her extremities. She clenched her hands experimentally—hopefully, her grip was strong enough to move Ozzie.

Mercy strolled by, juggling an armful of weapons she'd confiscated from her fellow Aeronoth citizens. She stationed herself next to the door and flicked her bullwhip. "Get out while you can, loves."

"This isn't over, Pascal!" Baron Muk croaked, all six of his legs twitching in the air.

The inventor grunted, fastening his utility belt as he walked toward the doorway. "Good to see you again, Mercy. Sorry about the mess. I'll keep an eye out for Vicarious."

Alex locked her elbows under Ozzie's armpits and dragged him backwards across the floor, dodging bodies and debris.

"*PASCAL!*" Bryce raised his arm cannon, his fur spasming as if thousands of volts were coursing through his body. The Triple-Action Bolt Cannon's gaping mouth gave Alex new reserves of energy.

"Faster!" Ozzie said.

Pascal waited at the doorway to let the twins pass. He waved a finger. "The manual clearly states the cannon is for outdoor use *only*, Bryce!"

Havoc the Plague sneered.

Shnick

Alex shielded Ozzie's body.

Bryce shook his arm.

Shnick

Shnick

Shnick-schnick-schnick

Pascal frowned. "Did you reset the combustion valves?"

"Don't help him!" Alex yelled.

"There's such a thing as pride in your work," the inventor said.

Bryce twisted two dials on the side of the cylinder, then snarled and hammered the weapon with his fist.

"Calm down, Bryce. Did you prime the ignitor?"

The mercenary mashed a row of buttons on the rim of the cannon.

"No, the red one—not that one, the other one," Pascal said. "Wait, sorry, I meant yellow."

A low hum turned Alex's stomach. Havoc the Plague sighted down his forearm with a nasty smirk. "Farewell, *friend*."

"Seriously?" Pascal said. "Don't expect a discount in the future."

Fwip

Mercy's bullwhip wrapped around the barrel, and the old woman threw her body into diverting the cannon.

WHOOSH

A horizontal cylinder of fire forced Alex to the deck. When the blast of heat dissipated, she looked up. Bryce had blown himself across the room and through the far wall. Rubble spilled off the giant's shoulders as he shook his arm to douse the smoke pouring out of his gun.

"Time to go!" Pascal yanked Alex to her feet, then slung Ozzie over his shoulder. A klaxon warbled, and a PA system crackled, "*Code Red, Code Red. Fire crew to the Pit.*"

The inventor charged through a wall of flames without slowing. "We need to reach the dock."

Alex craned her neck to check on Bryce, but the smoke was too thick to see anything. "What about Mercy?" she said.

"The fire crew will save her." He kicked a door open. "I'm more concerned about the Maelstrom investigating the commotion."

Water sprinklers chattered, cheerfully dispensing warm mist that doubled the smoke. The walkway trembled.

"PASCAL!"

Alex coughed. "Bryce is coming."

"Is that what that deranged scream was? I assumed someone was cheering me on." He nudged her forward. "Keep moving."

They sped through a doorway and narrowly avoided plunging into a massive hole that occupied the center of Aeronoth. Pascal teetered on the catwalk that lined the perimeter of the hole as Alex grabbed a handrail and searched for an escape route. Aeronoth was an inverted pyramid of rings, each level wider than its downstairs neighbor. Businesses packed the top donut, advertising their wares with flickering billboards and garish flags. A few stories below, colorful living quarters teemed with laundry and the mundane pageantry of daily living. Industrial machinery dominated the lower tiers, bottoming out at the Pit's circular walkway.

A gust teased Alex's hair into her face. She looked down at the distant ground. Had Aeronoth been this high when they came on board? Clattering footsteps drew her gaze upward. The fire crew were snaking down counter-weighted ladders and staircases to the Pit.

"I'm coming, Pascal!" Bryce howled.

He was close. Too close.

"Get ready," the inventor said.

"For what? There's nowhere to run!"

"To jump."

"What?" Ozzie said, flopping against Pascal's back. "Did you say *jump?*"

A ghastly figure emerged from the smoke on the far side of the circle. The Sauracian was taller than Layla, with a stockier build.

Updrafts whipped a tattered, blood-red cloak against the warrior's tree trunk legs. Three red stripes gouged the left side of the creature's face, highlighting a wolfish grin that sank Alex's hopes.

Pascal groaned. "Skhaar."

The Annihilator read his name on the inventor's lips, gave a mocking bow, then limped in their direction. Billowing smoke swallowed him whole.

Pascal pushed Alex back the way they had come. "He has to circle the Portal. We have a few seconds—"

Bryce exploded out of the hallway with a triumphant roar and slammed into the safety railing, twisting it like a pretzel. Only lightning-fast reflexes and a desperate heave saved the mercenary from tumbling to his death. He flipped onto the catwalk, which buckled beneath his weight.

"This isn't a good time, Bryce." Pascal backed away from the panting giant. "There are recent developments you should know about."

"You talk too much," Bryce said, swinging his arm cannon like a bludgeon. A breeze from the near-miss caressed Alex's cheek. The gun clanged into the wall, crimping its barrel. At least he couldn't shoot it again. A flicker of motion caught her eye—Skhaar was halfway around the Portal.

"Seriously, Bryce," Pascal said, "there's something you should know. We're not alone."

The mercenary sighted down his arm, but his weapon's brief career as a hammer had crushed its barrel. Even to Alex's untrained eye, firing a crippled Triple-Action Bolt Cannon topped the list of Bad Ideas.

"Don't do it," she said.

Her warning widened Bryce's delirious, evil grin.

He triggered the cannon.

---

1. A Shetland pony-sized yak native to the Leviathan mountains. Popular with locals for their impressive load-carrying capacity and ability to anesthetize wounds with a lick of their tongue.

CHAPTER 15
THE THERMALS

WHUMP

As flames erupted from Bryce's arm, Pascal flung Ozzie's body at Alex, knocking her into the Portal. She tried to scream as she fell, but only managed a strangled cough. Ozzie suffered no such impediment.

"AAAAAAAAAAAAAHHHH!"

POOOOF

A pillow of canvas slapped Alex's back, pitching her sideways. Friction torched her fingertips as she clawed snowy fabric. Open sky swallowed her legs, then a viselike grip seized her wrist. She looked up to see Pascal hanging upside down, leg hooked over a line of rigging and right arm cradling Ozzie's limp body. Alex bumped into a canvas wall and stared at her reflection. Mirror Mode. She was dangling beside *Angelus'* envelope!

The Dromedarian winced. "Ow."

"Everyone okay?" Layla shouted.

"No," Ozzie groaned.

"Swing," Pascal croaked, blushing a deep shade of red.

Alex kicked her legs to generate momentum. Pascal released her at the apex of a swing and she floated, weightless, for an exhilarating second before slamming into a tangle of rigging. She glanced up at Aeronoth, half-expecting Bryce to leap after them, but unless the mercenary's mutations included wings, *Angelus* was out of range.

Her eyes locked on a hulking figure standing at the edge of the Portal. Skhaar's foot was planted in Bryce's back, and he thwarted the mercenary's struggles with bored detachment. The Annihilator pointed at Alex, drew a claw across his throat, and laughed.

Pascal unspooled a grappling hook from his belt winch, looped it around Ozzie's waist, then lowered him to the deck. "Injury, starboard side," he shouted.

Crimson lightning flashed, sending Alex scrambling down the ratlines.

CRACK

Two Maelstrom airships dove at *Angelus* like bloodthirsty birds of prey, electricity sparking across their black hulls. A dissonant horn blast goaded enthusiastic roars from their crews. Alex dropped onto the deck as Layla banked hard at the Thermals.

Pascal slammed into the pilothouse like a wrecking ball, then untangled his belt winch. "How did you know to come to the Portal?" he shouted.

"Sirens and smoke—I recognized your handiwork. What happened?"

"I *told* Bryce not to fire his cannon indoors." *Angelus* lurched, and the inventor corralled a runaway box of parts. "I'm going to delay his neural splatimizer build until he apologizes."

Alex fought the urge to shake the inventor by his shoulders. "Stop arming mercenaries who want to kill you!" she said.

Pascal chuckled. "Then who would I sell to? Besides, Bryce is a horrible shot."

Layla growled, "Did you speak to Mercy?"

"We chatted, somewhere between getting roughed up by a Guild accountant and running from Bryce. Head for the Archive."

Layla's upper lip curled. "Why?"

"Apparently, the Professor is dead set on perishing at the hands of lunatics."

Angelus juked and skidded across the sky, but maintained

course for the base of the storm. Day turned to night as they dove beneath the edge of the mushroom cloud. A rumble, like continuously crashing surf, grew louder. Turbulence flexed the hull, popping nails. The Maelstrom vessels fell back, their captains recognizing a suicide mission when they saw one.

Alex snaked an arm around Ozzie's shoulders to stabilize his head.

"Is he hurt?" Layla asked.

"Don't be silly," Pascal said. "He's only temporarily paralyzed."

The Sauracian groaned. "You used shempum saliva."

"In my defense, the child touches *everything*."

"You are an imbecile." Layla whirled the helm, dodging a Maelstrom lightning bolt.

Pascal pulled himself to his feet. "We saw an old friend," he said.

Layla fishtailed the airship. "Anyone I know?"

"Skhaar." The inventor's somber expression was the most frightening thing Alex had seen in the past hour.

Layla slapped her tail against the deck, cracking two planks. She tightened her goggles. "We will escape in the Thermals."

A lightning bolt scorched the bow.

"More altitude!" Pascal yelled. "The lower windwall will crush *Angie*." He secured a frazzled strand of rigging with a deft knot.

"She can take it!" Layla barked.

Angelus accelerated, inhaled by the storm. Waves of brown sand shot into the sky, blotting out the horizon as a low-pitched rumble, like ten thousand bowling balls rolling down a lane, grew in volume.

Maelstrom warriors lined the railings of their ships, watching their quarry flee to certain doom. Alex, never one to pass up the chance to poke an enemy in the eye, smiled and waved, provoking a fit of furious weapon shaking. Scarlet lightning smacked into *Angelus*, scorching canvas and frying Mirror Mode. Alex lowered her hand and caught the full brunt of Layla's incredulous glare.

"Was our day not bad enough already?" Pascal thundered, gesturing to the windwall.

She blushed. "Sorry. I didn't—"

A downburst dropped *Angelus* ten feet, but left Alex's stomach behind.

"Secure the boy below!" An olive green respirator mask muffled Layla's command as she struggled into a twelve-point harness.

Pascal and Alex carried Ozzie downstairs and strapped him to a lab table. Increasingly violent turbulence drew a chorus of alarmed burbles and bleats from the terrarium wall.

"It's going to be okay, Ozzie," she said, buckling restraints on his ankles.

He groaned. "I seriously doubt it."

"That's the spirit!" Pascal said, cinching a leather strap across Ozzie's forehead. He uncorked a vial of red fluid and dribbled it into her brother's mouth. "In an hour or two, you'll be on your feet again or buried beneath an ocean of sand—either way, things are looking up!" The inventor rummaged through a drawer and retrieved two human-sized respirators. "The storm is strongest at the base of the windwall, so sand is going to be a bigger problem than usual." He tossed a mask to Alex and strapped the second to Ozzie's face. "I have to keep mechanicals from seizing up and Layla needs to pilot. The intercom is useless, so you run messages between us if we need to communicate." Pascal buckled a utility belt around Alex's waist and tapped its mini-winch. "Clip in and shelter beneath the cowling." He handed her a pair of red-lensed goggles, then vanished down the engine room corridor.

"What's a cowling?" Alex yelled.

Too late.

She fumbled with her belt winch until it spooled enough cable to clip in at the top of the stairs. Her respirator reeked of wet socks, but the sound of her labored breathing was oddly comforting. She tightened the strap on her air canister bag, then threaded the breathing tube so it wouldn't snag on anything.

When *Angelus* crossed the windwall, a violent updraft thrust her bow skyward and sucked the ship into the sandstorm's maw. The vessel pitched and yawed, rocketing higher as the Thermals lashed her from every direction. Alex clung to a handrail, battling to stay upright. Sand infiltrated her mask, and she resorted to shallow breaths to combat the sensation of being smothered by a pillow. *Angelus* corkscrewed and the railing knocked Alex's respirator off her face. She choked on gritty air as the Thermals flogged her against the stairwell like a rag doll on a string.

"RRRRAAAAAAAAGH!" Layla's roar was a mere squeak in the storm. The airship leveled, sending Alex crashing to the stairs. She jammed her respirator against her face and exulted in its heavenly stench while the Thermals punished *Angelus* with halfhearted blows. The sky gradually lightened to amber as dust clouds thinned, revealing the Sauracian slumped against the helm.

Alex unspooled her tether, traversing the deck with the care of a climber summiting Everest. The airship's gyrations had snapped Layla's harness, and indentations in the steering wheel testified to the brute force she had used to stay on board. Heavy wheezing filtered through the Sauracian's mask as she straightened, sending waterfalls of sand cascading from crevices in her leathery skin.

Pascal emerged from the cowling. "I *told* you *Angie* could handle the windwall."

Layla lifted her goggles and scowled. "Why is your fur singed?"

The Dromedarian adopted an expression of wounded innocence. "I indulged in some system upgrades."

"My engine room is off limits."

"When you see how much better our fuel economy is, I think you'll—"

Layla elbowed him aside, then trudged downstairs.

Pascal waited until she was out of earshot, then said, "It's been months since I set hoof in the engine room and the cooling system was a prime candidate for an experimental stankwerm lubricant." An outraged bellow and *clang* from belowdecks made the inventor wince. He frowned at Alex's bloodied shirt. "What happened to you?"

"The cowling," she said. "Out of curiosity, how was I supposed to deliver messages between you and Layla in the middle of a hurricane?"

"Painfully, from the looks of it." He gauged the clouds overhead. "Excellent! A little higher and we'll be in the northbound trade winds."

The temperature dropped as *Angelus* climbed, but at least the sand was dissipating. Pascal unearthed a blanket and draped it over Alex's shoulders.

"I should check on Ozzie," she said.

"He's fine. The antidote is taking effect, but he needs rest."

She shivered and pulled her blanket tighter. "Why did the Maelstrom stop chasing us?"

Pascal grinned. "Skhaar's lackeys may be bloodthirsty, but they aren't looking to die for the cause—only plummeters enter the windwall as low as we did. It's a miracle we didn't get shredded."

"Plummeters?"

"High-speed messengers with a death wish. Plummeters ride disposable platforms up to the Dome, then soar to their destination in wingsuits. It's expensive, but the fastest way to deliver messages or small packages across Terravenum, provided the plummeter survives."

"That's crazy," she said.

"That's not the worst of it. The higher they launch, the farther they can travel—but if they wait too long to jump, they risk dying inside the Divide."

"Unless they have one of your sivsuits."

The inventor coughed. "True, but try to avoid talking about sivsuits in public. There are good reasons to keep that invention quiet." He spun the helm to dodge an ominous cloud bank. "Even when plummeters avoid the Divide, they're exposed to pure dynami close to the Dome. That's how mutations happen."

"Aren't *you* a mutant, though?" Alex stammered to frame her question in a less offensive way, "I mean, without dynami, aren't you just a camel?" She withered inside.

Thankfully, Pascal didn't take offense. "Mutations are unpredictable. Some creatures grow vestigial armpit hair, while others triple their teeth count, sprout an extra nostril, and declare war on anything that smells like licorice."*[1] He tapped his chest. "Thanks to Dromedaria's proximity to the Divide, my ancestors experienced explosive cognitive growth, stood on two legs, then experimented with and eventually outlawed folk dancing."

"How many species live in Terravenum?"

"The five biggest populations are humans, Sauracians, Dromedarians, Arthropids, and Trenchians. Add the handful of sentient outliers who evolved in the Barren—lorebadgers, garganchu trolls, and creatures like Bryce—and you've got a mutation melting pot."

"Does everyone get along, apart from the Sauracians?"

"Most factions are locked in power struggles, barring occasional truces for the sake of making klunk. Species tend to stick together." He met Alex's stare. "Remember Muk and his henchbug, back at the Pit?"

She nodded.

"Baron Muk's ancestors evolved into number-crunching geniuses, then founded the Merchant Guild."

"They didn't like you very much."

"Arthropids don't tolerate anything that interferes with their bottom line. They live for profit, and my loyalties are negotiable." Pascal looked aft, then frowned at their compass heading. He pulled the throttles back. "We've lost thrust." The inventor hobbled to the stern, peered over the rail, and groaned. "Sand clogged the tricogent flange on the starboard engine."

"That sounds bad."

"Only if you want to escape an Annihilator."

"Can we get by with one engine?"

"In the Thermals, it would be better to have three. Even if we weren't being chased by the Maelstrom—and believe me, they're coming—we don't want to lose propulsion up here. At this altitude there are currents, counter-currents, and counter-*counter*-currents—not to mention the possibility of a Moribund Gale."

"A Mori-what?"

"An unpredictable, terminally violent downburst that—" Pascal saw her expression. "Never mind. Nothing to worry about."

"It *sounds* like something to worry about."

"You'll clean the flange while I troubleshoot from here."

She sized up the light scaffolding that extended from the hull to the engine. "You want me to climb across that?"

"Not exactly." He kicked a locker open and pulled out a rusty slab of metal. "It's a proof-of-concept prototype, but if it flies, it's going to revolutionize mid-flight engine maintenance." Pascal handed her the contraption. "I call it a cloudwhip."

The board was lighter than it looked and weighed even less after a layer of rust flaked off in her hand. "If it *flies*," Alex mused under her breath, her heartbeat quickening. The kidney-shaped cloudwhip was contoured like an airplane wing—thick in the middle and tapered toward the edges. Adjustable leather foot straps dangled, waiting for a victim.

A red flag waved frantically in the back of her mind.

"Wait. *If* it flies? You don't *know*?"

"The aerodynamics are sound." Pascal clipped an air canister to Alex's belt. "I'll unspool cable from the winch and monitor your progress as you float back to the engine." He see-sawed his hand, like a leaf wobbling on a breeze.

The plan was undeniably crazy, with a generous side helping of awesome.

And she loved awesome.

"Has anyone actually *flown* this thing?" she said, offering her right foot.

Pascal tightened a strap, cutting off circulation in her toes. "Not so much 'flown' as 'spun wildly out of control,' but I had a break-through with the spontaneous inversion problem—it's a simple matter of weight distribution. Just don't lean back." He thought for a second. "Or forward. It's best not to lean at all."

Alex ground her teeth and watched Pascal unspool cable from the winch drum on the starboard bow. He clipped a carabiner to her belt, then helped her climb the railing. She glared at the engine and replayed Pascal's rushed advice:

Keep your knees bent so they don't sprain when—I mean IF, the board inverts without warning. Which probably won't happen. Although it could. This close to the Dome, static builds up with friction and can trigger lightning, so take all metal out of your pockets. If a noxious gild-

*abeast*² *soars by, try to grab it. Isobel gave me a scrumptious recipe for gildabeast with plum sauce. Did I mention not to lean back? Whatever you do, don't stray too far from Angelus, or the Thermals will rip you from the board like a dryptiff from a slothhound's beard.*

Years of extreme sports had honed Alex's instinct for the relative sketchiness of an idea, and all indicators were pegged on "Impending Tragedy."

But she'd never been one to back down from a challenge.

Pascal hit a switch and the starboard propeller clattered to a grateful halt. Gray smoke puffed from the overheating engine, leaving a trail of periods, like a skywriter building anticipation. The inventor said, "Nothing fancy, just glide back and clear the flange. And above all..." He gestured her closer. Alex leaned in, sponging last minute pointers like her life depended on it, which it probably did. "Watch for noxious gildabeasts. They're drawn to smoke." He winked, then limped to the winch drum. "Plum sauce! Think of the plum sauce!"

Alex rolled her eyes, then blew warmth into her frigid fingers, grateful for the jacket she'd found in her parents' closet. With a little imagination, the smear of clouds below looked like a halfpipe. She adjusted her goggles. "Come on, Alex. You've got this."

Angelus lurched sideways in a gust, dropping her rail. Alex slid into empty sky with a startled shriek.

---

1. According to *The Ledger*, the Merchant Guild's journal of record, the gum-fanged snortlug is responsible for twenty-seven percent of candy-related assaults.
2. Noxious gildabeasts possess the wingspan and grace of an albatross in flight— and thanks to a steady diet of loftgrass and frenzied gymbits, the methane production of a cow herd. Near-constant flatulence gives them a boost when traveling long distances or battling headwinds.

    Ornithologists have long considered noxious gildabeasts as evidence that Mother Nature never graduated middle school.

CHAPTER 16
CLOUDWHIPS &
CONSEQUENCES

Free fall.

The winch cable jerked taut, crushing Alex's ribs as the cloud-whip spun her like a propeller. She grabbed the wire and angled her feet against the spin until the horizon steadied. Gusts buffeted her as she wobbled in place, looking to *Angelus* for assistance. Pascal pointed at the engine, in case Alex had forgotten why she was dangling from a cable ten thousand feet above the ground.

His cleaning instructions had been even less helpful: *Use your brush to scrub the tricogent flange—it's a yellow cylinder under the propeller. Be careful not to touch the magneto booster, it can discharge 100,000 volts. Don't worry, I painted it yell-...oh... Just try not to touch anything. On an unrelated note, do you have any important messages for Ozzie?*

Alex flexed her calves and bit her tongue when the cloudwhip shot thirty feet up, inverted, then resumed windmilling her body. She gasped, squeezing her eyes shut to block out the whirling horizon. Instinct flicked her ankles, countering the spin and standing her upright.

Breathe.

She forced herself to take stock of her surroundings. Far below, gray clouds bombarded each other with sheet lightning, but in the upper Thermals, the sky was crisp and inviting. Alex dipped her toes, carving a cautious turn through smooth air, like she was surfing a wave. She rocked her hips, and the cloudwhip tracked with her motion. A harder stomp rewarded her with a sharp turn, and she laughed.

Juddering tugs at Alex's belt yanked her attention back to the job at hand as the winch drew her even with the starboard engine. Pascal had spurned aerodynamics in favor of a clunky hodgepodge of gears, tubes, and twirly metal bits that relied on a propeller to give any clue to its purpose.

The inventor shouted, but rushing wind stole his words. He pointed behind her, at a towering thunderhead pancaked against the Dome. The cloud was ominous, but not a concern. He must have spotted a noxious gildabeast.

Alex shook her head. Plum sauce or no plum sauce, she had work to do.

KRAAAACCKKK

A blue lightning bolt scarred the sky and a savage gust swatted Alex against the engine. Her fingers groped scorching-hot metal, searching for safe holds among thick cables, extruding pipes, and for unknown reasons, a glass cage.

Plink. Plink. Plink.

A purple, furry beast lunged at the glass in a spirited attempt to disembowel her, each defeat compounding its fury. Alex wrapped her elbow around the propeller. Hopefully, staying closer to *Angelus* would lessen her chances of getting struck by phantom lightning.

PLINK. PLINK. PLINK.

The enraged furball tossed its head back, bayed like a bloodhound, and disappeared into the bowels of the engine as fast as its six tiny legs could scurry. Just when she thought the day couldn't get weirder.

Alex smacked the sand-caked engine with her brush, triggering a dozen mini-avalanches that vanished in the wind, unmasking yellow metal.

She gingerly probed a pipe with her brush.

"Raaaaooooorraaaaaaaooooooo!"

A howling purple missile launched out of a dusty tube, straight at Alex's face. She smacked at it, but the little terror saw the brush coming and welcomed its nemesis with six open arms. Bristles flew as scalpel-sharp teeth notched gashes in the brush handle. The beast froze mid-snarl and flicked a green eye at her. Alex panicked, slamming the brush against the engine like she was beating a carpet. The animal screeched and darted up her arm, claws tearing through her jacket.

Alex bellowed, and the creature responded with a triumphant howl. Fortunately, instead of mauling exposed flesh, the malignant furball focused on decimating her goggles. Alex shielded her face as minuscule teeth raked her lenses. Blind and desperate, she used her air canister as a club.

Whump! Whump!

Two direct hits gave the beast a new archenemy. It yowled, tore the bottle from her grip, and bounded onto the engine. Alex draped an arm over the propeller and tried to catch her breath, but the air was too thin to satisfy her lungs. The purple monster cackled and sunk its teeth into the canister.

Ssssssssssssss

Her air supply leaked into the atmosphere. If she snatched the bottle back, she wouldn't be able to fend off another attack.

At least the wretched beast was distracted. Alex swiped her brush at anything within arm's reach—yellow, green, flat, round… it all got swept. She kept her motions subtle to avoid drawing interest from the purring fuzzball. The walls of her vision narrowed as her breath shortened to gasps. The brush slipped from her fingers, and she tumbled off the engine like an autumn leaf.

The cloudwhip pitched Alex into a spin. Sky met clouds met sky in a despairing blur. How could so much wind contain so little oxygen? She smashed into a dark blob. Something snaked across her shoulder. The little monster was back! She slapped at it with feeble blows.

Hissssssssssssssss

An intoxicating scent invaded Alex's nostrils, and she gulped delicious lungfuls of syrup-thick oxygen. As she hacked and coughed her way back to lucidity, Pascal's concerned face materialized above hers. He tapped an air canister.

"You need these up here!"

Alex turned her head and discovered she was lying on the deck of *Angelus*. Still alive, then. Good. First things first. She grabbed Pascal's mask and wrenched his face down to hers. "What *was* that thing?" she panted.

"A dynami surge. I tried to warn you." He pried her fingers from his respirator. "Surges form when a thundercloud hits the Dome and funnels dynami from the Divide into our atmosphere."

"I'm not talking about lightning. Why is a furry murderball living in the engine?"

Pascal looked blank, then laughed. "You mean Socrates? He's a gruffletrunt—they're affectionate, provided you don't touch anything that belongs to them."

"Like a tricogent flange?"

"Exactly. Gruffletrunts are extremely territorial."

Alex shook her jacket's shredded arm. "You should have warned me!"

"Remember when you said, 'Stop listing what might go wrong, Pascal, let's just do this'?"

Alex tore off a foot strap and threw it at the inventor. "He tried to eat my face."

Pascal inspected the cloudwhip. "Be glad it was Socrates' engine. Snuggles is much more aggressive."

"Why are you housing psychotic animals in your engines?"

"Indiscriminate savagery cuts down on parts theft and sabotage. Also, they're cute."

Alex yanked her foot free of the remaining strap. "I'm checking on Ozzie."

Machinery, tools, and glass littered the lab like shrapnel from a science grenade. A vial crunched under Alex's foot, releasing a purple chemical that dissolved a hole in the floor. Terrarium tenants were splattered against their enclosures, but mercifully, the tanks were holding. A sizable dent in the coffee machine was going to bring a tear to Pascal's eye, though.

Ozzie, strapped securely to a table, sported a coat of dust. "Is someone there?" His hands twitched. "I can move now."

A lump lodged in Alex's throat at the sound of her brother's muffled voice. She unfastened his restraints and helped him sit up. "You missed all the action," she said. "Long story short—we're not dead yet."

Dust billowed off Ozzie's arms as he stretched. "What were you doing out there? I heard screaming."

"Pascal booby-trapped the engines with evil, six-legged, mutant kittens."

"Of course he did."

Alex glanced at the stairwell, then pushed her head close to his. "Things are out of control, Oz. Pascal got tortured, Bryce almost shot us, the Maelstrom chased us into a mushroom cloud—"

"A mutant kitten attacked you."

"An *evil* mutant kitten." She pointed at scratches on her goggles.

He chuckled. "My mistake."

"You wouldn't laugh if you saw its teeth." Alex lowered her voice, "Pascal and Layla are just as lost as we are."

Ozzie shrugged. "We won't find Grandfather without their help. Would you rather hide until the Noctem or Maelstrom hunt us down?"

"They can have the stupid journal."

His head snapped up. "Never! Grandfather—"

"Lied to us," she said, "just like Mom and Dad. If the world was ending, why would they keep it a secret? Exploring Terravenum was about ego and adventure. We need to go home."

"*Go home?* Look around, Alex." Ozzie gestured to the devastated lab. "Mom and Dad probably sat at this very table. Whatever they discovered here was important enough to risk their lives for. We have to protect the journal and find Grandfather."

Alex resisted the temptation to punch sense into her brother's shoulder. Since when did *he* want to take risks? She gritted her teeth. "Fine, but let's hide somewhere until we come up with a plan

121

that doesn't involve paralyzing you, getting clobbered by a pea-brained mercenary, or being professionally annihilated."

Layla's gravelly voice echoed in the hallway, "There is nowhere we can hide from Skhaar—Annihilators complete their mission and relish the cost." The Sauracian settled onto a bench and cleaned her goggles. Her eyes flitted to Alex's tattered sleeves.

"Socrates or Snuggles?" she asked.

"Socrates."

Layla grunted and raised her right forearm, displaying a gluttony of gnaw marks.

"They attacked *you*?" Alex said.

"Gruffletrunts adore large targets—there's more to bite," Pascal said, clomping down the stairs. "When Snuggles first nested, she intentionally triggered alarms on her engine to ambush Layla."

"Hang on," Ozzie said. "Not to change the subject, but who is Skhaar?"

Layla and Pascal exchanged an uneasy look. He spoke slowly, as if unearthing a confession from a shallow grave, "Skhaar is an Annihilator, an elite henchman the Fury King deploys on missions where collateral damage is a bonus. His exploits during the Siege of Quietus Pass made him a living legend in some circles and a walking nightmare everywhere else. Seven years ago, he..." Pascal choked back a sob, then continued, "he breached the Divide in a stolen sivsuit...and killed your parents."

Alex's stomach knotted as the bombshell stuck home. She watched her pale, fragile brother sway against the motion of *Angelus*.

"What happened?" Ozzie's respirator muffled his words, but his voice was flat.

The inventor stared at the floor. "A colleague stole my prototype sivsuit and gave it to the Maelstrom. I arrived at the launch site too late to stop Skhaar from going through the Breach, but managed to overload the system, shortening his time window. It trapped him in the Divide and sliced off his tail, but not before he murdered your parents."

"How long does a Breach last?" Ozzie asked.

122

"Forty-four seconds."

"Why forty-four?" Alex said.

"No idea. Something to do with particle physics—or possibly the color orange."

"Orange?"

"I said I don't know." Pascal removed his brass timepiece from his pocket and fiddled with its chain. "If I had secured my sivsuit, the Maelstrom couldn't have opened a Breach, and your parents would still be alive. It was my fault." He handed the clock to Alex. "But the Professor gave me this."

Elegant Roman numerals and intricate gears marked passing seconds with military precision. Her fingertips traced an inscription on the back:

There's always time for forgiveness, even of yourself. Forever your ally, QF

Quidby Forsythe.

She passed the timepiece to Ozzie. To her surprise, he barely glanced at it.

"So, what now?" he said.

Alex frowned at her brother. Maybe shempum saliva had scrambled his brain.

"Ozzie, Skhaar is—" she started.

"—a black-hearted murderer who killed our parents. Got it. I saw it happen, remember?" Ozzie pushed the clock into Pascal's palm. "After seven years of being told I'm delusional, now that I finally have answers, I'm not running away." His eyes had a steely glint Alex hadn't seen before.

"We'll find a place to hide you while Layla and I locate the Professor," the inventor said, "then we'll harvest enough dynami to get you home."

Ozzie folded his arms. "If you're right about the world ending, what's the point in going home? At least here, we can help find Grandfather."

Pascal pounded the table, sending a tray of Petri dishes clattering to the floor. "I have enough Forsythe blood on my hooves to last ten lifetimes!" His voice quaked as he met Ozzie's hard stare, "This is not a game. If Skhaar catches us, we'll be lucky for quick deaths."

Alex gnawed her lip. "I don't know, Oz."

"This debate is pointless," Layla rumbled. "By now, the Merchant Guild has issued a scrag contract on us, and every mercenary in the League is in the Thermals. *Angelus* is the children's best refuge."

Pascal read the inscription on his timepiece and squeezed his eyes shut. "It's all happening again," he groaned. "Skhaar, the sivsuit, the Maelstrom…"

Ozzie touched the inventor's arm. "Our parents accepted the risks, and so do we." He looked at Alex, and she nodded, reluctantly.

The Dromedarian pocketed his clock. "You don't *begin* to understand the risks, children. We're headed for the Archive, whose librarians collect Stone Lore at the tip of a sword. Not to mention that the Professor's research bred resentment among Stone scholars, who elevate backstabbing to an art form. If anyone at the Archive learns we possess his journal, we won't escape alive."

CHAPTER 17
AN INTERROGATION

Skhaar smirked when the Aeronoth fire brigade shoved past him without a second glance. For someone used to being the center of attention on a battlefield, blending in was a novelty. How like flesh-bags and grubs to focus on a small, peripheral threat while ignoring certain death strolling freely in their midst.

He plucked remnants of the bullwhip from his forearm. For a septuagenarian human, Mercy Malicious put up a decent fight—although she should have known that basic training renders Maelstrom warriors immune to whips. Drill Master Rook had made certain of that. Old Rooksy, so quick with a braided cord—though he likely wished he were quicker when Skhaar and Bzruk paid him a post-graduation visit. After Home Office completed their investigation of the incident, they abolished the tradition of students challenging former instructors to combat; then threw Skhaar and Bzruk into the dungeon. The next morning a gnarled warrior stopped by their cell and recruited them for the Annihilator program, with one catch: there was only a single slot available.

Skhaar occasionally felt a twinge of guilt when he sang Bzruk's name in his Deathsong, but survival requires sacrifice.

Mercy wouldn't quickly surrender useful information, and Skhaar didn't have time for a thorough interrogation, so he limited her injuries to a survivable level. No sense creating a martyr—especially in Aeronoth, a hub of Terravenum's rumor mill. If he accidentally triggered a war before the Fury King declared one, there would be unpleasant consequences.

Skhaar was vaguely embarrassed about threatening the Urtling girl by miming a throat slice. Cheap theatrics were beneath him, but fighting the mutant cat had roused his battlerage, and he'd gotten carried away. The human child would have to die, if only to preserve his reputation.

The Annihilator climbed to the level above the Pit, carefully ignoring the unobstructed view of the ground three thousand feet below. He wrinkled his nose as he stepped into a room that reeked of fear. His vanquished plaything—a mutant, cannon-armed cat—lay on the floor, a heap of fur and misery.

Skhaar cracked his knuckles and relished the sound of volcanic rocks exploding. Out of habit, he reached for the mace ball on his shoulder strap, then stopped himself and sighed. Home Office required him to file Post-Interrogation Reports because of his "pattern of blatant disregard for approved procedure." *Any further incidents will require your attendance at a mandatory five-day seminar on Ethical Conduct in the Field. You WILL change with the times, or get left behind.*

Skhaar had stopped keeping track of warnings and probations long ago, but if Home Office forced him to sit through another Ethics seminar, he was going to disembowel the instructor—and he was done hiding bodies.

Fine, he would do this by the book—even though he'd been around long enough to fight shoulder-to-shoulder with Nusk the Abysmal, the warrior who *trained* the desk jockeys who *wrote* the book. Skhaar fished around in a chest pocket and retrieved the crumpled Interrogation Prompt Card his supervisor insisted he carry at all times. For once, he was glad there were no witnesses.

Step One: Identify yourself and establish authority.

Easy enough. Skhaar kicked the cat in the ribs and growled, "You know who I am." The prisoner groaned.

Step Two: Build a rapport with the prisoner, then leverage your relationship to obtain information.

"Havoc the—" Skhaar stifled a snigger and tried again, "Havoc, the—" He burst out in a deep chuckle that rasped like sandpaper. "I can't call you that. What is your birth name?"

"Bryce," the cat mumbled through swollen lips.

"That's better." The Annihilator stepped on Bryce's wrist and applied pressure. "Bryce, was Pascal carrying a book?" Whimpering didn't count as an answer. Building a rapport was more difficult than expected. "I need to know where *Angelus* is going," he said. "Help me find Pascal, and your suffering will end."

Bryce moaned. "Don't know. Maybe...Rust?"

Skhaar sneered. Information volunteered so quickly wasn't worth a klunkling. Pascal wouldn't flee to the Scatterling city. He consulted his procedure card, mouthing the words silently.

Step Three: Reward compliance with positive reinforcement. Meet noncompliant behavior with calm resolve. Physical intimidation is a last resort.

"You can do better, Bryce." The Annihilator leaned harder, until a bone snapped. Skhaar seized Bryce's foot, spun in a circle, and hurled the mercenary into a wall, which buckled under the impact. When the dust settled, he said, "Remember anything yet?"

Bryce whispered, "Archive?"

Now that was an interesting possibility. The librarians were always up for hiding and protecting a book—the trick was prying it from their fingers once the danger had passed.

Step Four: Solidify rapport by thanking the prisoner for their cooperation.

Skhaar snagged Bryce's neck mange and dragged him out of the

127

room. The mercenary offered no resistance as his body flopped down the stairs and onto the catwalk.

"Thank you for your cooperation," Skhaar said. He nudged the mercenary over the lip of the Portal. Bryce plunged out of sight.

Skhaar hated to concede it, but maybe the desk jockeys were onto something—the interrogation had taken less time than usual and still yielded results. He flicked blood off the instruction card and smoothed its creases with a weathered claw.

Uh-oh.

Step Five: Secure and register the prisoner with Home Office as a future informant.

He gripped the rail, gulped a quick breath, and risked a peek over the Portal's edge. Bryce dangled far below, his claw wedged into a seam between two metal plates. Skhaar would need to summon a recovery team—and worse, admit a mistake—to retrieve the mercenary.

Neither of *those* things were going to happen.

The Annihilator sighed and turned away. More paperwork.

Black smoke enveloped Aeronoth's interior well. Nothing flight-critical had failed yet, but worried-looking welders with blow-torches and blueprints were making the rounds. Skhaar's knees complained all the way up the maze of stairs between the Pit and the upper level docks. Slack-jawed locals watched him lurch past, curiosity shifting to fear when they recognized the Fury King's brand on his cheek. Shopkeepers slammed their stalls shut as word of the Annihilator spread. Even Arthropod merchants, who viewed pillaging invaders as potential customers, stared at him silently instead of hawking their wares. By the time he reached the loading level, the docks were deserted.

A cheer from the Pit suggested the fire brigade had defeated the burgeoning inferno—an impressive feat in a rusting hulk like this. Maybe there was hope for Aeronoth yet...which was more than could be said for the captains of *Dreck* and *Karkis*, who had aban-doned pursuit of *Angelus* at the windwall.

If *Revenge* hit the Thermals low enough, they could reach the Archive in two days. Skhaar's stomach knotted in anticipation of the high-G maneuvers now necessary, thanks to the cowardice of his two captains. His tail stump twitched. Time for another lesson in consequences. He marched across *Revenge's* gangplank and barked, "Prepare for departure!"

Traumatic journey aside, he was looking forward to visiting the Archive. A line of scar tissue circling his neck was a daily reminder of the price of breaking the Booksworn's strict "No Books May Leave the Reading Room" policy. The prospect of revenge was enticing.

Skhaar grinned. He was getting ahead of himself. As Nusk the Abysmal famously said, "Never plan your enemy's funeral before you kill him, or you will fight a living ghost."

For Pascal, he was willing to make an exception.

CHAPTER 18
THE JOURNAL

Ozzie rolled out of his hammock and dropped into Grandfather's creaky chair. He stretched his arms and eyed the respirator hanging on the wall, grimacing as his tongue picked sand from his teeth. Supplemental oxygen wasn't necessary at lower altitude, but Layla insisted everyone keep a breather nearby in case the Maelstrom forced an emergency ascent. He smiled when he spotted grandfather's journal on the desk, where Pascal had promised to leave it.

Ozzie pressed the arrowhead into the cover, then leaned back as dynami outlined the frame with blue light. Pascal had only managed to dial the activation sequence down to a "survivable tingle," so he waited until the sizzling faded before gingerly touching a corner of the book.

"Ow!"

A spark zapped his finger. Ozzie winced, then smoothed the title page flat, ignoring protests from the book's spine.

Observations on Terravenum and Insights into Stone Lore, by Quidby Forsythe III

He forgave the bland title upon reading a random entry:

Humboldt—Ozzie's pulse quickened at his father's name—*believes flora and fauna native to the Barren are sentient in proportion to their dynami exposure. Certainly, the calypsicum matrimonius that sank its fangs into Humboldt's right ankle was vocal in its bleak opinion about the flavor of his socks.*

In the tradition of Darwinian naturalists, Grandfather catalogued and sketched wildlife he encountered in his travels. An alarming number of blood-spattered pages testified that indigenous creatures were equally fascinated by Urtlings—and in particular, how they tasted.

Hyperopic (far-sighted) Gulpums

- *Few natural enemies, thanks to a massive mouth and a propensity to swallow anything within range of its chameleonesque tongue.*
- *Gulpum tongue is a regional delicacy, or so I'm told (after a Rummage Lord presented me with a bushel of Yollibelli dung at the last annual Bargain Feast, I steer clear of Scatterling dishes unless their edibility is first demonstrated).*
- *Klunkian legend claims myopic (near-sighted) gulpums populated the Shatterjoy Swamp until the entire colony fell into the Trench due to poor depth perception.*

He flipped to the next page.

Overproud Lumberhen

- *Whatever mutation allowed chickens to grow to the size of a pony did nothing to prevent them from becoming the most territorial creatures I've encountered (with the notable exception of Gruffletrunts, who are in a class unto themselves). Thankfully, lumberhens limit their possessive aspirations to the tree they hatch in—a strategy which would be more successful if they did not propagate in litters of fifteen chicks. Overproud lumberhens spend the vast majority of their lives waging war with siblings, until their home tree topples beneath the weight of its portly tenants, crushing all parties.*

Fascinating observations, but hardly worth the risk of crossing the Divide. Ozzie skimmed to the middle of the book, which featured a sketch of a mountain with a question mark floating over its peak.

All signs point Northeast, but the Sky Gate—that sounded promising —is likely little more than legend. Supply convoys who venture into the highest reaches of the Leviathan mountains are unwilling to risk my presence, due to a rumor I might be Unlucky. Apparently, I'm being blamed for the accidental ignition of the Mountain Watch Signal Pyre Beacon Chain. In my defense, options for kindling wood were limited, and my tea was not going to brew itself.

References to an author named Garrilus the Unread dominated the journal. Grandfather invested a lot of time exploring the intricacies of Garrilus' writings, but his conclusions were baffling:

THREE mentions of eating midnight hatchclaw snacks in the "Sleepwalking Epics," but only TWO in the "Lorebadger Master Concordance." Coincidence, or is another trip to Tory's Descent in order?

After reading Garrilus' "Ballad to a Sneeze," I'm fully convinced the key to the Shudder Stone's location lies at the bottom of Scrum's sacred Sniffling Well.

A lower, hastily scrawled entry declared:

Following an ill-fated expedition to Scrum and three weeks in jail, I'm fully convinced the key to the Shudder Stone's location does NOT lie at the bottom of the Sniffling Well.

Ozzie leaned back and ran his fingers through his hair. He

132

needed context. Until he learned about Garrilus the Unread, Grandfather's notes were gibberish.

Alex cleared her throat and Ozzie nearly fell out of his chair. How long had she been standing in the doorway?

"Pascal wants to check your translapede scar." Mom's stretchy gray pants and black long-sleeved shirt fit Alex like she'd bought them off a rack. "Find anything?" she said.

Ozzie tugged his father's oversized collar. "Mostly animal sketches and scattered thoughts about a guy named Garrilus the Unread." He flipped through illustrations.

"Wait!" Alex said. "Go back."

Ozzie obeyed, then gasped. An illustration of the Stella Signum dominated the left page, opposite sketches of Alex's bracelet and his sword hilt.

Armillam and Hilt recovered from an underground tomb in the Northern Feral sands. Both artifacts are constructed from volantium and bear the Stella Signum, presumably indicating power and importance to the Ancients.

Armillam (bracelet) - Exceedingly rare. Use unknown. Glows in presence of ambient dynami.

Hilt - Potentially one-of-a-kind. The "Custos Luminis," a prophecy of the Ancients, suggests the existence of two such artifacts, but attempts at locating a source willing to discuss the prophecy have met with little success. Hearsay suggests a connection to the Fury King. Further investigation required.

"He found mysterious artifacts buried in the desert, suspected they were powerful, then gave them to us." Alex slapped her forehead. "You and I are the only members of our family who think before we do things."

Ozzie recalled the visceral terror of watching his sister free solo Keeper's Rock without ropes, but kept his mouth shut. "Let's go see Pascal before he sells an antigravity cannon to a mercenary who's trying to capture us."

The inventor was tangled in the electrical guts of a two-foot square black cube. Each side of the device housed a speaker cone, like the teeth-rattling subwoofers Lamswoolian teenagers used to drown out low self-esteem.

"Cranking some tunes?" Ozzie said.

"This device generates harmonic tremors across a wide range of frequencies." Pascal clipped a wire, then snapped the case shut. "At least, it's supposed to—so far, it's mostly a convenient place to set coffee. I call it Screechbox 3000."

A hiss stuttered from the speakers.

Alex said, "What happened to the first two thousand, nine hundred and ninety-nine versions?"

"Scientific progress is often indistinguishable from a series of preventable calamities." The inventor grinned. "Let's try a low-power test."

Ozzie gave a thumbs-up and sheltered behind a bench with Alex.

Pascal triggered a handheld remote. "Activating!" Screechbox coughed, then thrummed a sub-harmonic note that quivered Ozzie's innards. Glassware jumped, sloshing chemicals. The inventor scribbled on a notepad, then spun a dial. The cube bounced, screeching a piercing note that made everyone in the room clap their ears.

Ozzie weathered the storm from a fetal position as Pascal stabbed his remote with increasing urgency. Fault lines appeared in terrariums. Tools danced off workbenches. The inventor smashed the remote against a table, and the volume of the shriek intensified. Layla stormed down the stairs, snatched the controller from Pascal's hand, and hurled it at Screechbox 3000, rupturing two speaker cones. The cube gargled, spat a plume of smoke, then hissed resentfully.

"A weapon that incapacitates its wielder is useless," Layla thundered, then stomped out of the lab.

Pascal winced, bobbing his hoof in universal sign language for

Shout quieter, please. "I concede nothing but have noted your feedback for Screechbox 3001." He swept fragments of his ill-fated cube into a trash bin.

Ozzie lowered his hands and stared at bloody secretions dripping from his fingers. "Um, Pascal?"

"Fascinating," the inventor said. "Your translapede attempted to escape." He blotted behind Ozzie's ear with a handkerchief while Alex made grossed-out noises. "I've heard of this happening with belchgoat shepherds, but it's very rare." Pascal scribbled in a notebook and whispered, *"Observe children to monitor the mortality rate of translapede host rejection."*

"Mortality rate?" Ozzie said.

The inventor frowned. "That was a private note."

"You said those *exact* words out loud."

"I processed verbally, expecting you would do me the courtesy of not eavesdropping. Clearly, I made a mistake."

Alex scowled. "Your *mistake* was putting insects in our heads that might kill us!"

"That's overdramatic, but fair." Pascal snapped his notebook shut, as if that settled the matter. "What did you discover in the Professor's journal?"

Ozzie pressed the handkerchief against his incision. "Typical explorer's stuff...beast illustrations and notes about booby-traps. There's a lot about Garrilus the Unread."

The inventor grunted, but he didn't look up from buffing his coffee apparatus. Ozzie dangled more details, hoping for a stronger reaction. "There was something about him looking for a stone in a sacred Sniffling Well."

Pascal barked a laugh and twirled his polishing rag. "I warned the Professor about the well priests. It took three crews and a lurg-beast stampede to break him out of jail. Last I heard, local apprehenders raised the bounty on the Professor's head to five hundred klunklings. He wears a fake beard if we fly within twenty miles of Scrum." Pascal blew on a beaker of bubbling chestnut liquid, then wiped it clean with the air of someone relishing a pleasant jog down memory lane. "As for Garrilus the Unread, he was a self-important meddler who lived long enough to stick his nose into everyone else's business. You'll see what I mean at the Archive."

"What *is* the Archive?" Ozzie said.

"A fortified library inside Mount Typhon that stores rare, one-of-a-kind texts, the vast majority of which were written by Garrilus."

The corners of Ozzie's mouth twitched at the prospect of a treasure trove of research material.

"You weren't happy when Mercy mentioned Grandfather was going there," Alex said.

Pascal adjusted the rotation of a corkscrewing pipe. "The Professor thinks the librarians are noble defenders of Stone Lore, while I recognize them for what they truly are: lethal, chauvinistic thugs who would slit your throat for a pamphlet."

Coming from someone who sold weapons to Bryce, that was a sobering accusation.

"Which reminds me," the inventor said, "if you're dead set on helping us find the Professor, you need to learn how to fight." He tossed his rag on a table and beckoned the twins to follow him upstairs. Ozzie gave Alex a worried look and winced at the dread clawing his chest.

CHAPTER 19

SHADOWS AND SUNLIGHT

Layla stood amidships, twirling what had to be the famous "cloudwhip" Alex raved about. "Combat skills are honed through self-discipline and wise instruction. Since Pascal lacks both, it falls to me to train you." She threw the board to Alex, who caught it with a confident grin. The Sauracian tossed a flash of silver at Ozzie, who bobbled the catch. He retrieved the hilt from the deck, silently cursing the genetic coordination lottery.

"Swords first," Layla said. "Mirror me." She brandished a metal tube in a fighting posture.

Ozzie pressed the hilt's hidden button.

Shhhhhhhppp

He mimicked her stance, sword whipping through the air like a car antenna.

"Block." The reptile demonstrated.

Ozzie swept his arm across his body, like he was cleaning a window. Alex picked up a stick and executed a block with casual ease.

"Strike!" The Sauracian lunged, impaling an invisible opponent.

Ozzie thrust, tripped, and buried the tip of his sword in the deck. His sister assassinated an imaginary foe with the grace of a ballerina. "Maybe Alex should handle the sword," he said. "I'll use something blunt."

Layla growled, "You learn faster when mistakes have consequences. Repeat those motions until you can execute them without damaging *Angelus* or disarming yourself."

Block. Strike. Alex's muffled snickers didn't help.

"Again, but less like a frightened scurriluk."

Block. Strike.

Pascal tapped Ozzie's shoulder with a stick. "Mastering fundamentals is important, but might I suggest a strategy that buys you precious time to plan your next move? I call it—"

Layla palmed her face. "Pascal…"

"Whirling Wall of Death!" The inventor spun in circles, slashing random patterns in the air. "If you can't defeat an opponent with skill, make him fear your incompetence." He stumbled to a halt and leaned against the railing, panting. "It helps if you scream 'Whirling Wall of Death' while you do it."

"You are not helping, Pascal," the Sauracian said.

The inventor wiped his brow. "Once blades start swinging, technique is forgotten - the boy needs a way to survive long enough to get rescued."

Layla cocked her head, then nodded. "Good point." She turned to Ozzie. "Remember the Whirling Wall of Death, but for now… block and strike."

Ten minutes passed in a blur of semi-swordsmanship.

"Have you heard of a 'Custos Luminis'?" Ozzie panted.

Layla lowered her pipe. "Where did you hear that name?"

"Grandfather's journal mentions it on the page about this hilt."

The Sauracian stepped back and formed an "x" with her claws, as if warding off evil.

"Did I say something wrong?" Ozzie said.

Layla rasped, "The Custos Luminis—the Guardian of Light—is a warrior prophesied to lead Terravenum out of darkness. Most Sauracians hold the prophecy was fulfilled by the Fury King."

"How can the Fury King be the Guardian of Light if he destroyed so much of Terravenum?"

"The sun casts a shadow. Heroes and villains are a matter of perspective."

Layla refused to discuss the prophecy further, and given how spooked she was, Ozzie was glad when Pascal suggested a break from swordplay to focus on cloudwhipping. In no time at all, Alex was carving effortless arcs behind *Angelus*, whooping with joy.

Ozzie slouched next to Layla and dangled his forearms over the railing. "That cloudwhip is pretty awesome," he said.

"I look forward to watching your turn."

"I'll stick to swords for now, thanks. I started out Completely Useless, and if I don't quit, I think I've got a real shot at becoming Merely Awful."

"You underestimate yourself," she said.

"I stabbed the deck three times."

"A leg strike can be an effective combat strategy."

"I was aiming for an imaginary throat."

"You would be wise to limit yourself to short opponents."

Ozzie snorted. "Layla, you made a joke!"

She grunted as Alex whizzed by with a ten-thousand watt grin. "Keep your guard up at the Archive," the Sauracian said. "Stone Lore scholars distrust outsiders, and doubly so a Forsythe."

"Trust me, no one is going to care that I'm there."

"You are Ozzie Forsythe, son of Humboldt and Adeline Forsythe, and grandson of the greatest Stone Lore researcher alive. Academics will dissect your every syllable for clues."

Ozzie ran his fingers through his hair. "But I don't know anything—and even if I did, how would I succeed where Grandfather failed?"

"The Professor knew he was putting the weight of two worlds on your shoulders when he bequeathed you his journal. He believes in you."

"Well, that makes one of us." He shook his sword. "This is ridiculous."

The rest of the journey to the Archive was filled with embarrassing swordsmanship on Ozzie's part and annoyingly fluid cloudwhipping from Alex. By the time Mount Typhon rose from the featureless Foraging Plains, Layla declared Ozzie officially "Less Likely to Accidentally Stab Himself."

On the night before arrival, Pascal insisted on concealing Grandfather's journal in the smuggler's hold. "The Booksworn have an entitled perspective on Stone Lore documents," he said, securing the door with three padlocks, two of which were booby-trapped decoys. "If they discover we have the Professor's journal, we'll have a war on our hands."

"What if they search *Angelus*?" Ozzie said.

"Then we'll wish we'd given the book to Skhaar."

At dawn, the crew gathered at the bow and stared at Mount Typhon, two of them in awe, and two with grim resignation.

"Why did no one mention the Archive is inside an active volcano?" Ozzie asked, wrinkling his nose at the sulphur stench.

"Lava keeps the tourists away," Pascal said.

Layla powered up the radio. "Archive Control, this is *Angelus*, requesting permission to approach."

A businesslike voice squawked, "What is the pass phrase?"

She looked to Pascal for help.

He said, "Try...whence the wellow-fellow pets, the pillow-willow wets."

Her eyes widened. "You say it."

"It's protocol. You hailed them—it has to be *your* voice."

The Sauracian ground her teeth and keyed the mic.

Pascal coached her in a whisper, "*Whence..*"

"Whence—"

"*the wellow-fellow...*"

"—the wellow-fellow—"

"*pets, the pillow-willow wets*"

"—pets the pillow-willow...wets?"

"Incorrect!" the speaker barked. "You have one attempt remaining. As a relevant point of interest, twenty lava guns are currently tracking your vessel."

Layla stared at the radio helplessly.

Pascal burst into raucous laughter, hand and hoof on his knees. "I just wanted to hear you say it!"

"Idiot!" She punched the inventor in the shoulder, knocking him sideways.

The Dromedarian rubbed his arm, smiling. "Give it to me." He keyed the mic and said, "The arrows of my enemy are water to my thirst."

Ozzie held his breath and counted three long seconds of static.

"Permission granted," the voice crackled, tinged with a note of disappointment. "Cutting it close, *Angelus*—another two seconds and you would have been target practice. Observe protocol next time."

Layla snatched the mic from Pascal and bludgeoned him with a glare. "Our apologies, Archive Control. Beginning our descent."

The heat built in earnest when *Angelus* drew level with the mouth of the volcano. A constant background rumble forced Pascal to raise his voice. "See those fires along the rim?" He swept his arm in an arc that encompassed the volcano's lip. "That's the Crucible, the Archive's primary line of defense. Those lava guns are manned by bored, trigger-happy librarians. Visitors who don't follow protocol don't make it through—not in one piece, anyway." He peered over the railing, and the twins followed suit. A blistering updraft torched Ozzie's sinuses. Far below, an incandescent river of lava meandered inside the volcano.

Angelus shuddered and swayed as noxious, scalding bubbles of air raced for open sky. Layla angled the airship for a craggy shadow suspended in the center of the enormous, fiery chamber. As Ozzie's eyes adjusted to the dim light, the dark form took shape. He gasped.

Libraries are second homes to children of archaeologists. Ozzie spent half his childhood chasing Alex through serene, red-bricked buildings while their parents scoured rare documents for clues to ancient riddles. But in all the monasteries his family visited, no architect had been deranged enough to build an abbey on an island suspended inside a volcano.

The Archive's eight buildings were fortresses with cathedral aspirations. The main hall was longer than a football field and branched into twelve wings, each protected by a turret. An enormous shimmering envelope hovered over the complex like a disco ball while dozens of small, spherical balloons lined the island's edge, their reflective canvas mirroring the lava's orange glow. Six robust anchor chains flexed and stretched, keeping the Archive centered in the volcano as air currents buffeted the floating island.

"Amazing, right?" Pascal grinned, enjoying the twins' astonishment.

"It's incredible! How is this possible?" Ozzie said. "I thought heliovapor was flammable."

"It is. I developed heat-shielded canvas to protect their balloons, but a network of chains and counterweights is all that prevents the Archive from becoming a tragic, and somewhat predictable, bonfire."

"You work for the librarians?" Alex said.

"On the rare occasions they decide to be reasonable," he sniffed.

"Do not provoke the Booksworn this time, Pascal," Layla said. "The boy will not survive."

The inventor waved a dismissive hoof. "He can block and stab the deck. He's ready."

Ozzie frowned. The *boy* was standing right here.

"I should come with you," Alex said.

Ozzie sighed. His sister never had a problem when *she* was taking risks, but toss a few unhinged librarians and a volcano into the mix, and she became a mother hen.

Layla spun the helm and growled, "Females are forbidden from setting foot on Archive grounds, on pain of death."

A gust smacked *Angelus* sideways into the island's loading dock. Pascal and Layla secured the airship with a frantic flurry of line handling and only minimal shouting. When the last knot was tied, oppressive silence fell over the vessel.

The dock fronted a courtyard where an army of bronze statues welcomed visitors to the Archive. It would have been charming, were the librarians not using the plaza as a staging ground for a show of force. A wall of spears and arrows tracked the crew's movements. Heavy weaponry—was that a battering ram?—suggested the welcome wagon was hoping for a brawl. Ozzie kept his hands in plain view and tried to look harmless. Fortunately, he was playing to his strengths.

Pascal, in contrast, regarded the stalemate as an invitation to kick a hornet's nest. He cleared his throat, plonked his foot on the bow rail, and bellowed, "Which weak-kneed coward among you wants his head handed to him?"

CHAPTER 20

THE BOOKSWORN

A hooded, brown-robed librarian stalked forward and raised a speaking cone. "Your words doom you, honored guest. How may I hasten your quest for an early grave?"

"We come seeking truth," Pascal said, glancing at Ozzie and rolling his eyes, "and your head."

"You seek my head, do you?" The librarian threw his arms wide and bowed in mock surrender. "Then come take it!"

The inventor sharpened his hoof with a file. "Were crushing a feeble worm worth the effort, I would."

"Prepare yourself for an exquisitely painful demise!" The librarian hurled his megaphone at the ground, howled, and launched into a fierce display of aerobatic swordsmanship. Pascal yawned and polished his hoof on his chest.

Ozzie met Alex's horrified stare.

"Pascal…" Layla rumbled a warning.

"Fine, fine." The inventor folded his arms and said, in a sing-song delivery, "Very well, let us meet on the glorious battlefield to honor our ancestors in combat, like slithering blubberflumps."

A dozen archers aimed flaming arrows at *Angelus'* envelope.

"Pascal…" Layla's growl contained a note of rising concern.

"I *said*—Very well, let us meet on the glorious....wait—" The inventor turned to Layla and whispered, "Is today Tuesday or Wednesday?" The Sauracian clenched her fists. Pascal counted on his fingers, then called out, "Sorry! I meant: Very well, let us meet on the glorious battlefield to honor our ancestors in combat, like *steel-chested krubskunks*. Sorry, everyone. Totally my fault."

A pause, pregnant with the effort of heavily armed men reciting words in their heads, froze the courtyard. The lead swordsman frowned, mouthing sentences only he could hear. He lowered his blade and grinned. "All good, boys."

Archers eased bowstrings and extinguished arrows. The platoon scattered into pockets of laughing librarians as musclebound giants wheeled squeaky siege engines into corners of the courtyard. Foot-thick doors creaked open, admitting a stream of warriors into various buildings. The aggressive swordsman waved. "Nearly had you there, Pascal."

Pascal chuckled. "Sorry to disappoint you, Brother Scorchedearth. I'll double check my calendar in the future."

"No problem, it's easy to mix up the cadences. Kill you next time!"

"I hope not. Your swordplay is improving, and I'd hate to defeat you before you master *all* seventeen Monstrosities of the Lotus."

Brother Scorchedearth sheathed his sword with an elegant flourish, gave an exaggerated bow, then jogged after his brethren.

"What just happened?" Alex hissed, passing a surge quantizer nervously from hand to hand.

"I bungled the ending of a Booksworn Pass Challenge and nearly got us obliterated." Pascal turned to Layla, who was powering down *Angelus* and looked ready to do some obliterating herself. "I *said* I was sorry. The exact phrasing is different each day of the week."

"Calling him a 'feeble worm' is part of the phrasing?" Ozzie asked.

"It's Tuesday," Pascal said. "You just witnessed *Eternal Dance of the Headless Earth-Ingester*, one of the Booksworn's most venerated and ancient Pass Challenges. You're lucky, few people survive to watch the entire ceremony."

"What did he mean by 'Kill you next time'?" Alex said.

"A misspoken Pass Challenge triggers a death duel."

"That's insane."

"The Booksworn devote their lives to guarding a stack of dusty scrolls. It's no surprise they're spoiling for a fight."

A bone-thin figure glided up the gangplank and threw back his hood. Ozzie stiffened. The last time he'd seen those tribal tattoos, their owner was trying to impale him in the North Sea. A high-pitched whine from the quantizer told him Alex had noticed the tattoos as well.

The librarian stepped onto *Angelus* and steepled the longest, thinnest fingers Ozzie had ever seen. "Welcome, Pascal Trahir and...companions." The bald man's tone flirted with loathing. "I am Novice Slapsneeze. What is the purpose of your visit?"

"We're here to speak with Brother Deathfist," Pascal said.

The novice flared his nostrils. "Brother Deathfist is patrolling the Scandalous Documents Vault.*[1] He is unavailable to entertain *visitors*."

Pascal dropped the bomb with a smile. "Tell him Professor Quidby's progeny are here."

Slapsneeze's eyebrows shot up. "How...unexpected." His eyes strafed *Angelus'* deck, no doubt searching for any sign of a secret cargo hold bursting with Stone Lore. "I will petition Brother Death-fist on your behalf. You may wait in the courtyard if you wish, but females must not set foot on Archive property."

"Why?" Alex snapped. "What are you afraid of?"

Slapsneeze's hand flew to the dagger on his belt.

Ozzie stammered, "I apologize, Novice Slapsneeze." He glared at Alex, who jutted her jaw in defiance. "My sister is still learning the importance of honoring other cultures' traditions."

The librarian's mirthless half-smile said Alex had just earned herself a spot on his List. "No offense taken, but I recommend avoiding any suggestion that I or my brethren are 'afraid' of *anything*, unless she seeks an honor duel." His index finger tapped his dagger's hilt. "Females were banned from the Archive after the Sisterhood of the Notched Blade raided us twelve hundred years ago. It is not our intention to discriminate, merely to take precautions against one of our fiercest and most devious enemies." Slapsneeze spun on his heel and flowed down the gangplank with a flutter of brown burlap.

When the librarian was out of hearing range, Ozzie asked Alex, "You saw his tattoos?"

She nodded. "That guy is definitely Noctem."

"Slappy?" Pascal snorted. "He's all talk—just don't ask him for a high five."

"The assassins at St. Jude's had the same facial tattoos," Ozzie said.

The inventor leaned against the railing. "The Booksworn add tattoos as they progress through training, to boast of their increasingly nasty bags of tricks."

"That guy felt wrong," Alex said. "He doesn't want us here."

Layla grunted. "Probably because Pascal spilled coffee in the Fragile Documents room, destroying nine hundred pages of Garrilus the Unread's *Contemplations on a Nostril*."

The inventor scowled. "*You* try reading that without sneezing."

"Or *perhaps*," she continued, "it was because Pascal dumped a crate of priceless Labyrinthian parchment into the lava river."

"That box was labeled *Throw It Away, Please*," the Dromedarian said. "How was I to know it was the title of six years of meditation on a bootless ferret's*[2] hoarding instinct? I'm just going to say it: Garrilus had weird hobbies."

Layla silenced him with a glare. "Do not disparage Garrilus the Unread here. The Booksworn devote their lives to protecting his legacy, so try to resist desecrating more of his work."

Pascal rolled his eyes. "Don't worry, I won't touch anything."

"IF I HAD A KLUNK-TON FOR EVERY TIME I HEARD THAT, I'D OWN A SWARM OF RUTFANGS," a thunderous voice boomed. Ozzie didn't have to work hard to identify the eye of the storm. Novice Slapsneeze marched across the courtyard, trailed by three librarians who defied the adjective "large," but might begrudgingly tolerate "mammoth."

All three wore sleeveless robes that revealed bulging biceps and V-shaped torsos. Any of the trio could easily crush Ozzie with a casual hug or absentminded fist bump, but the giant in the middle was a force of nature unto himself. A head taller than his companions, with a smile to match his shoe size, he advanced like a benevolent landslide. Even Layla tilted her head back to make eye contact with the bald giant. The librarian's heavily calloused hands were the size of dinner plates—not salad plates, mind you, but banquet platters for serving shrimp on toast. Ozzie doubted his fingers could wrap all the way around one of the man's gargantuan digits. The gangplank moaned, pondering collapse under the librarian's tonnage.

"Brother Deathfist!" Pascal sounded genuinely happy.

"Hello, Pascal." Deathfist shook the Dromedarian's hand, then nodded at Layla. "Sorry to keep you waiting. Had to break up a fight in the Scandalous Document Vault—another pair of hotheads would rather cross swords than admit they might be wrong about a punctuation mark." He turned to the Forsythes. "You must be the Professor's progeny. I am Brother Deathfist, Head Librarian of the Archive. Welcome." His hand swallowed Ozzie's like an orca eating a baby seal.

"I'm Ozzie." He gritted his teeth, shocked at the staggering pressure on his hand—and this from a *friendly* handshake. Brother Deathfist was aptly named.

Alex introduced herself, but didn't flinch in the Head Librarian's suffocating grip. Ozzie resuscitated his hand by slapping it against his leg. He had a vague suspicion he'd failed some kind of test.

Deathfist said, "So how can the Order of the Booksworn aid Pascal Trahir? If you plan to drop manuscripts into lava, I doubt I can stop Brother Flyingfury from seeking vengeance. Well, I could, but I won't."

"I'm on a fact-finding mission."

"You've never shown the first interest in Stone Lore. Finally come to your senses?"

"Not exactly." Pascal straightened his long neck to peer over the librarian's shoulder, then dropped to eye level and whispered, "The Professor has gone missing."

Brother Deathfist cracked his knuckles with the sound of icebergs calving. "Professor Quidby visited the Archive three months ago, then left—for Amnesia, I believe."

Ozzie's hopes fell. Amnesia, again.

"Where was he researching?" Pascal said.

"The Haiku Wing. I don't know what he discovered, but he left in a hurry. Come, we'll speak with the duty librarian."

After they disembarked, one of the human walls planted himself at the bottom of the gangplank. Ozzie shrugged at Alex, who shoved her hands in her pockets and fumed from the deck.

Ozzie and Pascal followed Brother Deathfist through a parade of bronze statues. Ozzie ran his hand along a wall, relishing the scrape of the porous surface. Lava bricks were the Booksworn's construction material of choice. Every building, wall, and cobblestone in sight was red and volcanic, including the bone-dry ornate fountain in the center of the courtyard, which served as a poignant tribute to the futility of outdoor plumbing in a volcano. The main hall resembled a fortified abbey, complete with a bell tower, turrets, barred windows, and a set of oak doors thick enough to withstand a nuclear blast.

A pair of sentries waved Brother Deathfist past a checkpoint at the top of the stairs. He jerked a thumb at Ozzie and Pascal. "They're with me." Shriveled academics waiting in line glowered at the newcomers. A monocle-wearing scholar swept his beard aside to reveal a double-headed axe.

"I'm with him!" Ozzie pointed at the Head Librarian and hustled to catch up. Cool air, tinged with mothballs, greeted him inside the door. Centuries of shuffling feet had polished black pumice tiling to a smooth veneer. Artificial light filtered through stained glass windows, adding elegance and drama to the vaulted ceiling.

The first stained glass panel depicted a youth riding a sedan chair borne by four Galapagos tortoises. In the next window, an adult was shoving his arm down the throat of a startled ostrich-sized chicken, who was choking on a book. At the end of the hall, a blue and purple panel depicted an old man trapped inside a thirty-foot jellyfish.

BANG

Two Booksworn stationed on either side of a doorway conjured battleaxes from the depths of their robes and approached a scruffy man who was scrabbling to retrieve a parcel of books scattered across the floor. The man stammered, "I-I tripped. I'm sorry. Please..." His bowtie quivered beneath a trembling jaw as he clutched a book like a shield.

The closest librarian leaned down, an executioner listening to a condemned man's confession.

A single finger raised to a cowl.

"SHHH!"

The guards floated back to their posts by the archway as the terrified man exhaled a low groan and collapsed.

Ozzie caught up with Pascal and Brother Deathfist beside a painting of a middle-aged man sprinting across a desert plain, pursued by a herd of elephant-tusked giraffes. A brass plaque titled the piece, *"Attempt Not to Ride the Stilt-legged Beasts, or Suffer the Chase - Ode to Poor Judgment, Volume Nineteen, by Garrilus the Unread."*

"Who *is* this guy?" Ozzie blurted, drawing a spiteful glare from a passing scholar.

Deathfist barked a laugh that woke his ancestors. The Archive's moratorium on noise must not apply to anyone who could crush a skull between their thumb and index finger. He threw his arms wide. "Ah! The ten-thousand klunk question that topples empires and ruins men. You've come to the right place, boy."

---

1. The Scandalous Documents Vault contains the most volatile documents in the Archive.

When a poem such as *I Sneezed, Did I Knot?* schisms the academic community (Is the 728 volume epic a reflection on how sneezing makes the body feel knotted or a tragic misspelling?), it is removed from general access until tensions die down. Scholars may view the document in the SDV, but only under close supervision, unarmed, and with their feet bound.

2. Similar to a regular ferret, but lacking boots.

CHAPTER 21

GARRILUS THE UNREAD

Deathfist locked his fists behind his back. "The region of Insomnia is famous for two things: detestably sour sheep's milk, and every few generations, birthing a human who lives hundreds of years and requires no sleep."

"That sounds wonderful," said Ozzie, veteran of a thousand all-night research marathons.

The librarian smiled. "Insomnians consider the mutation a curse. Most of the afflicted choose a life of solitude to spare themselves the pain of watching friends and family die. Garrilus became a traveling poet."

They strolled past a marble statue of a hunched, bespectacled old man frozen in the act of kicking a baby bird out of his path. A plaque at the base of the statue declared, *"Stop that infernal racket!"* in flowing calligraphy.

Brother Deathfist hoisted a gate and motioned for Ozzie and Pascal to continue down the spiral stairs to the basement. "Garrilus maintained a stream-of-conscious record of his every waking moment, documenting his life in poetry and prose." The librarian pushed a door open, raising an arm to endless rows of bookshelves and cabinets. "Welcome to the Haiku Wing."

Scholars hunched over manuscript-laden tables, scribbling notes in the dim light of glow orbs. Ozzie's elbow nudged a mobile book-shelf, which squeaked like a mouse and rolled two inches. As one, the academics dropped their quills and unsheathed weapons. They relaxed when Deathfist walked in.

"If all these people study Garrilus' work, why is he called 'the Unread'?" Ozzie whispered, trapped in a staring contest with an academic who was picking his teeth with a stiletto dagger.

"Due to the sheer volume of documents," the librarian said, "you could devote your entire life to studying his work and only scratch the surface—many have. Scholars occasionally form alliances to share their findings, but those efforts are invariably tainted by mutual distrust."*[1]

Ozzie watched an unblinking researcher drag his finger across a page at a sloth-like pace, straining with the effort of total concentration. "It can't be that hard to speed read a mountain of scrolls."

Deathfist quirked an eyebrow. "You've clearly never endured stream-of-conscious prose detailing a ten-hour internal debate about which shade of beige to paint a wall." He offered a handkerchief to a white-haired scholar sobbing in a corner. "Garrilus' poetry is widely regarded as some of the worst ever written."

"Why is it worth so much trouble, then?"

The Head Librarian brightened. "Fourteen hundred years ago, a Probationary Apprentice Librarian named Roncordiant Flog embarked upon a Codex Quest, a Dome-wide search for undiscovered manuscripts that might elevate him to a full apprenticeship in our brotherhood. His hunt was fruitless until, on the verge of defeat and the cusp of despair, he stumbled across the impossible: a lore-badger den, deep in the Wildermess."

Rustling paper quieted as scholars stopped to listen.

"Roncordiant knocked on the door, and to his shock, a legend answered—Henna, the last surviving lorebadger."

A mustachioed researcher's jaw dropped, sending his monocle bouncing across his desk and onto the floor. Deathfist smiled. "Our brother couldn't believe his good fortune. Lorebadgers are the Klunk Standard for record-keeping, thanks to their perfect memories and meticulous attention to detail. An astonishing hoard of documents were catalogued and collated in strongrooms attached to Henna's den. When asked what the vaults contained, the lore-badger uttered three words that forever changed the world: *Garrilus the Unread*."

A wizened academic who could barely see over his table sighed and rested his chin in the crook of his elbow.

"Garrilus' mission to transcribe his every waking thought was too ambitious for one man, so he employed Henna as his personal scribe. She accompanied him on mundane adventures to every corner of Terravenum, recording his deplorable prose. When Garrilus reached the end of his three century lifespan, the lore-badger compiled his writings, relying on her faultless memory to fill gaps in the timeline." Deathfist paused for dramatic effect. A bare-chested warrior-scholar wearing a fur loincloth swiped a tear from his cheek with the back of his hand. Someone sniffled.

"Roncordiant spent eighteen months randomly skimming Garrilus' work. On the sixth day of the nineteenth month he found his first reference to a fractured Borealis Stone. He couldn't believe what he was reading—the world had given up on finding the Stones centuries ago, but here, buried in an atrocious sonnet about baking a spineapple cake, was a clue to the location of one of the three lost Borealis Stones! Garrilus accidentally cast light on the mystery of the greatest treasure known to man or beast."

A handful of researchers whispered a library-appropriate cheer.

Deathfist nodded to his appreciative audience. "Roncordiant Flog redoubled his efforts, reading every line of every poem with painstaking care. Two years later he found his next clue, this time in an epic poem about an hour-long fit of hiccuping."

"*O Storm of Ceaseless Hiccumphrences that Plagueth Mine Breast, I Shall Vanquish Thee*," chittered an arthropid researcher, waving its antennae in blissful reverence.

The librarian nodded approval. "Brother Roncordiant proposed building a facility where academics across the Dome could study Garrilus' writing. Henna, wanting to enshrine her friend's work for posterity, agreed, provided the Booksworn pledged to guard it with our lives. Within a week of opening, the

Archive welcomed its first wave of pilgrims." Deathfist gestured to his rapt audience. "A steady flow of Stone scholars have patronized us since."

An awed hush hung over the room, then someone cleared their throat and broke the spell. Maybe it was the reminder that a great treasure was at stake, or perhaps they were embarrassed at being drawn in by sentiment, but around the room, heads bowed and paper rustled as hardened intellectuals dove into research with renewed vigor.

Deathfist motioned one of his brethren over. "Brother Pugnacious was on duty in the Haiku Wing during the Professor's last visit."

Pugnacious was roughly the same age as Ozzie, but a head shorter and twice as thick in the chest. A three-corded braid of black hair ran from the back of his otherwise clean-shaven scalp down to his ankles. The young librarian scowled at Ozzie and mumbled under his breath.

Brother Deathfist glared at Pugnacious until the younger librarian set his jaw and bowed to the minimum degree necessary for civility.

"Tell us about Professor Quidby's last visit," the Head Librarian said, in a voice that promised a future conversation about attitude.

"The Professor requested all twelve volumes of *Arguments with Hermits*, the first sixteen scrolls of the *Just Because You Claim to be Wise, Doesn't Make You the Boss of Me* collection, and *I Need Your Axioms Like a Hole in my Head*."

Deathfist grunted. "A fairly standard request—all classics. Did he read them all?"

"I don't know, sir. That was a busy week. A dispute over the color of Garrilus' favorite socks escalated into a turf war in the Eastern Cabinets."

The elder librarian sighed. "That blasted Sock Conundrum refuses to die."

"Yes, sir. I had to send five scholars to the infirmary."

"Did you at least notice when the Professor finished his research?"

"Yes, because he screamed, 'Eureka!' then rushed out, leaving a heaping mess of documents for me to clean up."

Pascal said, "We'd like to see whatever the Professor was reading, please."

Brother Pugnacious' eyes flicked to Deathfist, who nodded. A twinge of annoyance flashed across the young librarian's face. "Wait here." He disappeared into an adjoining chamber.

Ozzie scanned the room. At every table, scholars pored over manuscripts and scribbled notes, weapons close at hand. A few worked in pairs, taking turns standing guard while the other read. Each academic wore makeshift body armor that protected vital organs while permitting their fingers maximum dexterity. Grandfather, clothed in khakis and armed only with a stiff upper lip, must have appeared a suicidal madman to his battle-ready colleagues.

A grunt announced Brother Pugnacious' arrival, his sweaty forehead barely visible above the mountain of scrolls stacked on his squeaky cart. How were they going to find a clue to the Professor's location in *all that*?

Deathfist's stare convinced the nearest academic to surrender his study space and take an early lunch. Pugnacious' mood brightened with every document he slapped on the table—he was positively grinning by the time he balanced a binder of pamphlets on the papery summit.

Ozzie grabbed a handful of scrolls and read their titles.

Of Course Fallen Trees Make Sounds, Have You BEEN to a Forest?

If You're So Clever, Why Aren't Your Sayings on a Mug? - Vol. III

Beauty is in the Eye of the Beholder, is it? Thanks for the Tip (and Other Sarcasms)

"Garrilus didn't like philosophers very much," he said.

To his surprise, Brother Pugnacious spoke up, "These haikus chronicle his encounters with the Hermits of Mumblemere, whom he took particular exception to."

Pascal shuffled through a handful of books. "What did the Professor read last?"

"No idea."

Ozzie opened a scroll titled *Tell Me to "Surrender to the Universe" ONE MORE TIME, I Dare You* and started reading in the middle.

> What did you call me?
> I am rubber, you are glue
> My slap hand itches
>
> Think you're safe up there?
> Ladders are easy to make
> Prepare to be slapped
>
> You think I'm joking?
> Here comes the thunder, big boy
> Nowhere you can run
>
> Wretched spire, so steep
> Tipping ladder, gusting wind
> I build a slingshot

Ozzie asked, "How do haikus exist in Terravenum? I don't know a lot about poetry, but even *I* know they were invented in Japan."

"Cultural flotsam," Brother Deathfist said. "Storms in Urt blow items from your world across the Divide, which the Thermals distribute in the Feral. Scatterling tribes rummage the plains for breachfall, then sell it to collectors and historians. Over centuries, detritus from your world trickled into Terravenum, influencing our vernacular, technology, and in this case, poetry."

BOOM

Pascal slammed his forehead into an open leather-bound book, earning scowls from the rest of the room. "This is impossible," the inventor said.

Brother Pugnacious crossed his arms and pursed his lips, his body smugly saying, *I told you so.*

CLANG-ANG-ANG-ANG

A chiming bell jolted the Haiku Wing into action. Scholars leapt to their feet, reaching for weapons with one hand and cramming notes into satchels with the other.

"Brother Deathfist!" Novice Slapsneeze whisper-yelled, as he skidded into the room. He spotted the giant in the corner and dashed over to hiss in his ear. Deathfist's eyes widened, and he signaled Brother Pugnacious, who joined two of his brethren by a capstan. The three librarians threw their weight into the winch, winding chain onto a drum. Invisible machinery lowered gratings over a series of paintings depicting Garrilus punching a mime. A librarian rushed past, securing bookshelves with an ornate iron key. Inch-thick steel bars clanked down, blocking access to the main corridor.

Librarians collected documents from each table and deposited them in an armored book cart. To a man, scholars scribbled notes furiously until their manuscripts were forcibly removed. A loin-clothed barbarian, frantically writing, swung his axe to challenge the interruption of his work.

SMACK

If Loincloth Guy was lucky, he might wake up in a couple of days—and if he was *really* lucky, he might remember his name. Either way, whiplash and a five-fingered bruise on his cheek would remind him of his foolishness for weeks to come. So *that's* why they call him Slapsneeze.

"What's going on?" Pascal said.

Brother Deathfist barked, "Establish the defensive perimeter!" He glared at the inventor. "For the first time in decades, three Maelstrom ships are floating above Mount Typhon, requesting permission to dock at the Archive. Who did you cross, Pascal?"

Ozzie's sweaty fingers closed around the sword hilt in his pocket.

"That has nothing to do with me!" Pascal lied.

"Why is the Maelstrom chasing you? Do you possess the Professor's journal?"

"Maybe they're returning an overdue book—Sauracians read too, you know." The inventor folded his arms. "Don't be such a cliché, Deathfist."

"Pascal…" the Head Librarian growled. He dropped a meaty fist on the inventor's shoulder and marched him out of the Haiku Wing. Ozzie followed, trailed closely by Brother Pugnacious and Novice Slapsneeze. More librarians joined the procession as they stormed upstairs. By the time they reached the courtyard, their group numbered thirty Booksworn.

Ozzie's mouth went dry.

Angelus was docked bow-to-bow with a Maelstrom airship named *Revenge*. The angular Sauracian vessel was a study in contrasts to Pascal's rounded, jury-rigged home. *Angelus*' envelope was a patchwork quilt of mismatched, oft-repaired fabric, while *Revenge* sported red, silken material. The Maelstrom hull was formed from triangular, overlaying panels of black armor that started small at the bow and enlarged as they progressed to the stern, creating the impression of a claw poised to disembowel its prey.

A bass drum pounded slow, ominous quarter notes from somewhere belowdecks. Ozzie's shoulders tightened as Sauracians lined the railing of their ship, weapons ready. A brawny, red-cloaked warrior waited at the top of the gangplank, smiling.

Skhaar.

"Last chance," Brother Deathfist said. "Give me the journal and I can protect you."

Without breaking eye contact with Skhaar, Pascal hissed, *"I don't know what you're talking about."*

"I was speaking to the Professor's progeny," the Head Librarian said.

Ozzie counted snarling Sauracian warriors, glanced at the two Maelstrom airships circling above the Crucible, then gauged the stony faces of the librarians surrounding him. Deathfist was right—the journal would be safer here than on *Angelus*.

He said, "Pascal, maybe—"

The inventor threw Ozzie a ferocious warning glare that choked the sentence in his throat.

The drumbeat stopped. Weapons *clinked*, eager for combat. Skhaar limped down the gangplank, chains jingling, unconcerned by the arsenal targeting him. The Annihilator spread his arms.

"I come bearing death."

---

1. Allied efforts to divide Garrilus' work into bite-sized chunks peaked with The Limerick Armistice of 1190. Four hundred scholars agreed to temporarily shelve their differences for the sake of cataloguing the Limerick Wing once-and-for-all.

   Palindrome Specialist Liplark Tonunga detailed the events in his diary:

   "Twas but a smattering of minutes before mild disagreement blossomed into open warfare. It seemed a shame, but research could not progress in good conscience without first agreeing on the definition of *Nantucket*. Sides were formed (mine own feet firmly rooted in the conviction that *Nantucket* is a regional colloquialism for fried eggs) and lines were irrevocably crossed. Brothers clashed. Masters and apprentices warred. Families were torn asunder.

   By the end of an hour, no less than seven different interpretations of *Nantucket* were sworn allegiance to. A nation-state formed, was annexed by a party of rival academics with superior weaponry, then collapsed beneath the weight of its own bureaucracy. Were it not for the onset of lunch, I have no doubt the Archive would have burned to the ground that day. Curse you, *Nantucket*, and your delicious, eggy origins."

CHAPTER 22

PEGASUS PROTOCOL

Deathfist shoved through a wall of archers. "What business does the Fury King's lackey have here?"

Skhaar's jaw dropped in mock offense. "Is this how you greet an old friend, Deathfist? What of the Archive's legendary hospitality?"

"The Inkblood Accords are all that restrained my brethren from stoning you out of the sky, Annihilator. We reserve our hospitality for guests who *haven't* attempted to steal Dr. Haloopit's *Clues to the Lost Borealis Stones (with Bonus Tongue Twisters from the Zwp Tribe of Kol!).*"*1 The Head Librarian flexed his fingers. "I enjoyed providing you a lesson in etiquette on your previous visit. Do you require another?"

Skhaar folded his paws behind his ragged cloak and lurched forward like a world-weary bulldozer. The librarians parted, inviting the Sauracian deeper into their ranks. By the time the Annihilator reached Deathfist, a circle of spears and cocked bowstrings surrounded the two behemoths.

"As entertaining as that would be, I'm only here as a courtesy." Skhaar nodded at *Angelus*. "I thought you might wish to know you're harboring fugitives from Maelstrom justice."

"The Archive remains neutral to outside conflicts," Deathfist said, "as evidenced by your continued ability to draw breath."

A flicker of movement on *Angelus* caught Ozzie's eye. Layla and Alex were skulking on the bow, aiming a barrel-shaped device at the *Revenge*. He breathed a secret sigh of relief—he'd half expected his sister to sneak onto Archive grounds out of sheer pigheadedness.

Skhaar tapped a spear tip with his claw. "Neutral," he mused, "how adorable." His head twitched with reptilian speed, focusing one bloodshot eye on Pascal, who was failing to hide behind Brother Deathfist. "Pascal Trahir. Such a pleasure to see you again." The Annihilator's eye snapped down and his scratchy voice took on a silky purr. "And I see we have a new player in our little game."

Ozzie shivered at Skhaar's contemptuous sneer. In all the times he'd imagined confronting the monster who kidnapped his parents, he'd never expected to feel like a deer locked in a gunsight.

"What is your place in this, fleshling?" Skhaar sniffed the air. His golden eyes shot open, and he hacked a belly laugh that shredded the remnants of Ozzie's courage. The Annihilator clapped his paws together and rumbled, "How *poetic*—the inventor and his collateral damage, conspiring to save the world." His upper lip curled. "I knew your parents, child. They died painfully and without honor."

Ozzie would have given his left kidney for a snappy, action-hero comeback, but it was all he could do to hold back tears.

"What do you want, Skhaar?" Pascal said.

The Sauracian sighed. "So many things: eternal despair to my enemies, vengeance upon those who so richly deserve it, a new fangbrush...but today, I will settle for the Professor's journal."

"Sorry, I can't help you with that. But I know a good fangbrush guy—what's your favorite color?"

"Come, Pascal. My warriors are spoiling for a fight. Must I indulge them?"

Brother Deathfist flexed his shoulders and said, "Please do."

Skhaar clucked his tongue. "So quick to violence, Deathfist—

162

and coming from me, that's saying something. You have thirty minutes to surrender *Angelus* and her crew before I lay waste to your precious Archive. More Maelstrom vessels are on their way."

"*Surrender?*" The Head Librarian's cheeks blushed crimson. Skin stretched white over his knuckles. "Do not mistake our restraint for cowardice. You have thirty *seconds* to leave my Archive before *I* lay waste to *you.*"

Skhaar smirked. "Excellent. We understand each other." He brushed a spear point aside and nonchalantly lurched back to the *Revenge.*

Pascal shoved Ozzie toward *Angelus* the moment Skhaar moved away. The pair was halfway up the gangplank before anyone realized they were missing.

"Pascal!" Deathfist cried.

The inventor hissed, "*Go!*", but Layla had already fired the engines up and slammed the throttles against their stops. Alex cast off a dock line and thumped the barrel she and Layla had positioned on the bow. A lance of flame shot out, flattening *Revenge's* crew to their deck. Librarians shouted, forming ranks against a new, fire-spewing threat. Ozzie dropped the stern line, and the airship reversed away from the Maelstrom vessel.

"*Pascal!*" Brother Deathfist bellowed. "Give me the journal!"

The inventor waved.

"Shouldn't we be going up?" Ozzie said.

"Working on it," Layla grunted, but kept reversing.

"We're running out of room!" Alex pointed at the approaching volcano wall. Below, the lava river belched a bubble of sweltering heat.

"Brace yourselves!" The Sauracian slammed the throttles forward and flew *Angelus* into the center of the scorching elevator. Ozzie clung to the rigging, fighting the urge to vomit.

Whoosh

A flaming rock the size of Ozzie's head whizzed past *Angelus*.

"Take cover!" Layla shouted. "The Crucible is firing at us!"

Yellow lights blinked around the volcano's rim. Five seconds later, a storm of comets rained.

Thud

A glowing ball ricocheted off the envelope and landed on deck, setting fire to a plank.

"Pascal!" Layla yelled.

"Got it." The inventor used his prosthetic hand to heave the blazing stone over the railing. A deluge of sizzling projectiles hissed past *Angelus*, and soon Pascal's arm glowed orange from removing balls that struck home.

"I thought the Booksworn would be better shots!" Alex said.

The inventor plunged his hand in a bucket of water, releasing a cloud of steam. "Look down."

With *Angelus* centered over the Archive, Crucible gunners couldn't target them without putting the library at risk. "What happens when we reach the mouth of the Crucible?" Ozzie said.

"Nothing good." Pascal slapped a fiery projectile away from a bottle of heliovapor.

"But if they shoot us down, they'll destroy the journal," Ozzie said.

The inventor diverted a ball away from the stairway to his lab. "Librarians are experts at sifting through wreckage."

"It's a volcano! There won't be wreckage."

"I'll mention that to the gunners when we reach the Crucible. They seem reasonable."

Layla spun the wheel to dodge a salvo. "I need options, Pascal!" she snapped.

"I'm working on a two-step plan."

"What's step two?" She gunned the engines.

"Don't you want to hear step one?"

"Not unless step two is *Survive*."

"Fine, now it's a *three*-step plan. Happy?"

"No!"

"Guys!" Ozzie and Alex yelled, in unison.

Pascal pointed at *Revenge*. "Step one: Get closer to the Maelstrom ship. If we get lucky, the librarians will miss us and shoot Skhaar down."

Layla slammed the throttles in reverse, throwing Ozzie off his feet. "Makes sense," she yelled. "What's step two?"

The Dromedarian didn't answer.

"Pascal, *what's step two?*"

"Pegasus Protocol." He winced.

"Absolutely not."

The inventor put his hands on his hips. "I worked the bugs out."

"Injecting purified dynami into an engine isn't a plan, it's a disaster! Last time, the turbine melted—it took Snuggles two months to grow her coat back!"

"I'm happy to amend my plan, but—spoiler alert—step two is going to be *Cartwheel Into Lava!*"

Layla slammed her fist on the heavily dented railing next to the wheel. "Fine. Initiate Pegasus Protocol, but jettison our surplus heliovapor first."

"I need it for experiments!"

"Three-step plan," she said. "*Survive.*"

Ozzie and Alex hoisted heliovapor bottles over the railing, bombarding *Revenge*, who was directly beneath *Angelus* and closing like a hungry shark. Most canisters missed their mark, but two rocked the Maelstrom ship with satisfying explosions.

CRACK

Red lightning blew the roof off the cowling that protected the stairwell. The two reserve Maelstrom ships had entered the fray— one strafing *Angelus*, the other engaging the Crucible.

Alex helped Ozzie to his feet. She nodded at the last remaining heliovapor bottle, with a dangerous glint in her eye. Ozzie groaned —he knew that look. Something stupid was about to happen. His sister unspooled cable from the stern deck winch and looped it around her waist.

Oh no.

Alex threw open a locker and retrieved the cloudwhip.

"Drop the heliovapor over the starboard side when I signal," she said.

"This isn't the time for crazy ideas, Alex." Ozzie's scalp itched as a bolt of lightning flashed past the port side.

"Just trust me!" She leapt over the rail, locked her feet into the cloudwhip, and plummeted out of sight. The winch cable snapped taut.

"What is she doing?" Layla shouted. "We're starting Pegasus Protocol!"

Ozzie grunted, wrestling the bottle of explosive gas onto the rail. "Alex has an idea."

"She will be sliced in half if Pascal initiates while she's riding the whip!"

"*Sliced in half*? What *is* Pegasus Protocol?" He didn't hear the Sauracian's answer, because just then, his sister glided into view, legs pumping to speed up her board. Alex swung in a wide circle and gave him a thumbs-up. Ozzie grimaced apologetically at Layla, then pushed the bottle off the railing.

Alex flipped into a steep dive that sped her beneath the airship on a pendulum swing. Ozzie held his breath as *Angelus* veered to avoid a lightning blitz. Layla's evasive maneuver threw Alex's timing off, so instead of effortlessly grabbing the bottle's handle like an extreme sports superhero, she lunged for it in a desperate, headfirst dive.

Ozzie sprinted to the far rail in time to watch his sister rise, tangled in a jumble of cable, bottle clenched in her left hand. She soared above *Angelus'* envelope and released the heliovapor at the top of her arc. It was a perfect throw—the bottle exploded on contact with the bow of the attacking Maelstrom ship, spilling flames across its deck. The lightning cannon fell silent.

"Get her on board *now*!" Layla bellowed.

Ozzie ran to the winch and slapped a button labeled *Emergency Retrieval - Do Not Touch*. The drum whirred into action, spooling cable at wire-smoking speed. Alex flopped over the handrail and bounced across the deck. Ozzie slapped a row of red switches, searching for an emergency stop, but the drum sped up. *Angelus* lurched sideways, throwing him against a vertical lever.

CHUNK

The clutch disengaged, releasing the cable. Ozzie trembled with relief and adrenaline as he untangled his sister.

"Are you hurt?"

Alex moaned. "That was more awesome in my head."

"It looked pretty awesome from here." He unclipped the wire and helped her stand. "We're doing a Pegasus thing, and it was Pascal's idea, so we definitely need to strap in."

The ship rolled sideways, and the untended winch cable bounced over the rail. Ozzie yanked the transmission lever, but the clutch wouldn't engage. More cable spooled over the side as Alex helped him force the lever down.

CHUNK

"Ten seconds until Pegasus Protocol!" Layla shouted.

clunk-Clunk-CLunk-CLUnk-CLUnk-CLUNk-CLUNKCLUNKCLUNK.

The winch cable jerked, and *Angelus* shuddered from stem to stern. A geyser of smoke and flame engulfed the starboard engine as the propeller screeched, broke off, then embedded in the volcano wall like a ninja star.

"What was that?" Layla roared.

"Ready to initiate," Pascal's voice squawked over the intercom.

"The children are not harnessed," the Sauracian said.

"Then they're about to learn a valuable physics lesson."

"We lost the propeller on the starboard engine!" Alex shouted.

"What?" Layla turned and gaped at the swath of destruction behind *Angelus*.

CRAAACCKKKK

The Maelstrom vessel had doused their flames and recharged their lightning cannon.

Whoooosh

A flurry of bombs careened past the bow, trailing smoke. *Angelus* floundered at the lip of the Crucible, surrounded by a flickering circle of lava guns.

"Initiating Pegasus," the speaker crackled.

Layla gathered the twins in a one-armed hug.

Pegasus Protocol *sounded* like shrieking engines, splintering

167

planks, and giant robots slap fighting in a typhoon. Ozzie's chest burned with the effort of breathing, but he was grateful for Layla's iron grip when acceleration lifted his feet off the deck. G-forces melted Alex's smile into a grimace.

Angelus somehow, impossibly, continued to speed up, her roar crescendoing to an anguished wail. Mount Typhon shrank until the Crucible's lava guns twinkled like stars. The airship breached a high bank of cumulus clouds, and not a moment too soon—her starboard engine was belching twenty-foot flames.

Layla snarled something the translapede couldn't interpret, then hit a kill switch. Normal gravity returned as *Angelus* glided through a layer of clouds in silence.

Pascal's voice buzzed over the speaker. "We had a slight issue down here, but nothing I couldn't handle. On a related note, we are out of fire extinguishers." Static fizzed for two seconds, then he blurted, "And you need a new bed."

Layla punched the control panel and rounded on the twins. "Your foolishness doomed us," she snapped.

Alex gnawed her lip, a sure sign she was about to argue, so Ozzie jumped in. "It's my fault. I should've locked the winch."

"Pegasus Protocol was an attempt to escape *without being followed*." The Sauracian pointed to a line of smoke behind the airship. "Thanks to your escapade, a blind badgadder could track us."

An avalanche of debris announced Pascal's arrival on deck. "At least we made some distance before the engines slagged," he said. "Not bad, all things considered." He caught sight of the warped, propellerless engine and stopped wrapping gauze around his forearm. "What happened?"

Layla skewered the twins with a glare and spat, "Heroics."

"Oh. I hate those." The inventor slumped against the railing and released a long sigh, deflating his chest like a balloon.

The Sauracian said, "We need to eliminate our smoke trail."

Pascal snorted. "We have a bigger problem—if the starboard engine didn't burn purified dynami, Skhaar can track our energy signature." He pushed upright and wobbled over to the winch drum. "We might as well paint *Angie* orange and welcome our Maelstrom overlords with a pot of scourge."

Angelus drifted aimlessly in thick, soupy clouds while Pascal rappelled down to inspect the ruined engines. His investigation yielded a crate of torched parts and two infuriated gruffletrunts. Frustrated bellows and clanging sounds from the engine room suggested Layla's quest to generate propulsion wasn't faring much better. After an hour, Ozzie summoned the courage to approach Pascal, who was sketching diagrams on a notepad while Socrates and Snuggles brawled at his feet.

"Any hope?" he asked, endeavoring to sound more like a helpful bystander than a co-architect of their current predicament.

"Pegasus melted most mechanical components, and your finesse with the winch finished the job. We're not going anywhere without a major refit at a shipyard." The inventor held up a sketch of a snail that had glass tubes inserted into its nostrils. "But I invented a way to use lurp mucus to filter coffee."

"That's...good."

"The trick is getting rid of the lurp flavor."

"We can't stop now," Alex said. "Grandfather needs us."

Pascal scratched Socrates' belly, provoking the furball into a spirited assault on his finger. "Even if we *could* get moving, the Professor would never forgive me if I took you to Amnesia. It's too dangerous."

"We aren't going anywhere." Layla emerged from the stairwell and dropped a mangled ball at Pascal's feet. Snuggles edged Socrates out by leaping on the smoldering part first. "Reverters, coolant heads, actuators...we slagged anything remotely associated with an engine."

The inventor nudged the sphere, which cracked open, disgorging a puff of steam. "I may have slightly over-enriched the dynami."

"So, what now?" the Sauracian said.

"Isn't it obvious? We crash in the Foraging Plains and hope whoever captures us reveres us as gods."

"I am serious, Pascal."

169

"Be nice, or I'll tell my followers you taste delicious."

Layla sighed. "A controlled descent it is. Let us start by figuring out where we are."

Pascal released a blast of heliovapor from the envelope with a twist of his wrist. "Ready," he said.

Layla steered into the wind. "Use a light touch. Once we vent, the only way to ascend will be to lose weight or luck into an updraft."

The inventor rolled his eyes. "This isn't my first unpowered emergency descent, you know. I did them all the time before you joined the crew."

"Why?"

"Let's not get bogged down in details." Pascal cracked the valve. Two seconds later, Layla barreled across the deck and slapped her paw over the opening, sealing it.

"I know what I'm doing," the Dromedarian protested.

Layla nodded at the dark silhouette of an airship ghosting through a cloud beneath *Angelus*.

The Maelstrom had found them.

---

1. Dr. Haloopit, displaying unusual marketing instincts for an academic, recognized that while the world contains a relatively small number of potential treasure hunters, it boasts a virtually limitless supply of potential customers who love tongue twisters.

    Unfortunately, he neglected to translate his bonus material, so readers were left to puzzle through the native tongue of the Zwp Tribe of Kol (a language containing no vowels and only seven consonants).

    His most popular tongue twister, "Pwqtbt ybtpbp ytytytqp bptbtpzq ybtbbqt pwatbt, tqptpqt qptbqyptp pzqp," was a sensation in beekeeping circles after they discovered that screaming it made bee swarms turn left.

CHAPTER 23

CHILDREN OF CONTRIVANCE

Pascal locked the valve. Snuggles and Socrates sniffed the air, then ran in circles, growling. The inventor mimed popping the envelope open, and whispered, *"Icarus."*

Layla bared her teeth and shook her head. *"Skhaar will not fall for the same gambit. He will search for wreckage."*

The shadow whisked past the bow and into a bank of impenetrable white fog.

Pascal stroked *Angelus'* railing and sighed. "We can't let them capture us." He beckoned Ozzie and Alex closer, then untangled a pair of T-shaped handles from the rigging. "These are escape pods. Each wire connects to a balloon containing enough heliovapor for an individual emergency descent." He pointed to a red cord that ran through the handle. "Pull this to vent gas. Drop below Skhaar's ships fast, but conserve buoyancy so you don't smash to a pulp when you land."

Layla handed the twins a pair of harnesses. "We will regroup on the ground."

"How high are we?" Ozzie asked, sliding his arm into a mishmash of webbing. This seemed like an important question.

"I'd say, around 5000 feet," Alex said.

"*Shhhhh.*" Pascal pointed at a dark shape coasting overhead. It moved slower than the first vessel.

Layla snatched Ozzie's harness off his arm, untangled it, and whipped it over his shoulders. With two sharp jerks, she tightened the straps, stealing his breath and putting his hands on a fast track to purple.

"Ow!"

"Would you prefer to separate from your balloon mid-air?" she growled.

He pointed to his waist strap. "A little tighter here, please."

All four crew members perched on the bow. Ozzie's fingernails dug into the wooden railing as intermittent gusts bullied him. At least Alex looked nervous, too, for once. Pascal grimaced and tightened his satchel strap. He insisted on carrying the Professor's journal, since Layla was the heaviest and the twins might panic during the long descent.

Layla raised a claw.

Tick-tick-tick-squeak. Squeak-tick-tick-tick-squeak.

A triangular yellow flag sliced like a shark fin through the pillowy cloud off *Angelus'* port side. Repetitive clicking sounds grew louder as the flag rose, revealing a smudged canvas envelope.

"*Pedal faster, lads! The signal is strengthening!*"

Discontent murmured through the haze.

"*We would climb faster if you helped pedal instead of shouting instructions.*"

"*I invented the Dynami Scope, so I get to operate it and YOU get to pedal.*"

"*I studied exercise science to judge OTHER people while THEY exercise. It's MY airship, after all.*"

"*Scientific progress is bigger than one man's possessions - besides, pedaling is doing wonders for your calves.*"

"*Thank you.*"

Ozzie gave Alex a perplexed look. *Doing wonders for your calves?* Behind closed doors, Maelstrom warriors were significantly less savage than they appeared. Layla and Pascal wore matching expressions of shock. The Sauracian slowly lowered her arm.

Pascal groaned. "Let's jump."

"We might not survive the landing," Layla countered, "and if we do, we will be stranded in the Feral without supplies."

"Sounds like a fun challenge. I'm jumping."

"*Pascal…*"

"I'll start a tribe—we'll invent cheese, then build a dairy empire."

"*What's going on?*" Ozzie whispered.

"*Is that a Maelstrom ship?*" Alex hissed.

"Worse," Pascal said, "that ship belongs to the Children."

A cloud parted, and the vessel drew level with *Angelus*. It was impossible to say who was more surprised: the four white-coated, long-bearded men on the bicycle-propelled airship, or the Forsythe twins.

"Capital!"

"Well done, Dr. Hernov!"

"Thank you, Dr. Gunvig."

"Quickly, the chrono-fluctuator!"

"Right!" The rearmost cyclist hopped off his perch and grabbed the handle of a swiveling, gimbaled pitchfork. Bolts of blue energy crackled between the weapon's tines.

The portliest man—the only non-pedaling crew member—raised a speaking cone to his mouth. "I am Dr. Demotoclesp Hernov, and this fine vessel is the *Asthmatic*. Please observe the prototype weapon in my capable colleague's hands and surrender in the name of science."

A grumbled argument broke out between the three pedalers. Hernov raised an apologetic finger to *Angelus'* crew, then dove into the dispute. After wild gesticulations and multiple requests for clarification, he resurfaced.

"My apologies," he shouted, a harried edge to his voice. "My colleagues request that I afford their respective fields of expertise the respect they deserve." His words took on a sing-song quality. "Please observe the prototype weapon in my capable colleague's hands and surrender in the name of…" he glared at his three bearded crew mates, "*in no particular order*, Spontaneous Gravitation, Exercise Science, and Highly Combustible Vegetables—"

"With an emphasis on Volatile Starches," volunteered a wild-haired pedaler who was missing two digits on his upraised hand.

"—with an emphasis on Volatile Starches," finished Hernov, through gritted teeth.

His shipmates muttered satisfaction.

Pascal waved weakly. "Hello, Dr. Hernov."

"Hello, Pascal," the doctor nodded politely. "Now, do you surrender, or..." His voice trailed off as his brain caught up to his mouth. "*Pascal*? What are *you* doing up here?"

"Failing to escape, mostly."

"When I saw the outlandish readings on my Dynami Scope, I should have surmised your involvement. We *must* compare notes on...oh my." Hernov put his hand to his mouth. "I apologize, but I am obligated to take you prisoner. It's nothing personal, but—" The doctor spotted Layla, and blood drained from his face. He tried to speak and fell into an explosive coughing fit. "*What is <cough> SHE <cough, cough> doing...here?*"

His fellow scientists, sensing a straightforward capture going off the rails, craned their necks to see what the commotion was and, as one, gasped.

"*Ooooh, my sweet Aunt Agnes. It's—*"

"*I heard she ate the guards who tried to Banish her.*"

"*Everyone notice I'm not looking in her direction. If the Chieftess asks, I didn't make eye contact with anyone who doesn't officially exist.*"

"*I think the brilliant inventor of the Dynami Scope should have full credit for this capture.*"

"*Oh, you'd love that, wouldn't you, Gunvig? You've always coveted my corner lab.*"

"*We could destroy their airship. I've got a bag of napalm lentils here somewhere.*"

A disturbingly thoughtful pause followed that suggestion, so Ozzie jumped in. "Not to rush you, but three Maelstrom ships are chasing us."

The scientists burst out laughing.

"The Maelstrom!" snickered Dr. Hernov. "A slovenly pack of low-tech amateurs."

"Skhaar the Annihilator is leading them," Ozzie said.

The laughter ceased.

"Why would an Annihilator venture so far into Terravenum?" Dr. Gunvig said.

"No idea," Pascal lied, "but Skhaar will be here shortly, so either take us prisoner or let us escape, please."

The scientists huddled.

"The Chieftess will have questions."

"But she banished Lay—...the four-hundred pound reptile standing over there who doesn't exist."

"That sounded dangerously like an open acknowledgement of her existence. You're on shaky ground, Julius."

"Let the official report reflect that I did not make eye contact with anyone who doesn't exist."

"Gentlemen," Dr. Hernov stood up. "Annihilators automatically trigger a Level Thirteen Sigma protocol. Regulations are clear: we must bring them in."

The decision to "bring them in" was less contentious than the debate on how to move *Angelus*.

"A sixteen-ton granite counterweight should do the trick."

"If we direct the blast from a bushel of combustible radishes—"

"With so much pedaling, we need to monitor lactic acid build-up."

Ozzie watched the gunner abandon his weapon to argue with his colleagues for a third time. He said, "What would happen if I walked over and took control of the chrono-fluctuator?"

"They'd ask you to join their crew," Pascal said.

"Tempting. Do you think they know the Icarus Initiative or Pegasus Protocol?"

"I doubt it."

"Then I'm not interested. What's the point of air travel if you aren't crashing?"

"Oh, they crash. A lot." Pascal selected a pastry from a platter of delicious baked goods their captors had offered them. He took a bite and said, "The Children are completely bonkers, but they appreciate a good snack."

"How do you know these lunatics?" Alex asked.

"It's a long story." Pascal licked his lips and watched two scientists shake each other by the shoulders until both had to sit down. "But it looks like we've got time. The Children of Contrivance are the most brilliant minds in Terravenum. Their ranks include experts at the forefront of all scientific disciplines, including many they invent."

"So they're geniuses," Ozzie said.

"They certainly think so." Pascal nodded at the mass of squabbling white coats. "Minds that sharp are only a danger to themselves, unless an outside force organizes them—which is where the Chieftess comes in. Hundreds of years ago, the original Chieftess emerged from the Feral, recruited the first Children, and laid the foundations for Contrivance, a city devoted to the advancement of knowledge. Their mission attracted the best and brightest minds from across Terravenum, all hoping to score a coveted internship. In my case, a nomadic inventor named Professor Upmooth saw my potential and provided a letter of introduction."

Alex snorted. "You were one of these guys?"

"I didn't last long enough to earn my coat."

"What happened?"

"The Children don't have many ironclad rules, but the few they have are rigidly enforced. Purified dynami research was frowned upon at the highest levels." Pascal shrugged and popped a strawberry in his mouth.

"Why are they pretending Layla doesn't exist?" Ozzie said.

"That's her story to tell."

A scientist whacked his colleague in the head with a clipboard.

"Speaking of not existing," Alex said, "we need to get moving before Skhaar gets here. Can we speed this up?"

Layla stomped past, a chunky, braided rope draped over her shoulder. She climbed the railing and dropped onto *Asthmatic*, rocking the vessel. Children dove out of the reptile's path, stammering excuses to avoid acknowledging her.

176

"Oh! I've dropped my spectacles!"

"Your deck planks have such lovely grain, Enzo!"

"Never a bad time for a spot of yoga!"

"Oops, I tripped on my...beard?"

Layla secured the rope to a stern cleat, pointed at the bicycle seats, and roared, "Skhaar is coming! Pedal!"

White coats scrambled to avoid being the non-pedaling loser in a life-or-death game of musical chairs. Dr. Hernov leap-frogged two of his colleagues to claim the final vacant seat.

Gunvig grabbed Hernov's collar and tried to displace him as Layla advanced. He shouted, "Let me pedal! It's *my* airship!"

"Wouldn't *dream* of exposing you to lactic acid, old chum."

The exercise scientist hissed, *"There's no such thing, now get off!"* Gunvig shrunk when the Sauracian's shadow drifted over him. They stood belly-to-nose: a six-foot, four-hundred pound reptile and a quivering academic feigning sudden onset blindness. Layla slid a claw beneath the scientist's trembling chin and lifted. He screwed his eyes shut and whimpered.

The Sauracian whispered, *"Go."*

Six pale, spindly legs pumped as if someone had fired a starter's pistol. *Asthmatic* lurched forward at an impressive clip, then slowed to absorb the weight of *Angelus*. After a few tow line adjustments, the airships settled into a steady groove.

Pascal unfolded a table and emptied a picnic basket, preparing a smorgasbord of crackers, vegetables, cheese, and...was that *chocolate*?

Alex scraped jelly on a slice of artisan bread. "Where did you find this?"

The inventor said, "I liberated it from the Children while they argued about whether Layla exists."

POW

Ceramic shards and slimy orange chunks pattered *Angelus'* deck like hail, courtesy of a former plate of carrots.

The expert on Highly Combustible Vegetables With an Emphasis on Volatile Starches yelled, "Use kale to douse flames—it's all the wretched plant is good for!"

177

"Are any of you doing research into crackers, chocolate, or cheese?" Ozzie shouted over squeaking cogs and chains.

"Don't be ridiculous!"

Pascal reached past a bowl of fizzing asparagus to claim a slab of chocolate. He said, "When dealing with Children, always remember Rule Number Two: Don't volunteer to be a test subject." The inventor wrinkled his nose at a suspicious green dip, then shrugged and ladled it onto a cracker. "When you're tempted by promises of game-changing breakthroughs—and you will be—always ask yourself: *Do I WANT to grow gills?*"

"I think having gills would be awesome," Alex said.

"Really? What happens when your lungs stop working because you *only* have gills and can no longer breathe outside of water?" Pascal's voice hardened. "Contrivance is a city of consequence-blind egomaniacs. While I was there, a biomutationist bred a twenty-foot tall fangorius lump that had eleven additional tentacles, and five Children got eaten trying to teach it to fold socks."

Ozzie nodded. History is forged by people who don't know when to quit, and nearly all of them meet their end at the epicenter of a catastrophe. His family was a perfect example—"Why Not?" might as well be engraved on his parents' tombstones.

"What's Rule One?" Alex said.

Pascal waved a croissant. "Don't trust the Chieftess."

"Nearly home, gentlemen! Pedal with haste!" Moans and jeers met Dr. Gunvig's rallying cry, but *Asthmatic's* propeller accelerated with giddy squeaks.

Pascal beckoned the twins to the bow as *Angelus* emerged from a cloud bank. "The Children of Contrivance do so many silly things, it's easy to forget the impressive stuff." He swept his arm as if pulling back a curtain.

Ozzie gasped.

Contrivance wasn't just a city, it was a beacon of light in a wasteland. Seven corridors extended from a central hub like arms of an alien starfish, each lined with strings of glowing windows that stretched for miles. Cranes and industrial machinery dotted the city's enclosed roof, conducting experiments and fortifying defenses. Scientists labored in each lab window to the tune of warning klaxons and billowing smoke—the birthing pains of innovation.

A roof tile slid open halfway down the length of the northern-most arm. As they drew closer, Ozzie couldn't shake the feeling of being lured into a deep-sea predator's mouth. Pascal vented helio-vapor and sunk his airship into the growing rectangle. When they entered the landing bay, the roof swallowed *Angelus* with clattering, mechanical satisfaction.

CHIK-CHIK-CHIK-SKREEAAAWWWWWW...DOOOOM

Clamps secured the roof as lights blinked on, illuminating a hangar that boasted enough room to house two *Angelus*-sized airships. A squad of white-coated Children toting improvised weapons waited at the bottom of the gangplank. Scowls, folded arms, and tapping feet suggested that *Angelus'* unscheduled arrival had interrupted important experiments. When guards caught sight of Pascal, one or two gave a begrudging nod, then shoved up in line to be the first to greet him. Layla's appearance at the railing sent a ripple through the group, who tussled for the honor of guarding the square foot of real estate farthest from the gangplank.

"Welcome to Contrivance, the most paranoid city under the Dome," Pascal said. "Don't walk anywhere by yourself, don't eat or drink anything from a test tube, and whatever you do, don't sign any contracts. Things just got hairy."

CHAPTER 24
CONTRIVANCE

Two guards glowered at Ozzie and Alex while five of their colleagues quarreled about the best way to tie dock lines. Everyone wore variations on the unofficial uniform of geniuses: a white coat, disheveled hair (unless balding), and acid-stained trousers. A solitary Dromedarian scientist loitered near the exit, head bowed and knees knocking. When Layla stomped down the gangplank, the guards fumbled with their weapons and stared at the floor.

A door slammed, echoing through the hangar like a shotgun blast.

"I'm here!" A bearded, bespectacled scientist huffed across the room and stopped at the gangplank. Salt-and-pepper hair burst from his scalp like a shock wave from a brain explosion. He mopped his brow with a beefy leather glove that extended to his elbow. "I am Dr. Doolot, head of the Perilous Omnivore Department, and this month's designated Speaker for the Children."

He uncorked a curved, opaque tube hanging from his shoulder and slipped out an eighteen-inch, yellow fang. Orange liquid dribbled from its needle point tip, forming a sizzling puddle on the floor. Doolot said, "This is a fang from a nesting blistercheek—the word 'poisonous' does not begin to describe the potency of its venom, so please behave." His brow furrowed. "Protocol dictated

180

me to arm myself—I hope I haven't overdone it." Doolot plunged the fang into its holster. "Best not keep the Chieftess waiting." The guards formed a loose perimeter around *Angelus'* crew, and the group trudged across the hangar.

"I didn't know the Children had an official speaker," Pascal said.

"It's a new initiative, thanks to an incident in which Dr. Venchian unilaterally declared war on the city of Rust after one of their chefs under-seasoned his soup. The Rustian council retaliated by laying siege to Contrivance for a week."

"Did Dr. Venchian apologize?" Ozzie said.

The nearest guard grunted. Doolot's eyebrow quirked, as if he'd never considered such a bizarre possibility. "Hardly. No one noticed the Rustian blockade until our cafeteria ran out of low-fat pronk milk, so we were too late to stop Dr. Venchian from unleashing a swarm of impossiburbles onto their militia. Once the psychotropic ooze melted, we did our best to convince the survivors their limbs weren't made of rubber, then escorted them home." The Speaker kicked a door open and hustled through without breaking stride. "Our pronk milk supplier refused to make any more deliveries, so the Chieftess determined we need an official spokesperson to handle public relations. We rotate monthly."

"Does Dr. Venchian get a turn as Speaker?" asked Alex, grinning.

Doolot winced. "Thanks to an unfortunate bureaucratic mix-up, Venchian *was* Speaker for the first three months of the initiative, resulting in five wars*[1], mostly prompted by unsatisfactory food preparation. But after the Follicle-In-My-Salad Skirmish, we banned Dr. Venchian from the rotation, and a committee of concerned Rustian citizens hired him a personal chef."

Shepherding Layla without officially acknowledging her existence was a challenge. Guards compromised by waving weapons in the Sauracian's direction and belting stilted conversation.

"FANCY A LEFT TURN AT THIS CORNER, DR. GISDO?"

"A CAPITAL NOTION, DR. ULMPH. WERE I FORTY INCHES TALLER, I MIGHT HAVE CONCERN ABOUT BUMPING MY

HEAD ON THE EXPOSED DUCTWORK JUST IN FRONT OF ME."

Dr. Doolot signaled a stop, licked his thumb, and rifled through a clipboard overflowing with memos. "South tunnels are closed for de-gooping. We can detour through the Deranged Botany Lab."

A tall scientist shook his head, waist-length beard waving like a somber flag. "Juvenile daffodiles are teething. Dr. Fester lost three toes yesterday."

Doolot said, "Cross-breeding flowers and reptiles is an intriguing proposition, but the man needs to rethink his fondness for open-toed sandals."

A portly scientist brandished a thermos. "Fancy a splash through the mint tea swamp? I could use a top-up."

Doolot flicked through memos, frowning. "Sorry, Dr. Juvenius. Wrenchers drained the herbal marsh this morning. Project Prometheus strikes again."

The guards murmured a tune in the key of disgruntlement.

Ozzie nudged Pascal. "Don't they know the way?"

"These corridors have been cannibalized and rebuilt a dozen times since I haunted them," the inventor said. His lip twisted as a guard directed Layla up a staircase by waving an electric fly swatter at imaginary insects. "Though some things never change."

More detours drove the group deeper into Contrivance's underbelly, much to Dr. Doolot's memo-shuffling consternation. Lubricants stained Ozzie's hands brown as he tiptoed across catwalks that spanned bubbling vats of toxic chemicals. Spray-painted equations appeared on walls, carpeting the corridor with math from floor to ceiling. Numbers and variables shifted like flowing water—complete gibberish, but inescapably beautiful. The equation captivated him, promising secret knowledge that would change his life forever. He wanted—he *needed*—to know the answer.

"Ozzie!"

He jumped. Pascal beckoned from the rear of the group, which was walking away from the graffiti. Ozzie jogged to catch up, shaking fog from his mind.

The inventor grinned. "Tempting, right? Someone is waging a turf war."

Ozzie looked back at the shrinking equation—at this distance, the numbers were a blur of rainbow chalk. "I wanted to understand it."

"That's how math snares work. Mathematician gangs use them to ambush rival number jockeys. The Chieftess deploys eraser squads to keep things civil, but Math Law has always ruled the Undergrease." Pascal laughed and pointed to a bold, red-lettered sign.

BEWARE OF DROG

The inventor punched the air with his fist. "Drog lives!"

Guards gasped and formed a circle, aiming their weapons into the shadows. When nothing attacked, Doolot scowled at Pascal. "How do you know about Drog?"

"I built him."

Fingers whitened on triggers. A hunchbacked scientist shook a twelve-pointed spear. "Why would anyone *intentionally* build Drog? Are you consumed by hate?"

"Who is Drog?" Ozzie asked.

"A mechanized pet I designed with a former colleague," Pascal said. "The behavioral programming had a few bugs."

"*A few BUGS?*" spat a guard wearing fluffy pink ear muffs. "Drog pilfered my screampea patch. He's a menace!"

A droopy-eyed scientist raised a finger. "He drank my tear duct samples! Do you know how long it takes to cry eighteen gallons of tears?"

Dr. Doolot tore a dog-eared Wanted poster from a community bulletin board and thrust it into Pascal's chest. A rough sketch of a blocky, canine-shaped machine topped the bulletin.

DECOMMISSION WITH EXTREME PREJUDICE. Reward of ONE KLUNK-TON for evidence of DROG's destruction. If DROG captured alive, CAPTURER will be PUBLICLY SHAMED and SUBJECT TO

IMMEDIATE EXPULSION FROM CONTRIVANCE on grounds of UNFATHOMABLE STUPIDITY - by directive of THE CHIEFTESS.

Pascal chuckled and raised a placating hoof. "I'd like to take credit for Drog's escapades, but I can't—his clockwork needs winding every twenty-one hours. You have a traitor in your midst." He rolled up the poster, oblivious to his flabbergasted audience. "Can I keep this?"

Pascal's revelation watered seeds of mutual distrust among the Children, who rattled weapons and mean-mugged each other, but stopped short of physical confrontation.*2 Then a rotund scientist accidentally triggered his egg cannon, blasting two colleagues with rancid, pink yolks.

"Oh dear," he said.

The hallway erupted.

Layla lounged against the wall, picking grease from her claws as scientists brawled around her.

Ozzie said, "It's hard to imagine you fitting in here."

The Sauracian gave him a flat look. "The Wrencher program is renowned throughout the Dome. I graduated with Honors in Field Maintenance and Improvised Fabrication."

A guard shoved a fizzing trident into Ozzie's hand, cleaned his glasses, then charged back into the fray. Pascal high-fived him as he ran past.

Layla punched the inventor's shoulder. "We need to speak with the Chieftess."

Pascal scowled. "Fine." He blasted a shrill, two-note whistle, then shouted, "This is all very productive, but I'm fairly certain the Chieftess would like to hear about the Annihilator chasing us *before* he arrives at Contrivance." Clumsy combat ground to a halt as a game of telephone rippled through the guards. "Besides, this Drog thing has Corridor Eight written all over it."

Thoughtful silence was broken by shuffling feet and mumbled apologies.

"What's Corridor Eight?" Alex whispered.

"Mad Scientist wing," the inventor said. "It's populated by Children who push the boundaries of science too far in the wrong direction."

"The 'wrong direction' meaning…"

"Any combination of shovels and graves."

A cloud of resentment shrouded the rest of the journey, as guards ignored their prisoners in favor of glaring at each other. Thankfully, after two more detours and a sprint through an orchard of screaming trees, Dr. Doolot stopped in front of a vault. Black, leaden golf balls whizzed along tracks that wound through a maze of brass gears, springs, and counterweights on the door. The Speaker rang a bell and a triangular viewing port opened.

"Password?" snipped a reedy voice.

Doolot flipped through his memos, then looked for help from his colleagues, who shrugged. He said, "I was not aware we have a password protocol."

"A new initiative started today. I wrote a memo."

The Speaker waggled his gloved fingers. "My apologies. I was feeding faulty trills when the morning memos arrived."

"How *convenient*. For all I know, you're plotting to assassinate the Chieftess."

"How dare you?" Doolot thundered. "I am a senior department chair!"

"That's *exactly* what a conspirator would say." The port slammed shut.

Dr. Doolot pounded on the door, leather gloves muffling his blows. "Open the door, Dr. Weedle!"

The viewport clicked open. "Password?"

"Admit us immediately, or I'll slather your office in snawlbrawl pheromones and release a juvenile male."

"Oh! Threatening the Head of Security, are we?"

"You've been Head of Security for nine hours!"

"And I've already foiled three assassination attempts!"

Pascal cleared his throat. "Out of curiosity, how many of those plots involved a tray of food or tea?"

"Who told you? How did you know that?" A beady eye strained at the hole and widened when it saw Layla.

185

A razor-sharp female voice snapped, "Oh, for the love of Aristotle, let them in, Weedle."

There was a beat of silence, then a mumbled, "Yes, Chieftess."

Gears ratcheted, tumblers rose, and metal squealed as the vault door creaked open.

Pascal fidgeted with his prosthetic arm, and said, "Remember Rule One."

Layla pulled Ozzie and Alex close. "Guard your words, children. The less the Chieftess knows about your family and our purposes, the better."

A pudgy scientist with bloodshot eyes and a nervous twitch appeared in the doorway. "I am Dr. Weedle, this month's Head of Security." He flourished a glassware bazooka, loaded with pink slime. "Please give me a reason to vaporize your atoms. The Chieftess will see you now."

----

1. According to the Children's official records, the "Venchian Food Wars" include:
    1. "Burn-My-Steak-And-I'll-Torch-Your-House" Blood Feud
    2. "Don't-Tell-ME-It's-Too-Salty" Scandal of the Seven Popped Corns
    3. "Who-Puts-Mayonnaise-On-Fried-Potatoes" Vendetta of the Unforgivable Transgression
    4. "What-Do-You-Mean-Waffles-Aren't-A-Lunch-Food" Bare-Knuckled Brawl
    5. "Follicle-In-My-Salad" Skirmish
2. They preferred revenge served cold, with a side order of ironic physics. An epidemic of falling pianos loomed.

CHAPTER 25
THE CHIEFTESS

Illuminated floor panels led to a cavernous room where a spotlight bathed a single chair and circular desk in clinical splendor. Seven glowing paths extended from the central workstation like spokes from a hub, each leading to a vault door. The layout made sense—if Ozzie were in charge of these lunatics, he'd want to see them coming from any direction, too.

Chittering machinery powered a dozen overhead conveyor belts that deposited documents in baskets around the desk. In the hurricane's eye, a white-cloaked figure spun in her chair, scribbling missives and dispatching messages into hungry pneumatic tubes. She didn't glance up as the party assembled for inspection.

The Chieftess' silver hair streamed halfway down her back, gradually shifting to a somber gray as it passed her shoulders. Her flowing white lab coat had more in common with an evening gown than laboratory garb. Intense red lipstick and a pair of volantium spectacles with triple flip-down lenses were the only splashes of color on her ashen, humorless face.

The old woman straightened a sheaf of papers, clicked new lenses down, and studied her guests. Her unblinking gaze lingered on the twins, giving Ozzie an uncomfortable sensation of being catalogued and tagged as "Mildly Interesting".

"So this is the crew of desperate brigands Dr. Hernov risked life and limb to capture," she said. Her voice carried the self-assuredness of someone comfortable with authority, so long as she was the one who had it. "I'm disappointed—after reading his mission report, I expected you to arrive with blood dripping from your cutlasses." She dismissed the guards with a wave of her hand, triggering a grateful, clumsy stampede.

Dr. Weedle remained at the Chieftess' side, finger at the trigger of his atomic vaporizer.

"Leave us, Weedle," the old woman said.

"Madam, as Head of Security, I cannot allow—"

"I'm perfectly safe, Doctor."

"But I haven't searched them for poison! They might have hollow teeth."

The Chieftess rapped an impatient cadence on her desk with ivory fingernails. "Dr. Weedle, I hear rumblings of an insurgent plot on Level Nineteen in need of suppression."

"At once, Chieftess!" The security guard threw a salute that would have brought a tear to a drill sergeant's eye and sprinted away.

The old woman watched him leave, then tapped a button on her armrest. "Inform Master Wrencher Deeno to stage a malfunction in the clutz raptor cages on Level Nineteen." She thought for a moment, then added, "Use large nesting females."

"Yes, Madam," the speaker hissed.

"Hello, Pascal." The Chieftess' piercing stare drifted to the inventor, who dipped his head in the shallowest version of a polite nod. "I daresay neither of us expected you to set hoof in Contrivance again. Your former colleagues think of you frequently, and with considerable passion." She gestured to an overflowing basket of memos. "Since your arrival, I've received dozens of requests to—what was it again? Oh, yes: *Force that blasted fool Pascal to deactivate Drog before it triggers a cataclysm that swallows the city.*"

Pascal grinned. "Glad I made an impression. Memories of my brief time with the Children never fail to amuse me."

188

The Chieftess focused on the Forsythes. "And who are your companions?"

"Passengers bound for Scrum."

"Indeed? I was given to understand they are progeny of the illustrious Professor Forsythe."

Ozzie's shoulders tightened.

Rule One: Don't trust the Chieftess.

"What are your names, children?" the Chieftess asked. After the space of a few pounding heartbeats, she snapped, "Come now, I can't be bothered to know *everything* in advance."

Alex raised her chin defiantly. "I'm Alex. He's Ozzie."

"The sister answers for the pair. Intriguing." The old woman tilted her head, filing the observation away. "Welcome to Contrivance, Alex and Ozzie Forsythe. Your grandfather's talent for antagonizing powerful enemies brought me great entertainment over the years. I was sorry to learn of his disappearance."

Pascal frowned. "Disappearance? Where are you getting your information?"

The Chieftess rested her chin on the knob of a white staff inlaid with veins of volantium. "First, the Professor would never permit his grandchildren to cross the Divide given what happened to their parents. Second, *Angelus* is not in the habit of transporting passengers." Her voice sharpened, "And finally, I know the Professor disappeared because *you*, Pascal Trahir, are standing in the last place either of us desires you to be."

Ozzie searched the room for an exit, but the vault doors were sealed. How did the Chieftess know about his parents? Was she working with the Noctem? The Maelstrom? If she knew about Grandfather's research, was she after the journal?

The Chieftess rolled her eyes at Ozzie's alarmed expression. "Calm yourself, child. If I desired the Professor's journal, I would simply order my Children to search *Angelus*." She shut down Pascal's burgeoning disavowal with a frown. "Save your hollow denials. I have no time for trivialities—though your book would be an effective bargaining tool with any number of interested parties."

The old woman sighed—an oddly vulnerable noise—then

turned to Layla. "And what am I to do with you?" The Sauracian stiffened, staring into the distance. "Banished, yet here you stand— an open wound in the heart of Contrivance." She struck her staff against the floor with a *clang*. "You broke the Code."

Layla rumbled, "I do not regret my decision, only your actions."

"Do you know how many wrenchers I deploy across Terravenum? If I permit anyone to break the Code, it creates a dangerous precedent."

"I am grateful for the education I received here—" Layla said.

"Education?" the Chieftess snapped. "I gave you purpose and a future. A *family*—one you betrayed, and for what?"

Guilt flashed across Layla's face.

Pascal stepped in front of his friend. "You trained her, but you don't own her. Kill us, imprison us, or throw us to the Annihilator, but spare us your pompous rhetoric."

The Chieftess' icy glare could have frozen the sun. She stabbed a finger at the inventor. "Do not accuse *me* of vanity, Pascal Trahir, lest ghosts from your past return to haunt you. If not for your meddling, Layla would not be banished, and these children would not be orphans."

The inventor's face bloomed a dark shade of purple. Layla growled a warning, and he swallowed his protest, folding his arms.

The old woman glowered, then stood with a swiftness that belied her age. "To your good fortune, our interests temporarily align." She glided out from behind her desk, tapping her staff against the floor like a disapproving headmistress. "Follow me."

The blistering pace left Ozzie panting. In between gasps, he marveled at the first corridor in the city that hadn't been scavenged for parts.

"The Professor's last reported destination was Amnesia," the Chieftess said. "It so happens that Dr. Bloomvilt is a month overdue from an expedition to that accursed island. Two of her colleagues launched a rescue mission, but only one returned, and he cannot remember his own name."

"She was foolish to go," Pascal said. "Amnesia is unexplored for good reason."

190

The Chieftess sniffed. "As head of our Malicious Vegetation and Disloyal Shrubbery Department, Bloomvilt is a jungle survival expert, and her would-be rescuers were graduates of our Treacherous Ecology program. They were equal to their task." She handed Ozzie a photograph of a stocky, unsmiling woman brandishing a test tube, as two men flanking her repelled furry beasts with long poles. Ozzie stifled a laugh. He'd met enough seasoned explorers to know that "survival experts" have a hunted look in their eyes and a tendency to dive for cover at sudden noises. These Children might thrive in controlled laboratory conditions, but survival experts, they were not.

Pascal glanced at the photo. "Outside these walls, diplomas just make you a well-educated snack."

The Chieftess ignored his jibe. "In exchange for the use of my repair facilities, you will travel to Amnesia, broadening your search for the Professor to include Dr. Bloomvilt and her missing colleague."

Layla and Pascal exchanged a skeptical look. He said, "Why not send more jungle experts to rescue them?"

"Because they are experts. *Within* these walls, diplomas make you valuable."

Pascal said, "Amnesia is an unknown quantity. We can't make any promises."

"I can." The Chieftess' tight-lipped smile didn't extend to her eyes. "I promise that if you return to Contrivance without my missing Children, the Maelstrom's pursuit of a silly book will be the least of your concerns."

"This is blackmail!" the inventor protested.

"This is wisdom. *Blackmail* would be threatening to unleash hundreds of highly motivated, vindictive geniuses against an enemy whose clockwork canine abomination has plagued their research for years."

Layla thrust her arm across Pascal's chest. "We will do our best, Chieftess."

"I am certain of it. You depart at first light."

Pascal scoffed, "*Angie's* engines are slagged. Even with help

191

from every wrencher and scientist in the city—which will never happen, because I won't let those idea poachers within a hundred feet of my tech—we can't get her flying by dawn."

"Correct," the Chieftess said. She stopped in front of a hangar and inserted the base of her walking staff into a hole in the floor. A lock *clanged*, and a door squealed open. Glow panels lit the perimeter of a dusty, abandoned repair bay. A boxy contraption perched on a hydraulic lift, cloaked by a grimy tarp. Layla's eyes lit up. She tugged the sheet, uncovering a greasy, angular frame that housed an enormous engine block.

"*Spark!*" she breathed.

The Sauracian caressed the metal chassis, humming a low-throated purr. When she reached the engine, her happy rumble mutated into a growl. "Who re-routed the cooling vents?"

"An apprentice wrencher commandeered your racing skiff in a misguided attempt to impress a coworker." The Chieftess cast a disinterested eye across the airship skeleton. "Following his rather spectacular accident, the vessel was cannibalized for parts."

"He crimped the after-pipe injectors! What g'zudnuk wrenchie crimps injectors?"

The old woman scowled. "Someone destroyed your machine. Welcome to the never-ending battle against stupidity, or as I like to call it: Wednesday. Need I remind you banishment means you cannot return to Contrivance *on pain of death*?"

"I did not ask to return!" Layla snarled.

"Yet here you are," the Chieftess said. "A dawn departure gives you eight hours to rebuild *Spark*. You'd best begin."

Pascal said, "We won't all fit on a racing skiff."

"I fail to see how that is *my* problem."

Ozzie lifted the tubular frame. It was surprisingly light—designed for speed, not hauling cargo. The Chieftess had to know all four of them wouldn't fit on board. A solution was obvious, and if he forced the words out fast enough, maybe the idea wouldn't sound as crazy as it did in his head. "Layla and I will go to Amnesia while Pascal and Alex stay here and repair *Angelus*."

Alex slapped a toolbox. "No! I won't twiddle my thumbs while you fly to certain death."

Ozzie shook his head. "There isn't room for both of us, and Pascal is going to need your help."

"What if you disappear?"

"We'll be fine. I have four hundred pounds of Sauracian brawn and a headful of conversations with Grandfather to back me up."

"Excellent," the Chieftess said, in the weary tone of someone who spends too much time wading through other people's drama. "I leave you to your machinations." She paused at the door. "Return with my Children, and much may be forgiven. Fail me, and the consequences will be dire."

CHAPTER 26
SPARK

Layla ripped into *Spark* while Ozzie, Alex, and Pascal followed guards back to *Angelus*. The Sauracian's outraged howls encouraged a brisk retreat.

"She's taking this personally," Ozzie said, ducking as metal shrieked behind them.

"You can't get emotionally attached to property in Contrivance," Pascal said. "In exchange for a nourishing environment where no one frowns on tweaking the genetic codes of absurdly venomous creatures, Children surrender their intellectual rights to anything they create or discover."[*1]

"I don't think Layla got the memo," Alex said.

"*Spark* was always a problem. Children resented competing with a wrencher for resources."

"Did they try to stop her from building it?"

Pascal shook his head. "The Chieftess redirected their outrage by commissioning an airship design competition. The ship that captured us today, the *Asthmatic*, descended from those prototypes."

"Bicycle-powered airships don't seem like the future of air travel," Ozzie said.

"No, but they illustrate how the Children gravitate more to

problems than to solutions. They excel in the kind of thinking that launches doomed rescue missions to save failed rescue attempts of ill-conceived expeditions."

Within minutes of returning to *Angelus'* hangar, Pascal was neck-deep in a mound of scrap, searching for engine parts. Ozzie headed to his cabin to collect his things. As soon as they were alone, Alex punched him in the shoulder.

"Ow!"

"That's for your idiotic plan!"

Ozzie pulled a canvas bag from the closet. "What choice do we have? The Chieftess is eight moves ahead of us, and possibly even playing a different game. You have to watch Pascal's back."

"Who's going to watch yours?"

He ignored the question. "We're hostages until *Angelus* can fly. Help get her ready."

Alex set her jaw, but she didn't argue.

Ozzie dumped his treasures on the desk. The Trovian slumber-dart pipe might be useful for hunting food. He palmed the four remaining balls of Panacea clay and felt a pang of guilt about wasting so many in bored target practice at St. Jude's. Oh well, no point in crying over spilt, ridiculously rare medicine.

The corners of the Labyrinthian glide chute bore smudge marks. He'd badgered Layla into demonstrating how to open the parch-ment, then practiced until he could perform the thumb flick without looking. The minor victory boosted his morale after sword fighting lessons. He had half a mind to leave the hilt. What if he lost a fight? What if he *won*? The weapon gleamed in his palm, resting comfortably in the contours of his knuckles.

Alex plucked the hilt from his hand and tossed it in the bag. "You're taking it."

Ozzie sighed. "I can't kill anyone, Alex."

"A sword might be useful to open coconuts or defend yourself from man-eating eggplants." She slid the armillam onto her wrist and adopted a posh British accent. "This trinket, however, shall remain with me. Lady Hawthistle does not share jewelry."

Ozzie grinned. Lady Frantosia Hawthistle was Alex's alter ego when they played dress-up as kids, a lifetime ago. Frantosia split her time between investigating treachery in the royal court and hunting for treasure in Egypt. He cleared his throat and polished his vowels. "As always, Lord Persivinius respects his Lady's wishes."

Ozzie skimmed his notebook for the few Amnesia references he'd copied from his grandfather's journal.

Amnesia is simultaneously the Least Explored and Most Discovered island in history. At last count, twelve different expeditions attempted to claim and colonize the atoll. In one notable case, Ophelius Teerak became so disoriented by memory loss he discovered the island eight successive times in twenty minutes.

Amnesia boasts an arsenal of natural defenses and dangers, including (but not limited to):

- *Ferocious insects ("The Wakeful Terrors," per Garrilus the Unread's "Sonnets I Can't Remember")*
- *Catapult ferns (Referenced by multiple sources)*
- *Weltling? (Details are scant, beyond consistent mentions of teeth and a tail - most likely a tedious, opossum-like creature)*
- *Frequent earthquakes of unknown origin*

NOTE: All information remains anecdotal and speculative until an expedition successfully returns.

Ozzie flipped his notepad shut, hoping he wouldn't find out what a weltling was.

Pascal knocked on the door. His fur was tousled and smeared with grease, but he sported a satisfied grin.

"What happened to you?" Alex asked.

The inventor looked down, sniffed his arm, and wrinkled his nose. "I salvaged an overflow power regulator from a dumpster. They're usually impossible to find, but our neighbors in the next lab are growing sentient watermelons." He cleaned his hoof with a rag. "Ready?"

"This Amnesia thing is a bad idea," Alex said.

"Agreed!" Pascal heaved a canvas tool bag onto his shoulder. "Let's go make some questionable life decisions."

Layla was buried beneath a rat's nest of cables and wiring, tail twitching as she grumbled promises of retribution. In less than two hours, she'd stripped *Spark* to a bare chassis and organized piles of components.

"How did she do that without tools?" Ozzie said.

A claw emerged, waved a screwdriver, then disappeared into the jungle of wires.

Pascal grinned. "Wrenchers are worth their weight in klunk-tons." He dropped the tool bag, kicking up a cloud of dust. "More weapons for your war, Layla."

The Sauracian grunted and rifled blindly through the bag.

Pascal scratched his chin. "You know, if you doubled the size of the manifold, you could—" A deep-throated rumble stopped him in his tracks. "Looks like you've got everything under control," he continued. "We'll watch from the door." The inventor shepherded Ozzie and Alex to the wall, where two guards were doing their best to blend in with the ductwork.

Layla disassembled, inspected, and rebuilt her airship one component at a time, in a whirlwind of efficiency. Nuts and bolts tinkled across the floor as she discarded parts that didn't meet her standards.

Ozzie asked a guard, "What happened to *Spark* after Layla—I mean, the Prisoner Who Doesn't Exist—got banished?"

The scientist packed tobacco into a pipe and leaned against a stack of crates. "Tale as old as science: a Child scavenges parts, builds a sophisticated flying machine, gets hungry, then converts it into a deadly pizza oven."

His partner nodded sagely. "Happens more often than you might expect—especially on Mondays, when the cafeteria recycles leftovers."

Layla roared and punched the chassis with an impact that rattled the walls. She stalked over to the group.

Pascal said, "You gentlemen may want to find something to

guard outside," but the scientists were already out the door. The inventor forced cheer into his voice. "Almost done?"

Layla glowered. "It will take *days* to fix this mess."

"You can do it in a few hours."

"Of course I can," she snapped. "That is not the point. *Spark* deserved better than to be a victim of Mystery Meat Monday." The Sauracian scowled, then lowered her voice. "You must leave Contrivance as soon as possible, even if we have not returned from Amnesia."

Alex crossed her arms. "We won't abandon you."

"You misunderstand, child," Layla said. "If things go as I anticipate, Ozzie and I will need you to rescue us." She yanked a pipe off the wall and dragged it to *Spark*, muttering, "Mystery Meat Mondays..."

Ozzie stayed out of the way, fell asleep on a mound of canvas, and woke to the screech of the roof ratcheting open.

"Stand back!" Pascal yelled. Hissing filled the hangar, as if a thousand snakes were bursting into song. Ozzie hopscotched through levitating rigging as a patchwork envelope climbed to the ceiling. Sunlight streamed through the open roof, bathing the airship in a warm glow that was only outshined by Layla's smile.

Spark was twenty-five feet long, eight feet wide, matte black, and openly scorned the laws of aerodynamics. A gargantuan engine hoarded the aft third of the hull and boasted a ten-foot diameter propeller. The bow housed gas cylinders, valves, and all the arcane plumbing required to thumb a nose at gravity. *Spark's* cockpit was slightly forward of amidships and home to panels of gauges, dials, and an unsettling number of warning lights. Two chairs sat in line with the engine, the back one twice as large as the front, but each with its own set of piloting controls.

"Get on board!" Pascal shouted, straining at the bow line.

Layla strapped into the big chair, flipping switches as alarms wailed on her console. *Spark* lifted off the ground, and Ozzie leapt into his seat.

Alex yelled, "Be careful!"

He fumbled with his harness and threw a distracted wave.

"Hey, Ozzie!" Pascal bellowed.

"What?"

"Remember the *Whirling Wall of Death!*"

Ozzie gave a wordless thumbs-up.

Layla chuckled, a sound like rocks rolling down a cliff. "I did not have time to tune the engine—until I do, we will be lucky to match *Angelus* for speed." She stabbed a button, and the motor ticked over, then hissed. A gentle morning breeze jostled the airship. Layla muttered a curse, unstrapped, and slid her head under the engine. She re-emerged a minute later smelling of burnt wiring. "Mystery! Meat! Mondays!" The wrencher emphasized each word with a punch to the engine block, her last blow shivering *Spark's* fuselage. The motor revved, and the skiff sprung forward like a spooked mustang. Layla yanked the throttle back to a rough idle.

Slowly but surely, *Spark* reclaimed her place in the sky. As the airship ascended, so did Layla's spirits. Even at low throttle, they had to raise their voices to be heard over the chuffing propeller.

"How long to Amnesia?" Ozzie said.

Layla twisted a valve. "Once we attain cruising speed, two days."

"Then what?"

"Find the Professor. Trust no one. Escape with our lives."

"So, the usual."

"The odds are against us, Ozzie. If something happens to me in Amnesia, *you* will have to fly *Spark* back to Contrivance. Pascal will know what to do."

"You want *me* to fly this thing?" The engine coughed, sharing his skepticism.

Layla released her joystick. "It is not difficult. Take the controls."

"Shouldn't we do ground school first? Maybe some diagrams?"

"Vicious malarks learn to fly when their mother shoves them off a cliff."[*2]

He shook his head and slid his hand around the control yoke. "It just sounds like bad parenting. Also, I have no idea what a malark is."

"Use slight movements to steer," she said.

Ozzie nudged his hand and the fuselage responded immediately, swinging high to the left. He oversteered to compensate, skidding *Spark* in a wild curve.

"*Slight* movements!" the Sauracian snapped. "Tilt your wrist."

"I am!"

"You shifted your arm as if slapping a rimrat!"

"I don't know what that is either!"

"Stop slapping rimrats!"

"Stop referencing weird animals I haven't heard of!" An untethered heliovapor cylinder bounced over the toe rail and tumbled into open air. Ozzie dangled from his harness as *Spark* yawed sideways. He overcorrected, veering the airship even higher in the opposite direction. Alarms blared, and the engine revved wildly, belching flames from its exhaust.

"Release the controls!" Layla barked.

He white-knuckled his chair as the Sauracian hit emergency shut-downs. The engine sputtered to a halt, leaving the airship swinging quietly in a cool breeze.

Once he could breathe normally, Ozzie said, "That went well."

"Do not speak," the wrencher growled.

---

1. With the notable exception of Dr. Kilmagreed's work in the Flatulent Propulsion Lab, which no one wants.
2. While factually true, ornithologists are quick to note that the legendarily sheer cliffs of Slaughter's Bluff are thousands of feet high and descend into deep canyons. As Dr. Tivium Shrewspit, Chief Avian Behaviorologist of Scrum's Ornithology Institution, famously said, "Given the prodigious height involved, it's possible for fledgling malarks to brew themselves a cup of tea and author a book of poetry before they hit the ground."

CHAPTER 27

AN ANEMOI BLADE

Ozzie thumbed the Labyrinthian glide chute as Layla rewired *Spark's* control systems for the third time in as many hours. "Sorry if I broke anything," he said.

To his surprise, instead of grunting, the Sauracian growled, "You did no worse than the Children who salvaged her for parts."

She'd stopped sulking! Ozzie leapt at the chance to move past his piloting misadventure. "You never said how you ended up in Contrivance."

Layla glanced up, but kept working. "As the runt of my clutch, I was exiled to die in the Barren. Nomadic scavengers saved me and taught me to survive. In time, my aptitude for machinery drew the attention of an ethnobiologist, who sponsored my wrencher apprenticeship." She stretched her right forearm, displaying a tattoo of a triangle framing a wrench.

"*You* were a runt?" Coming from a six-foot reptile, the notion was ridiculous.

She closed the access panel. "Sauracians sacrifice the smallest hatchling in every clutch to ensure continual improvement of their clan's bloodline."

"That's horrible!"

"It is their way."

"Don't you mean *our* way?"

She scowled. "I am rejected by Sauracians, unwelcomed by humans, and disavowed by the Children. My way is my own."

The unspoken message was clear: back off. Still, she was in a talkative mood, so Ozzie pushed his luck. "I didn't see other Sauracians in Contrivance."

"The Cloud War fostered animosity between Terravenum and Sauracia that persists to this day. The Chieftess made a rare exception in my case."

"Why did she banish you?"

"Wrenchers are renowned for our mechanical skills, so the Chieftess deploys us across the Dome as her eyes and ears."

"You were a spy."

"A bad one. I was stationed in Aeronoth's Pit, but most humans do not trust Sauracians, so the only gossip I heard was about me. Then I met an inventor who could not find a mechanic willing to repair his ship because of his reputation for second-guessing their work."

Ozzie grinned. "Pascal."

She nodded. "He slagged an engine on a botched smuggling run. I took pity on him and had *Angelus* up and running in two days."

"And that's when you became friends."

"He criticized my work, then left without paying. On his next visit to the Pit, I saved him from a team of bounty hunters."

"And *that's* when you became friends."

"I threatened to chop his ship into parts and sell them on the black market. Lacking money, he offered me a position on *Angelus*. Weary of being an outcast and a puppet on strings, I informed the Chieftess of my intention to leave Aeronoth."

"I'll bet she wasn't thrilled."

"She hired killers to make an example of us." Layla rubbed a scar on her chest. "After three failed assassination attempts, the Mercenary League voided the contract, and the Chieftess settled for banishing me." She cranked the engine to life, steered toward a cluster of clouds on the horizon, then clamped her controls in place.

"Speaking of life and death struggles, Amnesia holds no battles we can afford to lose. It is time to hone your fighting skills." She removed a length of pipe from a tool bag.

Ozzie unstrapped from his harness, stood up, and took a wobbly step. "This is dangerous, Layla."

"Fighting is inherently dangerous."

"At least turn the engine off!" Ozzie's foot tangled in his bag strap. As he toppled backwards, he shoved his hand in his pocket, whipping the hilt up in time to block the Sauracian's strike.

SSSCCCCHHHHHP

CLANG

He staggered to his feet. "Seriously, there's no room. Someone is going to get hurt."

"Endeavor to make it your opponent," Layla said.

Ozzie deflected another attack with a desperate parry and felt a whisper of cautious optimism. He wasn't winning—but for once, he wasn't losing! He blocked another strike, then accidentally nicked a wire suspending the fuselage from the envelope.

"Sorry, I—"

Layla unleashed a flurry of blows with a snarl.

"Time out!" Ozzie struggled to form a "T" with his hands without lowering his guard.

"What?" The Sauracian knocked his blade aside with a jolt that chattered his teeth.

He raised his hands. *"Time out* is a universally recognized expression meaning *please stop hitting me."*

"My apologies. I am certain Skhaar will give you a *time out* if you ask politely." She smacked Ozzie's right bicep and he yelped, dropping his blade.

"Ow! How am I supposed to fight if I can't hold a sword?"

"Excellent question—one worth keeping in mind."

Ozzie retrieved the hilt and slumped in his chair. "This is hopeless."

"Pain is the price of skill, child." Layla lowered her pipe. After a moment's deliberation, she pursed her lips and grunted. "I have a theory about your sword. Given the Professor's checkered past

203

with recovering rare artifacts and your discovery of the Custos Luminis entry in his journal, it is possible your weapon is an Anemoi Blade."

"A what?"

"A legendary sword possessing unique qualities. Are you willing to test it?"

"Will it make me better at sword fighting?"

"I said 'unique qualities', not miracle properties."

"Then, no thanks."

She spoke slowly, as if navigating a minefield of half-truths, "You will not gain unearned skill, but an Anemoi Blade *will* make you vastly more dangerous."

"It sounds like we're increasing the chance I might accidentally cut off my arm. What could go wrong?"

"Many things. You could sever an artery or—"

"It was a rhetorical question!"

Ozzie swished his sword aimlessly, carved an "O" into the fuselage, then rotated the hilt like a doorknob. "Can you be more specific about what I'm supposed to do?"

"According to folk tales, imagination and emotion are key to activating the Anemoi Blade."

"So that's a *no* on being more specific."

The Sauracian closed her eyes and exhaled, like she was meditating. "Imagine a raging fire, then attach an emotion."

"You sound like a pyromaniac monk."

"It is from a rhyme I learned as a child: *A mind's desire shall breathe to life a blade of fire to curse the night.*"

"I'd go with the monk thing if I were you."

Layla's upper lip curled, exposing carnivorous teeth. "Imagine fire."

Ozzie rolled his eyes and focused on the blade.

Fire.

Nothing.

Campfire.

Fireplace.

Lava.

204

The hilt was unimpressed.

Layla swung her pipe close enough to Ozzie's head to ruffle his hair.

"Hey!" He jabbed at her belly, and she slapped his sword down.

"You are unworthy of your weapon, boy."

Ozzie retreated, relying on the classic "Hysterical Slashing" technique favored by novice swordsmen everywhere.*[1] He parried Layla's blows, forearm stinging, as she backed him into the engine. "Stop!" he yelled. Machinery thrummed, deafening and disorienting, as the Sauracian intensified her attack.

"STOP!" Ozzie howled. Time slowed as a blazing inferno raced up his spine and exploded into his right forearm. When he opened his eyes, flames were dancing on his blade.

Whoa.

Layla gasped and dropped her pipe.

Then everything went wrong.

The sword melted from its tip, flowing over Ozzie's hand in a stream of molten metal. He screamed as a silver blob engulfed his fingers like a lava flow, scalding skin and advancing to his wrist. Waves of searing pain subsided to a throbbing ache, and he dropped to his knees, cradling his arm. Layla killed the engine.

Ozzie winced and made a fist, marveling at the volantium glove enclosing his right hand. Metal flexed, allowing his fingers to bend with their usual dexterity. He touched the deck and felt the grating scrape his fingertips. At least his nerves still worked.

"What just happened?" he said.

"An Anemoi Blade." Layla's hushed voice bordered on reverent. "A blade of fire to curse the night."

Ozzie inspected the clean line that circled his wrist, forming the base of the metal glove. "Did you know the sword was going to melt?"

"I knew the only way to test the blade was to provoke you."

"Congratulations, you provoked my hand into Disco Mode." Ozzie frowned. Three flat, quarter-sized volantium circles were embedded in his right forearm, evenly spaced between his wrist and elbow. A light tap on one of the plugs radiated vibrations into bone. He rotated his hand and gasped at the Stella Signum pulsing on the back of his glove.

Layla said, "Can you manifest the sword again?"

"Are you crazy? We don't know what this thing will do."

"The Ancients did not waste volantium—the hilt performed as they designed it to."

Ozzie pried at the glove, but the metal was bonded to his skin. "Did they design it to come off?"

"Doubtful. Prophetic weapons demand commitment."

"What if I break it?"

"The Anemoi Blades were fashioned by Lorica Nightforge, Chief Armorer of the Ancients. You cannot break it."

Gently pulsating Stella Signum lines ran beneath the surface of his glove like blue neon veins. He clenched his fist, and the emblem conformed to the curvature of his hand. "I'll try to manifest the sword, but if this thing turns me into a supervillain, it's your fault."

Layla armed herself with a flame retardant blanket and retreated to the far end of the deck.

"Ready?" Ozzie said. Just a typical day, manifesting fire swords with a glove that melted into his hand. No big deal.

"Imagination and emotion," the Sauracian said. "Start with fire, since we know that works."

A blush crept into Ozzie's cheeks as he squeezed his fist and attempted to grunt fire into existence. The Stella Signum glowed brighter, but nothing manifested. After three of the most ridiculous and least productive minutes of his life, he gave up.

"So much for magical swords."

Layla folded her blanket. "This weapon is more than a sword, Ozzie—it is a promise. The Custos Luminis shall wield the Anemoi Blade to vanquish darkness."

"You mentioned that." He eyed his glove warily. "You also said most Sauracians believe the Fury King is the Custos Luminis."

"Until today, the only known Anemoi Blade in existence belonged to him."

Ozzie flexed his metal fingers. "And now there are two."

"Yes."

"Why is he called the Fury King?"

"For his ferocity in battle and merciless tactics. Under his leadership, the Maelstrom pushed humanity to the brink of annihilation."

"How do you know he *isn't* the Custos Luminis?"

Layla extended her claws. "When I was a clutchling, my adoptive mother's stories about the Custos Luminis inspired me to dream of saving the world from darkness. After the Maelstrom slaughtered my tribe and spared my life out of cruelty, they laid my helplessness bare." She paused. "My world burned to ash, prophecies and superstitions vanishing in the smoke." Layla took his hand, examining the glove. "Then I rescued you, a child drowning in events beyond his comprehension—a child who wields the blade of the Guardian of Light." She shook her head. "This cannot be, but is."

Ozzie pulled his hand from her paw. "I'm definitely not the Guardian of Light."

"We have no choice but to proceed as if you are."

"Seriously? We have *so* many choices!" He numbered points on his fingers. "We could pry this off, give it to an *actual* warrior, and point him at eternal darkness. Or we could throw it in the ocean and let destiny wash it onto a beach for a shipwrecked hero to find. Or—and this is probably the best idea—we could drop it in a volcano. Boom. Problem solved."

"That is not how prophecies work. If you are the Guardian—no, listen to me—if you are the Guardian, the fate of Terravenum hangs in the balance."

"I'm here to save my grandfather, not Terravenum." He shoved his hands in his pockets. "Let's just get to Amnesia."

Ozzie brooded while Layla negotiated a truce with *Spark's* finicky engine—a process they repeated frequently over the next two days. Further attempts to manifest the Anemoi Blade only yielded frustration, so they dropped the subject and focused on their mission. As they neared Amnesia, featureless wasteland became an immaculate beach, then an ocean. Layla throttled back to ensure an early morning arrival, then busied herself with a craft project that involved trimming material from her wrist guards.

Ozzie toyed with Labyrinthian parchment as *Spark* chugged over a blanket of moonlit clouds.

"That was your fifth sigh in two minutes," the wrencher said. "What is plaguing you?"

He flexed his fingers and watched the Stella Signum dance. "Just wondering why Grandfather didn't say anything to me about this—even a quick, *Hey, I'm not sure what this thing is, but don't put it in your pocket in case you accidentally declare yourself to be a prophesied warrior of legend.*"

The Sauracian tilted her head. "The Professor is consumed by Stone Lore. He did not know what the hilt was."

"Given our family history, he should have assumed it would be something disastrous."

Layla grunted and forced a needle through a bundle of leather. She inspected her handiwork, then tossed it to Ozzie. "Conceal your Stella Signum," she said. "We must avoid drawing attention to the Anemoi Blade."

The leather glove was a good fit. Cut-off fingertips allowed for grip, while opaque material limited the Stella Signum's glow to a gentle iridescence at his wrist.

"Thanks," Ozzie said. "What's this made from?"

"Lavaskink—difficult to catch, but worth the effort if you do a lot of welding." She slapped a leather gauntlet strapped to her forearm.

"Will it survive if I manifest the sword?"

"Not long."

He grinned. "I'll be sure to take it off before hunting any forces of darkness, then."

Layla stowed her sewing kit in her belt. "If Amnesia is as dangerous as I expect, the forces of darkness will come to us."

---

1. Hysterical Slashing is often denigrated as an amateur move, but elite swordsmen are known to utilize it in situations of extreme duress (most often,

208

when an army of henchmen unreasonably insist on attacking in unison instead of one at a time, as decorum demands).

Kasaromeo the Bladesman famously attempted to Hysterically Slash his way through a platoon of garganchu troll-riding mercenaries to rescue a kidnapped princess. He was crushed in seconds, but his valiant effort earned him a place in folk legend (Recounted for posterity in the epic poem *Flatter than Kasaromeo's Ego* and, rather less notably, in Doctor Limgi's graduate thesis *Physics Doesn't Care About Your Gallantry.*).

CHAPTER 28

AN ARMILLAM

Alex screamed, clutching her left wrist as her bracelet melted. Agony dwindled into a pulsing burn by the time Pascal loped into the engine room.

"Was it Socrates again?" He banged an air vent with a cricket bat. "Stop ambushing her!"

She shook her head and rotated her forearm, wincing.

Pascal flipped down a magnifying lens from his helmet and examined the flat two-inch wide band of volantium bonded to the skin below her left wrist. "That's new," he said. He tapped one of the three metal circles embedded in her forearm.

"Ow!" Alex jerked her arm out of his grip.

A trembling voice, pitched with dread, wafted from outside *Angelus*. "This is Dr. Strim. Do you require assistance?"

Pascal snaked his head into the hallway and shouted, "Everything is wonderful! Go away!"

Phosphorescent lines rippled like water under Alex's skin, forming a glowing Stella Signum on the back of her left hand. The inventor grabbed her wrist. "What have you been playing with?" he mumbled, frowning.

"I didn't do anything. The armillam melted."

"I've never seen Stone Tech fuse to skin and bone," Pascal said.

He prodded one of the metal plugs with his hoof, and an ache rippled the length of her arm. "This looks permanent."

"You can't take it out?"

"Not without cutting your arm off, which I don't recommend."

"Is it dangerous?"

"Given the Professor's penchant for stealing treacherous artifacts without reading warning labels, almost certainly." He shrugged. "But anything is dangerous, if you look hard enough for the pointy end."

Alex blinked away pain in her wrist. She said, "Let's finish these repairs, then find Grandfather so I can yell at him."

CHAPTER 29
A STANDOFF

Contrivance. Of course Pascal's dynami trail led here.

Skhaar pounded *Revenge's* railing and glared at the industrial complex below. The Maelstrom should have wiped these lunatics off the map centuries ago, but even the fools at Home Office knew better than to defy one of the Fury King's "No Kill" orders. For the life of him, Skhaar could not fathom why the Chieftess deserved protection.

The radio operator cleared his throat. "Captain, the Children are contacting us."

A pompous male voice piped out from the speaker. "Unauthorized Maelstrom ship, this is Contrivance Tower. Declare your intentions."

Skhaar snatched the microphone from the ensign. "This is Skhaar the Annihilator, Hand of the Fury King and Butcher of Quietus Pass. My *intentions* are to go where I please, take what I wish, and bathe in the blood of my enemies."

The radio crackled with white noise.

"Sorry, did you say *bathe* in *blood*? That sounds unhygienic. Stand by, let me patch in a consultant."

The Annihilator looked at his radio operator, who shrugged.

Skhaar keyed the mic. "Do not bandy words with me, fleshling. The Maelstrom—"

"I'm back!" the speaker chirped. "And I've brought Doctor Ubluk, this month's Assistant Lifeguard in the Non-Swimmable Liquids Department. He has concerns about your blood bathing plan."

"Correct." A prim voice coughed, then continued, "A recent study of berserker warriors concluded that bathing in blood increases exposure to bludge gnomes—which, as we all know, contribute to accelerated hair loss. While these findings remain controversial, I cannot in good conscience recommend bathing—"

"*CEASE YOUR IMBECILIC RAMBLINGS!*" Skhaar howled. "*Release the vessel Angelus to me at once, or face my wrath!*"

"There's no call for rudeness," Doctor Ubluk said. "I was only concerned for your hair."

"*He doesn't have hair,*" Contrivance Tower whispered in the background.

"He doesn't? Sorry, what species is he? Bludge gnomes are also bothersome for large-nostrilled amphibians."

The Annihilator growled, "I shall take pleasure in discussing my appearance with you in person, shortly."

"Hold on," Contrivance Tower said, "just to be clear: are you threatening to attack?"

"Annihilators do not threaten," Skhaar rumbled. "We promise."

"Stand by, please." Wood creaked, wheels scraped, and papers shuffled through the speaker. "Ah, here it is. According to Protocol Binder Sixteen Beta's *Contingency Plan for Hostile Aerial Threats*, I must inform you we are currently targeting your vessel with fifty-eight anti-aircraft weapons—well, fifty-nine, if you count Dr. Wellid's experimental Pie-Flinger."

On Contrivance's roof, projectile turrets, ratcheting flamethrowers, an extendable boxing glove, and a robot hand holding an enormous pie swiveled toward *Revenge*.

"Protocol dictates you have five seconds to evacuate our airspace," Control said. "Five...Four -"

"Evasive maneuvers!" Skhaar shouted. "Charge the lightning cannons!"

Both engines roared, skidding *Revenge* sideways.

"Two...One..."

"*Stop the countdown!*" a female voice shrieked.

When no pastries fired, Skhaar signaled his helmsman to kill the throttle.

"This is the Chieftess," the radio snapped. "What manner of idiot am I speaking to?"

The radio operator bit his lip and twiddled knobs. Skhaar keyed the mic. "This is Skhaar the Annihilator, Hand of the Fury King and Butcher of—"

"I see. Another hammer doing a scalpel's job. And what business does a mindless tool have above my city?"

Skhaar ground his teeth, but let the insult pass. "You are harboring fugitives from the Maelstrom. Surrender *Angelus* and her crew, and I will spare your lives."

"*Surrender?* You greatly overestimate your ability to intimidate me."

"I am on a mission from the Fury King."

The radio hissed.

When the Chieftess spoke, her words came in the measured tones of someone clamping a lid on panic. "Neither of us wants a petty conflict to escalate, but I will not accede to your request. Crawl back to your master, Annihilator. The situation is in hand."

Skhaar narrowed his eyes. "So be it. We will depart your airspace following completion of a minor engine repair." The Annihilator tossed the mic to his radio operator. "Scan the city for compulsion transponders. Let us see what assets we have under the Chieftess' nose."

The ensign dialed in a warbling signal tone. "Only one contact, sir." He opened a binder and matched the audio signature to a dossier. "Home Office classifies this fleshling as *Notoriously Unreliable*."

Skhaar glanced at the photo and chuckled. "Oh, this is better than a frontal attack. Open a secondary channel and broadcast a compulsion code to the asset. Overload his pain receptors until he responds. I will speak with him before we leave."

CHAPTER 30

AMNESIA

CHAPTER 30
AMNESIA

Sunrise illuminated a puff of clouds on the blue horizon. By late morning, Ozzie could make out details in the lush vegetation carpeting Amnesia. The sand-crusted, hilly island was dominated by a single jagged spire and encircled by frothing reef. A turquoise interior lagoon promised serenity to anyone willing to brave bone-crushing surf. For a notorious island of death, Amnesia did a convincing imitation of a tropical paradise.

Ozzie massaged his metal hand. Fear had given way to fascination at the thin layer of volantium that flexed like normal skin. When Layla wasn't looking, he punched *Spark's* airframe and winced.

Note to self: all nerves are fully functional. So much for his vigilante career as the Disco Hand of Justice—as a general rule, superheroes don't choke back tears when they hit things. He slipped his lavaskink glove on.

Violent headwinds battered *Spark* as she circled the atoll in search of a landing site. Ozzie scoured the beach for any sign of his grandfather or the lost scientists, but no one had been thoughtful enough to write "*HELP*" in the sand.

Layla guided *Spark* away from the island and hovered outside the reef pass. "Conditions are too dangerous to land," she growled. "We must swim in."

He stared at the turbulent water. "The wind wasn't so bad. You can drop me on shore and come back after I look around."

The Sauracian untangled a mess of wires. "We encountered headwinds the entire time we circled Amnesia, which is impossible, unless the island itself is generating wind. Something is amiss, and we cannot risk damaging *Spark*—she is our only hope of escape."

Surf pounded the reef like a drum, amplifying Ozzie's dismay with chest-compressing thuds. "If you say so." He cringed as a gust thumped the envelope.

"You can wait on board if you wish."

"I want to help," he lied.

Layla clipped two wires together, activating a blinking red light. "Are you a competent swimmer?"

"Decent enough, in a pool."

To calm his nerves, Ozzie inventoried gear. Now that the Anemoi Blade had taken up residence in his arm, all he had left was a Labyrinthian glide chute, the Trovian slumberdart pipe, and a few balls of Panacea clay.

Layla tossed him a thick-walled, transparent pouch. "From the Seaweed lab in Contrivance," she said.

"Thanks." He dumped his treasures into the container, tightened the seal, and dropped it in his shoulder bag. Pascal claimed Labyrinthian parchment was waterproof, but there was no point taking any chances.

Spark idled twenty feet above the water while Layla lashed an antenna to the rigging.

"What is that for?" Ozzie said.

"Our escape plan." The Sauracian handed him a necklace that matched her own. "Once I activate sentinel mode, *Spark* will circle offshore until summoned." She pointed to a yellow button in the center of the pendant. "If something happens to me, press this to activate the homing beacon. When *Spark* arrives, fly her to Contrivance."

He nodded and looped the cord around his neck.

"See you on shore." Layla slapped a button on the console, then dove headfirst into the water with reptilian grace. Ozzie shook his head. Four-hundred pound creatures should make much larger splashes. He grabbed the rail as *Spark* lurched, turned away from the island, and climbed—Layla had activated sentinel mode before she jumped! Ozzie slid off the chassis and dangled from the fuse-lage. No point delaying the inevitable—every wasted second added height to his fall. He closed his eyes and let go.

Ozzie hit the water feet-first, bent at his waist. Every nerve in his torso and face shrieked, then went numb, vowing revenge. He floated on his back, moaning, as *Spark* disappeared into a bank of clouds. At least the water was warm—he probably had permanent nerve damage, but he wouldn't freeze to death.

A mountainous wave trundled past. He craned his neck and caught a glimpse of Layla slaloming between watery Himalayas with ease. Ozzie swam for shore, but his shirt and pants clung like leeches, draining his energy with every stroke. Panic slashed through a paper-thin wall of delusion—what was he thinking, jumping into surf fully clothed? A breaking wave bullied past Ozzie's lips, forcing a coughing spasm. He thrashed, gasping for air as the next set closed over his head.

Layla adjusted Ozzie on her shoulder and seethed, "You claimed to be a good swimmer!"

"I was trying to impress you with my courage." Ozzie retched bile onto the Sauracian's torso.

"You impressed me with your stupidity." She dropped him in ankle-deep water and stomped onto the beach like an amphibious assault vehicle.

Ozzie rejoiced in the sand that caked every inch of his body. He relaxed on a wonderfully solid rock that made no move to drown him. "Thanks, Layla. I owe you one." He would never forget the sight of the Sauracian thrashing through the heavy surf to rescue him.

"When we find the Professor, consider your debt paid. Until then, stay out of water."

BOOM

The ground trembled. Ozzie sat up and scanned the beach. Layla, absorbed in studying a wall of jungle foliage, gave no sign of noticing the sound.

"Did you feel that?" he said.

The Sauracian grunted and swept a clump of vines aside. "Wait here until I return." A gust convulsed the palm trees, masking her noisy passage through the undergrowth. Ten seconds later, a disconcerting quiet blanketed the island, underscored by high-pitched whistles of lonely insects.

What did a weltling sound like, anyway?

An eternity passed while Ozzie sheltered under a tree, weighing his options. Maybe Layla had found Grandfather and was bringing him back to the beach. Or maybe she had fallen victim to Wakeful Terrors and catapult ferns. Ozzie toyed with the homing beacon and watched the clouds for any sign of *Spark*.

Five more minutes.

He walked down the beach as far as he dared, but saw no signs of human presence. Aside from occasional subterranean rumbles and turbulent winds that shook the rainforest canopy, Amnesia was an unassuming island paradise. He cracked a coconut open with a rock, slumped under his tree, and waited five more minutes. Eleven times in a row.

Shadows lengthened.

She wasn't coming back.

Ozzie stood at the water's edge and stared at the darkening horizon. Layla's escape plan had more holes than a wheel of Swiss cheese. Assuming *Spark's* homing beacon worked and he survived the swim through the surf, he'd still need to pilot and navigate an airship by himself for two days. Then, on the slim chance he found Contrivance, he'd confess his cowardice to Pascal, Alex would punch him, and the Chieftess would feed everyone to a mutant hedgehog.[*1]

He wiped his brow and approached the wall of foliage that

219

protected the island's interior. Whispers of ancestral pride reminded him that his grandfather and parents lived for moments like this. A louder, more cynical voice pointed out his family tree's tendency to prune itself.

Ozzie counted to three, then plunged headlong into the mangrove, clearing a path with wide swipes of his arms until he noticed trails of blood where barbed leaves skittered across his skin. His plucky pace slowed to a cautious creep.

The rainforest gave Ozzie a crash course in jungle survival. First, it taught him to give a wide berth to pink flower buds, whose rubbery thorns delighted in separating scalps from skulls. Then he learned not to kick gelatinous blobs that house squadrons of parachuting jellyfish. As Ozzie stumbled through the brush, tingling hairs on the back of his neck warned he was being stalked.

"*Layla?*" His voice modulated with unbidden falsetto.

The jungle held its breath, then smirked and resumed thwarting Ozzie's advance.

A thin streak of mud masquerading as a walking path led him to a clearing. He stretched, reveling in the ability to widen his arms without provoking an attack from acid-spitting mushrooms. To his infinite relief, a worn footpath crossed the far side of the glade.

At last, evidence someone lived on Amnesia!

An island no one escaped.

His grin faded.

The path wound a sensible route through the rainforest, avoiding brightly colored plants and fording streams at narrow points. Ozzie knelt by a babbling creek and splashed water on his face while a school of piranha-jawed minnows circled, daring him to lean down for a drink. Did *everything* on this island want to hurt him?

He sped up to make the most of the dying light—spending a night alone in a jungle wasn't high on Ozzie's bucket list. He jogged around a blind corner, tripped over a leathery tail, and tumbled into undergrowth.

"Layla!" Ozzie scrambled to the Sauracian's head. She lay perpendicular to the path, eyes closed but breathing. He jostled her shoulder. "Are you okay?" She exhaled a long, hissing breath, but didn't respond. Ozzie slapped her cheek.

Ow.

"Please wake up," he pleaded, shaking life into his stinging fingertips. What could have knocked her out? He looked around but didn't see anything capable of felling a giant lizard. Maybe she was dehydrated. "I'll get water!" he shouted, in case she was paralyzed, hard of hearing, and awake.

Ozzie sprinted to the last stream he'd crossed. He could fold a bowl out of a leaf, then use his shirt to filter minnows from the water. He misjudged his speed on a corner and teetered into a patch of albino strawberries.

Thwop

White fruit expanded like airbags in a head-on collision, converting Ozzie's forward momentum into a canopy-scraping cartwheel that dropped him in the waiting mouth of a ten-foot-tall carnivorous plant.

Stiff hairs raked Ozzie's face as he slid headfirst down a fleshy bag that hung beneath the plant's mouth like a pelican's throat. His fingers clawed slimy skin but didn't slow his journey down the gullet. Desperate, he flexed his ankles, snagging the plant's lower lip with his toes. The upper jaw slammed down like a castle gate but couldn't dislodge Ozzie's sneakers. Blood rushed to his head as he breathed through his teeth to avoid drowning in goo. If he was careful, he might be able to—

The plant lurched sideways and slammed its trunk against the ground, flattening Ozzie, who yelled and punched the fibrous folds of the chin bag.

Whump

Another body slam. Ozzie groaned and cradled his head.

WHUMP

He curled into the fetal position.

WHUMP

He whimpered and lay still.

The plant straightened with a satisfied shiver.

Ozzie had learned to find silver linings in the storms of life:

when his parents disappeared into a trans-dimensional vortex, it led to years of therapy, but fostered his curiosity and sharpened his investigative instincts. Growing up with a name that attracted bullies like a magnet taught him to read people quickly, so he could escape before the shoving started.

But here, awash in a plant's digestive fluid, just fifty feet away from an unconscious friend he'd failed to help, Ozzie struggled to paint the scene any color but black. The faint glow filtering through the plant's skin faded, leaving him stewing in darkness until fumes and humid warmth lulled him to sleep.

---

1. Although Ozzie couldn't have known it, this scenario was surprisingly plausible, thanks to Dr. Plumbeet's successful Woodland Creature Inflation initiative.

222

CHAPTER 31
THE FORGOTTEN

Ozzie tumbled through the Divide, flailing his fire sword at a pack of Belua. Tentacles wrapped his legs, and a sixteen-eyed megasquid wrenched him into shadows beyond *Angelus'* halo. It opened its beak, then whistled a cheerful melody through buck teeth. Both combatants froze, perplexed. The monster tried to screech, but whistled a folk tune, much to its bewilderment. An earthquake shook the Divide, chasing the Belua into darkness. An aftershock jostled Ozzie awake.

He opened his eyes to find himself half-submerged in a puddle of foul-smelling stomach juice.

Perfect. He'd traded one nightmare for another.

He pressed his hand gently against the plant's digestive sac, glad for the morning light that silhouetted his fingers. Noise piqued his ears, and he sat up. A high-pitched, warbling melody drifted through the wall of his putrid prison. Someone was out there!

"*Help*," Ozzie whispered, as loudly as he dared. The plant shifted, preparing to wallop him into submission. He cocked his arm to punch the wall when a muffled voice said, "Look at your belly, luv! What delicacy have you caught me today?"

Fingers scratched cardboard. The plant slumped to the ground, drowning Ozzie in goo. Daylight streamed through the garage-door mouth, then a laughing head appeared. "And still alive, at that! You surrendered before she flattened yer gob. Wise man." Fingers scratched cardboard with greater intensity, and the plant vomited Ozzie unceremoniously into a puddle of mud.

Ozzie sprawled facedown on the path, savoring the sweet smell of grass and earth. He spat out a mouthful of odorous slime and addressed the makeshift sandals in front of his nose. "Thank you."

"You're most welcome, lad." A hand descended from the general direction of the friendly voice, so he took it. Skinny fingers led to a wiry arm, which became a shoulder, and shortly after that, a grinning, wrinkled face. Wispy tufts of ivory hair shot out like rockets from the man's scalp, in sharp contrast to his closely trimmed goatee. "You're a quick one for making friends with the locals," the old man said.

"I guess." Ozzie backed away from the carnivorous plant, which was giving him the botanical equivalent of a spiteful glare. "What *is* that thing?"

"A gluttonous maw—little more than a mouth, stomach, and a ferocious appetite, but quite a sophisticated hunter. She works in congress with heaveberries," the man pointed at the patch of white strawberries, "which, I'll wager, you also met."

Ozzie scraped pale residue from the soles of his shoes with a stick. "Why would anyone allow these things to grow next to a walking path?"

"I brought the path to them! Gluttonous maws are first-rate game traps." The old man scratched the plant's stalk, and it wiggled like a dog's tail. "My ravenous friend here provides a tasty meal once you drain the fluids." The maw flexed her stem, cracking powerful fibers for an appreciative audience.

Ozzie's rescuer was built like a pot-bellied asparagus. His undersized shorts and buttoned-up collared shirt were classic jungle explorer garb, but instead of khaki, his were sewn from brown fibrous material.

"I feel like we've met before," Ozzie said.

"I wouldn't know." The man's handshake was honest and on

224

the painful side of firm. "I'm Vicarious. Vicarious Quibble—or so I'm told."

Mercy's husband! "We're here to rescue you and my grandfather!"

"Are you? Delightful!" Vicarious clucked his tongue. "Unfortunately, I'm afraid my rescue will have to wait, as I've just taken you prisoner."

"What?"

Vicarious grimaced. "Only a formality, but Hugo insists we follow protocol with new arrivals." He held up a rope and shrugged apologetically. "Shall we?"

Ozzie looked at the jungle—if he ran, he'd only get eaten by something bigger than a gluttonous maw. He sighed and held his hands together. "My friend is unconscious on the path. She needs help."

The explorer tightened a knot around Ozzie's wrists. "Oh, I'm familiar with what ails *her*. Don't worry, the lads will sort it out." He strolled deeper into the jungle. "Off we go. Hugo gets prickly when he isn't the first to know things."

The journey was less a forced march than a guided tour of the world's most dangerous grocery store. Vicarious gave a running commentary, stopping every twenty feet to harvest fruit, inspect plant traps, and check homemade snares.

"Pink-striped blossoms taste like candy but accelerate hair growth alarmingly, as Furry McScruggins learned."

"Ah, Regret-Me-Probablys—marvelous anesthetic for medical procedures. Unfortunately, they come in two flavors: brown petals with pink stripes, which numb pain, and pink petals with brown stripes, which amplify nerve sensitivity tenfold." He scratched his head. *"Or possibly the other way around."*

"Every Monday, this orchid flowers at dawn and screams like a homesick brinemoose until lunchtime. It's called a workweeper. No one knows why, but they taste sweeter after Wednesday."

"Yellow blossoms are a dead giveaway for a distractaplant. At the first flash of yellow overhead, check behind you for strangling creepers."

By the time a herd of miniature six-legged warthogs ambushed them (*"Whizboars! They hunt in packs. Delicious, but deadly."*), two things had become abundantly clear:

1. He was incredibly lucky to survive his blind bash through the jungle yesterday.
2. Eating an Amnesian salad was taking your life in your hands.

Ozzie kicked the last whizboar into the undergrowth, and the herd retreated, squealing. "Mercy sent us to find you, Vicarious."

The explorer stopped whistling. "Sorry, who?"

"Your wife, Mercy Malicious—she sent us."

"I don't recall being married."

"She does."

"Mercy Malicious." Vicarious tasted the name like he was choosing a wedding cake. "A woman with a personality to match a moniker like that would be a handful."

"You don't know the half of it."

"Careful! That's my imaginary wife you're talking about."

"Sorry."

They walked in pensive silence.

"She carries a whip," Ozzie said, exhausting his limited store of facts about the old woman.

Vicarious doubled over in a coughing fit. He choked out, "Does she, now? Lad, did you come to our fair isle to play matchmaker?"

"I came to rescue *you*."

"And your grandfather."

"Yes—Professor Quidby Forsythe III. He's your friend. You invited him here."

"Did I? Never heard of him, but if you're looking for professors, you'll have your pick. Half the Forgotten stake claim to higher education, and the other half are lying."

"The Forgotten?"

"Our humble tribe of stranded souls. We forgot the world, and it returned the favor."

"There's an entire tribe?"

226

"Aye. Though none recollect our path here, we call Amnesia home. 'Tis a lovely island." The explorer laughed, "Or so we conjecture—no one remembers what anywhere else is like." They climbed a small rise, and Vicarious spread his arms. "Welcome to Oblivion, lad."

The postcard-worthy scene of fifteen thatched huts nestled against the island's pinnacle was a welcome relief from tiptoeing the knife edge of killer botany. Vicarious nodded at tribe mates as he led Ozzie across the village square. Handsewn, beige clothing was the popular fashion, with tattered white coats thrown in here and there. If Dr. Bloomvilt was in Amnesia, this is where he'd find her.

Vicarious stopped at a vegetable garden adjoining the largest hut in the village, where a gardener was smoothing furrowed earth with a trowel. The explorer untied Ozzie's hands and announced, "We have a new guest, courtesy of a gluttonous maw on the western slopes. He's traveling with the Sauracian."

The gardener rose, adopting a hunchbacked posture that kept his head level with Ozzie. His clothes were sewn from the tribe's ubiquitous brown cloth, but fashioned into a lumpy robe instead of shorts and a shirt. The overall effect was of a bald man being eaten by a potato. "It has been an age since a conscious visitor graced our shores." A respirator muffled the man's voice, but his emerald green eyes were bright and penetrating. "I am Hugo, Chief of the Forgotten. What is your name, boy?"

"Ozzie."

"And how did you come to Amnesia, Ozzie?" Hugo repeatedly flicked a string of prayer beads with his thumb, sprinkling their conversation with nerve-wracking *clicks*. Something about the unwavering intensity in the chief's stare warned Ozzie to lie.

"Our airship crashed offshore, and we swam in."

Hugo's left eyebrow raised, so Ozzie beefed up his alibi with a partial truth. "I'm looking for Professor Quidby Forsythe."

"Forsythe?" Prayer beads clicked. "No one by that name lives here. I'm sorry, but your journey was wasted."

"Vicarious mentioned that some of your villagers have experienced memory loss," Ozzie said.

Hugo smiled coldly. "True."

"Is it possible Professor Quidby is here and doesn't know it?"

The chief met his gaze with an impassive stare, then his eyes flicked to Ozzie's metal fingertips. "Anything is possible. On the subject of unlikelihoods, how did you come to travel in company with a Sauracian?"

"Layla is my pilot. Is she okay?"

"Aside from unavoidable side effects of her malady, she will recover." He jerked his wheeled oxygen cart out of its ruts with a grunt. "Let us go see your...pilot."

BOOOOOM

Hugo and Vicarious didn't react when the ground shook and a violent gust of wind flogged the village, whipping up a dust devil. Ozzie brushed dirt from his shoulders. "What was *that*?"

Vicarious gestured to the black pinnacle towering over the village. "That spire houses a blowhole we call Mother's Bane. When waves pound in Amnesia's womb, Mother breathes, and the island trembles. You get used to it."

The trio resumed their stroll through the village. Smoke from a bonfire in the main square left an acrid taste in Ozzie's mouth.

Hugo rasped, "Pardon my curiosity, but what is the function of your bionic enhancement?"

Ozzie glanced at his exposed metal fingertips and stammered, "This? Uh, industrial accident—hand got caught in a turbine. The Children of Contrivance built me a prosthetic. It's glitchy, but it lets me comb my hair, so...yeah." He slid his hands into his pockets. "What happened to Layla?"

"She fell victim to Amnesia's scourge: concussive beetles." Hugo pointed at a group of villagers emerging from the rainforest. "Observe Professor Ceeval's helmet—seven concussions taught her the importance of cranial protection." The academic heard her name and nodded, jostling a battle-scarred gourd strapped to her head.

228

Vicarious waved. "She spearheads an effort to purge concussive beetles from the island."

"How is that going?" Ozzie asked. Two more villagers trudged out of the jungle, toting an unconscious comrade on a stretcher. The front porter staggered into a tree, then dumped his wounded colleague in the mud.

"Poorly," the chief said.

Muffled shouting got louder as they approached a two-story hut. "Our storehouse is the only building in Oblivion with a doorway large enough to admit your companion," Hugo said, as Vicarious slid a barn door open. "Fortunately, we—" He stopped and frowned at the crowd occupying the octagonal hut.

"No, no, NO! You've got it all wrong. Lift with your back, that's the ticket!"

"Does anyone here have engineering expertise?"

"I sometimes dream about numbers."

"Having a fondness for numbers doesn't mean you know about load displacement or tensile breaking strength. Hey, listen to me—I sound like an engineer!"[1]

A calm female voice entered the fray. *"Why don't we lift as a group?"*

"Oh, great. Lucille is here to save the day."

Lucille defended herself, *"I'm not an expert,*[2] *but we're stronger when we work together."*

"We should use a catapult."[3]

"What if we dig a trench and lower the hut instead of lifting the beast?"[4]

Squabbling cooled to a simmer as Hugo's labored wheezing and squeaky oxygen cart parted the crowd. Someone had jury-rigged a system of bamboo poles, counterweights, and pulleys to lift Layla from her stretcher, then discovered Sauracians are heavier than they look. The wrencher's legs and tail were suspended three feet in the air while her head rested on the ground at an unnatural angle.

"Let the Sauracian be. She will wake soon enough," Hugo said. "Leave us, please."

Grumbles acknowledged the sensible solution, but no one

argued. Ozzie searched for Dr. Bloomvilt as villagers filed out the door. After the behavior he'd just witnessed, he was prepared to believe the entire tribe was from Contrivance.

Hugo raised Layla's eyelid, then felt her forehead. "She's the first Sauracian to set claw in Oblivion, but responding well to our standard treatment for concussive beetle attacks."

"What's the treatment?" Ozzie asked.

"Confirm she's breathing, then leave her alone."

"Oh."

"It's the wisest course of action. Our medical supplies are limited to what we can forage on the island, and more often than not, Amnesian medicine is worse than the ailment."

"I believe you—I was just expecting an herbal remedy from the petals of a night-blooming flower that grows on a treacherous peak guarded by disembowelling roses and razor-tongued wraithgoats."

"You're thinking of our toe fungus treatment." Hugo led Ozzie outside. "Your companion will not recover for hours. Why don't you accompany Vicarious to check game traps on the far side of the island? He can educate you on Amnesia's many eccentricities."

Vicarious cocked his head at the chief, then shrugged. "I'd be happy to. Come, lad."

Before they left, the explorer insisted on dousing Ozzie with buckets of fresh water to wash off the gluttonous maw's stomach juices.

"Believe me, you don't want to attract a slithergore."

Ozzie smiled, scrubbing crusty phlegm from his arms. "No, I don't." He pointed to his satchel, which had survived a near-drowning in digestive fluid. "What about my bag?"

Vicarious dunked the satchel in a trough, then hung it outside Layla's hut. "It'll be a little stiff, but good as new when it dries. Ready?"

They took a different path into the jungle, and Ozzie was careful to stay in the explorer's footprints. "It must be terrible not to remember anything," he said.

"I get memory flashes—blurry faces and laughter. I'm content to imagine they're from a happy past."

The air grew heavy, so Ozzie grasped for a new topic. "Hey, those are heaveberries."

Vicarious perked up. "Well spotted, lad!" He winked. "Want to do something truly ill-advised?"

"Uh...sure."

The explorer plucked a handful of albino berries from the center of the patch. "Gentle movements are key. Heaveberries are highly sensitive when planted, but once picked," he pinched a berry and reared his arm back, "they require significant force to trigger." Vicarious hurled the berry at the ground.

Thwop

A white explosion launched the explorer ten feet into the sky.

"Woooo!" As he fell, Vicarious threw another berry.

Thwop

A fruity trampoline inflated, throwing him even higher.

Thwop

The explorer bounced down the jungle path in the least stealthy manner possible.*[5]

Thwop

"Wooo-hooo!"

Thwop

"Marvelous!"

Thwop

"Haha!"

Thwop

"Wonderful!"

Vicarious twisted in the air, landing in the final heaveberry like it was a beanbag. He giggled and scrambled out of the deflating fruit. "Care for a bounce?"

Ozzie was already sprinting to the heaveberry patch. He reached down to pick a berry, when Vicarious' arm slapped across his chest. The explorer whispered, *"If you value your life, do not move."*

---

1. He wasn't. He was a rope salesman.

2. She was. Unbeknownst to herself, Lucille held three doctorates in Engineering.
3. Dr. Flingum, renowned psychophysicist and author of *Hurling Therapy*, had one string on his problem-solving banjo.
4. Per Dr. Proolev's timeless *Analysis of Improbable Likelihoods and Fanciful Realities*: "The Fourth Law of Relational Dynamics states that every group project includes someone whose sole contribution is to complicate a simple task."

    In this case, Folmis Bombo fell into the role, displaying the kind of logic that got him shipwrecked on Amnesia in the first place.
5. With the obvious exception of the Shrieking Axe Saunter, a mode of travel favored by the Clamorous Lumberjacks of the Scabbard Forest.

CHAPTER 32
AMNESIA'S SECRET

Ozzie froze. A steady crunching beside his left ear demanded investigation, so he turned his head *just* enough to see a creature lounging on his shoulder. The boxy insect was four inches long and neon blue, but its crowning glory was a snowplow forehead that screamed "Headbutt World Champion." The concussive beetle stared back at him, munching on a leaf.

Vicarious poked the insect with a stick.

"*Stop it!*" Ozzie hissed.

"Sometimes this works."

"*Sometimes?*"

The beetle blasted its wings for a split second and hopped onto the branch. Vicarious laid his stick down, then motioned Ozzie to back away. The insect cast a lazy eye over their departure but was too engrossed in lunch to care about two people tiptoeing like cat burglars across a pressure-sensitive floor.

The explorer dabbed his forehead with a handkerchief. "A near miss, there," he said.

"That thing was *huge*."

"It was just a drone. Throne guards and queens are twice his size and three times as spiteful." Vicarious crouched, scanning the surrounding rainforest. "A grainer nest must be nearby."

"Grainer?"

"Abbreviated from *migraine*." Vicarious crept to a hedge of thorny bushes, peeked over, then motioned for Ozzie to join him.

Hundreds of wings whirred like a fleet of hot rods revving at a stoplight. The nest was eight feet tall, six feet wide, and tapered like a volcano. Grainers swarmed every inch of the mound's muddy surface as a steady stream of drones zipped in and out of the crater entrance. A pungent aroma of damp earth permeated the small clearing.

"What does a queen look like?" Ozzie said.

"Bright green, mean enough to spit on your grave, and strong enough to crush your skull to powder. But don't worry, queens only leave a nest when their colony migrates." His eyes brightened. "Ah! A spot of luck—here's a juvenile drone." The explorer flattened his right hand across his forehead, then allowed an inch-long beetle to climb from a bush onto his left palm. "Grainers are docile until they take offense at an insult."

"An insult, like...?"

"Breathing. Whistling. Speaking. Not fleeing in terror. And they *hate* it when you do this." Vicarious flicked the beetle with his index finger.

Wings buzzed like an outraged chainsaw as the insect slammed into the explorer's forehead with unchecked fury.

Thud

Thud

Thud

Vicarious snatched the beetle from the air, threw it to the ground, and stomped it flat. An angry red welt swelled on the back of his hand. "Death by ten thousand headbutts is a heinous fate," he said.

"How does Professor Ceeval study them?"

"She waits until nightfall, when grainers sleep, drained from a day of pure evil. Their snoring is enough to drive a man mad." He stood. "Come, lad. Best leave while we can still walk."

Vicarious hopscotched across a creek, deftly kicking an eel who lunged at his ankle. "Apart from grainers, Amnesia is a wonderful home," he said.

Ozzie ran down a mental list of harmful wildlife he'd encountered, then nodded politely.

"Mind your toes!" Vicarious dumped a dozen piranha minnows out of a bamboo fish trap. Minuscule jaws mauled the grass. "These vindictive little creatures are called megajowls."

A megajowl chomped Ozzie's sneaker and glared at him. Do fish growl? That sounded like a growl. "What are you going to do with them?" he said, shaking his foot to an ascending snarl.

"Feast!" Vicarious scooped megajowls into his bag with a leaf. "They're delicious snacks."

Ozzie pointed in the general direction of the beach. "Does anyone go fishing in the lagoon?"

"Never more than once," the explorer said. "Vicious beasts ply these waters. Dr. Yoris started a daily habit of swimming around the island—for exercise, you know—and was ten minutes into his first lap when she ate him."

"She?"

"The Weltling." Vicarious shook his head. "A heartless brute. Professor Snoodle's ill-conceived water polo tournament suffered a similar fate—and don't get me started about Dr. Bobloon's Snorkel Safari Adventure. Trust me, stay out of the lagoon."

Ozzie struck out for a less depressing topic. "When did Hugo arrive on the island?"

"Many years ago. He founded Oblivion after a grainer attack left him the sole survivor of a disastrous expedition. The ordeal took a heavy toll on his health, but he eventually learned the ways of Amnesia and devoted his life to rescuing other grainer victims." The explorer smiled. "That's the legend, anyway—one downside to sharing an island with a tribe of scatterbrains is that details get fuzzy."

"But you still have flashes from your past."

"I'm a relatively recent arrival, with limited grainer damage. Those who've been here longest remember next to nothing of their former lives."

"You may not remember Mercy, but she misses you terribly," Ozzie said.

Crow's feet around Vicarious' eyes deepened at his wife's name, but he merely pursed his lips and kept walking.

By the time they reached Oblivion, lengthening shadows undercut the sweltering heat's tyranny. To Ozzie's delight, Layla was standing in the center of the storehouse, staring blankly at her medallion.

"Layla!" He raced across the room and wrapped the Sauracian in a full-bodied hug. "I'm so glad you're awake. You won't believe where we are. A tribe—an entire tribe!—of lost explorers and scientists live in Amnesia." When the wrencher didn't respond, he released her. "Layla?" Her eyes were dull and unfocused.

Vicarious rested a hand on Ozzie's shoulder. "Give her time, lad. I'll leave you to get reacquainted." The explorer padded out of the room.

Layla rubbed a purple bruise on her forehead, her movements bewildered and lethargic.

He said, "Layla, it's Ozzie. You saved me from drowning, then left me on the beach." He lowered his voice. "We need to get out of here and search the village for the Professor. Remember the Professor?"

The Sauracian growled a note of menace.

"She does not." Hugo's declaration was matter-of-fact, like a jaded coroner pronouncing a time of death. Ozzie spun around. The chief was perched on a stool, nestled in a shadowy corner, with Ozzie's satchel at his feet. Hugo raised a marble-sized ball. "Panacea clay—that's actually quite clever." He removed a jeweler's loupe from his eye. "And incredibly rare. Did your grandfather give them to you?"

Ozzie's tongue tripped in its rush to lie. "I-I don't know what you're talking about." It was a weak bluff, but his heart was pounding so loud he couldn't think. How did Hugo know he was the Professor's grandson?

"Professor Quidby and I share a passion for Stone Lore," Hugo said. "But even if I hadn't met your grandfather, I would know him

236

—would-be heroes and self-righteous world-enders are two sides of the same klunkling. Quidby's disappearance was inevitable." He tilted his head at Layla. "Meddlers must be removed from the equation."

Ugly suspicion chilled Ozzie's spine. "What did you do to her?"

Hugo snorted. "I merely guided her rehabilitation." He convulsed in a coughing fit, and added, "Amnesia's ministrations, however, are beyond my control." The bald man wheeled his oxygen tank across the room and stopped in the doorway. His fingers flicked through prayer beads as he stared at Ozzie. With a final *click*, he reached a decision. "Layla, won't you join us for a climb?"

The trio drew curious stares as they trudged through the village, but the stony look on Hugo's face kept spectators at a distance. The trail up Mother's Bane started behind the chief's hut, then ascended the pinnacle in a gentle spiral. Overgrown tree roots battered Hugo's oxygen cart as Layla lurched along in an unresponsive daze. Hundreds of feet below, the village bonfire glowed like a precious gem in the twilight.

Ozzie stalled for time. It was no use denying he was a Forsythe, since Hugo clearly knew more than he was letting on. "How do you know my grandfather?"

"We are rivals, of a sort." Hugo yanked his cart over a snarl of vexing roots with a grunt.

Ozzie took a leap. "So *that's* how you ended up on Amnesia. You were hunting for the Borealis Stones."

The chief chuckled. "Quite the opposite. My superiors assigned me here." A breath of wind whisked the baffling statement away, as if it had never happened. "Keep climbing, boy, your answers await."

Conversation ceased while they navigated a blustery network of wind tunnels that riddled the top of the spire. On the summit, knifelike ridges sliced Ozzie's palms as blasts of salty air tried to blow him off the pinnacle. The blowhole was fifty feet wide—a black portal to an invisible storm raging in the island's belly. Tornadoes of mist whipped Ozzie's hair and stung his eyes.

Hugo shouted over the thundering abyss, "Did Vicarious show you the concussive beetles? The *grainers*?" When Ozzie nodded, the chief smiled. "Shall I tell you a secret, Ozzie? Concussive beetles, while a nuisance, are merely a convenient deception."

A roar shook the spire. Hugo threw his arms wide as a tremendous gust flattened his robe against his back. Trees lining the summit thrashed, and the pinnacle became the epicenter of a circle of turbulence that rippled through the island. A cloud of white powder erupted wherever the wind convulsed the canopy, dusting the island with a fine, ivory mist.

"Amnesia's greatest gift!" Hugo cried. "Leethee pollen!"

The gust dwindled, declaring a fragile ceasefire as water churned in the dark pit.

"With every breath, Mother's Bane circulates leethee pollen across the island!" Hugo crowed. When Ozzie didn't react, he frowned. "Small white orchids, with orange lines on the petals? You didn't see *any*? They grow everywhere." He slapped his forehead. "No wonder you fell prey to a gluttonous maw. No matter—what's *important* is that leethee pollen, while otherwise inoffensive, is a potent memory suppressant."

Ozzie glanced at Layla, who was watching Hugo with a disinterested stare.

"What a pleasure to get that off my chest," the chief said. "Opportunities for honest dialogue are so rare."

If Hugo was openly divulging secrets, it didn't bode well for Ozzie's immediate future. He had to get Layla off the island *now*. There was too much wind up here for *Spark* to land, but if they could get to the beach, he'd figure something out. Ozzie inched toward the trailhead. "Why are you lying to your tribe mates about the grainers?"

Hugo sneered. "My *tribe mates* are the reason I'm here. A steady influx of foolhardy explorers and scientists succumb to Amnesia's defenses, but my primary directive is to detain Stone hunters."

Primary directive? *Detain?*

"This island is a prison!" Ozzie said.

"Of the most humane sort—one where inmates do not suffer

knowledge of their captivity." His voice took on a mocking tone, "After all, Amnesia is their home."

"These prisoners are hollow shells. You're stealing their past!" Ozzie grabbed Layla's arm. "Let's go." The Sauracian stared at him vacantly. He might as well have begged a statue to carry him down the trail.

"Would you prefer I take their lives?" Hugo asked. "When the Chieftess informed me you were coming, I hoped you might join my merry, compliant tribe—Sir Quidby's grandson would make a fine trophy. Alas, like most Urtlings, you proved immune to leethee pollen. Pity." Hugo unsheathed a blade concealed in the handle of his oxygen cart and targeted Ozzie's chest.

"The Chieftess sent us here to rescue her lost Children," Ozzie said. "She's going to come looking for us."

"She sent you because we ordered her to. The Stones must be protected."

A chill gripped Ozzie's heart. "You're with the Noctem. When are you going to realize my family isn't trying to hurt anyone? Just leave us alone."

Hugo snarled, "Leave *you* alone? We protect Terravenum from people who would doom it—people like the *indomitable* Professor Quidby and his self-aggrandizing ilk. People like *you*." He limped forward and pressed the tip of his sword to Ozzie's sternum. "I imagine you understand the burden of a surname better than most, boy. I labored under mine—*Deathfist*—through a tortuous youth." He grinned. "I know—Hugo Deathfist is a dreadful name, but since you met my brother Bartholomew, you can appreciate its etymology." Hugo groaned and straightened to his full height, vertebrae cracking like popcorn in a microwave. He opened his left hand, splaying oversized, malnourished fingers.

Ozzie's jaw dropped. From his sturdy, skeletal frame to his wide-set facial features, Hugo was a vitamin-starved, shriveled doppelgänger for Brother Deathfist, the Archive's Head Librarian. Confusion and anger swirled in Ozzie's mind. "What did you do to my grandfather?"

"Nothing, boy. The Professor never set foot on Amnesia."

Hugo's eyes twinkled as he shrunk to his customary crouch. "How could he? He's my brother's permanent guest at the Archive."

Ozzie teetered on the rim of the blowhole, buffeted by bafflement and outrage. *Of course* the Booksworn were Noctem! How better to protect the Stones than to monitor the search effort firsthand, ready to eliminate successful hunters? A spike of anger clenched his fists. *How close had he been to his grandfather at the Archive?*

"I'm pleased you didn't give the Professor's journal to Bartholomew," Hugo said. "If you had, you would be dead, and I would have been denied the pleasure of this conversation." He cracked his neck. "Confession nourishes the soul."

Ozzie steadied his footing as Mother's Bane trembled. When in doubt, stall. He said, "You'll never get away with this," and winced. The hackneyed cliché was cringeworthy, but bought him a few more seconds.

"*Never get away with this?*" Hugo chuckled. "That old nugget exists on Urt too? Now I'm embarrassed *for* you—besides which, I rather think I already *got* away with it." He nudged Ozzie toward the blowhole. "One lesser-known quirk of leethee pollen is how its victims are highly suggestible, provided you address them in the proper voice. Fortunately, I've had years to refine my technique. Allow me to demonstrate." Hugo stepped back, sword leveled at Ozzie's throat. He lowered the pitch of his voice, hardened his tone, and said, "Layla, dispose of our guest in Mother's Bane."

The Sauracian blinked, seized Ozzie's arms above his elbows, and lifted. Her eyes stared through him, uncomprehending, as he dangled over the blowhole.

"Don't do this, Layla," Ozzie said.

Her breath came shallow and strained.

"Please!"

She released Ozzie into gravity's embrace.

CHAPTER 33
MOTHER'S BANE

Spray pelted Ozzie's face as he fumbled the Labyrinthian parchment out of his trouser pocket. Hours of practice paid off when his thumbs cracked the square open without hesitation.

Thwip-thwip-thwip-thwip-thwip

An accordion of translucent cubes cascaded out, slowing Ozzie's descent, but taxing his grip to its limit. His left toe snagged a shelf as the shaft widened into a gaping, midnight-black cavern. The blowhole burped, ripping the chute from his grasp. He slid down the wall, pumice grating his skin, until a desperate lunge rewarded his fingers with a tiny ledge. An invisible cauldron of rage swished and hissed below as his precarious handhold grew slipperier by the second. He bicycled his legs, deeply regretting brushing off Alex's invitations to go rock climbing. Amnesia inhaled, transforming the pinnacle into a wind tunnel. Ozzie kicked his feet up, but couldn't find a foothold. When his legs swung back, his fingers slipped, dropping him face down into the void.

Mother's Bane exhaled.

A firehose of spray half-drowned Ozzie, punching him upward on a fist of wind, as if he were skydiving in reverse. He covered his head and slammed into the shaft wall, outcroppings shredding his skin and clothes like a cheese grater. He snagged a ledge, and with a desperate heave, torqued his body out of the wind column. Mercifully, the shelf was deep enough to allow him to curl into a ball until the gust died.

Ozzie shivered through two more wind cycles without attempting to rise, ears popping with the pinnacle's tantrums. Whenever he closed his eyes, he saw Layla staring down at him. The fact she wasn't in control of her actions didn't ease the sting of her betrayal. His adrenaline receded, opening the door to a flood of pain and an ocean of despair. He tore a strip of material from his shirt to bandage a gash on his left forearm, then sat upright, dangling his legs over the edge.

If Hugo was telling the truth, Grandfather was imprisoned in a fortress hidden inside a volcano guarded by belligerent fanatics famous for bearing grudges.*[1]

Not ideal. At least Alex would—

Ozzie's train of thought derailed.

Alex.

If the Chieftess was working for the Noctem, what did she have planned for his sister and Pascal?

He had to get back to Contrivance.

The Stella Signum flared, casting a blue glow on his wrist. Ozzie removed his lavaskink glove and touched the metal plug closest to his elbow. Heat blossomed in bone as a neon line glided beneath his skin to outline all three circles. Maybe he could manifest a tool that would help him climb out of here. *Imagination* plus emotion, right? In the belly of Mother's Bane, any straw was worth grasping.

Ozzie closed his eyes and imagined a grappling hook with a rope. After a minute, he mentally lit the rope on fire, just in case.

Nothing.

His imagination meandered through a range of climbing gadgets: flaming chalk bags, a flaming helmet, and a flaming harness. Nothing manifested.

Ozzie's ears popped. A big blow was coming.

He sheltered in the fetal position a split second before a blast roared up the pinnacle. As he pressed against the wall, waiting for the tempest to die, his thoughts wandered to Brother Deathfist. Heat surged through his forearm, prickling his skin.

Orange fire streamed from Ozzie's metal palm, forming a blade that skimmed his face. He gasped, and thrust his arm over the abyss, where spray hissed on contact with the flames. Ozzie clenched his fist, and a hilt solidified in his grip.

Victory and Glory!

The battle cry echoed in Ozzie's head, like his conscience had overdosed on caffeine and was goading him into battle. He opened his palm, and the sword flickered, then vanished.

Mother's Bane gargled, a dragon biding her time to feast on a knight lodged in her throat. Ozzie's anger drained, taking its energy boost with it. He ran his fingers over the pumice, wincing as the jagged surface raked his skin. If a grappling hook wasn't an option, he might be able to carve handholds with the sword. He closed his eyes and pictured the Anemoi Blade but couldn't muster any emotion beyond fatigue. Hunger didn't help—at this point, he was more likely to manifest a pizza than a weapon. A scrap of white paper wedged in a crevice caught Ozzie's eye. He plucked it off the wall and examined it under the Stella Signum's glow.

A shredded fragment of Labyrinthian parchment.

Air pressure shifted, forecasting another blow. Ozzie flopped on his side as Mother's Bane launched a geyser of water to the moon, plucking the parchment from his grip. He slid his hand into the air stream, then pulled back when the updraft threatened to knock him from his perch.

A desperate idea formed.

After two sopping wet hours of counting intervals, a pattern emerged. As powerful as the small waves were, for his plan, he needed one of the monsters that bashed the island every twenty minutes. The sequence was consistent: popping ears gave him a half-second warning before a mega wave pounded the rocks below, then a gust thundered up the pinnacle three seconds later. On the biggest waves, the blow lasted anywhere from nine to thirteen seconds.

He flexed his ankles to soothe his cramping calves. The thought

243

of Alex suffering at the hands of the Chieftess kept him focused, but it was only a matter of time before he fell asleep or lost his balance due to exhaustion. It was now or never.

Ten minutes later, high-octane suction of an incoming tsunami granted his wish, as Mother's Bane filled her lungs to bellow with rage. Ozzie scrunched his legs beneath him and dug his fingernails into rock. His Stella Signum couldn't illuminate the opposite wall of the shaft, so hopefully, it was at least twenty feet away.

BOOOOOM

One…Two…

Tendrils of wind reversed direction and built with mounting fury.

Three…

He closed his eyes as a monsoon whipped his face.

Four…

Ozzie gulped a breath, threw his arms forward, and leapt.

All hope of a graceful swan dive evaporated the instant his toes left rock. Panic seized Ozzie's limbs, turning his leap of faith into a windmilling tumble of doubt. Air current flipped him over, thrusting him skyward like an upended turtle strapped to the nosecone of a Saturn V rocket. He arched his back, desperate to stay in the center of the pinnacle as jet black walls streaked past. Ozzie's foot caught an outcropping, sending him spinning out of control. Mist crowded his vision as terror strangled his lungs.

Mother's Bane sneezed.

Ozzie's flight was invisible against the night sky, but anyone out for an evening stroll heard the moment his scream equalized his tortured ear canals.

"*AAAAAAAHHHHooohhhhhhhhhhh-oooooooooaaaaa-AAAAAAAAAAAAAHHH!*"

Peace washed over Ozzie as Amnesia's lagoon glistened in the moonlight. Time slowed. Life as a cannonball was blissfully uncomplicated—up here, with no grandfathers to rescue or villains to flee, his role was simply to hurtle through the air and figure out the landing later.

Tranquility abandoned Ozzie when he struck the first palm tree.

"Ow!"

He ricocheted through a grove of palms like a pinball. When he finally hit the mud, the pinnacle's steep slope kept him rolling while every tree on the island took a swing at him. Elastic vines snared his legs, slowing his descent until he lurched to a stop in a thicket of shrubs. Ozzie tested his limbs and groaned—miraculously, nothing was broken, although it was going to be a long time before he ate coconut again.

Long-stemmed flowers bent toward him, petals folding to form tiny mouths. One by one, they latched onto exposed skin.

"Hey!" Ozzie plucked a flower off his arm, eliciting a *pop* of failed suction and a trickle of blood where the plant pierced his skin. He swiped the other bloodsuckers away, then pushed to his feet. What was this island's *problem*?

The sound of crashing surf led him to a beach. Mother's Bane had spat him to the deserted side of Amnesia, away from Oblivion. Ozzie clutched *Spark's* homing beacon as tremors from the blowhole eroded sand around his feet. His thumb hovered over the button, but he couldn't shake the memory of Hugo's confession. Grandfather's motley squad of eccentric friends had honed Ozzie's ability to recognize a man wobbling on the tightrope of sanity—but while Professor Baxter's loose grip on reality manifested as a charming habit of wearing conquistador armor to the grocery store,*[2] Hugo was cracking under the strain of living a lie.

How far would the Noctem go to protect the Stones? They had already kidnapped and imprisoned Grandfather, dispatched assassins to St. Jude's, thrown him into a blowhole, and brainwashed Layla. For a secret society, they were really sticking their necks out. Ozzie let the medallion fall to his chest.

Enough was enough.

He started the long climb to the base of Mother's Bane. If history was any indication, this rescue mission wouldn't end well, but he had to try. That's what Forsythes do.

Ozzie wished he'd paid more attention to Vicarious' lecture on Amnesian ecology. He had a vague awareness the jungle was bursting with edible things, and complete certainty he was one of them. Moonlight painted shadowy teeth on every plant around him, so he resorted to the Golden Rule of Exploration: *When in doubt, touch nothing.*[*3]

A glimmer of white triggered warning bells. Ozzie shifted his foot to avoid the heaveberry patch, lost his balance, and pitched forward, landing next to the stout trunk of a gluttonous maw. The plant leaned down and opened its mouth, drenching him in rancid digestive juices. With sloth-like speed, he yanked the homing beacon from his neck, then tossed it into the heaveberries.

Thwop

A swollen berry vaulted the medallion into the air. The gluttonous maw swiveled to track the necklace's flight, then devoured it with a brutal chomp. Ozzie scrambled to get out of striking range, and the maw lunged, slamming into the ground between his outstretched legs. He crawled to safety as the plant pummeled the dirt with a barrage of crushing blows.

Ozzie touched the rising welt on his neck and fought back tears —that necklace had been his best hope of getting back to Alex. Theoretically, he could retrieve the homing beacon by letting the maw swallow him, but if he got trapped inside the digestive sac, he'd die—or worse, get captured by the Forgotten. It was too risky.

Darkness and fear heightened Ozzie's senses. A faint trickling sound led him through a gauntlet of scratchy undergrowth to a gurgling stream. He cupped his hands to scoop a drink, then froze as silver flashed beneath the surface. Ozzie grabbed a tree trunk and dipped his toe in the water, provoking an eruption of snapping teeth. He lifted his leg and sighed at a school of squirming minnows trying to tear his shoe to pieces.

Megajowls.

A dangled sneaker proved the perfect bait for murder guppies. Within five seconds of fishing, fifty snarling megajowls embedded their teeth in Ozzie's shoe. When he set the sneaker on the ground, the fish slapped their tails in a coordinated effort to hop their nemesis into the water, to savage it properly.

When his other shoe emerged from the stream unscathed, Ozzie risked a drink. Cool, sweet water sharpened his thoughts and

246

soothed his flayed skin. He gorged himself, then nudged his sacrificial sneaker with a stick, prompting growls as the shoe resumed its pilgrimage. Two minutes later, it stopped bouncing. He gave it another thirty seconds, then pried the lifeless megajowls off and arranged them in a pile. Even if Vicarious was right, and they *were* appetizing, their jutting jaws and scalpel teeth offered no clues how to safely eat them. Plus, knowing Amnesia, there had to be venom glands in there somewhere.

Ozzie's stomach, hungry beyond concern about consequences, rumbled impatiently. He grimaced and sunk his teeth delicately into a megajowl's belly. Paper-thin skin parted, and tangy liquid squirted onto his tongue. Ozzie choked on laughter—the thimble-sized killing machine tasted like sour candy!

Venom glands or not, megajowls were a delicious, nourishing snack. He nibbled each fish to its bones, not wasting a morsel of flesh. Each bite brought a trickle of energy that brightened his mood. Ozzie had no allies, *Spark's* homing beacon was being digested by a gluttonous maw, and the list of people he had to rescue was growing by the minute. But at least he wasn't hungry.

All things considered, a better-than-average day in Terravenum.

Ozzie's Stella Signum flared, illuminating a swath of white blossoms that dotted the overhead canopy like ornaments on a Christmas tree. No wonder leethee orchids spread pollen across the island—they were *everywhere*. He sucked peppery fluid from the last megajowls and watched the flowers spew ghostly particles as pieces of a bold plan clicked into place.

It took four attempts to find a tree that didn't want to strangle him. When Ozzie reached the canopy, he pulled his shirt collar over his nose, then plucked a leethee orchid from the tree. He unfolded its feathery petals and shook translucent dust into his palm. Holding his breath, he funneled leethee pollen into his pants pocket, then repeated the procedure with another thirty flowers. He sealed the stash with a folded leaf, then slid to the ground, careful not to spill his precious cargo.

On to Step Two of his doomed Two-Step Plan. Pascal would be proud.

Ozzie circled the pinnacle until he heard the distinctive pulsing buzz he was searching for. The grainer nest was larger than the one he'd stumbled upon with Vicarious. From the sound of it, hundreds of concussive beetles were snoring underground, but none detected his presence. He tiptoed to the nest and gently scooped dirt from the side of the volcano. Clumps of wet sand disintegrated, but the mound held its shape.

A labyrinth of tunnels and chambers brimmed with snoring, unblinking beetles. Progress was slow—each handful of dirt produced another drone to relocate with the care of a bomb disposal technician. He probed with his left hand—the last thing he needed was to start a war by accidentally manifesting the Anemoi Blade inside the nest.

Spiky weights pressed on his palm, so he cautiously drew his arm out of the tunnel. Vicarious hadn't been kidding when he said throne guards were twice as large as drones. The red beetle squeezed its pinchers absentmindedly and teetered beneath a bulletproof shell. To Ozzie's horror, when he set the throne guard down, it shuffled in a circle, disoriented by new surroundings. The beetle spread razor blade wings, then stowed them when its hind legs bumped into a drone. Reassured by its nest-mate's presence, the throne guard settled into a shallow slumber.

Ozzie reached into the nest again. How many throne guards would a queen have? If one woke up, things were going to go bad *really* fast. His fingers brushed a smooth surface. He grunted and pushed deeper into the side of the mound, ignoring a minor cave-in and a susurrus of wings. Six claws stepped into his hand.

There was no mistaking a grainer queen—incandescent green and ten inches long, she exuded regal power. Hairline cracks in her forehead warned of a fierce personality and a violent past. Everything about this insect screamed *DO NOT DISTURB*.

Ozzie set out for Oblivion, the queen snoring in his hands, a volcano waiting to erupt.

This was going to end badly.

1. The prison equivalent of a turducken (a chicken cooked in a duck cooked in a turkey)—which is, of course, the avian equivalent of bloporcudiles (a baby crocodile cooked in a porcupine cooked in a blowfish, commonly known as "the world's most dangerous delicacy", made famous by the Pippichuk Peril Chefs of Lower Solemnia).

2. Rumor had it that in Professor Baxter's younger years, the explorer ran afoul of a pack of rabid armadillos in the deep Amazonian jungle. They hunted him for three days until he escaped by swinging across a river gorge on a vine that turned out to be a boa constrictor.

   Whether the story was true or not, there was no mistaking Baxter's panic in the presence of round fruit and French baguettes. After multiple incidents, he was blacklisted by the Guild of Borderless Explorers and banned for life from the Cartographer's Bowling League.

3. Especially not a spider-webbed lever at the end of a corridor with wall carvings whose eyes are exactly the right height and diameter to fling arrows.

   The Silver Rule of Exploration ("*When all else fails, touch everything*") applies to situations where booby traps (spiked walls, rolling balls, skeleton warriors, etc.) are already in motion and you need to escape.

   Many promising careers end by mixing the two rules up.

CHAPTER 34
GRAINERS & THE LAIR

Ozzie raced the rising sun around Oblivion's perimeter, praying the crackling bonfire in the village square masked his twig-snapping footsteps. He crept past the storehouse, relieved to hear labored snoring through the open doorway—at least Layla had returned from the pinnacle safely. He ducked into the rainforest and forged a path to Hugo's hut, timing his advances with the blowhole's tree-shaking outbursts. The chief's door swung open at a touch.

He slinked into the hut, grainer queen nestled in the crook of his arm. Spartan furnishings—a desk, dresser, bed, and hand-cranked air compressor—bolstered Hugo's image as a simple man living a blameless life. An oxygen tank fed air through a canopy of fine white mesh that shrouded the chief's bed, protecting him from insects. Steady wheezing behind the curtain betrayed a man at peace with his conscience.

Ozzie's heart leapt at the sight of his treasures arranged neatly on the desk. He pocketed the velvet bag of Panacea clay and the Trovian blowdart pipe, being mindful not to rouse the queen, who was growing restless in the dawn light. The beetle flexed her front limbs and chittered. Ozzie jammed her wings against her shell, but it was too late—Queen Skull Crusher might as well have blasted a bugle in Hugo's ear.

"You!" The chief rose from the bed like a vengeful swamp monster, a blanket of mesh draped over his shoulders. He kicked his oxygen cart, sending it skittering across the floor. Ozzie side-stepped the bottle, but the air hose tangled his feet. He threw his arms up for balance, jostling the grainer. Her Highness thrashed her legs, seeking a culprit to punish for her present indignity.

Hugo writhed out of the mesh and dove headlong from his bed, catching Ozzie's left ankle in a bony, hydraulic grip. Ozzie screamed and flung the grainer queen at Hugo's head. The enraged monarch funneled her wrath into a ferocious headbutt deserving of capital letters.

CLONK

Hugo clutched his forehead and whimpered.

The queen battered her wings against her shell, generating a shrill whine that set Ozzie's teeth on edge. He tore the respirator from Hugo's face, then stumbled out the door.

"No!" The bald man's voice quavered, feeble without a mask.

Ozzie fumbled in his pocket. He jammed handfuls of leethee pollen into the respirator, then dropped it beside the doorway.

The queen's song permeated Oblivion like an air-raid siren during the London Blitz. Worried faces poked out of doorways, scanning the horizon and scrabbling with chin straps. Layla appeared in the storehouse, caught sight of Ozzie, and charged across the village square.

"Infantile wretch!" Hugo snarled, leaning against the threshold of his hut, hand covering his mouth. He snatched his respirator up, snapped it into place, and sucked a deep breath.

A circle of alarmed villagers blocked Ozzie's escape.

"What is that horrendous noise?" Vicarious asked.

"Grainer distress call," said a man strapping a watermelon to his head. "I've never heard one this loud before."

Ozzie craned his neck and spotted Layla, who was halfway across the square. He said, "There's a grainer queen in Hugo's hut!" Unfortunately, the revelation didn't sow seeds of hysteria—as flustered as the villagers were, they were scientists and explorers first.

"Did he say *queen*?"

"Queens don't leave the nest!"

"Why does Hugo keep a nest in his hut?"

A bony hand shoved Ozzie to the ground. The crowd fell silent, staring at their chief.

"Who do you think you are, *child*?" Hugo sneered.

Vicarious frowned. "What's going on here?"

Hugo fumbled with the handle of his oxygen tank, unsheathing his sword on the third try. "Surviving Mother's Bane was a neat... um," he shook his head, "...a neat, uh...*trick*." A perplexed scowl crossed his face, then he rallied, "Though I daresay you won't manage to...uh..." Hugo's brow furrowed as he checked the connectors on his breathing apparatus. He unclipped his respirator and traced its interior with a finger, producing a clump of leethee pollen. "*What have you done?*" he hissed. Madness danced in his eyes. "What...have you..." He looked up and focused on Layla, who was towering at the back of the circle. "Layla! Kill the boy!"

Vicarious stepped in front of Ozzie and placed a hand on the reptile's chest. "Hold, lass. This is lunacy." Layla shunted the explorer aside with a flick of her wrist and advanced.

A piercing hum from the jungle answered the queen's distress call. Villagers crouched, prepared to run in any direction. The pitch deepened into a moaning buzz. A line of convulsing vegetation rocketed toward the village like a cruise missile. Professor Ceeval sprinted out of the undergrowth, screaming, "Incoming colony! Take cover!"

A cloud of grainers burst through the rainforest wall. Long-term residents of Amnesia flopped to the ground, shielding their faces. Recent arrivals swatted the air, drawing clouds of attackers.

"Play dead!" Vicarious yelled. Ozzie collapsed and covered his head.

Beetles ricocheted off Layla's leathery hide as she shuffled forward. Sensing a worthy adversary, the colony banded together, strafing the Sauracian with an intensifying hailstorm of headbutts. Ozzie wriggled the Trovian blowpipe out of his pocket, flinching as grainers zipped past to join the assault on Layla. He untied the velvet pouch and rolled four balls of Panacea clay into his palm.

The Sauracian bellowed as a squadron of throne guards peppered her like artillery rounds.

Ozzie's shaky fingers struggled to load the blowdart gun. A tremor from Mother's Bane spilled the clay balls on the ground. Layla took an earth-quaking step as Ozzie slapped a round pellet into the tube. He sighted down the pipe.

Three...

A juvenile grainer bounced off his forearm, then sputtered away in search of more glorious conquests.

Two...

He dropped the arm covering his forehead, aiming the blowgun with both hands.

One...

Layla batted a throne guard out of her face, then threw her head back and roared defiance.

Now.

All his wasteful target practice paid off—the Panacea clay shot into Layla's mouth and disintegrated in the back of her throat with a puff of yellow dust.

"Yes!" Ozzie pumped his fist.

The Sauracian coughed, jerked her head, then howled. Ozzie clapped his hands over his ears and curled into a ball. Now that he thought about it, he wasn't certain how Panacea clay worked. What if he had poisoned Layla with too much?

Grainers took advantage of the Sauracian's distraction to rally a counterattack. A black cloud wheeled in a broad circle, then pummeled Layla's forehead with the full force of the colony. Hundreds of impacts cracked like machine gun fire above the incessant buzzing of wings. The Sauracian dropped to her knees, then folded, toppling like a redwood—right onto Ozzie.

"Wake up, lad!"

A stinging cheek slap demanded retribution. "I'm awake," he groused. "Stop hitting me."

Vicarious Quibble's grin filled the world.

Ozzie winced. "What happened?"

"A reptilian avalanche. Took five of us to roll your friend off after the grainers left. Could have done it sooner, but we had to stop Dr. Flingum from putting her in a catapult."

"Thanks," Ozzie said. Layla was next to him, on her back, and snoring. "How is she?"

Vicarious shook his head. "Your friend took the full brunt of the colony's attack—she'll be lucky to walk in a straight line, let alone remember her name."

A surge of adrenaline jolted Ozzie upright. Where was Hugo? He scanned the village square, but the warden had vanished. Layla snorted. Her breathing sounded like a bus grinding gears.

"Have you seen Hugo?" he said.

"Not since he ordered the lizard to kill you." Vicarious frowned. "Why did he do that?"

"There's a lot I need to tell you, but this isn't the best time." Ozzie's head swiveled, searching for any sign of the chief. Two vegetable-armored villagers passed, dragging a comrade on a stretcher. Moaned variations of *"Does my skull look dented to you?"* echoed through the square. He crouched by Layla's head and whispered, "Can you hear me?"

The Sauracian's eyelids cracked open like missile silos, and her slit pupils flared. Ozzie's mouth ran drier than the Sahara Desert, but there was nowhere to run. This was it—either the Panacea clay worked, or he was dead. He eyed her homing beacon necklace. Would the leather cord break if he grabbed it? Layla reached for his arm, and the world stopped.

"Ozzie?" Her voice was weak, but a flicker of recognition blazed in her golden eyes.

Relief swept Ozzie off his feet and onto Layla's chest. Human arms couldn't fully encircle a Sauracian, but he tried anyway. Hot tears washed away a lifetime of self-loathing as, for the first time, Ozzie saved someone. Layla grunted, but made no move to dislodge him.

They found Hugo lying in the doorway of his hut, mask askew. Swollen purple knots on his forehead attested to the queen's revenge. Vicarious surveyed the village, then grabbed one of his chief's arms.

"Help me, lad." They dragged Hugo inside and rolled him onto the bed. Layla shuffled in behind them and sat down, blocking the door. The explorer mopped his brow. "What was that about?"

"I'll show you." Ozzie opened the dresser and ran his fingers under piles of folded brown robes. There had to be evidence tying the chief to the Noctem *somewhere* in this room.

"Don't rummage through there," Vicarious said. "It's not right."

"He ordered Layla to kill me. Was *that* right?"

"We'll discuss it when he wakes."

Ozzie moved to the desk. "If what Hugo said on Mother's Bane is true, he has a method of communicating with the mainland. Does he often disappear into the jungle for long periods of time?"

"Hugo's infirmities confine him to the village." Vicarious stared at his slumbering chief. "What did he tell you on the pinnacle?" he asked, softly.

"That you need to keep a close eye on him when he wakes up."

A pile of stationary was stacked in the center of the desk, flanked by a feather quill pen and an ink bottle. A string of brown prayer beads dangled from a branch of driftwood. Ozzie removed the beads from their stand and surveyed the room, flicking wooden marbles with his thumb.

Click. Click. Click.

What was he missing? How did Hugo, isolated on Amnesia, communicate with the Noctem?

Vicarious cleared his throat. "Find your answers soon, lad. Once my tribe mates sort the grainers, they are going to have questions about what happened to Hugo." After a moment's thought, he added, "That's not entirely true...first, they'll argue nonsensical theories about what happened to Hugo, *then* they'll have questions."

A rough texture ground against Ozzie's thumb. He frowned and inspected a single, carved bead. Three lightning bolts extended from the center of a triangle, terminating with small circles on each of the triangle's points.

"Noctem." Vicarious' whisper dripped with disdain.

"You know them?"

"I remember little of my past, but I won't forget that symbol anytime soon."

"Hugo is Noctem."

The old explorer raised a skeptical eyebrow at the fragile man snoring on the bed. "That's a serious accusation. You'll need more than a bead to prove it."

Ozzie circled the room, rolling the carved bead in his fingers. What would Grandfather do?

Mother's Bane rattled the hut. The desk and bed bounced on the dirt floor, but the dresser didn't budge.

Hmm.

Ozzie rammed the dresser with his shoulder, but it was bolted to the ground. He probed its surface and grinned when his finger-tips discovered a shallow indentation on the side panel facing the desk. The bead with the Noctem logo slid into the triangular slot like a key.

Clunk

The dresser hopped a fraction of an inch. Vicarious gasped. A gentle shove slid the bulky furniture aside like it was on ice, revealing a staircase that led into darkness. Yes!

He tip-toed down the first few steps. "Coming?"

The old explorer glanced at Hugo, then nodded, his jaw tightening.

"Be careful," Layla said.

Ozzie grinned. "St. Jude's is riddled with secret passages and booby traps. I've been training for this."

Glow bulbs blinked to life as they descended the stairs. After witnessing Hugo's arrogance on the pinnacle, Ozzie wasn't surprised at the absence of security—years of operating an inescapable prison had made the Noctem chief complacent. The secret lair was roughly as large as the hut and featured a tall filing cabinet, a desk, a hand-painted topographic model of Amnesia, and an elaborate chemistry set. Crates of breathing filters and rows of oxygen tanks lined the far wall.

Ozzie tugged a bedsheet off a column in the center of the room, uncovering a chest-high volantium pylon. Its base was embedded in dirt, and all four sides angled in to form an obelisk. The top of the column housed a birdbath filled with blue liquid.

"Don't touch that!" Vicarious snatched the sheet from Ozzie and threw it over the pylon.

"What is it?"

"An echolith—Stone Tech for communicating over long distances. It only connects to other echoliths, but you don't know who might answer on the other side. If Hugo is a member of the Noctem, they monitor his transmissions."

The island rumbled, rattling glassware.

"Hugo is awake!" Layla's voice echoed down the stairwell. Ozzie took stairs two at a time and emerged to find Hugo sitting up, wincing at Layla's grip on his arm.

"Unhand me!"

"I don't think so," Ozzie panted, leaning on the desk to catch his breath. "As mayor of Crazy Town, you get a personal bodyguard."

"This brute is hurting me!"

Ozzie bit his tongue. It was hard to be nice to someone who had tried to kill him. "Lighten up a little, Layla." His voice hardened. "Who do you talk to on the echolith? Your brother?"

Hugo's brows knit. "What?"

"How often do you check in with your superiors?"

The chief looked from Ozzie to Layla, helplessly. "I'm sorry, I don't understand."

Ozzie clenched his fists. "*Where* is the Noctem holding my grandfather?"

The Sauracian must have squeezed, because Hugo flinched. "You've mistaken me for someone else. I don't know your grandfather. My name is -" He frowned. "My name...is—" His eyes widened, and his voice dropped to a whisper, "I don't know what it is."

Ozzie scowled, realizing the inherent flaw in his brilliant "trick

257

Hugo into inhaling pollen" plan. How could he know if the warden was faking memory loss? He clomped down the stairs and called over his shoulder, "Don't let Hugo outside or allow anyone to talk with him. We don't know who we can trust."

The filing cabinet was open, and Vicarious was staring at a file, mouth agape. He handed Ozzie a photo of Mercy Malicious threatening a photographer with a dagger. "I have a wife." The explorer's voice went hoarse, "and children." He pointed to another photo. "Grandchildren!" A tear rolled down his cheek, and he whispered, "Though mind knoweth not, the heart beats true.*[1] I knew it. *I knew it.*"

Ozzie patted the explorer's back. "Mercy will be so happy to see you again."

Vicarious clutched his folder like a life preserver.

Ozzie's smile faded as he sifted through files. Each dossier was dedicated to one of the Forgotten, detailing their arrival date, personal information, and memory status. He selected a file at random—it belonged to a woman he'd last seen elbow-crawling through mud after she'd bitten the head off a throne guard.

SPAWL, COLLETTE (*Sniveling Fungi Department Head, Contrivance*)
Forgotten Alias: *Natenya*
Arrival: *874 A.F.*

The log showed Dr. Spawl's memory had improved to the point of requiring Hugo to administer additional doses of leethee pollen, a procedure which *"had a harshening effect on her personality, but satisfactorily muted flashes from her past. Prone to violence under stress."*

Ozzie skimmed the next dossier.

PROTA, ELTUS (*Merchant Guild*)
Forgotten Alias: *Grom*
Arrival: *865 A.F.*
Observations: *Responding well to pollen. Compliant to verbal commands.*

258

An entry dated two months later:

Flashbacks growing in severity. Prime candidate for repollenation.
Commenced high-concentration serum trial.
Brain activity pacified. Increased propensity toward violence.

Ozzie jumped to the bottom of the page and nearly dropped the folder.

Subject terminated in Mother's Bane.

"Grom was before my time," Vicarious said, studying the photo. "Legend says he went mad and headbutted a grainer queen."

Ozzie handed him the paper. "Hugo lied, Vicarious. Grainers aren't responsible for your memory loss, leethee pollen is." He pointed at the chemistry set. "When the pollen stopped affecting Grom, Hugo gave him a concentrated dose—and when things got out of hand, killed him." The accusation felt empty. A life should count for more than a file locked in a cabinet. Anger stirred in Ozzie's chest. "Amnesia is a Noctem prison, Vicarious. Hugo is the warden and executioner."

He flipped through more dossiers. Some folders contained only a name, presumably belonging to someone the Noctem was watching or planned to imprison. His fingers trembled when he came to the "F" section.

FORSYTHE, QUIDBY
Aliases: The Professor, That Blasted Urtling, Blundering Temple Ghost
Background: High value target. Leading figure in Stone Lore research.
Skills include tomb robbing, cryptography, and blind luck. Wanted for
questioning by the judiciary in Rust, Labyrinth, Scrum, Thwart, and
Klunk. Bounties ranging from 500 klunklings to 1 klunk-ton.
Current Whereabouts: Detained at Booksworn Archive by Bartholomew
Deathfist

Ozzie's heart threatened to punch out of his chest as he folded the paper and slipped it into his pocket. Finally, hard evidence Grandfather was alive! A photo on the next dossier caught his eye, and a face he hadn't seen in seven years beamed at him.

Dad.

Ozzie snatched the file. The page was blank, except for three lines.

FORSYTHE, HUMBOLDT
Aliases: *None*
Background: *High value target. Active figure in Stone Lore research. Last seen two years ago in the southern Feral.*
Current Whereabouts: *Unknown*

Two years ago? Ozzie folded the paper, then climbed the stairs in a daze, burdened with more questions than when he arrived.

---

1. An oft-quoted line from Garrilus the Unread's timeless classic *Soliloquies for My Fallen Ham Sandwich, Purloined by Gravity.*

CHAPTER 35
THE WELTLING

Ozzie sat on Hugo's porch, trying to calm his storm of thoughts, as grim-faced villagers fed beetle carcasses to a bonfire. How was Dad alive two years ago? What about Mom? Did Grandfather know? Tinkling porcelain interrupted his brooding. Ozzie's eyebrows leapt as Vicarious sat down, carrying a filigree tea set on a bamboo tray.

The explorer coughed. "Sorry for the smoke, lad—keeps grainers away and soothes any stragglers." Vicarious was responding well to the Panacea clay—even now, the old man's eyes brimmed with tears as the medicine worked its magic, flooding his mind with revived memories.

"Where did you find a tea set?"

"Your grandfather gave it to me." Vicarious offered him a cup. "A fact I now remember, thanks to you."

Ornate cups, saucers, and a teapot contrasted absurdly with a jungle, but Grandfather was adamant about the importance of tea breaks in a debunker's life. *No crisis is too dire for a spot of tea, Ozymandias. A moment's reflection gives solutions an opportunity to present themselves.*

Ozzie took a sip and spat the repulsive liquid out immediately. "Sorry," he said, frowning at his cup, "I wasn't expecting that."

Vicarious sighed. "I should have warned you. I ran out of tea months ago, so I'm experimenting with local flora."

"And this is?"

"Chuffgut fern—it's terrible, but a vast improvement over spleen blossoms."

Ozzie risked another sip, this time with lowered expectations. He smiled through the taste of sweaty socks. "Thanks, Vicarious."

"You're most welcome."

Villagers prowled among vegetation in the square, poking leaves with long poles. Disturbed grainers bounced halfheartedly off their helmets, then retreated into the jungle. Across the clearing, an unlucky volunteer peeked inside the village's smallest hut while his tribe mates shouted encouragement from a safe distance.

"Why are they so focused on that little shack?" Ozzie said.

"Can't leave stragglers in the outhouse, lad. That's a mistake you don't make twice."

Layla squeezed through the doorway, then sat on the ground next to Ozzie. "Hugo is secured to his bed. Tell me what happened."

"What's the last thing you remember?"

"You lied about being a good swimmer, I saved your life, then I walked into the jungle to find the Professor."

There was a lot to catch up on, much of it humiliating. Layla spewed a cloud of tea from her nostrils when Ozzie described getting eaten by the gluttonous maw, but it was worth a bruised ego to see her laugh. After the Sauracian regained her composure, he told her about meeting Hugo and the Forgotten. She roared at the bombshell that Grandfather was a prisoner at the Archive.

"I will teach that librarian the true meaning of *death fist*," she rumbled, knuckles cracking like ice floes.

Layla grew still as she learned her part in throwing Ozzie into Mother's Bane. She exhaled a long breath. "I am sorry I failed you."

He waved her apology away. "You weren't yourself." The Sauracian's intense glare burned a hole in the ground, so Ozzie punched her shoulder. "I don't care what happened or whose fault anything is. You're okay now, and we know the Chieftess is

262

working with the Noctem!" He massaged his throbbing fingers. "We have to save Alex and Pascal, then rescue Grandfather."

Layla crushed a grainer with a flick of her tail. "I will deal with the Chieftess."

The Forgotten were more difficult to convince of Hugo's treachery. Shouts barreled across the crackling fire.

"A prison?"

"Oblivion is our home!"

"Who are YOU to make these claims? Where's Hugo?"

Amnesia's longest residents bickered, while recent arrivals, who still experienced flashes from their former lives, looked thoughtful. The tide of public opinion turned when Ozzie led the tribe to Hugo's underground lair and showed them their dossiers. After the chief fielded their outrage with a vacuous stare and baffled shrug, a vengeful mob proposed throwing him into Mother's Bane, but Layla blocked the path to the pinnacle. Vicarious confined the warden to a vacant hut and organized a rotating guard of villagers who hadn't been subjects of leethee serum experiments. It was more than Hugo deserved, but the Forgotten were going to need options when the Noctem realized their Amnesian prison was compromised.

By mid-afternoon, Ozzie was champing at the bit to leave. Every wasted minute put Alex and Pascal in greater danger, not to mention he had no idea how long Panacea clay would protect Layla from leethee pollen. They said goodbye to Vicarious on the edge of Oblivion.

"I wish we had room to take you with us," Ozzie said. "We'll send help as soon as we can."

"No rush, lad," Vicarious said. "I'll keep things in hand until the rescue party arrives." He gestured to the square, where villagers were crafting defenses from bamboo. "My tribe is uncharacteristically unified in purpose at the moment. If the Noctem come sniffing around, they'll regret it."

Ozzie handed the explorer the pouch of Panacea clay. "Grandfather would want you to have these. There's not enough for everyone, but it might help."

The explorer rolled the two remaining pellets into his palm and smiled. "I'll put them to good use."

Ozzie and Layla followed the path to the beach they had landed on two days previously. As they breached the jungle wall, Mother's Bane thundered a farewell, sending palm trees into convulsions.

The Sauracian touched her medallion. "*Spark* cannot land in these headwinds," she said. "We need to swim beyond the breaking waves to activate the homing beacon."

Surf crashed on the distant reef, blasting foam three stories into the air. Ozzie's stomach churned at the thought of facing the breakers again, even with Layla's help.

A long shadow rippled a swell in the smooth surface of the picturesque lagoon.

Ozzie grabbed the Sauracian's arm. "Did you see that?"

"What?" She scanned the jungle canopy for threats.

Red spines arced out of the water, then submerged with casual menace.

"The humongous snake!" He pointed.

Layla turned to the waves. "Was it green, with red ridges on its back?"

"Yes!"

"As long as *Angelus*?"

"Longer."

She grunted. "So, the Weltling is not a myth."

Ozzie had heard enough debunking anecdotes to know that any sentence starting with the name of a beast and ending with "is not a myth" was a bad omen. "What *is* a weltling?"

Layla waded into the water. "She is a sea serpent."

"A sea serpent *the size of a bus* lives in the lagoon, and you didn't say anything?"

"Would it have made a difference? The Weltling will ignore us if we do not resemble food."

"Vicarious said she ate a villager named Dr. Yoris, and a couple other guys, too."

Layla thrashed the water. "I am summoning *Spark*! You can

264

cower in Amnesia if you wish, but I will *not* allow the Chieftess to harm my friends."

Ozzie scowled at the tranquil lagoon. "I'm coming," he said. "Just give me a second."

The Sauracian held out a claw. "Stay close to me. If the Weltling attacks, I will attempt to draw her away. When we reach the reef pass, we should be safe."

Warm water swirled around Ozzie's legs. In the distance, white, cresting rollers pounded the reef, taunting him. There had to be another way to get past the Weltling. Could Mother's Bane blow them across the lagoon? No, that's insane...but that catapult-obsessed guy in Oblivion could probably heave them far enough. A flag waved frantically in the back of his mind. Hang on.

Heave…

"I'll be right back."

Ozzie plunged through undergrowth, scanning the ground for clues with the urgency of a condemned man skimming a law book for loopholes. Within five minutes, he found what he was looking for: a glistening patch of heaveberries.

Four gluttonous maws lurked in the gloom, feigning innocence. Ozzie belly-crawled to the edge of the patch and picked a handful of fruit. The nearest maw sensed movement and tilted toward him. Its jaw cracked open, slathering the grass with pungent saliva. Ozzie pinched a heaveberry between his thumb and index finger, then flung it into the bushes.

Thwop

All four gluttonous maws snapped to attention and searched the canopy, vying to catch whatever had stumbled into their trap. Ozzie snatched berries from the dirt, praying Vicarious was right about their increased stability once they were picked. He log-rolled out of the maws' striking range, then returned to the beach, holding a fistful of heaveberries in front of him like a stick of dynamite.

Thwop

Heaveberries floated even better than Ozzie hoped.

Layla prodded the inflated fruit with a claw.

Plllllbbbbbttttttttttththththtthhhhhhhhhhhhhh

The berry spun in place, skipped across the water, then spluttered through the sky, like a mortally wounded whoopee cushion. A gentle splash of a paper thin carcass punctuated the heaveberry's short, dramatic life.

Layla's incredulous stare was difficult to shrug off, but at least Ozzie's plan didn't involve doggie-paddling past a sea serpent. "We need to be careful with sharp objects," he said.

"My entire body is a sharp object," the Sauracian growled. "Those berries are thinner than a Pronk's tooth-hide."

Ozzie shrugged. "I can't outswim the Weltling. If a heaveberry holds my weight, how fast can you push me?"

Layla glanced at the lagoon. "Fast."

"Faster than a sea serpent?"

"Almost certainly not."

Great.

Thwop

Ozzie shimmied onto the glorified pool toy, clutching the last remaining homing beacon in his hand. Layla was reluctant to trust him with her medallion, but they needed to signal the airship as soon as possible once they cleared the island's headwinds. Anxiety ratcheted Ozzie's pulse to a deafening thud. Don't drop the beacon. Don't fall in. Don't get eaten.

Layla positioned her paws on either side of the float. "Ready?"

Ozzie looped the necklace over his head and kissed the medallion for luck. "No. Let's do it."

The Sauracian's steady thrust and a tailwind from Mother's Bane turned the first hundred yards into a pleasure cruise. When they entered deeper indigo waters, a sinister shadow glided beneath them. Layla corrected course and her claw tore a hole in the heaveberry.

PSSSHHHHHHHHHHHH

Stay calm, they'd rehearsed this.

"Hurry!" the Sauracian barked.

Green dinner-plate scales slithered through Ozzie's imagination as water surged past his knees. He shoved a hand in his pocket, selected a heaveberry, and gave the rubber-hard fruit a vigorous pinch.

Thwop

The heaveberry creased as he scrambled on board. A darkening menace circled, spawning confused waves that threatened to swamp his life raft.

"She's toying with us!" he shouted.

"I know." Layla powered them toward the reef pass—another minute, and they'd cross the surf line. The shadow dove.

PSSSSSSSSSSSSSSSSSSSSSHHHHHHHH

Ozzie's death pinch punctured the berry's tortured skin. He stabbed a finger into the hole, but only widened the gash.

"New raft," the Sauracian rumbled. "She is coming!"

A mound of water approached like a torpedo. Ozzie gave up on the floundering inflatable and snatched heaveberries from his pocket.

The Weltling rose, a railway car-thick water cobra preparing to strike. Her boxy Volkswagen head housed two milk-white eyes large enough to devour Ozzie with a blink. Four rows of twelve-inch apex-predator teeth flashed as sparks crackled up and down red spines lining the serpent's emerald body. She hissed like a ruptured kettle.

"New raft! NEW RAFT!" Layla's roar jolted Ozzie from his stunned reverie. He smashed a handful of heaveberries, then hurled them at the Weltling.

THWIP-THWIP-THWIP-THWIP-THWIP-THWIP-THWIP

Erupting white fruit filled the sky, in the Least Impressive Fireworks Show in History.[1] His throw wouldn't win any medals, but it bought precious seconds as the Weltling ravaged the armada of pillowy attackers.

Layla snagged a floating berry. "Get on!"

Ozzie climbed onto the raft, clinging as tightly as he dared until they churned past the surf line.

The Sauracian raised her snout out of the water. "Call *Spark*!"

"On it." Ozzie wobbled to his knees, thrust the homing beacon over his head, and stabbed the button with his thumb.

"HHHHHHAAAAAAASSSSSSSSSSSSSSSSSSS!" The Weltling charged through the field of decoy heaveberries, shrieking outrage.

Ozzie jabbed the medallion with the impatience of a man calling an elevator while being charged by a tyrannosaurus. Layla threaded the lagoon's narrow pass, shoving the raft into open water as the air sizzled like steak on a grill. Ozzie glanced back and nearly swallowed his tongue—the Weltling was in striking distance, her spines crackling with electricity. The serpent's mouth curved into an insidious smile.

Ozzie battled to his feet and waved the homing beacon at the heavens. Where was *Spark*?

Lava flowed in his right forearm.

At last, a worthy adversary! Drown the Weltling in a pool of blood! Victory and glory!

Ozzie shook the deranged voice from his mind. Attacking a sea serpent was a one-way ticket to an excruciating death, but the Voice of Appalling Life Advice was right: he had to make a stand. His metal fingers twitched as he embraced the heat in his arm.

Layla saw the shadow emerge from the clouds first. "*Spark!*"

Engine roaring, the plucky airship raced to rescue her crew.

Electrical charges skittered up ridges on the Weltling's back, birthing a globe of light in her belly that erupted from her mouth. Gigawatts of sputtering energy skimmed the waves as the Anemoi Blade materialized in Ozzie's hand. His panicked swing connected with the ball, then stabbed the ocean, dispersing a web of lightning in the water. He howled a mixture of shock and exhilaration.

"Did you see that?"

We feast on serpent flesh tonight!

Ozzie winced at the bellowing voice in his head as the Weltling marshaled another attack.

"Incoming!" Layla said.

He whirled his sword in a figure eight, then adopted a pose that might have been valiant, had the tip of the Anemoi Blade been steadier. Ozzie masked his desperation with a cocky smile and bellowed, in his best barbarian yell, "Bring it!" The epicness of his challenge was somewhat lessened when his lavaskink glove caught fire and dropped in the water.

The Weltling paused in the face of her prey's sudden confidence.

"*What are you DOING?*" hissed Layla.

"Stalling."

The Weltling's spikes flexed like a slinky descending a staircase. She screeched, then discharged a sputtering globe of energy that skipped across the water. Ozzie squeezed his eyes shut and swung his sword like a tennis racket. Thunder wrecked his eardrums as an electric shock rubberized his knees. White lightning crackled the length of the Anemoi Blade.

"*AHHHHHH!*" He flailed his sword.

The Voice of Appalling Life Advice rejoiced. *That's the spirit! Victory through intimidation! Kill the Weltling!*

"Calm down, Ozzie!" Layla shouted.

A tendril of electricity lanced from his blade to the Sauracian, who blocked it with her forearm. "Sorry!" Ozzie screamed. He thrust his sword at the sky, then gasped in horror when it blasted *Spark* with a bolt of lightning. Damage done, the Anemoi Blade blinked out of existence, as the airship pulled within arm's reach, aflame.

Layla seized Ozzie by the scruff of his neck, flung him onto the fuselage, then hauled herself on board. The Sauracian punched the throttle, and *Spark* responded like an eager puppy, oblivious to the fact her tail was on fire.

Flames carpeted the airship's control surfaces and licked at her rigging. With one paw on the yoke, Layla pried the lid off a wooden box and flung white powder over the rudder's skeletal remains. She snarled at the Weltling, who shrieked back. A lightning ball, smaller this time, hurtled past the envelope. The Sauracian tore smoldering wires from an instrument panel and pitched them over the side as *Spark* found refuge in a cloud bank. The engine hiccupped, gasped, and died.

Layla slumped at the controls, bandaging a nasty burn that charred her right forearm.

"Are you okay?" Ozzie panted, wincing as her glare struck him like a hammer.

"You nearly destroyed our only hope of saving Pascal and your sister."

"It was an accident!"

The Sauracian shoved a bolt of canvas into his arms and pointed at the rudder. "Accident or not, only one of us is light enough to fix it."

Ozzie swallowed his protests and inched along the twig-thin airframe, trying not to look down. "Imagination and emotion, Ozzie," he mimicked. "Manifest the blade, Ozzie—unless we're getting attacked by Shocky McShockface, in which case, stand there and get eaten." He stretched canvas over the rudder's damaged frame until Layla grunted permission to return to the safety of the fuselage. Ozzie flopped in his chair and fished the remaining heaveberries from his pocket. Their ivory skin had faded to mottled gray and hardened like stone.

Layla waved a wrench. "Dispose of those," she growled.

"I want to show Alex a heaveberry."

"If they inflate, they will endanger us."

"They're petrified now. I couldn't trigger one if I tried." He rapped a berry against the instrument panel, praying he was right.

The Sauracian rumbled, "I do not want them on *Spark*."

Ozzie waited until she looked away, then shoved the heaveberries into his pocket.

After an hour of threats, cajoling, and exasperated wallops, Layla convinced *Spark's* motor to clunk and clack again. "Your heroics cut our top speed in half," she said, revving the engine. "At this rate, it will be four days to Contrivance, unless we crash first."

"What will the Chieftess do when we show up?" Ozzie said.

Layla adjusted a valve, coaxing a snarl from the engine. "She will try to erase us, to pacify the Noctem."

"I can't believe that woman takes orders from *anyone*."

"The Chieftess betrayed us because it gained her a strategic advantage, but she will turn on her allies if it serves her purposes."

Great. Alex was trapped in a city of mad scientists ruled by a Machiavellian tyrant who was only *probably* going to kill her at the whim of a secret society.

"Can *Spark* go any faster?"

---

1. It wasn't. That honor goes to Rennigan Collow of Trove, who trained a sloth to spell out "Will You Marry Me?" with a sparkler, then accidentally stationed the slow-waving mammal on top of a hill half a mile away from his proposal site.

CHAPTER 36
FINDING PARTS

Alex tapped one of the circles embedded in her forearm and winced as vibrations transmitted to bone. In the three days since the armillam melted, throbbing pain had diminished to a tedious, dull ache. She yawned, then twisted out of her hammock. Time for another round of haggling with crazy people. She'd rather help repair *Angelus*, but after the Plasma Torch Incident, Pascal had demoted her to sourcing spare parts. It was a classic overreaction—and given the Dromedarian's checkered past, wildly hypocritical. It's not like she had *intended* to cut a watermelon-sized hole in the hull.

Alex downed a bowl of something distantly related to oatmeal and scanned Pascal's requests. *Two Reverters* topped the list again, but today the words were underlined, targeted by arrows, and highlighted with a note to *QUIT STALLING*. She grimaced.

As usual, her "security detail", Dr. Strim and Dr. Ploz, escorted her into the city. Once again, they had redesigned their weapons overnight, and were struggling to walk in a straight line as they tweaked their new inventions.

"Where to, Miss Alex?" Ploz said, pumping his stubby legs to keep up.

"Level Twelve. Pascal is getting impatient about reverters."

Strim said, "He needs to form a salvage squad to steal parts after lab hours." The doctor was built like a stick insect, and emphasized dialogue by waving his hands, which was fine as long as he wasn't holding anything sharp.

"Believe me, I'd love to kick a few doors in and get this over with, but Pascal says we can't afford to make more enemies." She nodded at his hands. "What's the Weapon of the Day?"

Dr. Strim smiled eagerly, eyes widening to rival the rims of his spectacles as he held up a pair of yellow, thrumming, ping-pong paddles. "A static blast array—it funnels power from ambient electromagnetic fields into convenient, hand-held shock paddles."

Alex dodged an enthusiastic forehand. "No backpack for this one?"

He chortled. "Backpack weaponry is an artifact of outmoded thinking."

Dr. Ploz, whose puffy eyelids testified to a night spent squeezing a ventralistimizer into the backpack he proudly wore, cleared his throat. "My colleague could not be more wrong. Observe the elegance of backpack weaponry." He squeezed his spear handle, disgorging a stream of green bubbles that wafted toward the ceiling.

Strim laughed. "You call that a weapon?"

The barrel-shaped scientist waggled his eyebrows. "Wait for it."

Dr. Strim reached out, popped a bubble, then shrieked as flesh melted from his finger, baring bone and gristle. Alex recoiled, but before she could scream, the damage reversed itself. Strim ceased wailing and flexed his healthy, pink finger in wonder. "You solved Ooplav's Quandary!"[*1]

Ploz grinned modestly. "I merely localized a chrono-shift to temporarily dissolve your flesh with acid."

"Astounding!"

"That was incredible," Alex said. "Why are you guys wasting time guarding me? You should be inventing things."

The scientists shared a doleful look.

"Indeed," said Dr. Strim. He gestured in the general direction of

273

the city's hub, sending Alex ducking for cover. "Regrettably, the system is holding us down."

Dr. Ploz slapped his colleague's wayward paddle out of his face and said, "In a completely unforeseeable sequence of events, we phase-drifted the Chieftess' cat into a parallel dimension." He hesitated, then added, "Probably. I mean, she went *somewhere*."

"I *told* you not to aim at Madam Fluffkins," said Strim. "It took days to clean the fur out of the carpet."

Ploz stowed his spear in his armpit with the air of a man rehashing an argument for the thousandth time. "If the feline had remained still, *as instructed*, I would have knocked the gunkaberry cleanly off her head. It was an honest mistake that could have happened to anyone."

"You are a halfwit, and you happened to me," said Dr. Strim.

The scientists bickered over the entire mile and a half walk to Level Twelve. Alex just rolled her eyes and kept to the designated Safe Zone—a yellow, striped line running down the center of every hallway. According to Pascal, anyone who strayed more than three steps from the line risked being eaten by a nub-toothed gumbeast, or worse, getting gassed and "volunteering" for an experiment.

A complicated barter system ruled Contrivance's limited resources. Alex spent hours untangling the convoluted supply chain, one link at a time, for each item on Pascal's list. The painstaking process yielded minimal results, especially with rare items like reverters—but yesterday, after another dead end, she overheard a scrap of a conversation between two scientists who thought she was out of earshot.

"*What did she want?*"

"*Reverters.*"

"*Ha! She might as well attempt to precipitate molecular substrate within two dipoles of an average mean.*"

"*Right?!? Although, between you and me, I hear Dr. Kuro is sitting on a stash.*"

Alex knocked on Dr. Kuro's door, then raised her hands to show she was unarmed.

"Enter."

She nudged the door open with her foot but waited outside. Her heart leapt when she saw a mound of reverters stacked against the far wall. Alex forced her politest smile. "Good morning, Dr. Kuro. My name is Alex. I'd like to barter for two reverters, please."

The scientist blinked and lowered his crossbow a millimeter. Politeness always threw the Children off. He shook his head. "Those reverters belong to Dr. Jorm, once she cleans my waste vault of yumlip pheromones."

Alex gritted her teeth and scaled a series of rusty step ladders to Dr. Jorm's lab on Level Fourteen.

"Sorry, I can't help you." Jorm lowered her shovel. "After I decontaminate Kuro's vault, I'm trading the reverters to Dr. Belpop for a barrel of Troomium Halide—it's just the thing for chapped lips."

Alex counted under her breath and marched to Dr. Belpop's lab.

"Reverters? Those are for Dr. Onti, once he trains my crustacean choir," he said, powering down a pneumatic eye-gouger.

Curiosity overruled her annoyance. "Crustacean choir, as in: *singing crabs*?"

"Not yet, but hopes are high."

Corroded metal stairways complained as Alex and her escorts descended to Level Two. Faint singing grew increasingly distinct as they approached what was, judging from the *Diphthong Research* sign, Dr. Onti's lab. She kicked the door open, startling the doctor, who was conducting music over a pond-sized aquarium. Gargling oysters continued to take direction from Onti's flailing arms as he fought to regain balance, scoring his awkward tumble into the water with ascending soprano wails.

Shame deflated Alex's frustration as Dr. Onti squelched out of the tank like a waterlogged flamingo. He wiped his monocle on a dripping coat sleeve, then fixed her with a dignified glare.

"May I help you?" It was the diction of a man who regards polished vowels to be the bedrock of civilization.

"Dr. Belpop sent me," said Alex. "I need two reverters."

"Reverters?" Dr. Onti tapped his lips with a conducting baton and searched the ceiling for inspiration. "Ah, yes! I shall soon have some I can part with."

Her shoulders sagged with relief. "Thank you."

"Certainly. And you are in luck, Dr. Belpop's crustaceans are vocalizing ahead of schedule."

"Wonderful! Not to rush you, but what kind of time frame are we looking at?"

"Difficult to say—it depends how quickly they learn Latin."

Defeated, Alex walked out of an enthusiastic lecture on the elasticity of lobster lips.

Detours and freshly cordoned-off hallways plagued the journey to *Angelus'* hangar. The ever-expanding Restricted Zone claimed more of Contrivance every day, and by the fifth dead end, Alex was ready to pull her hair out. She yanked down caution tape blocking a stairwell they used yesterday.

"Let's go this way," she said. Ploz and Strim gasped.

"Don't!" Dr. Strim reached for Alex, but was too late. When her foot crossed the threshold, a klaxon blared, yellow lights flashed, and steam filled the stairwell.

The PA system screeched, "*Unauthorized Restricted Zone incursion in Stairwell Delta, Epsilon Quadrant. Dispatch Perimeter Security Team Gamma.*"

Ploz threw an arm around Alex's waist, dragging her backwards. Strim guarded the hallway, paddles ready. Metal shrieked in the distance, accompanied by shouts.

"Get down!" Dr. Ploz dropped to all fours, scuttled beneath a sewage pipe, then gestured for her to follow. Alex flopped onto her stomach and squeezed next to him, wincing as Dr. Strim slammed into her shoulder.

Steel-toed sandals and laboratory galoshes pounded past the trio's faces. When the security team vanished into the stairwell, Alex crawled out, then helped her guards stand. They sprinted through the city, taking random turns until they were far enough from the Restricted Zone to claim a credible alibi.

Dr. Ploz crumpled beneath the weight of his backpack.

"Sorry," Alex panted.

Strim lifted his head and waved a finger. "Stay out...of... Restricted Zone."

She paced in a circle. "What are they doing in there?"

Dr. Strim slowed his breathing. "Only *lunkbrains*...in Ballistics...know...about Prometheus...and they don't...play well...with others."

"Blasted rocket jockeys," gasped Dr. Ploz.

After five minutes, they recovered enough to trudge to the surface levels, carefully avoiding the Restricted Zone. Alex dreaded returning to *Angelus* empty-handed—not because she'd failed, but because Pascal would only sigh, then add another item to his to-do list. There had to be some way to scrounge up reverters.

She leaned against a doorframe, waiting for her wardens to catch up. A block ago, Strim and Ploz had forgotten their mutual resentment of Ballistics and circled back to being disenfranchised colleagues.

"Phase-drifting is an inexact science! We know sloths are immune to the effects of—"

"Immune? You swapped my arms with a sloth for two weeks! Do you have any idea how long it took me to brush my teeth?"

"No, but that sloth set a few speed records with your arms. And— silver lining—you stopped dropping test tubes every thirty seconds!"

"Psst."

Alex turned to an empty hallway.

"*Psst!*"

The hiss came from a dark alley brimming with pipes and duct-work. A skinny arm shot out of the shadows and beckoned her closer. She glanced at her guards—Ploz was prancing on his tip-toes, straining to go nose-to-nose with Strim as they yapped insults at each other. Alex approached the alley, ignoring Ozzie's scolding voice in her head.

"What do you want?" she said.

After a moment's hesitation, a scrawny, middle-aged man stepped into the corridor. Close-cropped, scruffy white hair complemented the threadbare lab coat draping from his pencil-thin frame. Spectacles magnified frictionless, darting eyes. "Your life is in danger. Follow me," he whispered.

"No."

He frowned. "I *said...*your *life* is in *danger.*"

"I'm not going anywhere with you. For all I know, you want to harvest my brain for science."

The man rolled his eyes and exhaled, exasperated. "I can get you spare parts."

Her pulse quickened. "Lead the way."

---

1. Sominus Ooplav pioneered the field of chronological philosophy. His famous Quandary, "*How could you know what I know if I don't know what you knew when you knew what I know?*" is widely regarded by the scientific community as a key to unlocking time travel.

   In *The Journal of Reckless Inquiry*, Contrivance's weekly newspaper, no less an authority than Dr. Roodle Rexus, head of the Morbidity and Preventable Accident Commission, said, "I have no idea what Ooplav was blathering on about, but that's time travel for you. Let's go with it and see what happens."

CHAPTER 37

THORPE

The stranger wriggled through hidden passages like an eel, only stopping to cross his arms and tap his foot impatiently until Alex caught up. They navigated a labyrinth of abandoned labs, ducking past barriers that warned of *Radiation Leakage* and *Misplaced Explosives*. Her instincts screamed to turn around, but she'd lost her bearings ages ago. Following a paranoid scientist into a toxic waste dump—what could go wrong? She was eying a jagged pipe to make an improvised weapon when her gawky guide took a sharp left into a lab with boarded-up windows.

Broken glass crunched under Alex's feet as she crept past a sign dedicating the lab to *Inertial Defiance Research*. Bluish lights flickered on, emitting a gentle buzz. Rows of workbenches filled the room, boasting prototypes in various stages of construction and disrepair. To Alex's delight, a Chieftess' ransom in parts was stacked in the corner. She suppressed a grin—*this* guy would know where to find a pair of reverters.

The man paced in the center of the lab, muttering. He conjured a deck of cards and started shuffling, rectangles pirouetting and leaping between his fingers like ballet dancers. His eyes flitted to her face.

"Alex?" he said.

"Yes."

His fingers blurred. A dragon's head spewed a paper fireball, then melted back into the shuffle. "My name is Thorpe."

"Are you a Child of Contrivance, Thorpe?" she asked, unable to tear her eyes from his hands. A paper frog hopped, then submerged into the whirring deck.

He grinned. "Yes, but my principal training is in other disciplines." He spread his arms, bowed his head, and paused for dramatic effect. "I am a Master of Parchment Animation."

When she didn't react, he looked up.

"A Practitioner of Cunning Foldsmanship?" he said.

His brow furrowed at her blank stare.

"A Class Three Paper Mage?"

He dropped his arms and pushed his glasses up on his nose.

"I'm Labyrinthian. Surely you've heard of us."

"I think so," she said. "You guys make parachutes."

Thorpe tore a square from a roll of toilet paper mounted on his belt, performed a series of deft folds, then opened his hands with a flourish, revealing an origami bird.

"Wow." Alex tried to inject enthusiasm into her voice and failed.

He tweaked the creature with his thumbs, then blew it into the air. The origami bird flapped its wings, climbed to the ceiling, circled twice, then glided into its maker's waiting palm.

Alex clapped in spite of herself. "That was incredible! How did you do that?"

Thorpe grinned. "It's all in the thumbs."

As charming as the demonstration was, she needed answers. "You said my life is in danger. Is it the Chieftess?"

The scientist's face darkened, and his shoulders shrank. "It's *always* the Chieftess." Cards spun like liquid going down a drain. "But she's going too far this time."

"What is she doing?"

"I don't know, but—"

Alex balled her fists. "So, *your life is in danger* is all you've got for me? *Of course* my life is in danger! Welcome to my world—

where monsters kidnap people, librarians attack you with siege weapons, and weirdos lure you to their creepy lairs to dazzle you with card tricks."

Thorpe raised his hands defensively. "The threat is imminent. A countdown has begun." A distant rumble rattled ventilation ducts, showering the lab with dust. He flipped a chalkboard and pointed to a convoluted web of yarn connecting photos and question marks to a map of Contrivance. Alex's stomach sank—she'd met a lot of eccentric geniuses in the last three days, but this was her first conspiracy nut.

The Labyrinthian stabbed the map with an accusing finger. "Project Prometheus began six months ago in Corridor Eight, then expanded to include significant portions of every arm of Contrivance. All signs indicate we are entering its final stages."

"This doesn't sound like my problem," Alex said.

Shuffling cards formed a snarling face. "If I'm right about Prometheus, it's *everyone's* problem."

"What *is* Prometheus? Any time I ask someone, they rant about Ballistics, then change the subject."

A tornado whirled in Thorpe's palms. "I don't know."

Alex snorted. "How am I supposed to take you seriously?"

Thorpe scowled, marched across the lab, and tugged a sheet off a video monitor that occupied most of a wall. He threw himself into a swivel chair and knuckled buttons with a vengeance. *"Take me seriously?"* he grumbled. "She doesn't know a lurp from a lorebadger and *I'm* the one who isn't taken seriously?" Vacuum tubes fizzed and popped as he twirled a hand crank. A radiator grille burst into flames, but Thorpe snatched a blanket from a pile and smothered the fire without taking his eyes from the glowing monitor. His hand raked a control panel, tuning dials that summoned bursts of static. Lines zig-zagged across the screen, then coalesced into blurry footage of three scientists wrestling in front of a chalkboard.

"Ambient dynami plays havoc with video wavelengths," he said. "It's impossible to get a clean signal." Thorpe flipped a switch and dialed in a new feed. A welding torch flared on screen, spraying sparks across—wait, was that *Angelus*?

"You're spying on us!"

Thorpe rolled his eyes. "I'm watching your back. *Someone* has to." He coaxed a new channel onto the monitor. A scientist stilt-walked across a pit of hopping snakes, a dozen wriggling serpents dangling from his armored boots.

"The Elastic Reptile Lab," Thorpe said.

Another burst of static. An enormous boulder crushed a test dummy as scientists took notes.

"Inconvenient Physics Lab."

A blast of white noise crackled from the speaker and a blizzard of static lit the screen.

"This *was* the Slap Lab until the Restricted Zone swallowed it."

A splash of black, then more snow.

"Toxin Vault, now Restricted."

Black, then white.

"Pernicious Snail Pavilion, now Restricted."

White screen after white screen flickered as Thorpe scrolled through feeds.

Alex said, "Maybe they found your cameras."

Thorpe leaned back and riffed through his cards. "If the Chieftess caught me surveilling the Restricted Zone, I would have suffered three dozen industrial accidents by now. More likely, Project Prometheus involves enough dynami to completely over-whelm my video system."

"Why don't you just sneak in?"

The scientist pulled back his collar, exposing a scar on the side of his neck. "Children are implanted with a tracking device to keep absentminded faculty from wandering into feeding areas. Removing an implant triggers alarms across the city. I can't infil-trate the Restricted Zone undetected," his eyes shifted to hers, "but *you* can."

Metal clattered in the corridor. Thorpe whistled, and a knee-high door burst open, admitting a frenzy of golden limbs. The creature bounded across the room and skidded into Thorpe's legs. Internal springs *boinged* and bronze feet tapped a giddy rhythm.

"Drog! Good to see you." The scientist scratched the fawning canine's chin. "Who's a good boy? Whoosagoodboyden?" Gears shifted and a golden tail *clinked* like an ecstatic metronome. Drog spat an electrical component on the floor and barked.

Brrrk. Brrrk.

"What did you bring me?" Thorpe inspected the smoking module. "Another one of Dr. Vispoy's centrifuge brakes! She's in for an exciting day in the G-force Lab." He tossed the component into a crate brimming with identical brakes. "Good boy!" He patted the canine's head, inspiring shivered, mechanical delight. "Drog, this is Alex. Let her live."

Brrrk.

"Does Drog scrounge all your parts?" Alex gestured to the scrap littering the lab.

"A lot of it—some, I scavenge. When colleagues don't take security precautions with their resources, I teach them the error of their ways." Thorpe retrieved an oil can from a shelf. "Drog is an excellent companion, but lacks an eye for detail—he's just as likely to bring back an empty lunch box as a multitimbral logic core."

"I know a few people who would love to destroy him," she said.

Drog's neck hinges rasped as he swiveled to stare at her with sinister red eyes.

Grrrrckrrrrrrckrrrrrckrrrrrrrrrrckcrrrrrrrrrrck.

Thorpe chuckled. "I'm certain you do." He squirted oil in Drog's right hip and exercised a squeak out of the joint. The scientist removed a fan-shaped key from around his neck, inserted it into Drog's back, then cranked it clockwise. Springs *plunked* as machinery protested tension. A hind leg scratched a phantom itch.

Brrk.

"Can he think for himself?" Alex asked.

"Binary logic circuits associate stimuli with patterns. When I scold or reward Drog, he adjusts his behavior accordingly. Over time, he becomes a projection of my personality."

Alex pictured the Wanted posters plastering bulletin boards

across Contrivance, and steered the conversation in a safer direction. "Pascal said *he* built Drog."

Thorpe hefted a crowbar. "We built Drog together, using his clockwork tech and my circuitry. I'm not surprised he takes credit, though. Pascal loves the spotlight." He grunted and pried the lid off a crate. Alex's breath caught in her throat at the sight of a gleaming, pristine reverter. "How many do you need?" he asked, watching her face. Cards reappeared, teleporting between his hands.

Thorpe wasn't someone Alex wanted to owe a favor to, but the thought of returning to *Angelus* empty-handed was unbearable.

"Two." Hopefully, she didn't sound as desperate as she felt.

The scientist shrugged. "Help yourself."

She took a hesitant step and lifted a reverter out. The translucent tube was half the length of a fluorescent light bulb and twice as heavy. Green liquid flowed from one end to the other as she tilted it.

Grrrrckrrrrrrrckrrrrrrckrrrrrrckrrrrrrrrrrrrr.

Drog followed the tube with an unblinking, possessive glare until Alex placed it back in the crate.

Brk.

"One more thing…" Thorpe botched a shuffle, and a handful of cards spun to the floor. His face reddened as he crouched to pick them up. "Don't mention me to Pascal."

"Why not?"

"Dramatic pronouncements of betrayal, accusations of treachery, unbridled anger…" He stood up. "Take your pick."

"I can't keep secrets from Pascal."

The scientist snorted. "Good luck finding reverters, then. I'm sure those lobsters will get the hang of vowels any day now."

Alex bit her lip. "Fine, I won't say anything to him."

He grinned. "Tell me what parts you need and I'll have them ready when you return from the Restricted Zone. In the meantime, take a pair of reverters back to *Angelus* as a gesture of my goodwill."

Alex sighed and thrust Pascal's wish list at Thorpe. "How do I get in without tripping alarms?"

He flicked a sheet of paper, which careened around the room like a magic carpet. "I marked a route for you."

She snatched the map out of the air and glowered at a jumble of blurred text. The page was an incomprehensible mishmash of over-lapping blueprints, but Alex would rather spend a year wandering the Feral than admit she didn't know how to read it. She rotated the map, as if studying a complex problem from every angle. Thorpe's smile only made the puzzle more infuriating.

"Need help?"

"Looks good," she said. "I'll read it later."

"Corridor Eight is heavily patrolled, but a maintenance shaft in Subsection Seventy-Four of Corridor Nine will drop you into the thick of things."

"I'm going to need a code to unlock doors."

"The access code is 1-2-3-4. A few years ago, Cryptology programmed locks with codes so diabolical even *they* couldn't crack them. Riots started when no one could unlock the bathrooms. The Bladder Revolt led to the Relief Accords, which mandated a simple universal code on all access pads."

"What are these red 'X' marks?" she asked, seizing on the only map symbol she could decipher.

"Booby traps—sonic incapacitators, acidic gel clusterslams, wontletgos...Children of Contrivance make atrocious guards, but we're exceptional trap designers." He tossed her a bundle of cloth. The tattered, semi-white lab coat was tailored for someone six inches taller and a hundred pounds heavier.

"Do you have anything smaller? I'll look like a child playing dress up."

"You'll blend in. Just avoid talking to anyone, especially about math."

She scowled. "For all you know, I'm great at math."

"Oh, really? How are you at Battle Trigonometry? Can you defend yourself in an unsanctioned logarithm duel? How many sudoku bombs have you defused?"

Alex huffed, "Fine, I get it—no math. What happens if I get caught?"

Thorpe lifted his coffee-stained shirt to reveal a pink scar that ran from his sternum to his belly button. A zig-zagging trail of sloppy sutures bore witness to a long journey of suffering.

"Don't get caught."

CHAPTER 38
BREAKING TRUST

"Where have you been?" Dr. Ploz hissed, poking Alex with his spear. She backed away, visions of flesh-melting acid bubbles dancing in her head.

Dr. Strim waved a fizzing paddle. "If we lose you, the Chieftess will defund our research faster than an adolescent murmoot sheds his four vestigial tails."

Dr. Ploz lowered his weapon and turned to his colleague. "I think not—as fast as a *juvenile* murmoot faceblooms his blemish beard, perhaps."

Dr. Strim frowned. "As fast as an *infant* murmoot's ear wax dam bursts on Teething Day?"

Ploz raised a finger. "As fast as a *pubescent* murmoot's blue morning fever incinerates his shame fur!"*[1]

"Perfect!"

Alex was halfway down the corridor before her guards realized she was gone. They scampered to catch up.

"Wait!" Strim pushed his paddles into her arms and caught his breath. "Where were you?"

"I got lost," she said.

Dr. Ploz handed Alex his spear. "Please don't...get lost...again," he wheezed.

She juggled their weapons, raising a reverter to the top of the pile. "Look what I found."

Strim gasped. He stared at Alex, then turned to his colleague. "I knew we could do it," he said. Ploz gave a mute thumbs-up.

As the trio ambled down the corridor, shouts from *Angelus'* repair bay goaded Alex into a sprint. In the hangar, a mob of Children were rioting inside a circle of five chalkboards at the foot of the gangplank. Pascal's head bobbed above the mosh pit like a periscope, weaving between arguments. Alex shoved past scientists locked in a tug-of-war over a chalkboard eraser. A clipboard caromed off her shoulder as she neared the center of the storm. Pascal's voice cut through the bedlam. "*Pineapple?* You are seriously suggesting *pineapple* as a backup power supply? How would that even work?"

"If you don't know, I'm certainly not telling you!"

"Dr. Soroto, why are you in a Ballistics think tank?"

"I was told there would be snacks!"

Alex elbowed the hungry scientist aside. "Where did all these people come from?" she shouted.

Pascal scowled. "The Chieftess ordered Ballistics to consult me about dynami, but neglected to instruct them to *listen*." A chalkboard crashed to the floor, prompting a boisterous cheer.

"This is getting out of hand," she said, clinging to the inventor's elbow.

The Dromedarian shook his head. "You should see the cafeteria on Design-Your-Own-Salad-Dressing Thursdays."

"I got the reverters!" Alex offered her prizes for inspection, then wilted when Pascal gave them a passing glance.

He shoved a trio of combatants into the scrum and shouted, "Finally! Put them on board *Angelus*, then find the rest of the parts."

She stood on her tiptoes and cupped a hand to her mouth. "I need to go into the Restricted Zone."

Pascal's eyebrows knitted. He put his hoof on her shoulder and leaned down. "Levels only get restricted after a radiation leak or

288

when a gurglestench escapes the petting zoo - in either case, it's too dangerous!"

"I'm talking about Corridor Eight."

His eyes widened. "Absolutely not! Corridor Eight is the epicenter of lunacy."

A hairy arm flung a sheaf of papers into the inventor's muzzle, and a high-pitched voice screamed, "My life's work of calculations are WRONG, are they? Please, oh illustrious mega-genius, show me the error of my ways!"

The Dromedarian grimaced and hissed, *"Beg, borrow, and steal to get us parts, but do NOT go near the Restricted Zone or Corridor Eight."* He rounded on his attacker, shouting, "For the last time, Dr. Rottbom, equations that end in question marks do not qualify as a *life's work of calculations!"*

Alex barged through the crowd and boarded *Angelus*. In the time it took to dump the reverters in the lab and rustle up a mystery meat taco in the galley, the ruckus outside escalated to a junkyard brawl. Factions formed, with clumps of scientists weaponizing chalkboards to ram their colleagues' wood-crate fortresses. A stream of green bubbles and a smattering of shrieks by the hangar door meant Ploz and Strim had also engaged in the rigorous scientific debate. Perfect. She jogged down the gangplank and headed for Corridor Nine.

Thorpe's map was bewildering—lines intersected at random junctures, hatches overlaid each other, and doors jammed against walls. Even the text was a translapede-stumping hodgepodge of nonsense. She held the map to a glow lamp, cursing stupid Labyrinthians and their stupid Labyrinthian paper.

Wait.

Labyrinthian paper.

"Thumbs and corners," she groaned. She twisted blindly until the map took pity on her and released a pop-up, three-dimensional diorama of Corridors Eight and Nine. A red line plotted a round-about path through alleyways and narrow squeezes, avoiding booby traps and guard posts.

Word of a think tank spread quickly in Contrivance. A steady stream of intellectuals rushed past, tweaking prototype weapons as they prepared to debate theories with less enlightened colleagues. Even if Alex had been strolling down the hallway instead of belly-crawling through an air duct, no one would have given her a second glance.

Thorpe's route led through scorching culverts, beneath spiked rolling pins, and across a narrow beam that spanned a furry ice monster's cage. When Alex came face to face with a jiggling bed of poisoned needles, she began to question the wisdom of following a conspiracy nut's plan. She did some quick orienteering, kicked an air vent open, and dropped into Corridor Nine, directly on top of her goal: Maintenance Hatch 218C.

A keypad next to the hinges glowed red. Alex keyed in the universal code, praying that aftershocks from the Bladder Revolt had rippled as far as Subsection Seventy-Four.

1-2-3-4

Green.

CHUNK

She threw her weight against the corroded wheel lock, straining until it surrendered with a squeal that made her teeth ache. Light panels flickered on, illuminating a shaft eight feet in diameter and a hundred feet deep.

Rust chewed Alex's palms as she descended the aging, wobbly ladder. Grimy walls and two broken light panels suggested no one had used this shaft in a long time. She stopped to double-check the red "X" on Thorpe's map that warned of a booby trap on the bottom hatch.

Fusillade of Poison-tipped Darts (Calamitous Wretch venom)

Alex descended at a snail's pace, racking her brain for the definition of *fusillade*. When fifteen rungs remained, she untied her left sneaker, dangled it over the hatch, and let go.

SHHHPTPTPTPTPT

A dozen feathered darts impaled the shoe before it hit the floor. Three darts missed, ricocheting off the walls with sharp *pings*.

"Whoa!" Alex scrambled up the creaking ladder and collapsed in Corridor Nine, heaving lungfuls of grease-laden air. Traps were Ozzie's thing. At St. Jude's, she used to laugh when he pored over Grandfather's booby trap collection "in case he needed to infiltrate a secret temple someday." It wasn't so funny now.

She didn't want to face the fusillade trap, but she'd rather drink a *pitcher* of calamitous wretch venom than return to *Angelus* or Thorpe with nothing but an embarrassing anecdote. If Ozzie were here, he'd probably use Mayan burial rituals and Icelandic tide tables to disable the trap with a lampshade and an egg. Alex pounded the hatch with her fist. As the blow echoed down the unlit hallway, a glimmer of an idea formed. She combed Corridor Nine for debris, then dumped her bounty by the hatch. The haul was meager—a pair of pliers, two halves of a clipboard, and a wool sock —but it would have to do.

Alex descended the ladder, cradling her scrap collection in her shirt. She stopped ten feet above the fusillade trap, held a clipboard fragment over the hatch, and let it drop.

SHHHPTPTPT

Darts converged in a ball of feathers and clattered to the floor. She counted the projectiles, then dropped the other half of the clipboard.

SHHHPTPT

Only thirteen darts in that salvo—two less than the first time.

SHHHPT

Four darts transformed the wool sock into a pincushion.

She released her final sacrificial lamb: the rusty pliers.

SSSSS

Compressed air fired, but no projectiles emerged from the walls. The pliers crashed into the pile of spent darts with a bang that woke the dead. Alex removed her right sneaker with the finesse of a paranoid master thief.

Thump

The trap was out of ammunition. She eased down the ladder, straining to detect any whiff of an ambush. When she was eight rungs from the bottom, the shaft walls hummed, sending vibrations through her palms. As the whine rose in pitch, darts jiggled and clinked across the floor, then vanished into a black vent that circled the hatch. Worrying clicks hinted at something important happening behind the scenes. The trap was reloading! Alex scrambled up the ladder as a salvo of darts hissed by her left calf.

SHHHHHHtinkatinkapuhtink

Her abrupt weight shift overwhelmed exhausted bolts. She yelped as her section of the ladder fractured, bent backwards, and wedged against the opposite wall of the shaft. Years of rock climbing gave Alex the stamina to hang in place until she could formulate an escape plan—unfortunately, it didn't prepare her for ladder rungs that crumbled to dust in her fingers.

She fell, clawing for handholds. The fusillade trap's firing ports appeared in the corner of Alex's vision and she screamed, shielding her face. A river of heat flooded her left arm and streamed from her wrist band in a neon blue blaze that illuminated the shaft.

SHHHPPPP

Pingkt-pluckta-plugta-takty-tack

Alex slammed into the hatch, curled in a tight ball as fifteen venom-tipped darts clattered on the floor. She grimaced, twisting her throbbing forearm. A shimmering umbrella of sapphire energy tracked with the rotation of her wrist.

CRAAAAAAAAAWWW

The broken section of ladder screeched like a banshee, then plummeted.

CRACK

Twisted metal bounced off her translucent shield.

"Ow!" Her forearm plugs flashed orange at the impact, then her shield disappeared. Alex touched her armillam. The volantium was cold, and the Stella Signum on the back of her hand was barely visible. She flicked her wrist and rotated her arm, as if blocking a strike.

Nothing.

"Shield, engage!"

Not voice-activated, then. Alex relaxed her head on the hatch with a gentle *bong*. She'd grill Pascal about the armillam later, omit-

292

ting a few key details about the maintenance shaft. Tremors rattled metal plating beneath her, then died out.

Right. Time to check on the mad scientists.

She gathered her shoes, careful to crouch below the trap's kill zone. Evil-smelling purple liquid—presumably calamitous wretch venom—trailed black scorch marks down the sides of her sneakers. Fortunately, no venom penetrated the inner linings.

Alex cracked the hatch open, squinting as light spilled into the shaft. When no deranged scientists attacked her with shovels, she poked her head into the Restricted Zone.

---

1. Murmoots are universally held to suffer the worst forms of puberty in the animal kingdom. Once they reach adulthood, they devote their lives to avoiding eye contact with other members of their species. If not for the Murmoot Preservation Society's conservation, breeding, and morale program, murmoots would have gone extinct from shame centuries ago.

CHAPTER 39

THE RESTRICTED ZONE

In Alex's imagination, Corridor Eight, "Home of the Mad Scientists," featured sparking wires, Tesla coils, straitjackets, and maniacal laughter—basically, the exact opposite of what greeted her. The brightly illuminated passage buzzed with nervous energy, like a hospital ward. Equipment carts trundled past, laden with sensors and testing gear. At the far end of the hallway, a scientist crouched over an observation window, scribbling notes on his clipboard. Alex retreated into the shaft as a gaggle of Children swarmed past.

"Wells Three through Sixteen need power boosts."

"Commandeer the Anger Mismanagement Lab reactor."

"No way! They dropped Dr. Pillory in a dung pit when she borrowed their break room toaster."

The group disappeared around a corner. Alex slipped her lab coat on, then climbed down the wall-mounted access ladder, leaving the hatch cracked for a quick getaway. A colossal black pipe dominated one side of the hallway, forcing pedestrians to brush elbows when they passed. She read the nameplate on the closest door.

Doctor Wellid - Executive Director, Carnivorous Pastries Dept.

The lights were out in Wellid's lab. Alex wiggled the knob. Locked. She moved to the next door.

Doctor Breppinex - Spontaneous Pachyderms Dept.

Breppinex's lab was dark, too, and its double doors were secured by a humongous padlock.

On the opposite side of the corridor, a stack of caution labels obstructed an observation port in the pipeline.

- *USE PROTECTIVE EYEWEAR*
- *NO TOUCHING OR LICKING, BUT ESPECIALLY NO LICKING.*
- *CONTACT LEGAL DEPT TO ARRANGE AFFAIRS BEFORE OPENING*
- *WARNING: SANITY MAY BE COMPROMISED UPON VIEWING*
- *INELIGIBLE FOR SICK DAY IF EXPOSURE INDUCES TENTACLE GROWTH*

Alex wrenched the port open, choked back a scream, then slapped it shut. She fell to her knees, clutching her left wrist as heat consumed her forearm. Turquoise artifacts floated across her vision, thwarting her efforts to blink them away. The last time she'd seen that much dynami, a surge had nearly blasted her off a cloudwhip. What were the Children *thinking*? A blaring alarm jolted Alex to her feet. Had someone discovered the open maintenance hatch? Overhead lights snapped red, and a bored voice crackled through speakers.

"*Commencing Gravity Well Seventy-One test fire in three... two...one...*"

Lighting dimmed as a roar shook the corridor. Alex tiptoed to the end of the hallway, peeked around the corner, and groaned. Dozens of scientists were tapping instrument panels, reading gauges, and slap fighting with clipboards. A quick glance at Thorpe's map confirmed the large question mark hovering over the far end of Corridor Eight. She straightened her collar, took a deep breath, and sauntered into the lion's den.

Alex threw confidence into her stride, mirroring the perpetually puzzled facial expression favored by so many Children. One or two scientists glanced up from their work, but her magic white coat told them everything they needed to know. A purple, four-armed maintenance man wearing overalls and slathered with enough grease to lubricate a locomotive stood in a cloud of steam, battling a stuck valve. She tried to play it cool, but couldn't resist staring as she walked past. The mechanic was a head shorter than her, if you counted his twin, eight-inch eyestalks. But more shockingly, his eyes radiated a blue glow, like the assassins who attacked Grandfather's funeral. The creature met her open-mouthed gape with an appraising look, then returned to straining against a gigantic crescent wrench. She nodded and kept moving.

Yellow and blue flares silhouetted a cluster of Children grouped around a window. In the next room, an engine roared like a waterfall, spitting a fifty-foot tongue of blue flame. Alex sidled into the crowd unnoticed, until she bumped into a water cooler-sized specimen jar mounted on a pair of robotic legs. The jar spun and elevated. A storm of bubbles parted like a curtain, revealing a pink brain suspended in blue liquid behind spiderwebs of cracked glass.

"WHERE IS YOUR SECURITY CLEARANCE?" A light bulb on top of the jar flickered in time with the words barking out of the robot's speaker. Even amplified, the shout barely penetrated the background wail of the experiment in progress. Alex pointed to her ears and shrugged, feigning deafness. A mechanical arm ratcheted out of a flap in the robot's waist. A miniature clockwork hand, no larger than a child's, extended an index finger to poke her belly. *"WHAT DEPARTMENT ARE YOU WITH?"* She squinted at the tarnished nameplate welded to her inquisitor's body.

Doctor Genghis Vilyab.

Alex cupped her mouth and yelled scientific words interspersed with gibberish, *"HYGIENIC mrflrm bubblabroo DENOMINATOR jblwok EXTINGUISHING DEPARTMENT."* She pointed to a pipe junction and lowered her shout to an unintelligible volume. *"I*

BEFORE E EXCEPT AFTER C, MAY THE FORCE BE WITH MY PRECIOUS. YOLO." She gave the brainquarium a comradely nod. "AM I RIGHT?"

Dr. Vilyab glared at her with more intensity than a brain floating in a vat should be able to, then snapped his fingers. A green-skinned, lab-coated flunky materialized. His linebacker-thick neck, mullet haircut, and seven-foot stature were fronted by an expression of bored malevolence. Alex immediately christened him Frankenthug.

Vilyab pointed at the floor. "REMAIN HERE. WE WILL CONVERSE WHEN THE TEST CONCLUDES."

Alex gave a thumbs-up and flashed a winning smile. The brain turned to the observation window and clomped forward, bull-dozing colleagues and sparking a shoving match. Frankenthug waded into the crowd to clear a space around his boss.

The PA screeched, "TEST FIRE TERMINATING IN FIVE... FOUR...THREE..."

Alex spun on her heel.

"TWO..."

She broke into a jog.

"ONE..."

Her legs pumped like pistons. The engine cut thrust, and Alex's ears rejoiced. Hallway lighting blinked white.

"TEST FIRE SUCCESSFUL."

"Stop!" Vilyab cried. "She's a spy! Stop her!"

Alex ducked under a horizontal geyser of steam and slammed into the purple, four-armed mechanic. Two bulging eyes flared, swaying on their stalks like daisies in a breeze. A calloused hand snatched her wrist.

"Find what you seek?" His voice had a bubbly quality, but was hoarse, probably from a lifetime of yelling over machinery.

She pried at his fingers. "Please, I'm not spying. I'm just...looking."

The creature's fat lips sneered and one of its eyestalks twisted to glance up the hall as stampeding footsteps grew louder. He tugged Alex down, sniffed her hair, then let go. "Tell Thorpe to find better spy." The mechanic latched his Goliath-edition wrench onto a pipe and bowed his legs, barricading the hallway. "Go," he growled. Alex stumbled away, confused but grateful.

An alarm squawked, and yellow light engulfed the corridor. *"Restricted Zone Breach. Code Beta Thirty, Mark Seventeen Alpha, Subclause H. All personnel respond."* The lethargic announcer even made espionage sound mundane.

White coats charged from the far end of the hallway. Alex climbed onto the dynami pipeline, ready to fight, but no one gave her a second look—they were too busy flipping through reams of index cards.

"Was that OMEGA or DELTA Thirty?"

"Subclause J indicates a gelatinous ambiwulf is loose in the water supply."

"Again? I just cleaned these socks."

"No! It was clearly Subclause K, which is, let's see...a swarm of contentious chatterdaxes."

"Again? I just bought new pants."

"Did anyone bring a klunk-ton of muffins?"[1]

Heavy footsteps and garbled shouts preceded Dr. Vilyab's approaching mob. Quarrels about "What You, Good Sir, Can Do With Your Subclauses" escalated as Alex flew up the ladder. A frantic shove opened the maintenance hatch. She squirreled her legs into the shaft and ducked out of sight while the herd of scientists groused and bickered below.

When their voices faded, Alex closed the hatch and spun the lock, wincing as metal squealed. Blue flames raged in her mind's eye. If she'd witnessed a test fire of Gravity Well Seventy-One, were there *seventy* other engines like that in the Restricted Zone? And why did the mechanic help her escape? *Tell Thorpe to find better spy?* Stooping to avoid the fusillade trap, she maneuvered the twisted ladder until it angled across the shaft.

SHHHHHPTINGTING

Darts ricocheted off the stricken scaffolding. A deep ache in Alex's forearm warned her against trying to project a force field—

not that she knew how to. She balled up the wool sock and tossed it in the air.

SHHHPTPTPT

After six throws, the tortured sock was a porcupine, and the fusillade trap was drained of ammunition. She scrambled up the warped ladder as magnets plucked darts from the unlucky ball of woolly fuzz. When Alex reached the top, she kicked off the wall, launching herself across the shaft. Her fingers closed on the bottom rung of the fixed ladder as the trap spat a parting salvo.

SHHHPTINGTINGTING

Darts careened off walls, jingling disappointment. Alex hauled herself higher, ignoring blossoming fatigue in her arms until her feet found purchase and her legs earned their keep. The rest of the climb was a simple matter of defying gravity, but once she escaped the shaft, nothing would be simple.

---

1. Classified by most scholars as a semi-sentient species, contentious chatterdaxes are famous for their violent contrarian streak. They hunt by provoking their prey to reveal an opinion on a controversial topic, then loudly argue an opposing viewpoint until their prey collapses from elevated blood pressure.
   Hearty baked goods are the recommended defensive strategy, as it is impossible to surrender an opinion with a mouth full of cinnamon bagel.

CHAPTER 40
UNSANCTIONED

Alex was halfway down Corridor Eleven when a white projectile skimmed her nose and lodged in a crevice between wall panels.

Thwhip-p-p-p

Cards riffed between nimble fingers.

"You found me fast," she said.

"Not fast enough, if what I hear about Prometheus' timetable is true." Thorpe tried to scan the hallway in both directions at once. "What did you find down there?"

"A river of dynami and a gravity well."

The Labyrinthian stopped shuffling.

"It's a ridiculously loud rocket engine," she explained.

"I'm familiar with gravity wells," Thorpe said. "They're impractical—ludicrously powerful, but too volatile to control." He puffed his cheeks and exhaled, like he was blowing out a candle. "What do you mean by *a river* of dynami?"

"Enough to fill a six-foot diameter pipeline."

He snorted. "Impossible. Dynami research on that scale is Unsanctioned by the Chieftess."

"Unsanctioned, meaning: a big no-no?"

"Unsanctioned, meaning: public execution." Cards vaulted between Thorpe's hands.

"Well, it's sanctioned now," she said. "They were test firing Gravity Well Seventy-One."

Thorpe stiffened. "*Seventy-one?* No one could be *that* reckless."

"If you say so. Now, where are my parts?"

The scientist peeled a tarp off a handcart, uncovering a pile of components. "I raided my private stash for most of this but had to fabricate a few items."

Alex smiled. Pascal wouldn't brush off her bounty this time. She grabbed the cart handle, but Thorpe blocked her with a well-placed foot. His expression hardened.

"You have to go back. I need more information, and we're running out of time!"

"No way! A belligerent, walking pickle jar and its nefarious henchman saw my face."

Thorpe chuckled. "Vilyab? Unless you disguise yourself as a spreadsheet, he won't recognize you. No Children will."

"Someone will figure it out, then tell the Chieftess."

"And admit a security breach? Not likely. Vilyab won't take credit for anything that makes him look bad."

"What's the deal with the walking brain, anyway?" she said. "It's creepy."

"He was the first Child to successfully transplant his own brain—that kind of thing earns serious street cred around here."

Alex changed tactics. "A four-armed mechanic saw me too. He sniffed me, then said to tell you to 'find better spy'—he was right, by the way."

Pirouetting cards slowed in Thorpe's hands. "Was he purple?"

"Yes. He was half my size, had two giant eyestalks, and a long scar slicing his cheek."

The Labyrinthian clucked his tongue. "Deeno's wrenching in the field again." Cards fluttered into question marks. "When you go back in, ask him what he's working on."

"I'm not going back in," she said. "Who is Deeno?"

"Master Wrencher Deeno keeps Contrivance from self-destructing, despite her citizens' best efforts."

"Why does he have four arms and eyestalks? Is he a Contrivance experiment?"

"You haven't seen a Trenchian before?" Cards whirled in a vortex beneath Thorpe's skeptical stare. "The Trench is a highly radioactive zone, given to large-scale mutations. Trenchians rarely ascend above ground, but Deeno supervises our Wrencher program. Rumor has it, he owes the Chieftess a life debt."

"Why do his eyes glow blue?"

Thorpe frowned. "Long term exposure to purified dynami turns anyone's eyes blue. How do you not know that? Where are you from?"

Alex's heart thudded in her ears. She wanted to ask about neon-eyed assassins, but the last thing she needed was to raise questions about her background. Time to change the subject. "If dynami research is unsanctioned, why not tell the Chieftess what's going on?"

Thorpe scoffed, "If a river of dynami is flowing through Contrivance, the Chieftess is responsible for it—and if she's breaking her own rules, she's desperate. Prometheus has been in motion for months, and non-volantium pipes can't store dynami forever. Elasticity ratios will create sympathetic combustion." He read her blank look and riffed cards into an explosion. "Dynami go boom," he clarified.

"Given what I've seen from the Children, I'm surprised it hasn't already."

"You'd be amazed how competent we can be when the Chieftess directly supervises a project. You need to go back to Corridor Eight."

"I held up my end of the deal," she said. "We're done."

Thorpe folded his arms. "Best of luck sourcing the rest of your parts. Don't wait too long to come to your senses—we're running out of time."

One of the handcart's wheels developed a nerve-fraying squeak that stabbed Alex's eardrums all the way back to *Angelus*. The relief on Pascal's face when she rolled up the gangplank made everything better.

Hot solder stung her nostrils as she spread trophies across two lab tables. The gruffletrunts made their rounds, rubbing each component and squabbling over the largest ones. Pascal lifted a blunt-pointed star from the wagon and released a low, appreciative whistle. "You must be a wily negotiator—nexus hubs are scarce, even in the Crypt. Nice find." He rummaged deeper and scrutinized an octagonal metal thermos. "Where did you find this?" His brown eye, comically enlarged by a magnifying lens, bored into hers.

She shrugged. "I asked around."

"A reciprocating Hult Cylinder is a theoretical impossibility. I put it on the list as a joke."

She cursed under her breath. Thanks, Thorpe. "I got it from a guy who knew a guy who owed another guy for watering his plants, or something."

Pascal flipped his lens up. "Where did you find these, Alex?"

She winced. Here we go. "The Restricted Zone."

He slammed the Hult Cylinder on the table. "I told you not to go into the Restricted Zone!"

Alex put her hands on her hips. "You told me to find parts."

"Not by interfering in the Children's business!"

"You're the one refereeing a think tank!"

"To keep us on the Chieftess' good side!" he said. "If I refused to stop those lunkbrains from blowing themselves up, we'd be shoveling sewage in the Undergrease right now."

Alex took a quick breath, then blurted, "I saw something in Corridor Eight—"

"*Corridor Eight?*" He smacked his forehead. "Of *course* you saw something. Every day, Children devise six new ways to end the world before breakfast."

"But the Chieftess—"

"The Chieftess doesn't look past her own self-interest." He paced in a circle, flexing his prosthetic arm. "Did anyone see you?"

Alex grimaced. "A few people."

"Who?"

"A walking jar and his pet human."

"You tangled with *Vilyab*? Bad idea."

"Yeah, I figured that out when he incited a mob to chase me."

"How did you get away?"

"Luck, mostly." She grabbed his elbow. "Pascal, there's a pipeline in Corridor Eight—"

The inventor pushed her hand away. "I don't care."

"It's full of dynami!"

Pascal pounded the table. "Even if the Chieftess did something as monumentally stupid as harvesting enough dynami to fill a pipeline, it's not our concern." He tossed parts into a bin. "We've got to leave before she perceives us as a threat."

Hope swelled in Alex's chest—maybe she wouldn't have to deal with Thorpe again. "Does that mean we don't need more parts?"

He sighed. "A few more. We'll scavenge in the morning."

"You repair *Angelus*," she said. "Give me a list and I'll get it done."

Suspicion crinkled the corners of Pascal's eyes. "Stay out of the Restricted Zone."

"Not a problem." So much for coming clean.

Thorpe was going to get his spy.

CHAPTER 41
AN INCONVENIENT REPAIR

Apprentice Wrencher Zevv wiped his hands on his coveralls, bit a chunk from his clotblud sandwich, and double-checked his safety line. A quick glance at the pock-marked walls of Shaft 218C confirmed the security sensors were correct—a fusillade trap *had* fired multiple times. He shook his head. *Lunkbrains.* Once again, petty interdepartmental rivalry had escalated into guerrilla warfare, and a wrencher had to clean up the mess. At least there wasn't trans-dimensional slime everywhere this time.

Whatever they were doing in the Madhouse must be important for Master Wrencher Deeno to schedule himself on a routine maintenance rotation—or maybe Ol' Scarface was trying to keep Zevv and the other apprentices paranoid so they would triple check their work.

He closed his lunch box and pressed a negator wand against the fusillade trap's control module. When the telltale whine of revolving magnets faded, he waved a broomstick handle in front of the motion sensors. The Wrencher motto, *"Better safe than impaled by a lunatic,"* had saved his life four times this month.[*1] When no venom-tipped darts attacked the probe, he rappelled down to the access hatch. Warped ladder remnants and a collection of random debris lay scattered on the floor.

305

Zevv rubbed his front teeth with his tongue, relishing the familiar tang of industrial grease. He picked up a wool sock and poked a finger through one of thirty holes. The crime scene didn't add up. Children settled scores in the least efficient, most pointlessly convoluted ways possible. A lack of scientific paraphernalia —and a hole-ridden *sock*, of all things—suggested an amateur had tried to infiltrate the Madhouse. He skimmed the work order again.

Maintenance Shaft 218C - Security Sensors Triggered. Inspect defense mechanism. Leave no trace of your presence. Report directly to me.

Master Wrencher Deeno had signed it, an occurrence so rare, Zevv meticulously folded the yellow paper to save for his scrapbook. He nudged the sock with a steel-toed boot. It pained his wrencher soul to leave the wrecked ladder untouched, but orders were orders. Zevv clicked his belt winch into retrieval mode and listened to the wire complain until he stopped above the motion sensors to re-arm the fusillade trap.

Then Zevv indulged in one of the habitual overreaches that earned him these kinds of grunt assignments. Like all wrenchers, he longed for the prestige of capturing and destroying Drog. On the slim chance the clockwork canine had been here and might return, Zevv deployed an additional trap. Magnets snapped an articulated frame flush to the rounded walls, camouflaging the contraption against the riveted surface. With a single green flash of a glow bulb, the Highly Inconvenient Megabob snare declared itself armed and ready to deploy.

No point mentioning this in his report.

Apprentice Wrencher Zevv ascended Shaft 218C, oblivious to the ticking time bomb he'd left behind.

---

1. Other useful nuggets from the Wrencher Handbook include:
    "Never underestimate the destructive potential of a bored genius holding a red button."
    "A mysterious sandwich on a plate in the hallway outside the Genetic Manipulation Lab is not a delicious gift."

"Safety is our Number 2 priority, just behind Not Pressing Buttons."

"If it's smoking, put it out. If it's burning, douse it. If it's chasing you down a corridor, don't trip."

"If your feet are fleetin', you won't get eaten."

CHAPTER 42
NEW BETRAYALS

The world looked brighter after a few hours of sleep. Alex stalked an intoxicating aroma of hazelnut and mystery spices from her cabin to Pascal's lab, where a recently drained thermos anchored the inventor's latest—and hopefully, final—wish list.

1. *Fractal Atomizing Filter (Anything over 2 microns and we choke on irradiated particles, so check the label.)*
2. *Six Kobolex Rings (Look for yellow ones—blue ones smell like rotten cheese when they heat up, and the gruffletrunts eat them.)*
3. *Proxylinear Belt Lubricant (Ask Dr. Wisto, in the Vestigial Nostrils Department. If he argues, remind him of my help in the Taranticle Incident, then threaten a visit from Drog.)*
4. *STAY OUT OF THE RESTRICTED ZONE, LUNKBRAIN.*

Alex pocketed the list, retrieved Thorpe's handcart, and squeaked across the hangar.

Dr. Strim snapped to attention when the bay door screeched open. "Where did you disappear to last night?"

"If anyone discovers we lost you, we'll be transferred to the Undergrease," Ploz muttered, kicking the cart with his toe.

Her guards' forlorn expressions tugged Alex's heartstrings. Ditching them again would be like kicking two puppies—which was fine, since her plan was to win them over.

"Sorry! Yesterday, at the think tank, I heard a guy from Ballistics bragging about something called 'Project Prometheus'. It sounded cool, so I followed him into the Restricted Zone."

"*Into the Restricted* —" Strim hissed.

"Shhhh!" Ploz cut him off, then turned to Alex. "Ballistics, you say? Go on."

Bingo. She cast a line for old grudges, "I didn't see a name tag, but he claimed to be smarter than everyone else in Contrivance."

"Dr. Yurp? Dr. Burble?" Strim said, watching her face.

She nodded. "One of those sounds right. He wouldn't stop talking about how great it was to work on an elite project like Prometheus, and how pleased the Chieftess was."

Ploz scowled. "I'll bet they're fully funded."

She fanned the flames of jealousy. "Their pastry buffet *was* opulent."

"We need to report your activity to our supervisor," Strim said, but he didn't sound convinced.

Alex bit her lip. It was only a matter of time before someone connected the mysterious spy in Corridor Eight to her disappearance yesterday. "Good idea. He'll ask inconvenient questions about where you guys were, but security is important, especially with all those piles of unattended parts."

Ploz leaned forward, narrowing his eyes. "When you say *piles*... are we talking *mountains* or *foothills*?" His hungry stare warned Alex she was dangerously close to starting a gold rush.

"Mountains, definitely. And the only scientist down there was a walking brain jar."

Ploz clenched his fists. "*Vilyab.*"

"Yeah, that guy," Alex said. "I hid until he left, then grabbed a bunch of salvage and ran for it. I'm going to make another stab at the stockpile today. Do you want me to look for anything?"

Ploz rubbed his hands and chuckled like a supervillain with an inside track on a planet-destroying laser.

Strim threw his colleague a pained look. "We can't interfere in Restricted Zone business."

Alex started up the corridor. "You're right, we should leave Ballistics' supplies alone. They deserve to have everything they need."

Dr. Ploz choked an indignant cry, and both guards scurried to keep up. "Let's not rush to hasty conclusions," he puffed, glaring at his comrade.

Strim, wincing in time with the wheel's obnoxious squeak, nodded.

Alex feigned surprise. "Okay, if you're sure. What parts do you need?"

The tall scientist made a *keep it down* gesture. He bellowed, "WHAT IS THAT? YOU REQUIRE FOODSTUFFS?" The right half of his face twitched with rapid-fire conspiratorial winks. "LET US SEE WHAT IS AVAILABLE AT THE COMMISSARY." He whispered, *"I'm intentionally misleading eavesdroppers."*

She bobbed her head. "Smart."

Ploz handed Alex a strip of paper that was as long as he was tall. Her eyes widened—the list read more like an arms dealer's catalog than an inventory of scientific equipment. She gave Ploz a flat look. "Choose *one* item Ballistics might *actually* have and I'll look for it."

Dr. Ploz snatched his paper back and crumpled it with a snarl. "Fine. I want an angulating portal retro-stabilizer, but it better have a racing stripe."

Dr. Strim whispered, *"I'll take four globules of thermolytic metamucus."*

Alex gave a thumbs-up. "Sounds good."

Strim crept ahead of the cart while Ploz "covered their six," as if the squeaking wheel didn't torpedo any hope they had for stealth. Alex flinched every time the thin scientist screamed and leapt around a corner, windmilling paddles like he was swatting a squadron of flies. At least Thorpe wouldn't have any trouble finding her.

"Why are you guys so twitchy?" she asked. "We do this every

day."

Ploz answered without tearing his gaze from the hallway behind them, "Yesterday you were a hopeless rookie who couldn't barter to save her life." He clonked the wagon with the butt of his spear. "Now you're a proven scavenger, hunting in the open. Predators will smell blood."

Alex opened her mouth to argue when a flash of white whirled across the junction with Corridor Six and lodged between two panels in the opposite wall. She pocketed the quivering card without breaking stride and said, "I'll stash the cart here, so no one can track us to Corridor Nine."

Dr. Strim shifted his weight from one foot to the other, twirling his paddles impatiently. "Hurry," he said. Ploz knotted a red bandana around his forehead and tipped over backwards, providing a perfect distraction for Alex to dart down a side alley.

Thorpe fumed in the shadows. *Why did you bring the blunder squad?* he whispered.

"I had to bribe them so they won't turn me in."

"They work for the Chieftess!"

"Don't you?"

Furrows in Thorpe's forehead deepened. "Not for a long time. What did you bribe them with?"

"An angulating portal retro-stabilizer with a racing stripe and four globules of thermolytic metamucus." She handed him Pascal's wishlist. "This stuff is for me."

He scanned the paper. "The Taranticle Incident—those were the days." Two fingers flicked, folded the list, and slid it into his coat. "Get down there fast. They started a countdown on Prometheus."

Alex pointed at the cart and matched his chilly tone. "Just have the parts ready when I get back."

Ploz and Strim stationed themselves at the mouth of Corridor Nine. They would be at each other's throats within five minutes, but well-armed, bickering Children were an excellent deterrent to casual foot traffic. Alex made quick time to the maintenance shaft, where fresh boot prints in the grime chilled her blood. She held her breath, senses straining to detect any intruders. When a minute passed without an ambush, she spun the wheel lock, which swiveled freely and quietly. *Suspiciously* quietly. Fresh-grease-lubri-cating-the-hinges quietly. Given all of Contrivance's corroding infrastructure, what were the chances *this* particular shaft had received routine maintenance in the past eight hours?

A gravity well rattled Corridor Nine, taunting her. She hooked a crowbar she'd borrowed from *Angelus* onto her belt, then opened the hatch before she could change her mind. The shaft was every bit as dirty as she remembered, but its light panels no longer flick-ered like fluorescent bulbs in a horror film. The ladder groaned and jiggled beneath her weight—too bad her mystery maintenance man hadn't bothered to tighten a few bolts while he was at it.

Alex stopped above the fusillade trap and reassured her long-suffering sneakers, "Don't worry, I came prepared this time." She dangled her crowbar in front of the trap's targeting sensors.

SHHHPTPTPT-TING-PTINGGG

Purple venom sizzled on the bar, dribbling onto the hatch below. It worked! Piece of ca—

KUH-CHUNK

Metal bands sprung off the shaft walls, slapping her flesh.

Clack-Click-Clack-Chik-Clack-Chik-Ching

Flexible strips conformed to Alex's limbs, flattening her against the wall like a human hieroglyph. She strained against the bands until blood trickled down her right arm, but the magnetic locks didn't budge. Alex balled her fists. *Of course* someone had added another booby trap—in this city of malignant Einsteins, she was lucky the shaft wasn't *triple*-trapped. At least Ozzie wasn't here to see this.

She marshaled her strength, then fought her restraints with every ounce of energy she had left. Her right ankle slipped half an inch, but nothing else shifted. Alex slumped.

"*PSSSST*," Dr. Ploz stage whispered, from the shaft's mouth. "What are you doing?"

She winced at the agony of shrugging. "Just hanging out."

"This is no time to relax! Salvage parties are hunting us. I feel it in my bones."

312

"I'm trapped, Dr. Ploz. Climb down and let me out!"

"Traps are beyond my expertise. I'll get help."

"No! Don't leave me."

Too late.

The list of potential helpers was short, since Ploz wouldn't risk sharing a source of spare parts with his colleagues, and Dr. Strim's first instinct would be to submit a grant proposal for a Trap Extraction Device. No, there was only one person he would ask.

Twenty minutes later, gear rustled and clinked above her, but she didn't look up. A gently squeaking belt winch lowered into view the last face in the world she wanted to see. Pascal wore a polite smile, but bulging veins in his temple forecast a monsoon of anger.

"Hello," he said, brightly. Alex bit her lip and looked away. He flipped a magnifying lens down. "Don't blame yourself. It's my fault." Pascal inspected a strap binding her wrist. "Clearly, the translapede I implanted in your brain malfunctioned." His voice sharpened, rising in volume, "Why else would Dr. Ploz beg me to free you from a Highly Inconvenient Megabob snare in a maintenance shaft that services Corridor Eight, *after I specifically told you to stay out of the Restricted Zone?*"

She mumbled apologetic noises.

The tip of Pascal's index finger flipped up, deploying a mini-blowtorch. He lowered tinted lenses to shield his eyes. "I trusted you," he said. Her left wrist manacle surrendered to the flame, unleashing a flood of pins and needles. Another blast of heat emancipated her right wrist. She clung to the ladder while Pascal worked on her ankles. "Do you know what the Chieftess does to spies?" he said. "No? Me neither, because their bodies *have NEVER been found.*"

Alex said, "I was just trying to help."

Pascal punched the wall, denting the shaft with an echoing *boom* that summoned Ploz's head to the open hatch. When the scientist saw Alex glaring up at him, he gave two thumbs-up and ducked out of sight.

"I told you to scavenge parts, not provoke a mob of dullards to swarm *Angelus* with solar-powered pitchforks!" Pascal severed her leg shackles with two swipes of his blowtorch. "Where did you find those parts yesterday? There's no way the Madhouse just *happened* to have exactly what we needed."

Alex massaged her right ankle. Pascal was already angry—she might as well get his eyes on Project Prometheus. She pointed at the hatch below. "See for yourself, but watch out for the fusillade trap."

The inventor glowered. "Wait here." He activated his belt winch and squeaked down the shaft. When he breached the targeting zone, Alex shouted, "Look out!"

SHHHPTPTPT

Fifteen doses of calamitous wretch venom swerved harmlessly into the walls.

Chink-chink-clunka-chink-clank-clink

The inventor descended, unruffled and untouched, as the trap tried again.

SHHHHHPTPTPT

Chikka-kink-chik-chatter-chank

He stood next to the hatch, looking up at Alex with a smug grin. "Rule One of trap mitigation: always reverse the magnetic field."

Show-off.

Pascal spun the wheel lock and cracked the hatch, with an absence of screeching metal—someone had greased those hinges, too. He stretched his neck, popping vertebrae like firecrackers, then snaked his head into the corridor. After checking both directions, he descended into Corridor Eight.

Alex chewed fingertip calluses, counting seconds. There was no way Pascal could infiltrate the Madhouse undetected without a lab coat. What if he got caught?

Alarms shrieked. An apathetic voice announced, *"Perimeter Breach. Code Gamma Six, Mark Fifteen Omega, Subclause…um…hang on, I've got it here somewhere…Subclaaaause…M? Or possibly K. All personnel respond."*[1]

A crowd of people shouting about tranquilizer donuts thundered by as a dark shape broke the yellow light pouring in through the hatch. Someone was coming! Panic propelled Alex into motion. Halfway up the shaft, she glanced over her shoulder and yelped. Pascal's winch was smoking, and his eyes blazed with an animal fury that looked foreign on his normally affable face. He circled Alex's waist with an arm and accelerated upward. When they escaped the shaft, the Dromedarian slammed the hatch closed and slumped beside it, panting.

"They have lost their minds," he growled. "That much dynami will push elasticity ratios into—"

"Sympathetic combustion?" Alex finished his sentence.

His jaw dropped. "How do you know that?"

She sighed. "I have a confession to make."

---

1. Thanks to Dr. Weedle changing the coding system fifteen minutes previously, the announcer accidentally warned the Children in Corridor Eight of a rampaging Thumpergrout, whose only known weakness is an affinity for dense, high-sugar carbohydrates.

315

CHAPTER 43
OLD ENEMIES

The scowl on Pascal's face deepened with every turn of a maze he seemed to know by heart. Alex jogged to keep pace with the inventor's brisk strides. It was just the two of them, since Ploz and Strim had gauged the Dromedarian's mood, then claimed to have urgent business teleporting a hamster. Pascal stomped to a halt in front of Thorpe's lab and glared at the sign over the door.

She grabbed his arm. "Let me explain."

He bellowed, *"Thorpe!"*, kicked the door open, and charged through a cloud of sawdust. The Labyrinthian sprung from his chair, flicking a paper ninja star that Pascal slapped aside. Thorpe smashed a button, releasing a hail of spikes that plunged through the ceiling. The Dromedarian dove under a table, plucked a red ball from the depths of his trench coat, and heaved it at his nemesis. Thorpe twisted his wrist, unfolding a shield that blocked an explosion of droolug mucus.

Alex leapt between the former colleagues. "Stop it!"

Pascal cocked his arm to throw another slug grenade.

"Put it *down!*" she said. "You're acting like children."

The inventor clenched his jaw hard enough to make his teeth groan, then jammed the ball in his pocket.

Thorpe peered around the edge of his drooping shield. "He started it."

"You tried to skewer me!"

"I see you haven't lost your fondness for wallowing in self-pity. That was low grade pulp—if I wanted to skewer you, I would have used card stock. Meanwhile, you risked killing me by gluing my fingers together!"

Pascal folded his arms. "Of course—as usual, you're the victim here."

"I rely on pliable pinkies to fold battle edges!" Cards materialized between Thorpe's fingers like claws. "Not that *you* care."

"I care that you sent a gullible child into the Restricted Zone," the inventor said. "Are you trying to add another Forsythe to your murder tally?"

Alex's eyebrows, still frowning at "gullible child," shot up. *Another* Forsythe?

Thorpe gave her a sharp look. "So *that's* where he got you—well, that makes sense." He turned to the Dromedarian. "Congratulations, you sleuthed out my elaborate plan to destroy the Forsythe family, one halfwit at a time."

"Hey!" Alex said.

"I warned you what would happen if you crossed me again," Pascal growled.

"I wasn't listening."

The inventor twisted a crimson dial on his elbow. "You never do." Red light flared between segments of his arm.

Thorpe tapped his coat pocket, and blue light traced the edges of his cards.

A wave of heat rushed through Alex's arm, throbbing in time with her quickening pulse. She clutched her left wrist and muttered, "Calm down, guys." Her vision blurred.

Bolts of crackling red energy shot from Pascal's fingers as Thorpe's cards spun across the room like neon blades. Alex shrieked. Pressure in her arm burst its dam, projecting a translucent blue dome from her wrist that deflected the lightning into the ceiling and embedded the cards in a bench. A wave of exhaustion rolled down Alex's body, jellifying her legs. The shield blinked out of existence when she hit the floor.

"How did she do that?" Thorpe's voice was muffled and distant.

Alex flinched as fingers forced her eyelid open, permitting light to stab her brain. Someone twisted her forearm. "Dynami projection," Pascal said.

She groaned, commanding her body to sit up. When her muscles refused, she lowered her ambition to flexing a finger and was relieved when skin tightened around her knuckles.

"A shield that strong requires a power stone bigger than this room," Thorpe said.

"An armillam implanted itself in her forearm a week ago." The Dromedarian tapped one of her plugs, generating a spark. "I've seen Stone Tech do stranger things."

"Can you remove it?" Thorpe asked—a touch too eagerly.

"Not without cutting her arm off."

"Oh."

"Try not to sound so disappointed."

"I'm only disappointed she saved your wretched hide from a thrashing."

Pascal huffed. "I was one second away from gluing your hands to your forehead, and you know it."

Alex moaned, "Stop talking. I'd like to get up now, please."

Unseen hands helped her upright, then pressed a flask to her lips. She swallowed automatically, eyes widening as liquid fire torched her throat. Alex attempted to cough her lungs out, then waggled speech into her swollen tongue. "Why are you drinking battery acid?" she croaked.

Pascal looked hurt. "That was the last of my Miserabawl roast[*1] —it's impossible to get more, thanks to a quibbling hoardworm outbreak." He snapped the flask to his belt. "How did you project that shield?"

Alex flexed her arm, wincing. "No idea. It happened at the fusillade trap, too. I was going to ask you how it works."

He pointed to her arm plugs. "I think these nodes harvest ambient dynami, then the armillam projects it."

"Sounds cool."

Thorpe grinned. "It is."

Pascal rolled his eyes. "It's also how mutations happen."

"It might be cool to have a tail," Alex said. "Good for climbing."

The inventor stood up. "Even if it grows out of your forehead? Mutations don't come packaged in convenient boxes—you're just as likely to melt your joints to jelly as you are to sprout functional wings."

"He's right," Thorpe said. "Although, don't knock jelly joints—they're excellent for dancing."

Pascal turned to his nemesis. "You're not helping."

"Okay, let's talk about *helping*," the Labyrinthian said. "Did you see the gravity well?" Pascal unscrewed a panel on his prosthetic elbow, pointedly ignoring the question. Thorpe shuffled a deck of cards and said, "I'll interpret your complete lack of shock as an unqualified 'yes'. Then you know as well as I do something disastrous is in the works and we're running out of time to stop it. Dynami research has been unsanctioned for centuries, and suddenly a fully juiced pipeline is running through the Restricted Zone to power *gravity wells*. Why would the Chieftess break her own Black Ordinances?"

Pascal grunted. "Since when do *you* care about the Black Ordinances?" He jabbed a screwdriver at his former colleague. "I recall the limits of your morality with *astounding* clarity."

Thorpe palmed his forehead. "Are you stuck on the sivsuit? That's ancient history."

"Not to me!" The inventor turned to Alex. "Your *friend* here stole my sivsuit and sold it to the Maelstrom. That's how Skhaar crossed the Divide." He slammed the screwdriver down. "This man killed your parents, and you *lied* for him!"

Anger burned in Alex's chest with familiar heat, but the shame was new. She whispered, "I didn't know."

Melancholy shapes—a raven, flames, and a Sauracian—surfaced and disappeared in the shuffling cards. Sitting in the wreckage of a

319

neglected lab, the scruffy Labyrinthian cut a pathetic figure. Perhaps he'd gotten what he deserved. Maybe she had, too.

Pascal read her face. "Don't feel sorry for him. Thorpe knew what he was doing back then, and he knows it now."

The cards stopped. "It was a long time ago," the scientist said, staring at his hands. "If I'd known what the Maelstrom intended, I wouldn't have given them the sivsuit. I'm trying to make amends."

Pascal scoffed. "*Amends.* You won't lift a finger if it doesn't benefit you. What's your angle now?"

"Redemption," Thorpe mumbled. "Saving the world."

"The only thing you've ever cared about saving is your own skin." The Dromedarian pulled Alex to her feet. "We're leaving. Thanks for the parts." He snatched a handful of circuit boards from a workbench and tossed them onto an overloaded cart.

A metallic scuffle in the hallway froze Pascal in place. The inventor's frown creased to a smile as Drog blasted through the doorway like a bronze wrecking ball.

BRRRRK! BRRRK! BRRRRK!

Servos zipped and chattered as the canine danced around its creator, barking with robotic joy.

"Drog!" Pascal rubbed the machine's back. "You've been upgraded!" Drog spun in a circle, then spat a component at the Dromedarian's feet. Pascal glanced at the offering, and his brow furrowed. He picked up the square of black netting and examined it under a magnifying lens.

Thorpe templed his fingers. "When I saw you marching here, I knew you wouldn't listen to me, so I sent Drog to fetch evidence."

"Where did he get this?" Pascal said.

"Contrivance's outer hull—powersieve netting covers the entire city."

The inventor glanced at Drog. "Is he telling the truth, boy?"

Brrk. A mouthful of cogs and gears *plinked* on the ground.

"But why? What could she hope to accomplish with..." Pascal's voice trailed off.

Thorpe gestured to his video monitor, which displayed a vault door marked *Restricted.* "Think about it," he said. "The Chieftess secretly built more than seventy gravity wells—engines too powerful to be permitted under the Black Ordinances—then stockpiled enough dynami to supply all the wells while fueling the biggest powersieve in history."

Pascal's eyes widened as he finished Thorpe's thought, "She's taking Contrivance through the Divide."

---

1. Miserabawl Roast was ranked "Second Most Excruciating Caffeine Rush" by *Coffeenoisseur Weekly's* Annual Migraine Issue six years running.

   By necessity, Thwartian Coffee (street name: "Catastrophuccino"), a perennial first place winner, was awarded a special Perpetual Grand Prize and removed from future competition after every judge who sniffed it "experienced a brainplosion elevating them to a plane of consciousness beyond sleep, or indeed, blinking."

CHAPTER 44
BRAINSTORMS

For all their animosity, Pascal and Thorpe were on the same page when it came to brewing high-quality coffee. Alex licked delicious foam from her lips ("Perditian Roast! Bliss in a mug!") and watched the Dromedarian scribble calculations on a chalkboard while his archnemesis needled him.

"You're forgetting time bleed," Thorpe said. "Every twelve seconds spent in the Divide doubles the power drain."

The inventor reciprocated with a death glare. "Sorry, I forget—which of us *designed* a powersieve, *built* a powersieve, and then used it to cross the Divide?"

The Labyrinthian lowered his mug. "That was you?"

Pascal's eyes bulged as he realized he'd disclosed critical information to an enemy. He pursed his lips. "No."

Alex was impressed. In a city of ego-driven scientists who claimed credit for the sun rising, Pascal's denial was a Herculean display of humility—although, given the Dromedarian's purpling cheeks, the effort of not boasting was going to kill him. She cleared her throat and threw a lifeline. "Can seventy gravity wells really move a city?"

Thorpe pillaged a filing cabinet, then flicked a sheet of paper across the room in a physics-defying arc. "Here's data from the experimental trials."

Pascal snatched the page out of the air as if he'd done it a thousand times—which he probably had, in better days. He said, "What was the official reason for blacklisting gravity well research?"

"The whole 'destroying a quarter of Contrivance' thing was considered a significant design flaw—and that was only a single engine."

Pascal whistled through his teeth as he read the page. "Even if the city crosses the Divide safely, radioactive blowback from the power-sieve will destroy Terravenum." He looked up. "This isn't the Chieftess' style—she takes risks, but she's not reckless. Something is wrong."

Thorpe waved his mug. "That's what I've been trying to tell you."

The Dromedarian scribbled an equation on the board. "What's the launch window?"

"Within the next five hours."

The scratching of chalk stopped. Drog's neck squeaked as he looked from one master to the other.

"How do you know that?" Pascal asked, in a dangerously calm voice.

Thorpe tapped a keypad, and a colossal cylinder appeared on the video monitor. "Behold, the only place in Contrivance beyond the Chieftess' iron grip: the central cafeteria's coffee engine." Steaming, black liquid gushed through a mysterious gauntlet of copper pipes and glass canals until gravity dripped flawless caffeine into a waiting mug. "The Drippinator was designed to make a single cup of coffee as a proof-of-concept, but yielded such transcendent roast, no one dared to modify it. Thus, it brews one heavenly cup at a time, while geniuses wait in line and gossip." He twisted a knob and pointed to a queue of thermos-toting Children stretched around the cafeteria. Conversation burst from a speaker, syncing with the mouths of the fourth and fifth scientists in line.

"Did you hear? Dr. Rooshem started a Vegetable Combat Training Lab next door to a marshump nesting chamber."

"Oh, he'll be invaded by the weekend."

"He theorizes broccoli will defend itself if sufficiently threatened."

"Ludicrous. Broccoli is a well-documented pacifist."[1]

Thorpe huffed an impatient sigh and panned the camera left. New voices argued through the speaker.

"I'm telling you, it was an entire WAGON of parts. That child found the Motherlode!"

"The Motherlode isn't real."

"Oh, really, Dr. Skeptic? Why else would a mysterious girl roam the city at night hauling a wagon overflowing with volantium?"

"I heard it was a convoy of twenty carts pulled by Ghostly Marvin."[2]

Alex's cheeks blushed under the heat of Pascal's glare. Thorpe panned the camera further down the line of caffeine enthusiasts.

"At least Ballistics won't hog so many resources after today."

"Blasted rocket jockeys!"

"Project PROmetheus...more like Project AMATEUR-metheus, am I right?"

"That wasn't funny eight weeks ago, and it's less funny now, Odswold."

Thorpe turned down the volume. "Piecing together useful information from this crowd is like herding nipnards—difficult, but doable with enough patience and armor-plated trousers. The Chieftess kept a tight lid on Prometheus, but clues trickled out." He gestured to the yarn-covered chalkboard detailing his investigation. "When Alex described the gravity well and dynami pipeline, the true scale of the project came into focus."

Pascal tapped Alex's shoulder and nodded at the door. She followed him and hopped onto a lab table. He growled, "What did I tell you about Rule One?"

"This isn't my fault!"

"Let's recap: I asked you to scavenge a few parts, then you allied with Number Four on my Revenge List and booked us front row seats to the end of the world."

"I shouldn't have lied to you," she said, "but Prometheus was already in motion when we got here."

The inventor scowled and scratched Drog's chin as the canine's tail pummeled the floor.

Taktaktaktaktak

Alex cleared her throat. "Out of curiosity, who are Numbers One through Three on your Revenge List?"

"Depends on the day—usually it's Skhaar, my brother, and a shoeshine guy on Aeronoth who never has change for a klunkling, even though it's his *job*."

"Did I crack the Top Ten?"

"Not yet, but you launched a strong campaign by strangling the engine with a winch cable and lying about Thorpe. Don't give up, you have potential."

Alex grinned and tilted her head at the Labyrinthian, who was eavesdropping on the Drippinator queue. "Do you trust him?"

"I learned the hard way not to." Pascal lobbed a screwdriver across the lab and Drog scurried after it in a jubilant spasm of clanking limbs. "But Thorpe is right: Prometheus is an apocalypse waiting to happen."

Alex touched the inventor's hoof. "We can just fix *Angelus* and leave."

He shook his head. "I'm as close to an expert on dynami as there is, and the Chieftess knows it, so she played on my ego and had me correct the Ballistic Department's math. Before I showed up, the gravity wells would have blown Contrivance into next week. Whatever happens next is my fault." His lower lip twisted. "It's time to do something…heroic."

Thorpe scribbled *Operation: Prometheus Shutdown* on the chalkboard and diagrammed a map. "You can deactivate the gravity wells from the control room. The entry point is *here*."

"No." Pascal smeared the drawing, then scrawled *Operation: Rudderless Weaselface* on his half of the board. "If we use hallways, twenty goons from Ballistics will atomize us before we get anywhere near the control room. We need to enter through the vents."

Thorpe X-ed out the inventor's plan, scribbled *Operation: Archangel*, then sketched a man floating down to the city under a parachute. "Why not glide in through a skylight on a Labyrinthian assault chute? It will take me time to fold one that can take your weight, but—"

"I'm not riding anything *you* fold," Pascal said. He wrote *Operation: Never Trust Backstabbing Backstabbers*, then diagrammed a plan so complicated, it made the Normandy landing look like a jaunt to the mailbox.

"Pointlessly complex, as usual," Thorpe scoffed. He pointed to the upper right corner, where a peacock was torching a bicycle with a flamethrower. "What's this?"

Pascal folded his arms. "The ultimate distraction."

"Where are we going to find a petulant drawlbeak with opposable thumbs in the next hour?"

"Seriously? This is Contrivance—I saw five on my way here."

Thorpe clawed the air and huffed an exasperated sigh. "We need a *proper* plan, where you dangle over pressure-sensitive plates in a harness, using acid to melt through a padlock."

"We're going to dangle together, Thorpe," the inventor said. "If you want my help, you're coming with me."

The Labyrinthian's eyes widened. "I need to supervise the operation from here."

Pascal's stony expression left no room for negotiation. "You betrayed me once, and we both know you'll do it again. At least this time it will be to my face."

Alex raised her hand. "I'm coming too."

"No," the Dromedarian said. He sketched a Trojan walrus.

She clenched her fists. "I want to help."

"Then keep *Angelus* warmed up, and the hangar bay open. When Prometheus implodes, I'm going to come running like a swarm of ravening turfclaws are chomping at my heels—which they probably will be, if Dr. Stelk's grant got approved."

"*Angelus* isn't ready," she said.

326

Pascal sniffed. "She'll fly." He illustrated a new strategy, then stepped back. "What do you think?"

"Where I come from, we call that a human cannonball," Alex said. "For a genius, you devise a lot of flawed plans."

"The physics are sound," he protested.

"How strong is your helmet?"

Pascal sighed and turned to Thorpe. "We'll keep it simple, then. Protocol requires any experiment with potential for a Level Eight radiation leak or higher to use a Master Key. We'll break into the control room through a maintenance shaft, steal the key, then try to disable the gravity wells without cratering the city. If we get caught, you'll be my human shield."

"I hate this plan," Thorpe said.

"That's its chief redeeming quality. Let's go."

---

1. Broccoli scores a 12.7 ("Practically Guileless") on the Ludwik-Vildenholm Malevolence Scale. To give perspective: cauliflower's well-documented propensity to shove enemies off ledges, then feign innocence, earns it a score of 791.8 ("Don't Turn Your Back").

   The highest scoring plant in history (931.2 - "Likely to Declare Itself A Warlord") is Lady Misery, a sprig of rosemary that ruled a large valley in the Quarrel Mountains with an iron fist for the better part of a week, then got eaten by a belchgoat.

2. "Ghostly Marvin" (Dr. Marvin Korik) was infamous amongst the Children for his dragon-worthy parts hoard and underhanded scavenging tactics. His favorite ploy was to fake his death, then rob colleagues' stockpiles during his memorial service.

CHAPTER 45
THUNDERSKUNK DOWN

Alex paced *Angelus'* deck, glaring at the hangar door, as the starboard engine clattered to a stop for the third time in twenty minutes. She groaned and stabbed the ignition button while Socrates bellowed inside his nest bubble. The propeller stuttered, then begrudgingly rotated up to speed.

Pascal was half an hour overdue, and his newly minted plan, *Operation: Double-Crossing Thunderskunk*, was light on contingencies: *"If I'm not back in two hours, leave without me. What? You don't know how to fly Angelus? Okay, if I don't return, hide in the lower levels of Contrivance until Layla shows up. Wait, we're going to rescue Layla, aren't we? Fine, stand here and keep your hand on the throttle until I get back. On second thought, don't touch anything. Just stand here."*

Something had gone wrong. Maybe Thorpe betrayed Pascal to the Chieftess. Or maybe their mutual resentment had boiled over and they were hurling science at each other in an abandoned lab.

A gravity well test rattled ceiling girders. Alex shot Dr. Ploz and Dr. Strim a black look—after Pascal threatened to unleash Drog on their research if she escaped the hangar, the scientists had taken to guarding the door with infuriating diligence. A shrunken silhouette appeared in the doorway, and Alex ducked below the railing. There was no mistaking those four arms and swaying eyestalks—Master Wrencher Deeno had found her.

Whatever the Trenchian said to Ploz and Strim provoked them into an argument. Alex had been around the pair long enough to predict the ebb and flow of their fights. She waited until the yelling petered out, then risked a peek over the railing—to her horror, Deeno was halfway up *Angelus'* gangplank! She stood, straightening her clothes with the air of someone who wouldn't dream of infiltrating the Restricted Zone in a gorilla-sized lab coat. The wrencher waddled onto the main deck, his wry expression suggesting her performance fell short.

"Message from Pascal," he burbled.

Her heart leapt. "Yes?"

"Run." Mission accomplished, the wrencher put his hands on his hips and surveyed *Angelus'* deck with professional curiosity.

"That's his message?" she said. "*Run?*"

Deeno nodded and tightened a wayward deck screw with a fingernail.

"Where is he?" she asked.

The wrencher's four shoulders leap-frogged an elaborate shrug. "Captured. Pascal solve one, two, three, four traps, then fall into five, six, seven traps." His eyestalks bent low and twisted, searching the hangar for spies. "*You help,*" he hissed.

Alex nodded, as if mopping up sloppy espionage was something she did every day. Her mind raced to craft a cunning response that would probe Deeno's intentions without admitting any wrongdoing on her part. "So you're on our side?" she said. Strong work, Alex. Nailed it. She searched the deck planks for a crack wide enough to crawl into.

Deeno's eyebrows arched. "On side of life," he rasped. "Must stop Chieftess."

Alex rubbed her sweaty palms on her pants as an ache thrummed in her left arm. "What happened to Thorpe?"

"Pascal friend-enemy captured too."

"You're a wrencher—can't you sabotage a critical system doohickey to stop Prometheus?"

Deeno frowned, chewing her words a syllable at a time, "Cri-ti-cal sis-tem doo-hick—" His jaw dropped, and he stepped back, eyestalks wobbling. "*Sabotage? Break Oath?*" he snarled. Indigo tiger stripes flashed on his skin as his chest swelled like a vacuum cleaner bag. "*Deeno have no honor?*"

"Whoa." Alex patted the air in the universal symbol for *calm down*, praying the gesture wasn't Trenchian Hand Speak for *I Challenge You To A Slap Fight*. "Sorry, I wasn't questioning your honor—just trying to stay on the side of life and stop the Chieftess."

The wrencher deflated, scowling.

"So, just to be clear," Alex said, "you can't deliberately damage Project Prometheus without losing your honor."

Deeno's cheeks blazed red. He clenched all four fists and hyperventilated.

"Okay, okay." She made soothing gestures. "Should *I* sabotage Prometheus?"

The wrencher's eyes watered as his head inclined in the barest of nods.

"Can you show me how?" Alex said.

A vigorous head shake. She was on her own. Fine. "What do I do now?" she asked, keeping her voice gentle.

Four shoulders bounced. "You decide. Deeno deliver message."

"Thanks. Good pep talk."

"Pep-tok?"

"Never mind, it was a joke."

"Not funny joke."

Alex grinned. "You would get along great with Layla."

A sad smile wrinkled Deeno's face. "Layla good student. Bad servant."

"You know Layla?"

"Layla *wrencher*." The Trenchian pounded his chest with two left fists and watched Alex expectantly. After a few seconds, she cautiously mimicked him.

"*ROKAH!*" Deeno bellowed, eyestalks flailing. Indigo stripes flashed.

"Sorry." Alex spread her fingers in a placating gesture, but the

330

wrencher's gaze was laser-focused on her forearm. He gasped. Alex looked down and tapped the metal plug nearest her wrist band. "This thing? A bracelet melded to my bones and makes force fields when I freak out." She offered her arm to Deeno, who flinched. "Do you know anything about it?"

The wrencher whispered, *"Sentinel,"* then fled down the gangplank.

"So that's a *yes*?" she called after him.

Sentinel.

Pascal or Layla might know what it meant. Alex ran her fingers through her hair, pondering her lengthening list of People to Rescue. If anything happened to Ozzie…

She closed her eyes and imagined locking her fears in a wooden box—a trick she picked up from experienced climbers when she started tackling bigger walls. *Fear will kill you, lock it away.* Alex exhaled, releasing tension in her shoulders, then opened her eyes.

Operation: Double-Crossing Thunderskunk was over.

Time for *Operation: Rescue the Idiots.*

She punched the kill switches and walked down the gangplank as the engines clunked and wheezed into sullen silence. Drog trotted out from under a workbench. Alex said, *"You* vanished rather conveniently when Deeno showed up."

BRRRK.

"Whatever. Don't pretend you weren't hiding. Stay here until I call you, okay?"

BRK.

Ploz and Strim's argument had reached the Sulking stage, with both guards slumping against opposite sides of the doorway. Alex hurried to reach them before the next phase—Openly Challenging the Other's Intellect—kicked in. Strim saw her coming and tweaked his paddles so they hummed.

"You can't leave," he said. "We have orders."

"I thought you guys do whatever you want," Alex said.

Ploz glowered at his colleague. "My point exactly. I'm not scared of Ballistics."

"Are you scared of the Chieftess?" Strim asked.

Ploz grimaced, then poked his spear in Alex's direction. "Stay right there. Don't move," he said, in a defeated monotone.

Alex jerked a thumb down the corridor. "Did Deeno tell you Pascal got captured?"

The guards studied their sandals, confirming her suspicion. She whistled, and Drog bounded to her heel.

Grrrrrrck.grrrrrrrrrrk.grrrrckrrrrrrrrrrrrrrrrck.

Good boy.

"There's no need for threats," Strim said, his paddles trembling. Drog snarled, drooling screws and bolts on the floor.

A quake shook the hangar like a child looking for a prize in a cereal box. Glow bulbs snapped off the ceiling, carpeting the floor with shattered glass.

"*That* was Prometheus," Alex said. "The Chieftess intends to fly Contrivance across the Divide, and I need your help to stop her."

Strim gave Alex an incredulous look. "Don't be ridiculous. How could she fly a city?"

"Seventy gravity wells fueled by a river of dynami."

The scientists gaped.

"They wouldn't—" Strim said.

"Ballistics," muttered Ploz.

"But the power requirements—" Strim frowned.

"*Ballistics*," scowled Ploz.

"Through the *Divide*?" Strim tasted the idea, shaking his head.

"*Vilyab*," hissed Ploz.

The scientists stared at each other in mute shock.

"She would," Strim said.

"So would he," Ploz agreed.

They nodded in unison. "We're in."

"Good," Alex said. "Escort me into the Restricted Zone as your prisoner. If anyone asks, say the Chieftess sent for me. We'll rescue Pascal, then sabotage Prometheus."

Dr. Strim tapped his front teeth with a finger. "Intriguing. No one would anticipate such a stupid plan from us."

"It's a little pedestrian," said Ploz. "No flash or sizzle, but I like the sabotage part."

332

"Will it outsmart Ballistics?" Alex said.

Dr. Strim grinned wickedly. "Those microcraniums couldn't decipher an incipient enigma if you supplied them with a Twellis diagram and matching sockthumbs." The scientists shared a nerd-tastic snicker, tried for a high five, and missed.

"Let's go!" She started out the door.

Ploz raised his hand. Alex stopped and forced patience into her voice. "*Yes*, Dr. Ploz?"

"Your plan would benefit from a distraction," he said.

"Like what?"

The diminutive scientist pressed his fingertips together. "Like slathering ourselves in breeding pheromones, then sprinting through the Voracious Carnivore wing and directly into Corridor Twelve."

"And what happens when the voracious carnivore catches us?" Alex said.

Fascinated horror played across the scientists' faces. Strim cleared his throat. "Perhaps a less gruesome distraction..."

"No!" Ploz waved his spear. "Ballistics only responds to fear!"

She winced. "I can't believe I'm going to say this, but Dr. Ploz is right."

"Thank you!" The scientist beamed, then processed her statement. "Hey—"

Alex crossed her arms. "Who inspires fear in every department of Contrivance and is so universally hated, the prospect of catching him will grind this city to a halt?"

Three pairs of eyes tracked downward. Drog looked up from a cockroach he'd cornered.

BRK?

CHAPTER 46
THE WORST RESCUE

Competing alarms filled Corridor Twelve with pronouncements of doom. Living in constant danger from so many potential catastrophes, Contrivance relied on multiple public address systems to broadcast information throughout the city. Much to the annoyance of his fellow announcers, whoever was manning the anti-Drog system had seized the opportunity to pepper his colleagues with hot tips.

"Warning: Drog shoots lasers from his eyes—mirrors can cause ricochets."

It probably wasn't true—although if Pascal heard that, the canine would have plasma-cutting eye torches by the end of the day.

"Also, beware his seismic bark, which can rupture spleens from—"

A grumpy voice crackled over the speakers, *"Ten seconds until Bank Nineteen test fire."*

"—incendiary lice, although according to the charred fragments of Dr. Noometz's journal, Drog's flame-bark is limited to a range of—"

"Silence, Dr. Bronk. Commencing test fire NOW."

The hallway lurched, throwing Alex and her guards against the wall. A distant roar faded and the horizon leveled.

"Confirmed Drog sighting in Quadrant B! Don your armored under-garments and load your rapid-fire oxidation darts—he walks among us!"

"THAT'S ENOUGH, BRONK. Commencing cooldown phase in—"

"All Drog hunters converge on Level Nine!"

"SHUT UP, BRONK."

"YOU shut up, Engleman. DROG, if you can hear me, Engleman's lab is on Level Four, Corridor—"

"DON'T LISTEN TO HIM, DROG. LA LA LA LA—"

Dr. Bronk screamed, "CORRIDOR SEVEN!", then the speakers overloaded with static and incoherent shouting.

A pack of Children stampeded past, waving prototype Drog-catching gear. A net-toting scientist tripped, capturing two of his colleagues as he fell. Someone screamed as sparks flew from a wayward cattle prod. Alex looked at Strim, who shrugged. As distractions go, it was possible they had overdone it.

Dr. Ploz pulled Alex's elbow and bellowed, "CONTINUE AMBULATING, SCOUNDREL."

"YES, TRANSGRESSOR," Dr. Strim telegraphed a wink, "PROCEED WITH ADEQUATE SPEED."

"As you wish," Alex said, sticking to the script the scientists had insisted on. "Your weaponry is too well-conceived and impressive to resist." Fortunately, their middle school drama club production of *Two No-Nonsense Guards Escorting an Unruly Prisoner* was an insignificant footnote amidst gravity well tests, Drog sightings, and bounty hunter brawls, so the trio marched through the Restricted Zone unchallenged.

Ballistics specialists lined Corridor Twelve, analyzing data and scuffling over the finer points of physics while gravity wells fired in different arms of the city. Alex kept a close watch on Ploz's twitching spear hand as the group delved deeper into his sworn enemy's lair. It was almost a relief when the inevitable finally happened.

"STOP RIGHT THERE!"

The familiar tenor of outraged robotic authority drew an involuntary sigh from her lips.

Dr. Vilyab.

Alex turned around, and the brain's light bulb flared. "The spy!" He snapped his Vienna sausage fingers, and Frankenthug seized her by the collar. "How did you infiltrate the Restricted Zone?" Vilyab said.

Strim spluttered, "We, uh…prisoner transfer."

"None of your business, Vilyab," Ploz growled.

"Ah, Dr. Ploz. Here to scavenge crumbs of glory from my table?" Dr. Vilyab barged forward, bumping his pint-sized colleague in the chest. "Do you know *why* I excluded your department from Prometheus? Your antiquated backpack answers the question well enough—you lack *vision*."

"Backpacks are the future!" Ploz's cheeks flushed red, and he charged his nemesis. Dr. Strim grabbed his friend's waist, saving him from becoming a grease smudge on the floor, courtesy of Frankenthug.

"We're on a mission from the Chieftess," Strim grunted, foiling Ploz's attempt to stab the brainquarium.

Vilyab scoffed, "Are you? Then let's summon her." He pressed a wall intercom. "Prometheus Control, Dr. Vilyab, reporting unauthorized intruders in Corridor Twelve—a spy and two nitwits."

"*Frzzlt whtzit?*" the speaker fuzzed.

"INTRUDERS," Vilyab said.

"*Zrpipy gisnt?*"

"IN-TRU-DERS!"

"*Pilpappy. Pilpappy Gmdrup.*"

"INTRUDERS IN CORRIDOR TWE—" Vilyab released the intercom with a snarl. "Follow me, miscreants."

Frankenthug relieved Ploz and Strim of their weapons and herded the trio behind his boss. Gravity well tests shook the city, splitting pipes that blasted clouds of noxious gas into the corridor, but after twenty minutes and three detours, the group arrived at a vault door labeled *Control Room*. Vilyab tapped a code into a keypad, and the door ghosted open with a hydraulic hiss. Frankenthug shoved Alex into a brightly lit room as the Chieftess' voice chilled the air.

336

"Perhaps your apprentice, Alex, will persuade you to return the Master Key to me."

Pascal chuckled from the far side of the room, where he and Thorpe were seated on stools, arms tied behind their backs. "You'll never find Alex. The Professor trained her in the art of concealment, using skills he learned from Scabbard Forest Wraith Wardens. She will haunt your footsteps for years to come, leading a resistance from the Undergrease. Your days are numbered, so you might as well..." His voice trailed off when he caught sight of Alex.

The Chieftess sighed. "You were saying?"

Pascal squeezed his eyes shut and drooped his head.

"Are you okay, Pascal?" Alex said.

"You were supposed to run."

"I came to rescue you."

The inventor spat blood at the floor. "How's that going?"

"Awesome."

"I'm not with them," Thorpe said.

"Silence," the Chieftess snapped. "Where did you find them, Dr. Vilyab?"

"Skulking by a power matrix in Corridor Twelve." The brain jar tilted at Ploz and Strim. "These two claimed they were escorting the spy to you."

The Chieftess dissected her wayward Children with a surgical stare. "Indeed? Such devotion will not find me ungrateful. Return to your laboratories and await your reward."

Dr. Ploz snatched his backpack from Frankenthug and flounced to the door. Dr. Strim took a half-step and stopped. "I...have a question."

The old woman rubbed her temple with a bony hand. "Yes?" The ice in her voice could have sunk an ocean liner.

"Talk around the Drippinator suggests Project Prometheus will use unsanctioned tech to move Contrivance through a breach in the Divide." Strim twiddled his collar, smudging the white fabric with sweat. "Given the, er...ramifications of such an endeavor, shouldn't Children outside the Ballistics Department have input?"

The Chieftess' eyes flashed. "You wish to have *input*?" She thumped her ivory walking staff against the ground, shooting lines of scarlet energy through its volantium veins. Strim flinched, and even Dr. Vilyab took a step back. Her voice swelled in volume and wrath. "I am honor bound to protect my Children from the evil lurking outside our walls. *The Fury King comes, Child.* Doubt not my word or judgment."

Dr. Strim stammered an apology and retreated, clutching his static array paddles. The Chieftess watched him leave and said, "Pay your colleagues a visit following the completion of Prometheus, Dr. Vilyab. Remind them of the price of wandering loyalty."

"With pleasure," Vilyab said.

"The Fury King?" Pascal coughed and lifted his head. "You're sacrificing the lives of everyone under the Dome to escape a bedtime story?"

"You know nothing of what you speak, Pascal Trahir," the Chieftess said. "The threat is real and imminent."

"Oh, I know *that*—in about two minutes, Prometheus is going to level this city."

"Enough." The old woman crooked a finger. "Bring me the girl."

Frankenthug clamped his hand around Alex's neck and pushed her forward. The Chieftess gasped. A telescoping series of magnifying lenses dropped in front of her spectacles. "Where did you procure an armillam?" She rapped the knob of her staff against a plug, sending a stream of fire coursing through Alex's arm.

"Ow! What's an armillam?"

The Chieftess glowered. "Do not lie to me. Have you manifested anything yet?"

Pascal shook his head frantically in the background.

"I'm not...sure?" Alex said.

Vilyab tapped his foot impatiently. "The gravity well tests are complete, madam. Prometheus is ready! Focus on the task at hand!"

The Chieftess snarled and thrust her walking staff beneath Pascal's chin. She said, "*You* are going to tell me where the Master

Key is and *she* is going to explain how she came upon an armillam, or *I* am going to infuse your bones with enough dynami to mutate perl glands on a grobthank."

Pascal tutted. *"Language,* Chieftess." The staff pulsed red, and he winced.

Alex said, "Please, I—"

"Silence, child—your turn will come soon enough. The key, Pascal."

Another flash of red. The Dromedarian grunted.

"The key." Shadows darkened the Chieftess' face.

Deep-rooted heat swelled in Alex's left arm. She clutched her elbow and hunched over—the last thing she needed right now was to project a shield and collapse.

"Stop!" Thorpe said. *"I* have the Master Key." He extended his leg. "Check my boot."

Pascal moaned, "No."

Frankenthug yanked Thorpe's shoe off, dumping a thin paper rectangle onto the floor. He scratched his head and rotated the envelope, searching for an opening.

"It's a Labyrinthian pocket vault." Thorpe said, a hint of pride in his voice. "It only opens to the correct touchphrase. Untie my hands."

The henchman looked at the Chieftess.

"Do it," she said. "If he runs, snap his neck."

"No!" Pascal yelled, grimacing as her staff dug into his throat.

Thorpe slid off his stool. "I expected better of you, Chieftess. Violence is the first resort of desperate tyrants."[*1]

"Do you wish to plumb the depths of my desperation?" she said.

"I'd rather test the boundaries of your generosity." He rubbed his wrists. "I'll give you the Master Key if you let me go. I'm no threat to your plans."

The Chieftess arched a calculating eyebrow. "And what of your co-conspirators?"

Thorpe shrugged. "Do what you want with them, but wait until I'm gone if you're going to make the girl activate her armillam. I

339

saw what happened last time." His eyes flicked to Alex, who scowled back.

"You have my word, now give me the key."

The spineless scientist contorted his fingers into an alien shape, then squeezed the corners of the pocket vault. A fold creased the rectangle into an open envelope, and he slid a silver, triangular key into Frankenthug's waiting palm. As the brute stepped away, Thorpe's fingers blurred in a frenzy of precision folding. He shouted, "Now, Alex!" and flicked a ninja star, which curled like a boomerang, slicing a bloody line across the henchman's knuckles. Frankenthug roared, and the Master Key jingled across the floor. The enraged flunky swung at the Labyrinthian, but Thorpe was already halfway to the door, screaming, *"Project a shield!"*

The Chieftess aimed her staff at Alex, who shook her head.

"I don't know what he's talking about," she said.

Thorpe sprinted past, the snarling brute hot on his heels. *"Any time, Alex!"*

The Chieftess shouted a command, but her burly lackey was incensed beyond listening. He wrenched an instrument panel out of the floor and hurled it at Thorpe, who dove through the doorway. Frankenthug bellowed, then chased his elusive prey into the corridor.

Dr. Vilyab stooped to retrieve the Master Key, but Pascal threw a flying tackle from his stool, like a wrestler diving from a top rope. They rolled across the floor, butting head to glass and growling insults.

"You couldn't calculate a valid thrust ratio if I spotted you twelve decimals!"

"You tackle with the weak ankles of a hyperopic gulpum!"

"You have sloppy penmanship!"

"HOW DARE YOU? It's a robotic hand!"

The Chieftess pressed her staff into Alex's stomach. "Bring me the key," she said. "If you attempt to activate your armillam, I will make you curse the day it chose you."

Alex cradled her throbbing arm. "I can't control the bracelet—it does what it wants."

crawling through sewers with a knife clenched in his teeth. "I want to help." He winced as a voice in his head shouted:

Help? You want to HELP? You WANT to seize your destiny and lay waste to your enemies, so the world can taste justice!

Layla frowned. "Are you feeling well?"

Ozzie stared at his metal fingers. "I'm fine, just worried about Alex." It was probably true—stress could make anyone imagine a bloodthirsty, disembodied voice that wouldn't stop ranting about laying waste to enemies...right? He clenched his jaw to combat the relentless ache in his forearm.

Spark's engine coughed and sputtered as Layla skimmed the hard-packed desert on the approach to Contrivance. The fuselage swung like a pendulum, every desperate slalom scalping trees and vegetation.

Ozzie swiped a nest of chittering birds from his lap. "Can we please fly a little higher?"

"We must avoid detection!" the Sauracian barked, her voice taut with concentration.

They careened into a cloud of expanding dust, which made for excellent camouflage but terrible breathing. A black monstrosity loomed ahead, and Layla slapped the throttle into full-reverse. The airship shuddered under the strain of shifting inertia.

"They're going to see us!" Ozzie gasped, as his harness squeezed his lungs like a lemon.

Layla jammed her boot against a rudder pedal and pointed. One of the city's arms was lifting into the air! Rocks and shrubs tumbled into widening crevasses as rising foundations ripped chunks of earth free. Twenty pillars of blinding blue flame inched the awkwardly angled structure skyward, warming Ozzie's cheeks from a mile away. Without warning, the chest-thumping rumble died and Contrivance plunged back into its hole, accompanied by screams of tortured metal and a wailing gaggle of alarms.

"Was that normal?" Ozzie said. "For a city of deranged geniuses, I mean."

"No." Layla climbed *Spark* over the smoking complex and bee-lined for the repair bay.

The Sauracian bypassed the hangar's locking mechanism with a twist of a toothpick and a rap of her knuckles. Ozzie gaped at her as the ceiling squealed open beneath them.

"Can you teach me how to do that?"

"Not unless you want the Wrencher's Guild to issue a scrag contract on your head."

"Knowing how to pick a lock with a splinter of wood might be worth the risk."

Layla vented heliovapor, lowering *Spark* into the hangar. "Hacking security systems is a way of life in Contrivance. Wrenchers who cannot access the entire facility do not graduate." The airship touched down next to *Angelus* in what appeared to be the aftermath of a war between office supply stores.

Ozzie kicked aside a broken chalkboard and sprinted up the mother ship's gangplank. "Alex! Pascal!" The deck was bare, and spare parts littered the laboratory. Lukewarm coffee in the machine rang alarm bells—Pascal wouldn't let Ethiopian roast go to waste. "Anyone here?" He returned to the main deck and looked over the railing. Layla beckoned to him from the starboard engine.

"Still warm. Both engines were run less than an hour ago." The wrencher cleaned her paws with a rag and dodged a murderous lunge from Socrates. "The repairs are rudimentary, but *Angelus* appears airworthy."

A loudspeaker crackled. *"Bank Forty-One test fire commencing in three...two...one..."*

The ground buckled, and Ozzie hugged the propeller as the hangar swayed under his feet. After ten queasy seconds, the rumbling ceased.

"Test fire complete."

"Is it possible Pascal dared the Children to make Contrivance fly as a prank?" he said.

Layla shook her head and closed an engine panel, sending Socrates into a howling rage. "The Chieftess is behind this."

A breathless announcer commandeered the PA system, "CON-FIRMED DROG SIGHTING IN QUADRANT FOUR! *Warning: According to Dr. Tremdot's final, tragic diary entry, Drog's saliva is laced with lava, so do NOT allow him to lick your face.*"

A voice that would belong to a vice-principal in any other setting cut in, "*Dr. Bronk, this is Dr. Gupp, this month's Head of the Crisis Response Team. Terminate your broadcast or we will disable your equipment.*"

"*Dr. Gupp, from the Insomnian Geology Department? Shouldn't you be reading bedtime stories to pebbles?*"

"*THAT'S IT. We're coming in!*"

Pounding noises cut through static.

"*Bring it, lunkbrains!*" Bronk crowed. "*I barricaded the door with Drog safety pamphlets, and you won't BELIEVE how many of THOSE I have! DROG, IF YOU CAN HEAR ME, RUN! RUN FOR YOUR LI—*"

White noise hissed over loudspeakers.

Layla said, "*That* sounded like Pascal's handiwork." She raised a claw to her lips and whistled a tune that skirted the upper range of Ozzie's hearing.

"What was that?" he said.

Layla smiled.

A clatter of tinkling metal suggested a silverware factory had exploded on the far side of the city. Indistinct shouts and muted alarms echoed through the hangar. An inhuman scream chased goosebumps up Ozzie's neck. A symphony of shattering glass was drowned out by the rattle of ten thousand ball bearings raining onto metal plates. Clouds of steam parted at the door, hyping the arrival of a knee-high...dog? Two glowing eyes pierced the fog like headlights.

"*Don't move,*" Ozzie breathed. "*It might not see us.*"

The creature sniffed the air, then yelped, and charged like a missile. Ozzie ducked behind Layla, who bent low, welcoming her attacker with open arms.

BONG

The canine bounced off the Sauracians's chest like a basketball.

345

BRRRRRRK. BRRRRRK.

"Drog! I missed you," Layla said. The notorious poster dog for Inventions Run Amok spat out a mangled saw blade and rolled over, exposing his belly. "Who is wreaking havoc, then? Is it you? Are you wreaking havoc, boy?" Her claws pitted Drog's shell, to his shivering delight. "Did Pascal put you up to this?" The dog whined, then noticed Ozzie, and flipped to its feet.

Grrrr-ck-rrr-ckrrckrrrrr.

The machine's eyes shifted red as side panels flipped up, deploying an arsenal of barbed arrows, miniature grappling hooks, and goo-filled darts.

"Whoa." Ozzie raised his hands.

"Abort Kill Mode, Drog." Layla's voice had a playful, scolding tone. "Ozzie is a friend."

The Butcher of a Thousand Research Grants hesitated, then shuttered his weapon ports, eyes flaring a warning.

"Get it, boy!" The Sauracian tossed a wrench across the hangar and Drog charged after it with ecstatic joy. Heavy shelves toppled like dominoes in the wake of his frantic search for the tool.

Ozzie lowered his arms. "How do you two know each other?"

"Remember the Wanted posters all over the city? Imagine what the Wrencher's bulletin board looks like, since we repair the damage Drog inflicts. The Master Wrenchers offer a larger reward than the Chieftess does."

"Did you catch him?"

"Drog evaded me for months, until I got lucky with a mudgeon mucus trap," she said. "He torched my favorite tool bag, then escaped before I could puncture his outer shell."

"How many times did you catch him?"

"Three—each time, he destroyed something I cherished, then escaped. Eventually, we forged a bond of mutual respect and Drog accompanied me through long night shifts in the Undergrease."

The canine trotted back to Layla, proudly displaying his trophy wrench. He dropped the tool and wagged his tail with abrupt, jerky motions.

BRRRK. BRR—

346

Drog's head swiveled to the door. He whined, then skittered behind Layla's boot. The Sauracian stood up, hefting a sledge-hammer the size of Ozzie's head. "What is wrong, boy?"

An arrow whistled through the doorway and lodged in the ceiling, trailing a wire.

"Oh no," she groaned.

Ozzie's arm hair stood on end as a fizzing ball of light zipped up the cable, hit the arrow, and showered sparks across the repair bay. When the smoke cleared, a purple-skinned, overall-clad creature crouched in the middle of the hangar, swishing razor-sharp sickles in four hands. Its eyes glowed like dim blue headlights.

"Master Wrencher Deeno," Layla said. She bowed her head, but kept her sledgehammer ready.

"Wrencher Layla." The creature sounded like he was growling while blowing bubbles underwater. Two eyestalks tilted to peer around Layla's boots. "You shelter enemy."

"Drog has done me no injury."

"He dishonor your home."

"Contrivance is no longer my home," she said. "I am unwelcomed here by any but Drog."

Deeno chewed his lip and swiveled one eye to inspect Ozzie, who casually inched closer to a splintered stool, in case he needed to take a page from the Willowsby School of Pub Fighting. The master wrencher hissed, stowed his blades, then pounded his torso with two left fists. Layla lowered her hammer and returned the gesture. Ozzie started to mimic the motion, when the Sauracian's tail smacked his shins, bringing tears to his eyes.

"*Deeno* welcome Wrencher Layla," the purple creature said.

"I am grateful, Master Wrencher."

"You seek Pascal."

"I do. What has become of him and his apprentice?"

"Captured." It was a statement of fact, delivered without emotion or judgment.

"By who?" Ozzie said.

Deeno scowled at the interruption, then caught sight of Ozzie's forearm. He snarled, "*Sentinel!*" and crouched in a fighting posture.

Layla blocked his view of the volantium glove. "With respect, Master Wrencher, this is not the time for folk tales. Where are Pascal and Alex?"

The mechanic narrowed his bulbous eyes as dark stripes flashed on his skin. He murmured, "Fail to stop Prometheus. Caught by Chieftess."

"What is Prometheus?" she said.

Deeno burped. His eyestalks drooped. "Fly city. Use power-sieve. Cross Divide."

Layla grunted. "There are not enough engines under the Dome to generate *that* much thrust."

"Gravity wells."

Her sledgehammer thudded on the ground. "Show me."

Deeno cleaned his nails with the point of a sickle while Layla inspected the gravity well. Drog circled the Sauracian's ankles, growling whenever the Master Wrencher glanced in his direction.

"Madness," the Sauracian muttered, squinting into a pipeline viewing port.

"This thing is powerful enough to lift a city?" Ozzie said.

"With enough wells, you could lift a continent." Layla examined a schematic of Contrivance, then turned to Deeno. "Ninety-three engines?"

He burped an affirmative.

"Master Wrencher, you *must* stop the Chieftess. If the city enters the Divide, radioactive blowback will decimate Terravenum."

A wave of stripes rippled across four purple shoulders. "Deeno cannot harm Chieftess plan."

The Sauracian flexed her claws. "She is ending the world!"

"End with Deeno honor intact."

"Fine," Layla fumed. "I will sabotage as many wells as I can." She reached for a keypad and froze at the throaty rasps of four sickles scraping leather. Drog growled, his eyes blinking crimson.

Deeno stepped in front of the gravity well, whirling his blades. "Wrencher Oath! No damage wells. Layla *talk* Chieftess."

"She will not accept my council."

"Layla must try."

The Sauracian slumped her shoulders. "Very well." She turned to Ozzie. "Drog's logic cortex periodically requires organic nutrients. Feed him the remaining Amnesian berries."

"I threw those away, like you asked." Ozzie said, feigning bewilderment until her deep-throated growl motivated him to reach for his pocket. "Oh, you mean these? No problem." He thrust a fistful of steel-hard heaveberries at the canine's face.

Drog tilted his head, internal relays chattering as he watched Layla's silent hand signals. When she finished, he lunged at Ozzie's outstretched hand and devoured the berries with a single bite.

BRRK.

"Careful," Ozzie said. "Those are—"

"Drog is fine," Layla snapped.

Deeno motioned for her to lead the way. "Chieftess and Pascal in Corridor Twelve Hub."

At the Sauracian's first step, Drog shot out the door. Four arms snatched at the canine but grabbed thin air. Mocking barks echoed over the patter of clanging footsteps.

"How long have you chased him?" Ozzie asked, failing to hide a grin.

"Long time. Drog move through city like wrencher."

A faint mechanical howl declared victory in a distant hallway. Layla threw Ozzie a warning look, so he changed the subject before Deeno could speculate where Drog might have learned wrencher secrets. "I can't believe Pascal tangled with the Chieftess after all his bluster about Rule Number One."

"I am not surprised," Layla said, squeezing past a pair of wheezing bellows. "Pascal is burdened by occasional bouts of conscience."

Drog sprinted across a junction in the corridor ahead, yipping cheerfully. A clump of Children stampeded after him, throwing elbows and bickering.

Deeno sighed. "Chieftess change. Grow e-rra-tic." Consonants clicked in the back of his throat.

"Maybe that's why she sent us to Amnesia for the Noctem," Ozzie said.

Layla shook her head. "That was a strategic decision. Master Wrencher Deeno is referring to the Chieftess embracing dynami research after decades of forbidding it."

"What changed?"

"I intend to find out."

Traveling with two wrenchers made a march through Contrivance a breeze. Five invisible shortcuts and nine back alleys later, the trio arrived at Corridor Twelve.

Deeno pounded his chest with two fists. "Layla help Chieftess," he said. "Deeno go."

The Sauracian returned his salute.

BRRK.

Drog bounded up a side passage and skidded to a stop by Layla's boots. She leaned down. "Good boy! Did you follow my instructions?"

BRRK.

The dog spun in a gleeful circle.

"Instructions?" Deeno said.

"I told him to keep the Children occupied and out of our path."

"Drog *obey* Layla?"

"When I tell him what he wants to hear."

Deeno pounded his knees and croaked in what was probably a laugh. "If *Drog* listen Layla, Chieftess listen Layla."

"I seriously doubt it."

Drog's ears swiveled down Corridor Twelve, then the rest of his limbs followed suit. His eyes shifted red. Kill Mode.

"What is it, boy?" Layla said.

The robot trembled in place, focusing on the hallway with unnerving intensity. Layla gripped her sledgehammer, rearing back for a swing guaranteed to put someone in an early grave. Adrenaline pumped heat into Ozzie's right forearm.

Wield the sword! Cleave your enemy's heart!

350

Wonderful, the bloodthirsty voice was back.

Where would I go? I am part of you now.

Ozzie clutched his forehead. This can't be happening.

You doubt me? Manifest the Blade and test my words, hero!

He groaned as fire swelled in his arm.

"Out of my way!" A thin, white-haired man barreled up the hallway, lab coat streaming like a superhero's cape. Drog made an inquisitive sound, then pranced in place, eyes yellow.

Yip. Yip. Yip.

Layla lowered her sledgehammer. "Thorpe?"

"Hi Layla," the man panted, clutching his ribs as he stumbled past. "Pascal...Control Room." He frowned at Ozzie, and kept running. Drog howled, nipped Layla's tail, then scurried after him.

The Sauracian stared at the rapidly shrinking scientist. "This explains a lot," she said.

An earthquake shook the corridor. Layla sniffed the air, then shoved Ozzie to the ground, saving him from being trampled by a green, rectangular humanoid who thundered past with murder in his eyes.

At last, a worthy foe! Victory and glory!

By the time he struggled to his feet, the stampeding brute was gone. A flickering glow made Ozzie look down. To his shock, the Anemoi Blade was fixed in his right hand, dripping turquoise flames on the floor like liquid fire.

Deeno pressed against the wall and scrabbled at his weapons. He hissed, *"Cus-tos Luminisss."*

Ozzie flicked his wrist, and the sword sliced the air with the sound of crashing surf. Ice flowed through his fingers, soothing heat that raged in his arm.

The world shall taste justice!

He winced at the creepy voice and reached for his temple. Layla smacked the Anemoi Blade aside before Ozzie could scalp himself. The sword flared.

"Careful, child! Legendary swords are notoriously sharp," she said. "Take deep breaths, Master Wrencher Deeno."

351

Hyperventilation doubled the mechanic over, but his eyestalks curved up to watch Ozzie. "*Custos...Luminis,*" he wheezed.

Ozzie covered his Stella Signum and said, "We're pretty sure this was an accident, not a prophecy."

There is no accident. You are destined for glorious victory or the eternal shame of excruciating defeat. Given your skills, I'm leaning toward the latter.

"Shut up!" Ozzie yelled. The Anemoi Blade melted into tendrils of smoke.

Destiny cannot be silenced.

Layla threw him an exasperated glare that promised an uncomfortable conversation at a later date. An argument drifted down the hallway—one voice was unmistakably Pascal's, shouting about calculating thrust ratio. The Sauracian spun and barged down Corridor Twelve like a force of nature. Ozzie waved an apology at Deeno, then sprinted after her. After a handful of sharp turns, he staggered to a halt as Layla stepped through an open vault door.

"Is this a bad time?" The wrencher's gruff delivery dared anyone to challenge her.

Ozzie massaged his wrist and stepped into the Control Room.

CHAPTER 48
THE SHOWDOWN

Alex was on her knees in the center of the room, grimacing as the Chieftess threatened her with a glowing staff.

Ozzie shouted, "Alex!" and charged forward, but Layla blocked him with her tail.

At the far side of the room, an aquarium defeated Pascal in a wrestling match. Servos whirred as the specimen jar—holding a brain!—teetered to a standing position, then stepped on the inventor's neck.

"Hello, Pascal," Layla said, her eyes locked on the Chieftess.

"Hurgle."

"You survived." The Chieftess matched the Sauracian's flat tone. "Did you find Dr. Bloomvilt?"

"No, but we escaped your trap."

"I assure you—had I devised a trap, that would not be the case."

"You sent us to our deaths to appease the Noctem."

A mocking smile played on the old woman's lips. "So, you met Hugo. Be grateful I gifted you to that doddering fool instead of the Annihilator and *his* master."

Ozzie's glove tingled. He casually stretched his arm to avoid stabbing himself if the sword manifested.

The brainquarium kicked Pascal. "Madam, the launch window—"

"Silence, Dr. Vilyab. Grown-ups are speaking."

"This quarrel with the Noctem is not of our choosing," Layla said. "My companions and I merely seek the Professor."

The Chieftess scoffed, "Does a nipnard *choose* to be hunted by a taranticle?*[1] You are pawns in a game of titans."

"Perhaps, but my fellow nipnards and I are leaving. *Now.*" The wrencher's lips parted, giving teeth to her declaration.

"Relinquish the Master Key and you may go, but the girl shall remain with me."

"No!" Ozzie strained against Layla's tail. He feinted left, but the chunky appendage anticipated his move, poking him in the chest. "Stop it, Layla!" Her tail shoved him back another step.

The Sauracian rumbled, "Alex is coming with us."

"She bears an armillam," the Chieftess said. "Without training, it will kill her—but even if she survives, you know what will be said of an Urtling who bears the mark of the Ancients." A pulse of energy rippled down her staff, making Alex flinch. "Show her the mark, child."

Alex's arm trembled as she rotated her wrist to reveal a Stella Signum on the back of her hand.

Layla hissed, "*The prophecy.*"

Ozzie clenched his metal fist and imagined the Anemoi Blade manifesting in his hand.

What do you want?

He frowned at the grouchy voice in his head, then visualized the sword in greater detail, fire dripping from its edge like molten syrup.

Very pretty. Imagine a theme song too—something with a beat we can pillage to.

Ozzie opened his eyes. Was he going crazy?

That would be an improvement. I've seen inside your head—you could use a little fun.

He grabbed his temple, careful to use his non-sword hand. Who are you?

I am you. You are the Anemoi Blade. We are one.

Well, that's not sinister or panic-inducing at all. Okay, Disembodied, Spine-Chilling Voice—I need the sword.

So NOW you want the blade. Have you suddenly decided you are worthy of a great destiny?

I've got to help Alex. You keep telling me to attack things, so give me a weapon.

You should have trained more—your "attacks" are better described as "energetic losses."

What is your problem?

You nearly decapitated yourself three minutes ago.

"It was an accident!" Ozzie shouted. The outside world rushed in. Everyone in the room was staring at him with worried looks. He glanced down and was annoyed, though somewhat relieved, to find himself unarmed.

The Chieftess gaped at his metal glove. *"It cannot be."*

The intensity of her gaze made Ozzie uncomfortable. He folded his arms, and the Chieftess shrieked, firing a red bolt of energy from the head of her walking staff. An electric lasso wrapped around his torso, then yanked him forward, forcing him to his knees.

"Release him!" Layla roared.

Alex screamed, absorbed a blow from the Chieftess' staff, then collapsed, gasping for air.

"If anyone takes another step, the boy dies," the old woman said. Icy blue eyes probed Ozzie's face. "Show me your hand."

Vilyab's speaker crackled. "Madam, it is imperative—"

"Your hand!" Her shout echoed through the control room.

Ozzie uncurled his metal fist.

The Chieftess covered her mouth and, for a moment, looked frail. "How long have you had the Blade?" she said. He pursed his lips, and her staff fired a spike of searing heat through the lasso. *"How long?"*

Ozzie grunted. "A couple of weeks."

"Has it spoken to you?" Her iron voice was tinged with sorrow.

There was definitely a wrong answer to this question.

"Did it speak?" The veins on her staff flared and the lasso blazed, inflicting a torrent of pain.

Ozzie grimaced. "I don't know what you're talking about!"

"Chieftess!" Dr. Vilyab barked. "We *must* initiate Prometheus, or we will miss the breach window."

The old woman straightened. "Very well. Surrender the Master Key, Layla—or the boy shall suffer the consequences of your betrayal."

Layla gripped the key in a massive paw. "Prometheus will end the world," she rumbled.

"This world is already dead!" the Chieftess shouted. "He is coming!"

"Who?"

"The Fury King." The name sucked life from the room. Even Dr. Vilyab stopped punching buttons to stare at the Chieftess. She twisted her wrist, and the lasso brightened, burning holes in Ozzie's shirt and hissing where it touched skin. He yelped. The Chieftess said, "If you value this boy's life, insert the Master Key in the center console and activate Prometheus."

Pascal thrashed in his restraints. "Don't do it! The blowback will —" Vilyab kicked the inventor in the stomach, cutting him off.

Layla trudged to the control bank in the front of the room. She glanced at Ozzie, then slid the key into an elevated slot in the center panel. "Please reconsider, Chieftess. Prometheus will only bring devastation."

The old woman sent a pulse of energy surging into the volantium veins of her staff. Ozzie's eyes bulged as he struggled to limit his cries to a manly whimper. "Turn it," she said.

Layla obeyed.

Click

The city trembled and rocked as ninety-three gravity wells ignited. Status lights tinted the control room leprechaun green.

"Increasing power!" Dr. Vilyab bounced from foot-to-foot, spinning dials with a tiny finger. The Chieftess cracked a grim smile as Contrivance rose, engines roaring like a thousand subway trains arriving at a station.

"We have liftoff! Holding altitude at five meters!" Vilyab crowed.

As the Chieftess' pet project, Prometheus suffered few of the departmental rivalries and petty jealousies that plagued most projects in Contrivance. In every corridor of the city, meticulously crafted gravity wells gorged on dynami, spewing earth-shattering thrust with mechanical perfection. By any measure, Project Prometheus was the rarest of all scientific enterprises: an immediate success.

If only someone had thought to lock the firing chamber doors.

Ten minutes before the Master Key turned in the Control Room, a bronze canine coughed stony, mottled fruit into the inner workings of twelve gravity wells around the city, just as Teeth Face had asked him to do via claw-sign.

The heaveberries jiggled harmlessly until intensifying vibrations penetrated their calloused skin. One by one, berries inflated, crushing critical systems inside the wells. A few engines died immediately, but most redirected their thrust, slagging surrounding hallways and floors. The city's overtaxed cooling system failed, allowing the dynami pipeline to overheat in seconds.

Scatterlings in the deadlands bordering Rust heard the explosions more than one hundred miles away.

A single blinking red light was the first sign something was wrong. Within seconds, ten more joined it. Alarms wailed, gauge needles pinned, and pipes vented steam. Vilyab's jar was a cauldron of bubbles as he announced, "Four wells are critical!"

"Activate fire suppression," barked the Chieftess.

Flashing red lights gave the Control Room a bizarre Christmassy vibe as the floor tilted sideways. A string of concussions toppled machinery.

"Banks four through eleven are failing!" Vilyab stabbed buttons. "We're losing lift!"

Overhead lights blinked, and for two heart-stopping seconds, Ozzie was weightless. The Chieftess wailed as Alex kicked the walking staff out of her hand, killing the energy lasso. Contrivance struck the ground with an impact that flattened the Control Room and cratered the ceiling. Screams of buckling metal rent the air as skylights shattered, raining glass.

"Time to go!" Layla dislodged a girder pinning Pascal, then helped him to his feet. Ozzie grabbed Alex's arm, and the twins stumbled out the door.

The Chieftess' parting cry wafted above the sirens like a curse. "The Anemoi Blade will destroy you, boy! Seek me when you yearn for death!"

Thickening smoke obscured the hallway, and Ozzie plowed into Layla at the first junction. The Sauracian ignored him, flaring her nostrils as she sniffed each corridor.

Pascal leaned against a wall, coughing. He wheezed, "What happened to the gravity wells?"

"Drog planted heaveberries inside them," Layla said.

A smile crept across the inventor's face. "Did you tell him to do that?"

"I encouraged him to embrace his inner Pascal. We are fortunate he did not atomize us, then sell heaveberries to our enemies." She stomped down a hallway that looked identical to the others.

Ozzie jogged beside her, clutching his ribs. "Deeno will be furious that you sabotaged the wells."

"Master Wrencher Deeno hoped I would stop Prometheus. His honor remains intact."

"What if he'd caught you?"

"He would have executed me, of course." Layla clotheslined Ozzie with her outstretched arm a split-second before a pylon of flame consumed the passageway. Her leathery hide steamed as she helped him up. "Contrivance's thoroughfares are collapsing," she said. "We need to use the Undergrease."

Pascal blanched. "Absolutely not. Do you know what's down there?"

"All too well." Layla muscled a neglected maintenance hatch open with a grunt. "Hold your breath."

Ten terrifying minutes later, Ozzie crawled out of a nightmare, squinting under bright corridor lights. To his undying relief, the door of *Angelus'* repair bay was visible through the smoke. He climbed out of the manhole, then helped Alex up the ladder.

"Thanks." She dried her hands, smearing fetid slime across her shirt.

"I cannot believe you hit Albert with a shockbag!" Layla emerged from the darkness, seething.

"He nearly squeezed the life out of me!" Pascal said.

"He was playing!"

A boot-quaking roar pierced the subterranean murk. Pascal dove headlong into the corridor as something massive punched the floor from below, denting the walkway. A pale yellow tentacle as thick as a horse's thigh burst out of the hole, groping for a victim.

"He's not playing anymore!" Pascal yelled.

"*Bad* Albert! *Bad* sumpbeast!" Layla scolded.

The tentacle homed in on her voice and smacked the floor, only missing because Pascal shoved the Sauracian aside. Layla shook her fist. "No din-din for you, Albert—"

"We need to leave!" Ozzie tugged the wrencher's elbow as the ceiling down the hall caved in. He pointed to Pascal and Alex, who were sprinting up *Angelus'* gangplank. Layla snarled, then followed him into the hangar.

The airship's engines spluttered, then roared like ravenous beasts. Ozzie dodged toppling shelves, vaulted a splintered chalkboard, and tiptoed around a pool of chemical goo. He was halfway up the gangplank when Layla bellowed, "Ozzie! Release the docking clamps." She pointed at a vise gripping *Angelus'* hull beneath the bow. He dropped to the hangar floor and sprinted to his assignment as Layla tackled a stern clamp.

The corroded bracket didn't have an obvious release mechanism. He pawed at its grease-packed hinge, then tried to force it open with brute strength. Chunks of ceiling collapsed, bouncing off *Angelus'* envelope.

Alex's face appeared over the railing. "No pressure, but the sky is literally falling."

"Working on it!" Ozzie kicked the clamp, and twelve million nerve endings in his toe scolded him.

An explosion rocked the hangar, showering the airship with sparks and setting the gangplank on fire. Layla punched her clamp open. "Finished! Are you done yet?"

"Working on it!"

"Hurry! I am taking *Spark*!" The Sauracian bulldozed a path to her airship.

A twinge of heat raced down Ozzie's right arm. He gritted his teeth and forced himself to focus amid the chaos. Are you there, Ominous Voice of Doom?

Yes! Enjoying the show. Very dramatic.

I could use some help.

I was forged for epic conquests, not to spread jam on toast. This seems like a "you" problem.

Your prospects for glory are going to die with me if I don't release this clamp.

The boy who shies away from every mildly intriguing fight is suddenly chasing glory?

Absolutely—can't wait to attack someone twice my size, just as soon as I cut this clamp.

Promises, promises.

A wall panel screeched, then flattened workbenches by the door. The ceiling buckled, but Layla rammed *Spark* into the roof to buy *Angelus* time to escape.

Please help me! I need the sword.

Fine.

Ozzie swung his hand as lava pulsed through his veins. A translucent, blue-flamed blade manifested in his palm at the last instant, slicing the clamp in two. *Angelus* lurched skyward, and Ozzie snatched a dangling mooring line with his left hand. He swished the sword like he was trying to extinguish a flaming s'more on a stick. "Okay, we're good! Put it away."

That's it? No "thank you"?

"Thank you! Now, go away!" Sweaty fingers slipped, and he instinctively grabbed for the rope, severing it with the Anemoi Blade. He scrambled to his feet, watching *Angelus* ascend under full throttle.

"What are you doing?" Alex shouted. She tossed a new line, but it didn't reach the ground.

Ozzie scaled a stepladder, holding the sword away from his body. "Please go away," he begged.

I call that ungrateful.

The Anemoi Blade evaporated. Ozzie teetered on the top step, then leapt, snagging the end of the rapidly disappearing line. Adrenaline compensated for his chronically weak grip and he threw himself into scaling the rope hand over hand. If only Mr. Brofer, his middle school P.E. teacher, could see him now! Eighteen exhausting inches later, he lowered his ambitions to holding on for dear life.

Angelus squeezed past *Spark* and punched through the wreckage of the collapsing roof. Both airships clawed for open sky as gravity wells detonated across the city. Ozzie's fingers were begging for relief by the time Alex rappelled down to help him aboard. The harness squeezed his aching ribs, but he smiled through the pain as he scrambled over the ship's railing.

"We aren't clear yet!" Alex pointed to the far side of the city, where a one-man airship was climbing out of a hangar. Layla maneuvered *Spark* to intercept the mystery vessel.

"How is that thing flying?" Ozzie said. "It doesn't have an envelope."

Pascal groaned and pulled his head out of a mess of wiring under the helm. "Don't tell me: the ship is hopping around the sky like a hyperactive cranksnort while king-size bellows puff an over-head accordion."

"Uh, yes?"

"It's Labyrinthian."

Thorpe fluttered closer, feverishly pumping foot pedals to generate altitude from twitching paper wings. Springs and counter-weights kept his chair semi-stable while the rest of his airship jinked and juddered around him. He waved cheerfully.

Pascal folded his arms. "Don't encourage him."

BRRK. BRRK.

Drog spun giddy circles in the madly gyrating cockpit. The scientist saluted, then peeled away, bouncing northeast.

Once they found sanctuary in a suitably dense cloud bank, Layla secured *Spark* alongside *Angelus* and disappeared into the engine room.

Alex coiled a rope. "Where are we going?"

"Somewhere we can finish our repairs without lunatics trying to kill us every two minutes," Pascal said, tightening a bolt under the steering console.

"We need to go back to the Archive," Ozzie said.

His sister laughed.

The inventor said, "Perhaps I didn't properly explain all the nuances of my plan. You see—"

"The Noctem are keeping Grandfather imprisoned there."

Alex dropped her rope, then covered her eyes with a bruised hand. For the first time, Ozzie noticed how tattered her clothes were.

Pascal frowned. "Explain."

"The Noctem use Amnesia as a prison. The warden—who is Deathfist's brother, by the way—told me about the Archive, then dropped me in a bottomless pit."

"It is true." Layla emerged on deck, holding a tool bag. "I threw him in." She cracked an instrument panel open.

"We can't go back to the Archive," Pascal said. "We're definitely on the Overdue List,[*2] and the Booksworn don't just *nurse* a grudge —they nurture it through adolescence, send it to the finest grudge-building schools, then marry it off to another grudge to make cute little grudge babies that will someday strangle us in our sleep."

Layla lifted her goggles. "When the Noctem discover we escaped Amnesia, they will move the Professor or kill him."

"We won't get past the Crucible," Pascal said. "We broke neutrality pacts when we fought the Maelstrom on Booksworn turf. The librarians will not be inclined to talk things out."

"Of course not," Ozzie said. "They're Noctem."

"If that's true, it doesn't make anything easier. We need a plan."

"You'll think of one on the way to the Archive," Alex said.

"I'll think of ten," Pascal snapped, "but that doesn't mean it's a good strategy."

"This is our best chance to rescue the Professor," Layla said. "He would do the same for us."

"Of course he would! He's an abysmal tactician! Remember when the Professor tried to infiltrate Derelict's black market by hiding inside a cardboard horse outside the gate? He got stolen, then bartered eight times, before a family took him home for some kind of experimental Urtling anger therapy *pin-ya-tuh* session." The inventor winced. "Bruises covered every inch of his body."

Laughter started in Ozzie's belly and migrated north, an unstoppable avalanche that overwhelmed his senses, folded him in half, and swept his sister away, too. Layla grinned, flipped her goggles down, and soldered wires.

Pascal threw his arms up. "Great! We'll launch a frontal attack on the most fanatical, bloodthirsty psychopaths in Terravenum. At least they won't be expecting it."

---

1. Yes, but only when pubescent male nipnards goad each other into ill-conceived attempts to impress females.
2. Like all librarians, the Booksworn track borrowing transgressions with an Overdue List. But unlike their civilian brethren, they do not confine retribution to a token fine.

    More than one multi-generational war has been waged after the son of an aristocrat dog-eared a page in a book of poems about water lilies.

CHAPTER 49
SABOTAGE & SACRIFICE

Ozzie leaned into the gale from *Spark's* prop-wash and adjusted the tow line to minimize chafe on *Angelus'* bow. Two hundred feet ahead, the racing skiff strained against her leash, unaccustomed to traveling so slow. Ozzie gave the line a friendly pat, then worked his way aft, dodging piles of half-installed components in the junkyard that had taken over the main deck.

Layla slapped an instrument panel. "All conduit breakers are offline. What were you doing while I was gone, Pascal?"

"Saving the world," the inventor grumbled, from beneath the steering console, "though I'm having second thoughts."

"I was surprised you partnered with Thorpe."

"I decided I'd rather get stabbed in the chest than the back." Pascal held out his hand. "Number twelve socket."

Alex rifled through a tool bag. "Thorpe wanted to stop the Chieftess as much as you did," she said. "He didn't do anything to hurt us."

"Aside from abandoning us, you mean?" the inventor said.

Alex hammered the inventor's palm with a number twelve socket. "He was harmless."

Layla scoffed and flipped a switch. "Do not underestimate anyone who survived on the fringes of Contrivance." She pocketed

364

her soldering iron. "Breakers are operational. Where are the flow resistors?"

"In the lab," Pascal muttered.

"Ozzie, you are on watch. Maintain a heading of 300°." Layla stomped downstairs.

"Regale us with tales of Amnesian adventure, young Forsythe," the inventor said, wrenching a stubborn bolt.

Ozzie checked the compass and nudged the helm starboard. He started with their arrival at the island, skimmed over his near-drowning, and had to describe getting eaten by the gluttonous maw twice, because Alex was laughing too hard for Pascal to hear. Vicarious Quibble's appearance met with a jubilant cheer. Hugo's blowhole confession garnered universal outrage, although Pascal's fury was tempered by learning Brother Deathfist's name was Bartholomew. Alex mocked Ozzie's plan to capture a grainer queen, then nodded appreciatively when he dosed Layla with Panacea clay. The inventor whistled at his description of Hugo's lair. "An echolith? The Noctem are serious about Amnesia."

Ozzie's pulse quickened as he unfolded his father's dossier. The ink was smudged from submersion, but still legible. "Hugo had a file claiming Dad was alive two years ago."

Alex's smile faded. "What?"

Pascal craned his neck to read the page. "If Humboldt was in the Feral, I would have heard about it."

His sister shook her head. "Dad's dead, Ozzie."

"Then why would the Noctem store his file in a secret lair on an island no one leaves?"

"To spread disinformation if a prisoner found those records and escaped," Pascal said.

"That's pretty paranoid."

"Clandestine organizations generally are."

"PASCAL, GET DOWN HERE!" Layla's bellow vibrated the deck. The inventor lumbered down the stairs, Ozzie and Alex close on his heels.

Engine components were splayed across the lab floor. The

wrencher tossed Pascal a grapefruit-sized metal ball. "Recognize the handiwork?"

The Dromedarian flicked down a magnifying lens and rotated the part, as if inspecting a diamond for flaws. He groaned. "Not again."

Alex said, "What's wrong?"

Pascal pointed to a blinking red light on the sphere. "Thorpe, your friend who wouldn't do anything to hurt us, hid a transmitter in the parts he gave you."

"You did not check them before bringing them on board?" Layla said.

"I got distracted thwarting an insane plot to fly a city through a force field." He slammed the transmitter down. "I didn't discover Alex had joined forces with my archnemesis until it was too late."

"We needed parts!" Alex said. "I was trying to help."

"I'm certain whoever Thorpe is working for appreciates your help," the inventor growled.

It took an hour to uninstall and examine all of Thorpe's contributions to *Angelus*.

"Four transmitters." Layla arranged the offending doodads and thingamajigs in a row.

"That's only what we found," Pascal said. "There may be more. Thorpe thinks in curves."

"Why would he broadcast our location?" Ozzie said.

"Money, debts, blackmail...or just because it's Tuesday. More than likely, someone hired him."

"Who?"

"The Noctem, Maelstrom, Aeronoth City Council, Merchant Guild, Smuggler's Alliance, Mercenary League, Booksworn, Chieftess, and Children of Contrivance come to mind—but don't beat yourself up, we've only been at this a couple of weeks."

"If we destroy the transmitters, whoever is monitoring their signals will know we discovered them," Layla said.

The inventor dented the workbench with his fist. "We can't keep them on board. *Angie* is more vulnerable than a stubby-winged chunkfinch until we get her systems back online."[*1]

366

"How long will that take?" Alex asked.

"If I cut corners, and Thorpe didn't sabotage anything else, three days."

Ozzie raised his hand. "Can we buy time by releasing transmitters into the sky on separate balloons, so they scatter?"

Layla raised an eyebrow and looked at Pascal, who shrugged. "It is worth a try," she rumbled.

"Pascal will never trust me again," Alex fumed.

Ozzie knotted a line around a transmitter. "If it's any consolation, Layla is still mad at me for setting fire to *Spark*."

"What happened?"

"The Weltling attacked us and I deflected a ball of lightning vomit in the wrong direction."

"Rookie mistake."

"They say your first sea serpent is the hardest." He held the transmitter over the railing as gusts buffeted its canvas balloon. "Bombs away." The decoy bobbed in *Angelus'* wake and drifted north, chasing its three brothers.

"What's with the metal glove?" Alex said.

Ozzie straightened his arm next to hers. Their metal plugs were identical, but Alex's armillam had been replaced by a flat, two-inch wide metal band fused to her skin at her wrist. "Grandfather's sword hilt melted." He flexed his fingers. "It's pretty much a bedazzled normal hand, except when it manifests a fire sword."

"I saw you slice through the docking clamp," she said. "Can you punch through walls?"

"I'm not any stronger than I was, but the metal could probably take it. I'd feel everything, though."

"Why did the Chieftess ask if it speaks to you?"

"No idea." The lie came easy. After seven years of being dismissed by everyone important in his life—*especially* Alex—he was reluctant to pour lighter fluid on the Ozzie is Crazy Bonfire by admitting to arguing with a homicidal, condescending voice in his head. "She was freaking out," he said. "Does your armillam hurt?"

"Only when it randomly generates a force field."

"Nice! At least *you* can pick your nose without losing an eye."

Matching Stella Signums lit their grins.

Repairs progressed at a droolug's jogging pace, punctuated by roars from the engine room whenever Layla encountered system failures. Pascal was everywhere at once, jury-rigging solutions to a bottomless well of conundrums.

Ozzie nudged the wheel, fishtailing *Spark* as she strained against the tow line.

"Bored?" The inventor slurped from a gallon-sized coffee mug.

Ozzie adjusted course back to 300°. "I can feel an idea lurking in the corner of my mind, but I can't chase it down."

Pascal nodded. "In my experience, the key is to sidle up to the idea, then bash it over the head when it's looking the other way. Speaking of bashing things, what's the story on your upgraded hand accessories?"

Ozzie offered his palm for inspection. "The hilt melted, then this happened."

Pascal scrutinized the glove and forearm plugs. "Impressive workmanship—the Ancients knew what they were doing." A series of muffled thumps shuddered the deck. He moaned. "She's bludgeoning the bypass governors with a sledgehammer."

"Will that speed us up?"

"If you mean 'hastening our demise', then yes." The inventor patted the instrument console. "Sorry, girl."

"Thanks for agreeing to go to the Archive."

"You know me—I never pass up an opportunity to die in a completely avoidable strategic blunder."

Ozzie glanced at his sister, who was acting as a lookout on the bow. He cleared his throat. "Alex was only trying to help, you know."

"I'm not sure what the protocol for *helping* is on Urt, but in Terravenum, it doesn't include planting tracking devices on your own airship." Pascal looked at Alex and sighed. "It's my fault. I should have expected Thorpe would do this." He upended his coffee, then ambled downstairs.

A gust jiggled *Spark*, jerking the tow rope until the airships realigned. The inventor's voice rang in Ozzie's ears, *"I'm not sure what the protocol for helping is on Urt..."*

He sidled up to the idea lurking in the corner of his mind.

Protocol.

"Pascal!"

"Absolutely not," Layla said.

Pascal scribbled furiously in a notepad, then gnawed the end of a pencil. "It could work."

The wrencher frowned. "Pegasus Protocol slagged *Angelus* despite her fail-safes. *Spark* will not last five minutes."

"If we reinforce her vulnerable systems, *Spark* can tow us to the Archive faster," Pascal said. "She doesn't have to survive the trip." Ozzie, watching Layla's face, inched away from the doomed Dromedarian. The inventor soldiered on, oblivious to the ice cracking beneath his boots. "Worst-case scenario, we arrive at the Crucible with a fireship, ready to ram the ambush waiting for us." He looked up and finally registered the Sauracian's mood. "What?" Pascal pointed at Ozzie. "It was his idea."

Ozzie withered under the wrencher's glare. "I thought Pegasus Protocol might speed us up. I didn't know it would incinerate *Spark*."

Layla clonked the railing with her fist, then turned to Pascal. "When this is finished, you are going to scavenge parts to repair her."

"Only parts?" The inventor slapped her shoulder. "I'm thinking upgrades! With a little creativity, we can—"

"No." The Sauracian's jaw snapped like a bear trap.

"Sounds good," Pascal said.

Layla reinforced the towing harness while Pascal cobbled together a pipeline to inject purified dynami into *Spark's* engine. Within an hour, they were ready.

Ozzie tightened his harness for the hundredth time. "I can't believe we're doing this again," he muttered. Heat throbbed in his forearm.

I'm impressed! A risky plan born of desperation. Fate hinging on a throw of the dice. Now THIS is glory seeking at its finest.

Ozzie groaned. Not now. Why are *you* here?

Adrenaline and stress are music to my ears.

Not to be rude, but can you go away? I don't need a sword right now.

Perhaps you need guidance.

Not from you, whoever you are. *Whatever* you are. Hey, if you're going to keep popping in like this, I'd feel less crazy if you had a name.

I have gone by many names: Bloodseeker. Wrathblade. Slaughterstorm.

How about Slashy?

Don't you dare.

You're a sword. You slash things.

No one cowers before a weapon named by a toddler.

Perfect. Slashy it is.

This isn't over.

Quiet, Slashy.

"Everyone ready?" Pascal said.

Alex flashed a thumbs-up.

Ozzie sighed. "Not really."

Layla flipped her goggles down, gripped the helm spokes, and growled, "Go."

Blue fluid coursed through the makeshift canal leading to *Spark*.

Pascal crouched behind a barrier and counted down, "Initiating Pegasus Protocol in three...two...one..."

Spark's engine revved like a Tyrannosaurus preparing to sneeze, then choked. Ozzie opened his eyes as wind whistled a gentle melody through the rigging. "What happ—"

Turquoise flames erupted from the racing skiff's exhaust. The engine wailed, mortally wounded, but defiant. *Spark* surged forward, cracking the tow line like a whip. Ozzie clawed his harness to ease the pressure on his rib cage.

The world stretched like taffy.

---

1. Thanks to undersized wings, boneless bodies, and a habit of sleeping twenty-three hours a day, stubby-winged chunkfinches were voted #1 on *Nature Chef Monthly's* annual "Defenseless and Delicious List".

    Not coincidentally, the following month, stubby-winged chunkfinches were featured on the cover of the Creature Society's "Recently Endangered" pamphlet.

    Following the Creature Society's successful breeding program, the chunkfinch population increased to twice their original size. In addition, the Society trained the birds in self-defense to better protect themselves in the future.

    Unfortunately, exercise enlarged and tenderized chunkfinches' already delicious meat, only adding to their status as a delicacy.

    Things spiraled downward from there.

CHAPTER 50
AN IMPATIENT AMBUSH

Skhaar paced *Revenge's* deck, glaring at the southeast horizon. Days of loitering aimlessly over the Feral, waiting for Thorpe's signal, had worn his famously thin patience down to a cracking veneer. *Angelus* had been on a direct course for the Archive when the flesh-bag's transmitters went rogue, but three days' travel was too far to risk attempting a blind intercept. The Annihilator had no illusions about how much could change in three days—he'd toppled empires in a weekend—but his gut told him Pascal was returning to the Archive, so he set his trap above the Booksworn stronghold.*[1]

Dreck and *Karkis* circled overhead in their assigned patrol routes. Scout vessels were better suited for rapid strikes than an ambush, but Skhaar would rather plunge to his death in the Thermals than petition Home Office for additional ships—their snide condescension was insufferable. *Three swift ships were insufficient to accomplish your mission, Skhaar? Is line seven-hundred and eight of the Annihilator Creed not "One Blade, Many Necks"? How many blades do YOU require, Skhaar? Incidentally, we're still waiting for your Post-Action Reports from last year's Impaling Thornicorn incident. While you're here, file form 1073Y—in triplicate, please. And if you persist in using stankwerm blood instead of ink, you'll only have to do them over. Mind your penmanship.*

The Annihilator sneered and flicked his tail stump. He could think of a few necks he'd like to introduce to his blade. A grumble of concern rippled through the crew, who had learned to monitor their captain's mood closely—over the past week, he'd dropped so many warriors into the volcano, the vessel was operating shorthanded.

Skhaar's aversion to excessive altitude was a poorly kept secret in the Maelstrom, but it was also highly contagious—anyone who served on an airship with him soon found themselves equally concerned about altitude. During the Cloud War, Strategic Command limited Skhaar's air time to minimize collateral damage, but Home Office, in its infinite wisdom, sent him aloft regularly, to the dismay of the fleet.

Skhaar counted his remaining crew and ground his goreteeth. He'd isolated himself in the field—a reflexive habit for an Annihilator, but a costly mistake in ship-to-ship combat, where boarding an enemy's vessel was the ultimate goal.*[2] He would tackle *Angelus* by himself.

"Incoming rounds, Captain!"

The Annihilator cursed under his breath and risked a heart-thumping glance over the ship's rail. A salvo of lava bombs raced up from the Crucible, reached their apex, then dropped away in smoky arcs. He grunted. The librarians had boosted the range of their lava guns.

"Drop another hundred feet and hover over the center of the crater," he ordered. "Tempt them to fire, so their misses bombard the Archive." He grinned at the thought of Brother Deathfist sheltering from his own gunners.

A blast from *Karkis'* battle horn quickened Skhaar's pulse. Crew hustled to battle stations, armor and weapons clanking. The radioman barked, "Fast moving vessel to the southeast, sir!"

"Fast moving" was an understatement. The mystery vessel streaked toward the volcano like an avenging comet. Skhaar twisted his spyglass, bringing the threat into focus and confirming his suspicions.

Fireship.

A thrashing blob hidden in the airship's smoky veil triggered warning bells. Was there a second vessel?

"Dive!" he bellowed. A klaxon blared, and *Revenge* plunged. Skhaar's lunch tried to flee his stomach, but he kept his eyes fixed on his approaching enemy. The trailing ship broke away, and the fireship careened into the Maelstrom fleet. *Dreck* vented air, but never had a chance. The explosion shook *Revenge's* rigging and warmed Skhaar's face. He jabbed a claw at the airship diving for the Crucible.

Angelus.

"Ram them! I'm going aboard."

---

1. Ambushes ranked third on Skhaar's Least Favorite Forms of Attacking list, behind (#2) Tripping and Accidentally Crushing an Enemy with His Body Weight and (#1) Waiting for an Enemy to Perish of Old Age.

   There was no honor in loitering like an uncommon badgadder, waiting for unwitting quarry to stumble into your burrow.

2. Annihilators operate solo by necessity, as the trails of destruction in their wakes bolster fearsome reputations but do little to encourage teamwork.

   Recognizing this issue, Home Office revamped Annihilator training to include team building exercises and group therapy sessions.

   Following a string of incidents (referred to behind closed doors as *The Feelings Doll Massacres*), Home Office suspended the program.

CHAPTER 51
A DEATH SPIRAL

"Did you see *Spark* disintegrate?" Alex crowed. "That was incredible!"

"I pumped in extra dynami to amplify the explosion!" Pascal shouted.

Ozzie winced as Layla roared, diving *Angelus* at the mouth of the volcano.

CRACCCKKKKKK

Crimson lightning ripped past the port side. The wrencher punched a button, and a burst of speed popped deck planks loose.

"Don't over-modulate the throttle!" the inventor yelled.

Alex screamed, "Look out!"

A bowsprit carved with fangs and outstretched claws barreled past Ozzie's head as *Revenge* T-boned *Angelus*, crushing the port rail. Pascal's pride and joy lurched six feet sideways, her deck splintering like matchsticks. Air bladders snarled together in a jumble of rope and canvas.

Skhaar landed on the foredeck with a thump that shivered the rigging. Maelstrom warriors lined the railing of *Revenge*, but none moved to join him.

"Your foolishness does you credit, Pascal!" the Annihilator bellowed. "I enjoyed your fireship—prey rarely surprises me anymore." He flicked his tail mace up, caught the chain, and flung it in one motion. The inventor dove, and a bludgeoning blow caromed off his prosthetic shoulder. Skhaar yanked the ball back and spun it over his head. "Whoever surrenders the Professor's journal first will suffer the least."

Pascal wobbled to his feet. "Is this a new policy? Historically, Annihilators discourage survivors."

Skhaar smirked. "I did not say there would be survivors." He lashed the chain downward, burying the ball next to the helm. Layla snarled and cranked the wheel to regain control of the floundering airship.

Angry heat throbbed in Ozzie's forearm.

Seize your destiny!

Not a good time, Slashy.

He's not that big.

"Please go away," Ozzie groaned, cradling his wrist.

"The orphan whispers!" Skhaar said. Ozzie wilted as the Annihilator chuckled. "Speak louder, fleshling—will you choose a hero's death or a coward's life?" Skhaar reeled his chain in with a flick of his tail, then whirled the mace over his head like an aborigine bull-roarer.

Now's your chance!

To what? Die?

Everyone dies, few truly live!

Whose side are you on, Slashy?

Greatness!

A chorus of piercing whistles ended in thuds as lava bombs plowed into the envelopes. *Angelus'* elastic canvas repelled the shots, but a superheated ball found its mark in *Revenge's* balloon. Sauracian warriors formed a bucket chain, dousing flames with a gooey pink substance.

The Crucible's lip flared orange as it launched a fresh onslaught of bombs. Layla spun the helm, sending both airships into a corkscrewing death spiral. G-forces threatened to tear *Angelus* apart as Skhaar slid down the tilted deck. On the Maelstrom vessel, untethered Sauracians screeched, cartwheeling into the volcano.

Layla stabilized their altitude, then ducked as Skhaar's mace smashed the wheel to splinters. The Annihilator's claws tore furrows in the deck as he advanced. "Your fates are sealed!" he roared.

Pascal kicked a heliovapor bottle at Skhaar's feet and hit it with a shockbag. The concussion knocked Ozzie over, but when the smoke cleared, the Annihilator crouched unharmed behind his cloak. He snarled and unsheathed a wicked, curved sword from a bronze scabbard.

"I usually reserve Grieftongue for worthy enemies, but in your case, I'll make an exception."

The Dromedarian backed away. "Don't do me any favors."

Alex crouched to leap onto the Annihilator's back. Ozzie waved her off, but she ignored him. Why did everyone in his family think they're invincible?

Slashy?

Silence.

Slashy!

He named his sword Grieftongue.

So?

Mysterious. Intimidating. Slightly grotesque—with one word, it's clear his weapon has a past.

So do you. You slash stuff.

Silence.

Would you prefer to be called Sulky?

What do you want?

Do I have a chance against Skhaar?

Of course not. Since when does that matter?

Ozzie clenched his fist as heat flared, begging for release. Alex was about to jump.

Okay Slashy, let's—

Three Booksworn warriors flipped through the air, landing on *Angelus'* deck like jungle cats. A fourth slammed into the side of *Revenge*, then tumbled out of sight, screaming.

Skhaar hissed and stabbed Grieftongue in the deck. He whipped his mace in a broad circle, snared a librarian's leg, and swung him like a wrecking ball. A blade slashed the Annihilator's arm, drawing a spray of green blood, but the reptile only grinned, then crushed the swordsman's face with an elbow strike. Skhaar yanked Grieftongue free, blocked the last librarian's desperate crossbow shot, then cleaved him in half. He glanced up at the watching Maelstrom warriors and snarled, "Repel any further uninvited guests with lightning."

The Annihilator's eyes twinkled as he turned to *Angelus'* horrified crew. "Where was I? Oh, yes..." Grieftongue flicked, stopping a centimeter from Pascal's throat. "Surrender the journal and die quickly, or defy me and explore new frontiers of anguish."

The inventor raised a shaky arm to point at a storage bin.

Skhaar nodded at Ozzie. "Retrieve it."

CRAAAACKKKK

Angelus rocked as Maelstrom gunners shot a trio of Booksworn boarders out of the sky.

Ozzie unclipped his harness.

Any ideas, Slashy?

Stab Skhaar when you hand him the journal.

The journal is locked in the smuggler's hold! I don't know what Pascal's thinking, but if there isn't a metric ton of shempum saliva in this storage bin, we're in trouble.

You asked me for ideas. I'm nudging you toward your destiny, one stab at a time.

Ozzie unsnapped the locks on the bin with more force than necessary.

Is my destiny to become a shish kabob?

Maybe. What's a shish kabob? Are they glorious?

Forget it. I'll throw something at Skhaar as a distraction.

Will missing him be a distraction? I've seen you throw.

Just be ready. I'm going to need a sword.

Ozzie's heart hopscotched when he cracked the lid open and saw a black cube labeled *Screechbox 3001*. He picked the weapon up with the apprehensive touch of an amateur snake wrangler.

"What is that?" Skhaar said.

"A strongbox," Pascal rasped. "The journal is inside."

378

"Open it, boy. If this is a trap, I will flood this deck with Pascal's blood."

Ozzie rotated the cube, not daring to breathe. The device looked identical to the previous prototype, with the notable addition of a yellow On/Off button labeled *DO NOT PRESS, UNDER ANY CIRCUMSTANCES*. He winced, then triggered the button.

Click

He tried again.

Click

He held the button down longer.

Cli-ck

Nothing.

Pascal lowered his chin, eyebrows wriggling like panicked caterpillars. Ozzie stabbed the button again for good measure, then dropped the cube. When Screechbox 3001 struck the floor, a low pitch juddered his molars, then a high squeal bayoneted his ear drums. Alex tackled him as an expanding circle of deck planks exploded around the cube. *Revenge* fractured in two, pelting *Angelus* with a hailstorm of wood and metal. As seismic ripples snowballed, Skhaar heaved his mace at Screechbox, scoring a direct hit. The organ-crushing rumble blooped and burbled into indignant silence, but the damage was done. *Angelus'* envelope collapsed with a groan.

"We're going down!" Pascal yelled.

The airships tumbled through the Crucible, locked in a dying embrace. Layla feathered the throttle, coaxing the disintegrating vessels over the floating island and away from the lake of bubbling lava. "Brace for impact!" she shouted. *Angelus* slammed into the Archive bell tower, catapulting the twins at the side of a building. Ozzie curled into a ball, steeled for the worst, but a translucent blue shield downgraded the collision from Excruciating to Mildly Disagreeable. *Angelus* ignited in a fireball that swallowed both ships and collapsed a wing of the library, rattling the island's meter-thick chains.

Alex sprawled on the ground next to Ozzie, holding her arm aloft as bricks bounced off the force field projecting from her wrist band. When the rain of debris slowed, she dropped her arm. The shield flickered into nothingness, and bedlam rushed in.

"Alex!" Ozzie took her hand, carefully avoiding her frost-encrusted armillam.

"I'm okay, just give me a second…"

"That was amazing!"

"Thanks." She looked toward the crash site. "Pascal and Layla?"

"No idea."

An avalanche of wreckage and a belligerent roar announced the wrencher's escape from *Angelus'* blazing carcass. A series of explosions shook the Archive, and Pascal staggered into view, slinging a dilapidated leather satchel over his shoulder. He'd saved the journal!

Ozzie kept scanning the crash site. "Where's Skhaar?"

"Hopefully, crushed beneath a klunk-ton of debris," Layla growled, brushing pumice from her shoulders.

"Why haven't the Booksworn shown up yet?" he said.

The Sauracian tapped her ear. "Listen. There are skirmishes all over the island."

Now that she mentioned it, battle cries and clashing steel were drifting in from every direction.

Alex pointed to silhouettes battling behind stained-glass windows. "Why are they fighting?"

"It doesn't matter," Pascal said. "We can use the distraction. The dungeon is beneath the main hall."

Standing inside a volcano, the reality of infiltrating a Booksworn prison hit home in a way it hadn't when *Angelus* was soaring through the sky.

"That's going to be heavily guarded," Ozzie said.

The inventor scowled. "Remember back at Contrivance when I said returning to the Archive was a lunkbrained idea?" He gestured to the surrounding inferno, then pointed at the Crucible, where lava gunners were keeping the surviving Maelstrom ship at bay. "Welcome to the *I told you so* part of the plan."

"Let's stay positive," Alex said. "After we save Grandfather, how do we get out of here?"

"On *Angelus*, of course!" Pascal retorted, then slapped his forehead. "Wait, that won't work. If only someone had predicted this complete disaster."

"Enough," Layla rumbled. "How do we get out?"

The inventor crossed his arms, glaring at her. "The Archive has an emergency zip line exit in case of envelope failure. After we defeat an army of vicious, highly trained Booksworn warriors and rescue the Professor, we can access the zip line from the sub-basement. Assuming we don't fall in the lava, we face a second army of vicious, highly trained warriors who guard the ground-level Molten Gate. Then we escape into the Feral and evade kill squads." He smiled brightly. "It's almost too easy."

Layla sighed. "One problem at a time. We start with the dungeon."

They skirted the main courtyard, ducking behind toppled statues and shattered remnants of ornamental fountains. An explosion swayed the island, prompting a ragged cheer from a distant mob.

"Who is that?" Alex whispered.

"Probably a raiding party from a rival library," Pascal said. "Could be anyone, though—the Booksworn have a lot of enemies: researchers on the Overdue List, bookstore owners, secondhand book collectors, the Labyrinthians—"

"Congratulations, you made the list," a nasally voice sneered. Cloaked warriors stepped out of the shadows and surrounded *Angelus'* crew.

The speaker threw his hood back, revealing a bald head covered in tribal tattoos. Novice Slapsneeze smiled. "Welcome back, Pascal." His eyes snaked across the group. "Thank you for justifying your executions by bringing females onto Archive grounds."

Alex elbowed Ozzie. "I *told* you he was Noctem."

"It's good to be back, Slappy," the inventor said. "I'll give you one chance to surrender, for old time's sake."

Slapsneeze's cheeks reddened. "Summon Brother Deathfist," he snapped. A lackey sprinted into the main building. The remaining librarians dropped their hoods and assumed fighting stances. Layla

381

flexed her claws and growled. The two Booksworn closest to her exchanged a worried glance.

Slashy?

The hour of destiny is upon us!

Ozzie rolled his eyes, wincing as fire flowed to his hand like lava seeking a path to the ocean.

I need a sword, Slashy.

Ready and willing. A touch of manifestation and we're there.

I'm having trouble with that lately.

Try screaming.

You're joking.

Can't go wrong with a good berserker scream.

Ozzie groaned inwardly, then threw his head back and howled with every fiber of rage he could muster. Alex jumped, Layla frowned, and Pascal snorted. As battle cries went, it was a solid C minus, if you ignored the desperate gasp for air at the end. The embarrassed silence was more painful than the bonfire in his arm.

I stand corrected. In Terravenum, berserkers are warriors. Are they childcare providers where you come from?

Just help me with the Blade, Slashy!

Novice Slapsneeze's lip curled. "An appropriate final whimper for a—"

Ozzie tuned the librarian out and pictured orange flames dancing on the edge of his sword. Fire whooshed, exiting his glove in a cool wave of relief. He opened his eyes to find the Anemoi Blade gripped in his palm, just as he'd imagined, except its flames were green.

Slapsneeze choked on his monologue.

"Whoa," Alex breathed.

"*Custos Luminis.*" Layla's whisper echoed in the courtyard. Nervous murmurs rippled through the circle of librarians.

Attack while they are awed by our magnificence!

Maybe I won't have to. They're just staring.

This is what we in the business of Winning Fights refer to as "an opportunity." Attack!

I have their attention. Maybe we can talk things out.

Fire swords are not tools for talking things out. Attack NOW, before—

Novice Slapsneeze bellowed a rallying cry and charged.

—That happens.

Layla, Pascal, and Alex formed a circle around Ozzie. Why did they always assume he needed protecting?

Not this time.

He jumped in front of Layla and screamed the only phrase that came to mind.

"WHIRLING WALL OF DEATH!"

YES! The hour of destiny is—wait, what?

Ozzie spun in random circles, slashing the air with impotent fury, trailing green smoke with every stroke.

What are you doing?

"WHIRLING WALL OF DEATH!" He hacked the sky.

Stop! You're embarrassing us!

Ozzie parried a thrust, sparking green fireworks. A librarian ducked the Anemoi Blade, only to catch a swipe from Layla's paw. Two charging warriors discovered the torment of Pascal's shockbags.

"WHIRLING...wall...of death," Ozzie wheezed.

Running out of energy, genius?

It was a fair question. In ten seconds, Ozzie's fighting style had deteriorated from "Whirling Wall of Death" to the classic "Panting Guy Clutching His Side of Death" technique. With each exhausting swing, fainting became a bigger threat than a Booksworn blade.

If you're going to be this ridiculous, you need to work on your cardio.

Quiet, Slashy.

Had the Anemoi Blade always weighed a thousand pounds?

"Watch out!" Alex yelled.

Novice Slapsneeze's rigid fingers grazed Ozzie's chin. Only the proud Forsythe tradition of Not Knowing What Was Good For Him kept Ozzie on his feet. Time slowed as the librarian's backhand approached like a world-ending asteroid.

"Oooof!" Slapsneeze folded, Alex's foot buried in his stomach. His sister grinned—she was going to lord this over him for years.

A triple-corded hair braid whipped around Ozzie's metal glove. The other end was attached to the scalp of the grouchy haiku guardian, Brother Pugnacious. The librarian grinned, then performed a backflip, yanking Ozzie off his feet. Motivated by shame and the fact he really, *really* wanted to wipe that satisfied smirk off Pugnacious' face, he found a second wind.

"Cool move, Puggy," he said, regaining his feet. "I haven't seen a backflip that nice since my sister learned somersaults in second grade gym class."

Less patter, more stabbing.

The Anemoi Blade flared pink. Ozzie waved his sword, frowning at the cotton candy-colored smoke.

What's the deal, Slashy?

Different emotion, different fuel. Different fuel, different color.

What emotion is pink?

I haven't seen it before…I'm guessing anxiety. Maybe defeat?

Pugnacious torqued his neck, flicking his braid in a ferocious arc. Ozzie swung the Anemoi Blade, and by a miracle of blind luck, severed the hair whip.

"Yes!" he shouted.

I never doubted you! Taste the sweet elixir of victory!

Pugnacious yelled and launched a physics-defying tumbling run at Ozzie, who skittered backwards like a terror-stricken crab. The librarian double-flipped, landed on one foot, and cocked his leg for a death blow.

CRASH

A colossal bronze bust of Garrilus the Unread bounced down the stairs, flattening everything in its path before rolling over the edge of the island.

"CEASE FIGHTING, OR DIE." Brother Deathfist's command boomed like a proclamation from Mount Olympus.

CHAPTER 52

SCHISMS

All across the courtyard, tendons contracted mid-punch as Deathfist's ultimatum penetrated the fog of war. Relief washed over Ozzie when Brother Pugnacious retracted his foot. The Anemoi Blade fizzled and disappeared.

Slashy?

The blade didn't answer.

"Alex?" Ozzie said.

His sister's voice was muffled, "I'm here—just waiting for this meathead to let go of my leg." A pot-bellied librarian released Alex from a submission hold that, from the look of it, was named *Python Spitting Out Coconuts.*[*1] She stood up, scowling.

Layla grunted, bashed two librarians together like crash cymbals, then brushed an overzealous novice off her back. Pascal dangled upside down by the stairs, his teeth clamped around the ankle of a jumbo-sized warrior who was attempting to pile-drive him into the cobblestones. But *Angelus'* crew weren't the only combatants—all around them, Brother fought Brother in dazzling displays of martial arts. Grandfather's rescue mission had barged headlong into a Booksworn civil war.

Deathfist descended the stairs of the main hall, resting a six-foot wooden club on his shoulder.

385

WHUMP

A casual swing of his arm sent two squabbling warriors flying.

WHUMP

A second swing pulverized an archer as he drew a bowstring.

Word of Deathfist's arrival rippled to the outer edges of the battle. One by one, Booksworn brethren lowered their weapons, faced their leader, and resorted to subversive elbowing and toe-stomping.

Brother Deathfist stopped at the bottom of the staircase and spread his brawny arms like a hug-seeking apocalypse. "Pascal, you never fail to entertain." He snapped his fingers, and rough hands shoved *Angelus'* crew front and center.

The inventor tightened the straps on his prosthetic arm. "Glad to be of service, your megalomaniacship."

"This day does not have to end in your obliteration, old friend. Give me the book."

"Is this about that overdue copy of *Gardening for Super Geniuses Who Can't Keep a Fern Alive*?" Pascal said. "Because I requested an extension." He met Layla's incredulous stare with a shrug. "What? I have hobbies."

Slapsneeze yanked the leather satchel off the inventor's shoulder.

"Don't open that," the Dromedarian warned.

A geyser of shempum saliva erupted into the novice's face. The librarian collapsed, twitching in the center of a widening circle.

"Let's be honest," Pascal said, "no one is upset that happened."

Brother Deathfist cracked his knuckles with the sound of falling timber. "The book," he rumbled.

"No," Layla said.

Turbulence from the Head Librarian's club ruffled Ozzie's hair.

WHUMP

Librarian-shaped speed bumps were all that stopped the wrencher from knocking over a building in her flight across the square.

"Layla!" Ozzie started after her, but Brother Pugnacious' arm snaked around his neck. Alex grabbed the librarian's elbow, and he downed her with a knee to her solar plexus.

Heat flared in Ozzie's forearm. "You're going to regret that," he croaked.

Brother Deathfist glared at Ozzie. "You've done well to survive this long, child. Don't make me kill you in front of your sister."

Pugnacious loosened his grip enough for Ozzie to answer. "You can *try*, but you and your Noctem buddies have a pathetic track record—you failed at Grandfather's funeral, then at St. Jude's, and didn't even come *close* the last time we were here. Plus, your brother dropped the ball on Amnesia."

Deathfist's eyebrows gathered like storm clouds.

What are you doing?

Quiet, Slashy. I'm sick of these guys hurting my family. You have to stand up to bullies.

He doubled down. "By the way, you need a new prison warden, since I made sure Hugo can't remember his own name, let alone your secret handshake."

"Ozzie..." Pascal whispered.

Deathfist's club thumped the ground, cracking a stair. Way to go, Ozzie—you successfully agitated a man strong enough to punch a hole in the moon.

That was unwise.

If Slashy, who had the survival instincts of an overconfident lemming, was criticizing him for being too aggressive, he had definitely crossed a line.

"Hugo was always too soft," the Head Librarian rasped, "a flaw I have never been accused of having." The leviathan stomped forward, each step rattling Ozzie's spine.

Uh, Slashy?

Heat flowed.

Vengeance and glory!

When the Anemoi Blade appeared, Ozzie raised his arm as if preparing to slash downward, then slammed his head back, mashing Pugnacious' nose flat. Pressure on his throat disappeared, and he filled his lungs.

387

"WHIRLING WALL—"

Don't you dare!

"—OF DEATH!"

Amidst hysterical swordsmanship and Slashy's mortified disavowals, Ozzie couldn't help but be dismayed by his blade's purple flames.

"STOP," Pascal's cry pierced the burgeoning combat, "OR I'LL DESTROY THE PROFESSOR'S JOURNAL!"

An eerie hush set in—the kind you get when a gargantuan man has cocked his fist to crush a boy threatening him with a marshmallow skewer, and everyone wants to watch. For a dire moment, it appeared Brother Deathfist was going to unleash the cataclysmic fury of his namesake weapon, then he blinked and chuckled—an ominous, grating sound like a manhole cover sliding open.

"Do not count yourself spared, young Forsythe," he growled. "Once I secure the journal, we shall discuss my brother further. Spend this reprieve in contemplation of my capacity for protracted and excruciating revenge." Deathfist trudged to the top of the Archive stairs, where Pascal waited, holding the book over his head.

Ozzie's heart, surprised by his continued need for its services, resumed beating.

That went well.

Shut up, Slashy.

The Anemoi Blade flickered and died.

Pascal pointed to a glowing cylinder of dynami strapped to the cover of the book. "Harm my friends or make a move I don't like, and I'll detonate the journal."

Deathfist raised a wry eyebrow. "You believe I care so much about a book?"

"Beneath the Noctem nonsense, you're Booksworn—preserving documents is your sworn duty," the inventor said. "Here's what is going to happen now: You release the Professor, we zip line out of here, and you get to add the journal to your *Books We Stole Like Jerks* collection."

"You leave little room for negotiation." The librarian's sharklike smile was carved in granite.

"We both know it's the only way my friends and I are getting off this rock alive—and if we don't, at least I'll have the pleasure of driving a knife through your book-loving heart before I meet that Big Fist in the Sky."

"Bring the prisoner," Deathfist growled.

A haggard figure emerged from a cellar, flanked by two steroid-laced escorts. The prisoner's unkempt hair and silver stubble were a far cry from the Professor's meticulous grooming standards, but Ozzie recognized those khaki shorts anywhere.

"What is the meaning of this, Deathfist?" The man's colonial British accent polished his outrage. "It took me days to scratch that crossword puzzle into the wall, and your ruffians just smudged half my 'across' clues."

"Grandfather!"

Sir Quidby's jaw dropped. "Ozymandias?" He shielded his eyes and scanned the crowd. "*Alexandria*? What are you doing here?"

"Rescuing you," Ozzie said, contrary to all evidence. Alex waved an embarrassed hello from the clutches of an axe-wielding librarian.

The Professor scowled. "Where's Pascal?" He spotted the inventor, who winced. "You brought my *grandchildren* through the Divide? Are you *mad*?"

"Can we talk about this later?" the Dromedarian said.

"Believe me, we will." Sir Quidby marched up the stairs, ignoring his captors. "What is going on here, Deathfist?"

"Pascal seeks to barter your journal for your lives."

"Preposterous! He would never be foolish enough to bring my journal here."

Shuffling sandals and polite coughs broke the awkward silence as librarians cleared a space around Pascal. Sir Quidby adjusted his spectacles and squinted at the shrinking inventor. Blood drained from the old explorer's face.

"My wishes were simple." The Professor raised a trembling index finger. "First, to never bring more of my family across the

Divide, and second, *to keep my journal safe*. How you failed so spectacularly at both is something I shall ponder until my dying day."

Pascal said, "Things got complicated."

Sir Quidby gestured to the courtyard. "Really? How so?"

"Enough!" Brother Deathfist shoved the Professor at Pascal and snatched the journal from the inventor's hand. A flick of his finger tore the cylinder from the book, raising a dainty puff of smoke.

Pascal groaned beneath the old explorer. "It was worth a try."

Sir Quidby wobbled to his feet. "You are wrong about the Stones, Deathfist—they will save your world, not end it. But you can still choose—"

The librarian pounded the journal with a beefy palm. "Terravenum will not pay the price for your arrogance!" He turned to the crowd. "But the Professor is correct about one thing: this *is* a day for choosing. My brothers, for too long, the Noctem have lurked in the shadows. I extend amnesty to any of you who raised arms against us today, for as of this moment, the schism in our order is finished. Declare allegiance to the Noctem or meet your fate."

A wave of librarians drifted outward, forming a circle around a much smaller group in the center of the courtyard. To Ozzie's surprise, Brother Pugnacious remained beside him, glaring at the Head Librarian with unmasked animosity.

Deathfist held the Professor's journal high. "Behold, the catalyst of our dispute. The naïve among you believe our duty begins and ends where an author's quill runs dry. But those who have witnessed the self-destructive bent of stone hunters know better." His thick finger jabbed at Sir Quidby. "Meddlers, blinded by ambition and seeking personal glory, endanger us all." Deathfist smacked his chest with a blow heavy enough to crush a buffalo's ribcage. "We, the Noctem, stand on the edge of darkness! This is our moment, brothers. We—"

Brother Deathfist gasped and looked down, perplexed, as the tip of a golden blade burst from his chest. The sword extended further, lifting the mighty librarian off his feet.

"*RRRRRAAAAAAAAAAAAAKH!*"

With a roar of berserker rage, Skhaar the Annihilator raised Brother Deathfist over his head like a gruesome trophy.

---

1. Ozzie had no way of knowing *Python Spitting Out Coconuts* was forbidden by the Mortalis Council because of its propensity to dislocate the shoulders of everyone involved (including, in one infamous incident, an innocent bystander watching from half a mile away).

   The move that took Alex down was *Elephant Tickle in the Night*, a close cousin to *Python Spitting Out Coconuts*, but less severe thanks to a minor rotation of the left thumb.

CHAPTER 53
WHAT GOES UP

Maelstrom warriors vaulted into the crowd of shocked librarians, blades swinging. At the first clash of steel, the courtyard exploded into mayhem. All Booksworn, Noctem or not, found themselves allied against a common foe. Flying kicks, spinning punches, and snarling muzzles melded into a dance of destruction.

Skhaar plucked the Professor's journal from Deathfist's unresisting hand, then kicked the librarian's body down the stairs. The Annihilator met Ozzie's glare with a sneer.

Seize your destiny!

Skhaar had torn the Forsythe family apart.

Avenge them!

Heat surged in his arm.

You can bring justice.

Ozzie's hand shook as the sword fizzed into existence, spouting red flames.

The Sauracian's eyes widened. "An Anemoi Blade?" He slashed Grieftongue in a figure eight, as if conducting an orchestra. "You have earned my attention, fleshling. Perhaps with such a weapon, you will live longer than your mother did."

With a semi-respectable yell, Ozzie charged the monster who had shattered his life. He had only run a couple steps when a hand

392

snagged his foot, sending him tumbling to the hard-packed lava. Ozzie tried to kick free, but his grandfather, stretched flat on the ground, refused to release his ankle.

"Let me go!"

"He will kill you!" Sir Quidby said.

"Skhaar has to pay for what he did to Mom and Dad." He jerked his foot free.

"This is not who you are, Ozzie."

How would you know? He rushed the stairs, but by the time he vaulted two slain librarians and dodged a wounded Sauracian, Skhaar had vanished. A Maelstrom warrior leapt out of the shadows, swinging a jagged-toothed sword. Their blades locked at the hilt and inched toward Ozzie's neck like a guillotine.

Slashy, help me!

If you're looking for advice: in swordsmanship circles, your present strategy is known as "losing," and it's generally frowned upon.

Slashy!

There is one thing you can try, but—

Now!

Okay, but—

Ozzie screamed, and the Anemoi Blade spewed an arm-thick column of fire that severed the Maelstrom warrior's arm, instantly cauterizing the wound. The lizard bared his teeth and shrieked in Ozzie's face.

THUD

The warrior slumped, courtesy of a dented skull. Brother Pugnacious lowered Deathfist's club and snapped, "Get up!"

Ozzie pushed to his feet, clutching his throbbing wrist. "Thanks," he panted. Fury raging in the young librarian's eyes discouraged him from offering a handshake.

Pugnacious flourished his club and pointed at the edge of the island. "Get the book!" He took a step back, bellowed, "Dance with me!", then leapt onto three Maelstrom warriors, who were bounding up the stairs.

Bone-deep fatigue sucked at Ozzie's limbs like wet concrete.

Slashy?

The blade was silent. A bitter, frigid ache swelled in his forearm. Someone grabbed his elbow, but he was too exhausted to resist.

"Come on," Alex said. "Skhaar went that way."

"I can't," he gasped. "Grandfather's right, this isn't who I am. Skhaar will kill us, Alex. Look around." He gestured to the war zone. "We don't belong here."

She glowered at him. "Skhaar does *not* get to kill Mom and Dad *and* steal the doomsday journal. Not while we can stop him."

Ozzie looked into his sister's bloodshot eyes and sighed. "The Stupendous Twins never quit," he said, evoking their childhood superhero personas. Fighting monsters was more fun when they didn't systematically destroy everything he loved in the world. "Dibs on the Sword of Awesome."

"Whatever. Let's go!"

They found Skhaar skulking among the array of mirrored balloons lining the island's perimeter, muttering to himself and glaring skyward at the Maelstrom ship bombarding the Crucible. The twins crouched behind a low wall, searching for a way to approach the Annihilator without being spotted.

"He's waiting for a ride," Ozzie whispered. "We've got to reach him before his ship does. Can you make a shield?"

"Only when I freak out."

"Have you tried visualizing one? Imagination and emotion manifest my sword." He extended his palm and pictured a blade forged from orange, leaping flames.

Nothing.

He gritted his teeth. Fine, pink flames.

Nothing.

"You should see your face," Alex snorted.

"I'm still working out the kinks." He tapped the plugs in his forearm and turned his hand over. The Stella Signum was gone, replaced by the reddish-chrome sheen of volantium.

Slashy?

He felt an echoing emptiness, like he'd shouted down a well.

"Do you have a Stella Signum?" he said.

His sister wriggled her fingers, displaying the rippling translucent tattoo.

Ozzie risked a quick peek over the wall and shouted, "Incoming!"

CRUNCH

A fizzing metal sphere punched through lava bricks like they were made of paper. So much for the element of surprise.

A little help, Slashy?

"I gave you a reprieve, child," Skhaar's gravelly chuckle grated Ozzie's ears, "but foolishness runs in your blood." Metal scraped stone as the warrior retrieved his mace.

"*Psst.*" Alex pointed at a rock and mimed throwing it.

"*Have you seen me throw?*" Ozzie hissed. The menacing hum of a whirling chain knotted his shoulders.

CRUNK

Skhaar's mace rocked the wall, then rattled cheerfully back to the Annihilator.

Alex handed Ozzie a chunk of lava rock. "Throw hard, so it doesn't bounce before it hits him," she whispered. "We just need to keep Skhaar busy until the cavalry arrives." She nodded to the courtyard, where Layla and Pascal were dragging a siege crossbow through rubble.

"Is your shield ready?" Ozzie said.

She rubbed her armillam and grimaced. "Maybe."

"This is the worst idea *ever*—and that includes all of Pascal's plans."

"Just make sure you hit Skhaar." Alex jumped to her feet and shouted, "Hey lizard lips, do you annihilate anything besides walls?"

Cursing passive-aggressive swords and over-aggressive sisters, Ozzie palmed his rock and stood up in time to see the Annihilator hurl the mace. Alex screamed, and her shield manifested, sending Skhaar's ball ricocheting into the air. She twisted her wrist, clearing the force field from Ozzie's firing line.

"Now!" she yelled.

The throw was a thing of beauty, and unquestionably the

greatest athletic achievement of his life. Muscle and sinew unfolded in perfect sequence to hurl the rock directly at Skhaar's head. For a terrible second, Ozzie worried he might have underthrown, but adrenaline compensated for his sloppy technique.

Clonk

The stone bounced harmlessly off Skhaar's craggy forehead and *clinked* to the ground.

The Annihilator's roar shook the island. Ozzie checked on Layla and Pascal, who were struggling to load their jumbo crossbow.

"You dare to mock me?" Skhaar thundered, unsheathing Grieftongue.

Alex angled her shield to protect them. "Grab another rock!"

"*Are you insane?*" Ozzie hissed.

A horn blast reverberated through the volcano, halting the Sauracian mid-stride. He glanced up, snarled, and pivoted away from the twins.

"His ride is coming!" Ozzie searched the sky but couldn't spot the Maelstrom ship.

"I don't think so," Alex said. "Look!"

Skhaar grabbed a stabilizing balloon's chain and severed links near the ground with a slice of his blade. The island bobbed as the balloon ascended, carrying the Annihilator, Grandfather's journal, and the end of the world with it.

Alex dissipated her shield and sprinted for the edge, Ozzie trailing close behind.

"We need to grab him!" she said.

"I make swords, not grappling hooks."

"We have to do something!"

He threw his hands up. "Imagination and emotion?"

She grimaced and aimed her left arm at Skhaar. A pencil-thin line of blue energy darted out of her wrist band and snagged the bottom of the chain.

"Yes!" Alex dug her heels into the pumice, but she might as well have lassoed a passenger jet. He grabbed his sister's waist as the balloon dragged her toward the edge.

"Cut the line!" he shouted.

"I can't!"

Ozzie wrapped her in a full-body hug as their feet left the ground. A wave of suffocating heat strengthened his grip. He glanced down at the bubbling lake. *"Don't cut the line!"*

Alex grunted and grabbed her left forearm. The incandescent cord of energy hissed as it shortened, hauling them up.

Scorching gusts buffeted the balloon, whipping the chain in wild arcs. Alex, white-faced and exhausted, clung to the bottom links while Ozzie squirmed higher, like an ambitious inchworm. Skhaar's feet swayed just beyond his reach. The Annihilator had a death grip on the chain, and if Ozzie didn't know better, he'd swear the Sauracian's eyes were clamped shut. A guttural, low-pitched melody rumbled on the breeze. Was he singing?

A flaming bowling ball ricocheted off the balloon.

Fantastic. The Crucible gunners had noticed them.

Lava bombs rained, trailing smoke and sizzling as they hurtled past. A sulfuric gust shoved the balloon closer to the volcano's wall. Hoods poked over the Crucible's edge—in another fifteen seconds, the balloon would be face to face with a battery of lava guns.

Skhaar had fastened the journal to his belt with a leather strap. If Ozzie could climb past the Annihilator's gnarled feet undetected, he might be able to reach it.

Slashy?

No answer.

Please, I need help.

A low-grade burn in his forearm gave him hope.

What do you want? Wait, is that lava? Is that SKHAAR? I'm impressed. Stellar life decisions.

Where did you go?

I tried to warn you. Fire flinging is a massive power drain—I barely have enough juice to talk.

Can you manifest long enough to cut that leather strap?

I can manage a slice, but it might damage my power bank permanently.

One slice is all I need.

Let's seize some destiny, then.

397

The balloon skittered up the volcano wall, jostling the chain. Ozzie readied himself to lunge for the journal once they drew level with the Crucible. If he timed it right, he could sever the book strap, drop to the volcano rim, and run for it. Hopefully, the Booksworn gunners would be distracted by the four-hundred pound Annihilator, and he and Alex could escape in the chaos.

He looked up and gasped. Skhaar's golden eyes were locked on his, radiating malice. The Sauracian reached for his mace ball.

Now, Slashy!

Ozzie's arm was halfway to the journal when the Anemoi Blade manifested, boasting its most flamboyant pink flames yet. The sword sliced effortlessly through the leather strap, then evaporated. Ozzie's fingertips brushed the journal's metal-frame as it tumbled past.

"No!" he shouted.

Alex stretched like she was reaching for a last-ditch finger hold on a granite wall. Her left hand clamped the corner of the book's spine.

"Got it!"

"*KUUURAAAAAAKKKHHHHH!*" Skhaar crashed into the twins like a runaway semi-truck. A battle-hardened elbow rammed Ozzie's sternum. He fell, clawing at the chain until he ran out of links, then grabbed his sister's ankle. The Annihilator seized the journal and shook it vigorously, but Alex wouldn't let go. Skhaar lifted his arm, dangling the twins over lava. Ozzie bear-hugged his sister's leg as the Sauracian drew them close.

"You die without honor," he growled, his breath reeking of decay, "just as your parents did."

Skhaar bared his teeth to bite a chunk from Alex's arm, when an orange, flickering glow lit up his face. He frowned as the balloon crested the Crucible in front of a battery of waving, smiling gunners.

Alex lost her grip and screamed. As the twins fell, Skhaar mashed the arrowhead into the journal and brandished the glowing book in front of him like a shield.

Tongues of flame erupted around the volcano's rim. Lava

bombs plowed into the Annihilator with explosions of fire and blue lightning, rocking the balloon and chunking the walls with shrapnel. The Maelstrom airship dove into the expanding cloud of smoke, strafing the Crucible.

Alex grabbed Ozzie's hand and smiled, determined to spit in Death's eye. He nodded back. It wasn't much consolation, but at least they were dying as failed heroes, in the best traditions of the Forsythe family. A violent gust flipped them face down. Through tears, Ozzie could make out tiny figures darting around the Archive like ants. He squinted at a gleaming stabilizer balloon rising to meet them, carrying a long-necked, frantically waving figure.

Pascal.

The inventor released his chain, popped a Labyrinthian glide chute, and angled beneath the Forsythes. The twins careened into Pascal at breakneck speed, and Ozzie snagged the Dromedarian's prosthetic arm in a desperate grab that threatened to pop his shoulder from its socket.

The chute thrashed like a distressed tapeworm as parchment squares collapsed under the excess weight. Pascal steered for the Archive. "This is going to hurt!" he shouted. The island loomed closer—they were falling too fast.

"We have to slow down!" Ozzie said.

"Thank you for your valuable input!"

The Archive was two hundred feet away.

"Let go!" the inventor yelled.

"What?"

Pascal detached his arm, sending Ozzie and Alex tumbling head over heels. The horizon swirled lava orange and pumice black as they barreled into the Archive like a meteor. A flash of white swallowed Ozzie whole...then the world caved in.

CHAPTER 54

FALLOUT

The fetid stench of rotten vegetables swamped Ozzie's nostrils, jolting him awake. He gasped and tried to sit up, but restraints bound his arms to a cold stone slab. A rhythmic chant filtered through the wall of white curtains surrounding him. In a way it was soothing, but he'd read too much Mayan history to take ceremonies at face value. The monotonous voice spluttered into a coughing fit, then whispered, "Sorry, too much pepper in my tea." The mantra restarted, now with a hoarse undertone.

A deformed shadow lumbered past, warped by folds of fabric. Something monstrous huffed in the opposite direction, brandishing a beaker of chemicals with a pair of tongs. A squeaky wheel drew close, accompanied by purposeful footsteps. The curtain jerked open with an ear-splitting shriek.

"Awake at last! How are we feeling today?" A wafer-thin, white-cloaked librarian pressed two icy fingers to Ozzie's temple. "Your body sustained a significant impact, although I've seen far worse. Follow my finger." He panned his index finger at a speed a mongoose couldn't track, then clucked, unimpressed. "We'll have to do something about that. How high is your pain threshold? I only ask because we're low on shempum saliva and the next best anesthesia is my sleephammer." He nodded at a colossal wooden mallet on the cart.

"Wait!" Ozzie said. "Who are you? Where am I?"

"My name is Brother Terniket, and you've been recovering in the Probably Survivable Wing of the Archive Infirmary for the past four days."

Four days! He dropped his head against the cool stone and sighed. Might as well acknowledge the Weltling in the room. "Are you Noctem?"

The librarian flicked Ozzie's ankles, then scribbled on a clipboard. "You won't find many Booksworn who claim to be Noctem now. It took multiple skirmishes, a forty-hour siege, and an absurdly large hollow cake, but we resolved our differences."

Ozzie brightened at the good news and rattled his restraints. "Am I a prisoner?"

Terniket chuckled. "Hardly. You're an honored guest of the Booksworn, balloon rider. Your attempt to recover the Professor's journal has been deemed worthy of a footnote in the Scrolls of Renown."

Being hailed as a hero eased the sting of his shackles. "That's nice to hear."

The librarian shrugged. "Of course, your utter failure and subsequent humiliation earned you two chapters in the Tomes of Incompetence and an engraved portrait on the Wall of Ignominious Defeat, so it balances out."

"Get me out of these things."

Ozzie massaged his wrists, cringing as Terniket lowered a rack of yelping leeches onto a whimpering patient's chest. To his surprise, aside from a collection of minor cuts and deep bruises, he felt better than he had in weeks. The Booksworn's primitive holistic medicine worked miracles.

"Is my sister okay?"

"She'll drop by shortly, once she finishes desecrating some other area of the Archive with her presence," the physician said. He wrestled a squirming yellow creature out of a bubbling aquarium and thrust it into Ozzie's hands. "Hold this." The squidbeast gurgled and lunged for Ozzie's throat, but Brother Terniket intercepted the attack and sliced the tip off a thrashing tentacle. "Thank you. Please return Elmer to his tank."

Ozzie dunked the seething creature and jumped back, dodging a vengeful slap. "He's named *Elmer*?"

Terniket squeezed the severed tentacle, disgorging foul-smelling fluid onto a patient's gangrenous leg wound, eliciting a cloud of steam and a howl of pain. "His proper title is *Elmer, Devourer of Worlds, the Present and Coming Cataclysm*, but that's a mouthful—and frankly, he can be a little full of himself."

Ozzie wiped his hands on his trousers. "He doesn't look like a devourer of worlds."

"I suppose it depends how big your world is."

A mummified patient chained to the next slab glared daggers at Ozzie through a pharaoh's ransom of bandages.

"Novice Slapsneeze was collateral damage in Brother Pullmyfinger's attack," Terniket whispered.

Slapsneeze! That explained the humongous hand shackles. "What happened?"

The physician gestured to a dozen slabs, all occupied by mummies. "The perils of methane and fire." Behind him, a gauze-wrapped patient rose from his slab like a wraith, poised to leap.

"Look out!" Ozzie cried.

Terniket dropped his clipboard, grabbed the sleephammer, and pirouetted like a ballerina.

Whump

The would-be attacker flew through three sets of curtains and a cage of squawking chicken-rat creatures before hitting the floor and sliding to a stop. A novice groaned, shouldered a mop, and trudged toward the mess.

Brother Terniket sighed.

"Who was that?" Ozzie said.

"An assassin from another order—probably Muffinsworn, curse their carbohydrate-addled brains. We'll know more when we unwrap him." The librarian nudged a torn curtain with his sandal, uncovering a rudimentary dagger fashioned from hardened pastry.

402

"Muffinsworn. It's sad, really." He shook a finger at the mummy. "I only get four klunklings a year for new curtains, you know."

"Ozymandias!"

Alex's Converse sneakers slapped the smooth pumice floor. Ozzie received his sister's tackle with open arms, and the pair tumbled, laughing.

Brother Terniket sniffed. "Take it outside, please."

"Apologies, Brother," Sir Quidby said.

"Grandfather!" Ozzie threw his arms around the family patriarch. Wiry muscles, toned by a lifetime of overcoming impossible odds, crushed his ribs in return. Tears stained his grandfather's khaki shirt.

The old explorer patted his back. "It's all right, my boy."

Terniket cleared his throat and herded the Forsythes to the exit. "It's time for slurpentine-lick baths, so unless you wish to cleanse your toxins by peeling off four layers of skin..."

Alex's eyes widened, and she shook her head.

"We're leaving," Ozzie said. "Thank you."

"My pleasure."

A sullen figure sat alone on the slab nearest the door. Ozzie tensed when he recognized Brother Pugnacious and his freshly cropped ponytail. The librarian met his stare with dead eyes, then looked away.

"The young man is grieving his father's death," Grandfather murmured.

"His dad was a librarian?"

"Brother Deathfist."

"Oh." Now that Ozzie thought about it, Pugnacious' broad, flat nose and tenuous grip on sanity were obvious clues to his family tree. He felt a stab of pity for the young librarian.

The Archive greeted Ozzie with a slap of smothering heat that weakened his knees. "Can we sit down for a minute?" he said.

Sir Quidby smiled. "Certainly."

"I'll go stop Layla and Pascal from killing each other," Alex said. She squeezed Ozzie's shoulder and skipped down the stairs.

The steps were uncomfortably warm, but bearable.

403

"Did Skhaar escape?" Ozzie asked.

"After you fell from the balloon, a Maelstrom vessel retrieved him, then made haste westward."

"He used your journal to block lava bombs."

"Labyrinthian binding is astonishingly durable, especially when bonded to a power stone."

"So your journal is in Sauracia?"

"Most likely."

"Sorry."

His grandfather patted his hand and stared into the distance.

Ozzie frowned. "How did Alex and I survive that fall? The last thing I remember is a flash of white."

Sir Quidby pulled a six-inch rectangle from his pocket. "You landed in a prototype Labyrinthian Crashbox designed by my friend, Infernum the Wiser. It's a safety device for flight training—essentially, a pocket airbag." He twisted the corners with his thumbs and the parchment swelled, ready to deploy. "Unfortunately, it only works half the time, and if you get too close on deflation, it crushes every bone in your body. I was planning to use it to escape the Archive, once I worked out how to prevent lava from melting parchment."

Tap-tap-tap

A sculptor chiseled a wall on the far side of the stone garden that surrounded the infirmary.

Ozzie cleared his throat. "Grandfather, during the fight, when I said you didn't know me..."

The explorer smiled. "If we have to account for everything said in the heat of battle, son, Mrs. Willowsby would have gutted me with a butter knife years ago. It's forgotten."

They watched a team of librarians reassemble a bronze statue in the main courtyard.

"Does Mrs. Willowsby have a special forces background?" Ozzie said.

Sir Quidby laughed. "She came highly recommended by some rather humorless people. I've never had the courage to ask."

Tap-tap-tap-tip

404

A work crew fastened new stabilizing balloons to the edge of the island. The placid scene felt wrong. Everything was too normal. Blood shouldn't wash away so easily.

"Did we win? I was pretty sure we lost," Ozzie said.

"We survived. At my age, that counts as victory."

Taptap-tip-tap

"What about the Noctem?"

"Brother Deathfist was central to the Noctem's foothold among the Booksworn. His murder and the Maelstrom's attack brought… clarity. The brethren settled the matter with honor duels, and from what I can gather, the Noctem will find few friends at the Archive in the future."

Tap-tip

The stone sculptor stretched his arms, spotted the Forsythes, and yelped. He squinted at Ozzie, then dove into his work like a man possessed.

Taptaptaptaptaptaptaptap

Every few seconds he gave them a calculating look, then refocused on carving.

Taptap-tiptiptip-tap-tiptap

"What is he working on?" Ozzie said, dreading the answer.

"I believe that's the Wall of Ignominious Defeat."

"Let's go."

Musclebound librarians sifted through rubble and carted salvage to the main courtyard, where serious men with blueprints and protractors reconstructed ceremonial fountains.

"Alex told me about the armillam and Anemoi Blade," his grandfather said.

Ozzie winced. "They've been kind of useful, actually."

Sir Quidby shook his head. "I knew they were Stone Tech, but thought they'd be safe at St. Jude's, with no dynami to activate them. I never should have brought them home." Sorrow deepened worry lines in the old man's face.

A gentle burst of heat flared in Ozzie's right arm. "We'll figure it out," he said. "If anyone can reverse-engineer Stone Tech, Pascal can." He paused for a heart-thumping beat, wondering how much to say. "Layla has a theory—"

"The Custos Luminis," the Professor muttered.

"Right, but—"

"Has the blade spoken to you?"

The whispered question sucked the oxygen out of the conversation.

Ozzie couldn't stomach the thought of lying to his grandfather. "It, uh…comes and goes. Mostly it encourages me to attack things." He hated the pain that flashed in the old explorer's eyes, but the act of confiding in someone made it easier to breathe. "Please don't tell anyone."

Sir Quidby nodded. "I won't, but you must let me know if anything changes. You are not alone, Ozymandias."

"Thanks. Now I've got a question for you." He retrieved his father's dossier from his pocket and pressed it into the professor's hand. "Is Dad alive?"

The explorer stopped walking and stared at the paper. He sighed, but didn't look up. "I don't know. I've been searching for him for seven years."

"I found that a couple of weeks ago in the Noctem's hideout on Amnesia."

Sir Quidby smiled sadly. "I was proud to hear about your Amnesian expedition. Layla spoke highly of your resourcefulness."

Bitterness crept into Ozzie's voice. "If you had told me about Terravenum, I could have helped you."

The professor's face hardened. "For all the perils you've overcome, Ozzie, you cannot fathom the depths of danger I've faced, or what lies ahead. Skhaar the Annihilator is only the tip of the spear. The Fury King will not rest until he has the Stones."

"Was that what you told Mom and Dad? They sacrificed *everything* to find the Stones."

"I begged them to stop!"

"So it's their fault they got kidnapped?"

"Humboldt wouldn't *listen!*" Sir Quidby shook a finger in Ozzie's face, then clenched his fist. His shoulders slumped. "And it cost me the world." The invincible explorer was gone, replaced by a heartbroken old man.

Ozzie choked back his outrage. "So, what now?" he said.

Sir Quidby wiped his eyes and raised his head. "We move forward, one step at a time. The world is waiting..."

"—and it won't wait forever," Ozzie said, meeting his grandfather's gaze.

"*Angelus* is a vessel of science! She doesn't need a Sauracian deck cannon!" Pascal's reedy voice sliced through the clamor of construction like a knife.

"Is your *vessel of science* an experiment to discover how many ways we can die?" Layla's bellicose challenge echoed off distant buildings. "The Maelstrom is chasing us. How can you be against weapons? You design them!"

"Precisely! *I* design them, not some Sauracian think tank."

"I see. You only want weapons on board that self-destruct!"

"It's my ship!"

"*Angelus* became *our* ship when *you* turned *Spark* into a bomb. Do what you want with your half, but my half will be able to defend herself."

A mountain range of scrap surrounded the airship skeleton, growing ever higher as librarians sorted wreckage from *Angelus* and *Revenge* into piles. Alex jogged down the gangplank. "Come aboard," she said, "but whatever you do, don't mention *Spark*."

"Ozzie!" Pascal shouted. "You're awake!" He limped across the patchwork deck and cocooned the boy in a full-bodied hug. Socrates and Snuggles snapped at Ozzie's hair from the inventor's shoulders. "You're just the person to talk sense into Layla's ridiculous ban on purified dynami." Grandfather, Alex, and two librarians groaned, but the inventor waved them off. "While you were sleeping, I conceptualized a breakthrough in propulsion technology —I call it *Mini-Pegasus.*"

"No," Layla growled. She wrapped an arm around Ozzie's shoulder, shepherding him to the bow. "Are you well?"

"Shockingly, yes."

"Brother Terniket's methods are controversial, but he produces better-than-average results."

"He launched an assassin into orbit with a carnival hammer."

Layla tapped a librarian on the shoulder and pointed at a blueprint. "The Archive is under constant siege. Many in the Council of Brotherhoods are jealous of the Booksworn's prestigious responsibilities."

"Terniket said the guy was Muffinsworn."

Layla snorted. "Those halfwits are nearly as pathetic as the Turnipsworn."

Ozzie ran his hand over a splice joint, where angular Maelstrom styling merged with a round handrail. "Why are librarians helping rebuild *Angelus*?"

"Partly because we exposed the Noctem blight in their midst, but mostly because they wish to speed our departure."

Pascal, Alex, and the Professor joined them on the foredeck.

"You must be excited about incorporating Sauracian technology into your ship," Ozzie said.

The inventor sniffed. "Their dynami management is rudimentary, but they have an intriguing approach to armor plating."

"We discussed this," Layla rumbled. "*Angelus* needs to remain nimble—and if at all possible, airborne."

"You're the one who wants to cannibalize Maelstrom weapons!"

"A necessary weight sacrifice to ensure our survival—"

Grandfather clapped his hands. "Might I suggest a compromise?" Pascal and Layla fell silent, glaring at each other. "Time is of the essence, my friends. Now that Ozzie is awake, I propose we do the minimum to get *Angelus* flying, then head north, stopping at the Crypt for additional repairs as necessary." His face grew somber, and he lowered his voice. "The Fury King's search for the Stones will only intensify now that he possesses my journal. It is imperative we find them first."

Layla heaved a long sigh, then nodded. Pascal pursed his lips but didn't argue.

"I will ask the Booksworn if Ozzie and Alex can remain at the Archive," Layla said.

"Whoa!" Alex folded her arms. "Not cool."

Ozzie frowned. "We're coming with you."

"Layla is right," Pascal said. "Where we're going, we can't protect you."

"We don't need protection!" Alex argued.

"Without us, you wouldn't have survived Amnesia or escaped Contrivance," Ozzie said, conveniently overlooking all the times he and his sister had made things worse. "We can help."

"That may be true, but the risk is considerable," Layla said. "The decision ultimately lies with the Professor."

All eyes turned to Sir Quidby, who was polishing his spectacles on his sleeve with an expression of tight-lipped concentration. Deep wrinkles scarred the old explorer's face, a map of adventures, guilt, and grief. When the Professor replaced his glasses and looked up, his voice was weary but hard. "The time for caution is past." He squeezed his grandchildren's shoulders. "After I failed your parents, I tried to spare you the torment of knowledge. Perhaps that was a mistake. As much as it pains me to say it, you are both part of this now." His wiry, calloused hands grasped their wrists, straightening their arms. Twin Stella Signums pulsed blue light. "Forces beyond our comprehension are at work, and there is no time to lose. We *must* find the Stones. Together."

CHAPTER 55
AN EMBER

Skhaar marched down the black stone corridor as steadily as his limp allowed. Years of field experience had trained him to never show weakness—especially in the Royal Palace, where agendas were bought and sold in buckets of blood. When he passed into the Courtyard of Shattered Ambition, Skhaar dropped his tail mace, allowing it to rattle along the rough-cut floor as a warning to anyone considering an ambush. Grotesque shadows and cloaked contenders tracked his passage through the stone columns, weighing the risks and rewards of a confrontation with the old Annihilator.

Skhaar's tail stump twitched. Part of him hoped someone— maybe that *brakhta*, Deshk—would try to take the Professor's journal. Even with half the charred pages missing, it was a tempting prize—the Fury King would bestow favor on whomever delivered the book.

He flinched as the memory of the fleshling child's Anemoi Blade flitted through his mind again. Skhaar had already run through his post-action coping routine, but decades of hard-wired repression techniques couldn't erase the shocking image in his head.

Another Anemoi Blade had surfaced. That kind of information got a beast's tongue plucked from his mouth before the words died on his lips. Even in the throes of battlerage, the Annihilator couldn't bring himself to kill the boy, though the runt deserved it. If there had been Maelstrom witnesses to that pathetic rock "attack," he would have painted the Archive with the fleshling's blood.

Cloth brushed a column and Skhaar spun, dodging a tri-bladed gorespinner that whirled out of the darkness. He kept one ear on the spinner and scanned for movement among the pillars. A whisper of fabric gave him a bearing on his opponent. When the gorespinner streaked back on its return trip, he unsheathed Grieftongue and redirected the spinning blades with a flick of his wrist.

Chunk

Serrated metal burrowed into flesh.

"Hrk." A death gasp from punctured lungs.

"Anyone else?" Skhaar's challenge reverberated through the courtyard, unanswered. Torches on the wall blazed brighter as shadows retreated in search of easier prey.

The Cavern of Wallowing Pools brimmed with white-clad wellmakers tending the wounds of black-cloaked victors who survived the Trials. Given enough time in the healing waters, injured warriors could regenerate lost limbs. Wounded Annihilators had an automatic bid to compete in the Trials, but Skhaar turned the opportunity down, preferring to keep his tail stump as a reminder of the price of losing focus. Wellmakers and victors carefully avoided making eye contact with him as he limped past—shaming an Annihilator was bad for your health. No matter a healer's skill, they couldn't regrow your head.

No one challenged Skhaar on the Darkening Path until he reached the Catacombs.

"Where do you think you're going?" the on-duty sentry sneered. His partner, eyes wide, stepped back, his body language screaming *I'm not with him. Welcome to the dungeon, kind sir. Would you like to borrow my sword?*

Skhaar glanced at the insolent guard's rank. *Corporal*—high enough to draw attention if he went missing, and sure to create paperwork. Still, the Annihilator had crawled off too many battle-fields to allow a feckless slithernil to give him grief. "I go where it pleases me," he rumbled.

"Well, you're not coming in here without a Warrant of Prisoner Access, old timer."

The distant guard stifled a gasp at his partner's brazenly disre-spectful tone.

Skhaar flipped his cloak aside, displaying his mace. Annoyingly, the rude sentry didn't flinch—although judging from choking noises in the guardhouse, his partner had swallowed his tongue. If gossip about Skhaar the Annihilator no longer reached the dungeons—the bottom of the palace food chain—it was time to introduce himself to a new generation. The Annihilator casually unsnapped his mace ball and dropped it on the ground. The mouthy guard, who hadn't earned Catacomb duty for quick thinking on the job, frowned.

A flick of the chain launched an unstoppable surgical strike at the sentry's chin.

CRACK

The guard's head snapped back and his knees folded like a bad hand of tumblemonk. Fragments of teeth skittered across gravel as he collapsed in a heap. Skhaar pulled a Warrant of Prisoner Access out of his belt and dropped it on the body.

The other sentry emerged from the guardhouse, fumbling with a keyring. "Welcome, Annihilator Skhaar. I wasn't aware you had returned from the field, sir."

Skhaar grunted.

The sentry found the key on his third attempt, and the gate swung open with an agonized wail. The Annihilator nodded and stepped into the dungeon.

Down here, all cell doors featured three diagonal slashes of red paint, signifying High Value or Extremely Dangerous prisoners. In standard dungeons, temporary nameplates organized the ever-shifting prisoner population, but in the Catacombs, names were engraved on permanent plaques. Skhaar found the door he was searching for halfway down the hall, marked by an additional three

412

blue stripes. He slapped five rusty deadbolts back and cracked the iron door open.

The ceiling was lower than a standard cell, and bookshelves lining every wall heightened the sense of claustrophobia. A glow lamp in the corner illuminated a small desk, where a wild-haired, scrawny creature braced its elbows on an open book. Skhaar ducked under the threshold and invaded the room. To his irritation, the sweet fragrance of fear didn't waft up to greet him—if anything, the fleshbag smelled annoyed. He must be slipping. The Annihilator unwrapped the Professor's journal and dropped it on the desk, taking pleasure in the cloud of dust that blasted the pitiful wretch and his study materials.

"With compliments of the Fury King," he snarled. "Be ready." Message delivered and mission complete, Skhaar lumbered out of the room, slamming the door hard enough to topple two bookshelves.

Humboldt Forsythe swept hair out of his eyes, then touched the scorched remnants of his father's journal with trembling, unbelieving fingers. For the first time in longer than he could remember, an ember of hope glowed in the darkness.

THE END

THANK YOU

Thanks for reading Volume One of the Terravenum Chronicles! *Debunked* is a melting pot of things I love (haikus, swashbuckling, and clockwork dogs), so I hope it brought you joy.

Can you do me a favor? Word-of-mouth is the lifeblood of indie publishing. If you enjoyed *Debunked*, can you leave a review on your preferred retailer and recommend it to a friend?

Thank you for spreading the word and building momentum for more books in this series!

Dito

Join my mailing list to receive updates, special deals, and a FREE copy of Sir Quidby's Debunking Field Manual (and Bathroom Companion)!

www.ditoabbott.com

DOES YOUR WALL CRAVE ADVENTURE?

ACKNOWLEDGMENTS

As you may have gathered from *Debunked's* sky armadas, esoteric footnotes, and unabashed silliness, my aim for this book was to write a story I would have fallen in love with when I was 13 years old.

I chased that goal with support from some truly wonderful people:

My wife, Sarah, who brainstormed plot points, volunteered to be my first reader, and buoyed my spirit.

My kids, who pushed me to add spies, robots, and fart jokes into every scene.

My parents, who raised me to embrace adventure and showed me what is possible when you refuse to quit.

My sister, Wendy, who gave me the final edit I needed and challenged me to push myself.

Steve the Editor, who forced me to write more powerful scenes using fewer words.

Kirk at DogEared Design, who captured the spirit of an animal more elusive than Bigfoot.

Rachel the Proofreader, who threatened me with bodily harm unless I embraced US punctuation norms.

My beta readers, who caught mistakes that slipped through (notably, I got the cooking order of a turducken mixed up and accidentally wrote "ordinance" instead of "ordnance", which greatly reduced the stakes of a fight scene).

INFLUENCES

Sir Quidby's love of debunking mirrors the joy I find in exploring new places. I grew up surrounded by maps—first for planning trips in the Arabian desert, then for charting ocean voyages.

Living on a sailboat for a decade gave me a taste of the freedom embodied by airships.

Sailing taught me the importance of living in harmony with nature, especially when you are directly subject to its whims. A wise aeronaut keeps an eye on the Dome, watching for brewing Moribund Gales.

Literary giants like Terry Pratchett (my all-time favorite author) and Douglas Adams (king of the random footnote) taught me that whimsy and fantasy/sci-fi can be a match made in heaven (or purgatory, depending on an author's skill).

I should also credit Master Senora for teaching me Kung-Fu when I was ten years old. While I don't remember anything about self-defense, that experience planted seeds for the Booksworn.

And finally, a heartfelt thanks to you, Dear Reader. I hope *Debunked* lights up your life and earns a space on your bookshelf, to be dog-eared whenever you crave a smile and adventure.

Dito

ABOUT THE AUTHOR

Dito (rhymes with "Cheetoh") Abbott once spent three and half years animating a stop motion music video for his band, Too Many Drummers, in his garage. It featured a shot-by-shot remake of the exploding amp scene from *Back to the Future* (but with robots in a space junkyard, of course).

It's true. Search for "too many drummers fast asleep" on Youtube if you're willing to risk having your mind blown.

After completing such an epic project, he thought writing novels would be easy.

He was wrong.

Dito was born in Puerto Rico, grew up in Saudi Arabia, and sailed around the world with his family by the age of twenty-seven. His debut YA Fantasy novel, *Debunked*, draws on his love for adventure, googly-eyed slime beasts, and sarcastic swords of legend.

Now he lives in Phoenix with his wife, kids, and an invisible dragon named Clyde.

www.ditoabbott.com

Printed in the USA
CPSIA information can be obtained
at www.ICGtesting.com
LVHW031629220823
755973LV00025B/306/J